Once upon a time in New York City...

there lived a girl

    with skin as white as snow

        and hair as black as night.

Her name was Blanche Brier

    and she was loved by a Bear.

But one lonely summer,

    when he was far away,

    a jealous Queen took a

    sudden dislike to her,

    a dislike that was

        inexplicable and violent.

And soon the girl found herself

    alone

        and running for her life.

BLACK AS NIGHT: A FAIRY TALE RETOLD
BY REGINA DOMAN

Black as Night

a fairy tale retold

by regina doman

Regina Doman

CHESTERTON PRESS
FRONT ROYAL, VIRGINIA

for the McLachlan girls
Peace & good!

Chesterton Press
P.O. Box 949
Front Royal, Virginia
www.fairytalenovels.com
www.reginadoman.com

Summary: Over the summer in New York City, seven friars who work with the homeless find a runaway girl named Nora, while Bear Denniston searches for his missing girlfriend, Blanche, in a suspenseful retelling of the Snow White story.

ISBN: 978-0-9819-3182-1

Printed in the United States of America

This one's for the boys—
my brothers, my brothers-in-law,
my friends, my cousins,
my husband, my sons.

To all you members of the male gender
who have been my friends,
brothers, and comrades throughout my life,
I dedicate this book in particular gratitude,
with thanksgiving to the Father who made you,

and to all those boys
trying to survive the streets of New York City,
some of whom I knew for a brief time,

and of course,
to the Friars.

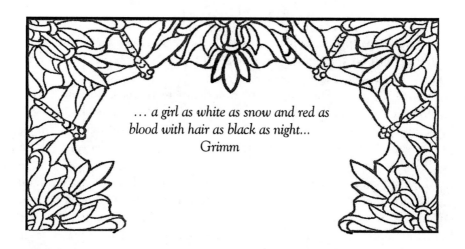

... a girl as white as snow and red as blood with hair as black as night...
Grimm

Chapter One

t was night.

In most places, Night is a time for sleep, calm, and mystery. But not in New York City.

In the tangled thicket of the urban landscape, millions of streetlights, arcade signs, neon tubes, and incandescent bulbs conspired every evening to murder the night, shedding their unearthly glow. The glow grew stronger as Night slipped in with her gray wool cloak and dropped it softly over the streets and subways.

The subway train rushed through the hot summer night like a sleepless dragon bellowing and hurtling along its metal track towards West 55th Street in the Bronx. Two youths slipped like phantoms from car to car, casing each jointed metal compartment for easy cash.

The older, fair-haired one first noticed the girl through the door window in the swaying car ahead. She looked lost, frozen. She didn't see the two vicious denizens of the Night, but they saw her—and they saw the purse clutched tightly in her lap.

This was it. This girl with her short, ragged, black hair, white skin, and eyes red from crying was their hit. She was alone in the car, staring at the floor, apparently not aware of anything around her. It was after three in the morning. As if on cue, the boys both checked over their shoulders to see if they were watched, grinned at each other and pushed through the separating door.

She looked up when they came in and she saw. At once. What they intended to do.

Her cry of surprise and fear was lost as the rocking car made a rough and deafening turn on the tracks. She stumbled to her feet, prepared to run. But there was nowhere to go.

It was too easy. They were fifteen and nineteen years old, and used to violence. The bleach-blond nineteen-year-old shoved her onto the car's dirty linoleum floor. She fell, her pale yellow flowered print dress splatting under her like a smashed flower. The younger, bigger one, with the earring, grabbed her bag.

The girl didn't seem to care. She scrambled to her feet, resurrecting quickly and silently, and jumped for the emergency cord. He lunged after her and knocked her against the seats. A wail and moaning seemed to break forth from the beast's belly, as the tunnel walls suddenly widened out. The girl screamed and shoved him away from her. He fell onto the seats and banged his head against the edge.

It was time to move. The train was coming to a halt, a station careened towards them. The bigger boy stuffed the purse inside his light jacket and burst through the doors as they opened. He leapt to the deserted platform, a slab of concrete in a burned-out neighborhood. The fair-haired boy was still staggering to get to his feet, furious. The girl dodged around him, and ran out of the dragon's belly, an escaping yellow flame. Surprisingly, she didn't stop to call for help. She just ran.

That was odd. Cursing, the fair-haired one regained his feet, looked after her and felt his blood stir to the chase. He sped across the platform after the fleeing form of the girl.

Greasy streetlights looming above in the humid night. Trash crushed in all the crevices of the broken concrete. No one around in the artificial light pools. Nocturnal creatures or nocturnal scavengers moving from shadow to shadow. A bleach-blond boy easily trailing a yellow cowslip girl, whose footsteps hammered to the beat of the cacophony of hidden nightlife, looking for someplace to hide.

His big pal joined him from out of a narrow alley, grabbing at his arm. "What're you doing?" he hissed, jogging to keep up with the other's smooth lope.

The fair one didn't even bother to answer, his eyes fixed on his prey. The girl had paused at a corner and looked around, breathing hard. She saw them, and darted down another street.

"She's not from this part of town. She's gotta be lost. She can't go anywhere," the fair one said, by way of explanation. He ran on, pulse racing. His companion followed.

Down beneath the train tracks, the dragon's skeletal feet, she ran, crossing a street, in and out of crosshatched shadows. Past a string of closed and barred and spray-painted stores—pawnshops, long-distance phone places, drug stores—

She had to be slowing down soon, the fair one figured. Soon she would be too disoriented and too beat to go much further...

Unexpectedly she halted and took off in a new direction, as though inspired.

They could see the girl was staggering now. A faint flickering figure with not much left in her... The two boys ran on, feeling sure that they were closing in. They wore sneakers, were used to racing for their lives.

Then the fair boy saw the church. It loomed in front of them, a gray-slabbed old mausoleum of heavy oak doors and a huge round window like a black spoked wheel that seemed to float ominously above their heads. The fair boy actually paused, but his pal, now intent on their goal, jerked him onward.

Ahead, the girl was running, stumbling, yanking at the neckline of her dress. She was hurrying up the steps; she was jamming something into the lock...

The fair one had seen that move before, a lady they had mugged shoving her car keys into the lock of her car, leaping in to make an escape...But this was a *church*, he thought. What sort of girl kept keys to a church?

Incredulous, the boys watched the door open, swallow the yellow and white and black figure, and close, like a mouth obstinately shut.

Cursing out of sheer disbelief, the boys jumped up the steps and seized the door handles. Locked. Neither door would budge.

"She's gone."

They hardly knew which had spoken. It was like a drug haze. Around them, the City continued in its dead sounds of machines and boom-box music sliding in and out of the streets, in and out of consciousness.

The bleach blond stared and finally turned to his friend. "Did we just follow a girl out here?"

"We swiped her purse." He tugged at the zipper of his jacket.

The church stood silent before them, betraying no secrets. No echo issued from beyond its walls.

At last, the older boy shook his head. "Some kind of weird. Like it never happened."

"But it did. Lookit!" the big boy had fished out the purse, unzipped it, and thrust it at his older companion.

A mass of hundred dollar bills stared out at them. Gingerly, the fair-headed boy touched one as though it were enchanted. But it was real, thick green and white paper beneath his fingers. This was something they understood.

They didn't know how or why a girl would come to be carrying thousands of dollars of cash in her purse in a subway late at night. And they didn't care. The important thing now was to move quickly, before she could call the police. Once again, in unspoken unity, the boys wheeled away from the door—their astonishment already forgotten in the hurry to get to a safe place to gloat over their treasure.

The church stood a silent soldier against the slow destruction of the night.

II

Brother Leon whistled softly to himself as he strode down the corridor in his bare feet after morning Mass. It was Sunday, and today it was his job to make breakfast for the six other hungry men in the friary, who would soon be finishing morning prayers.

Swinging the heavy knotted rope he wore as a belt, he loped into the kitchen with an easy stride and swung the refrigerator door open. Out on one hand came a box of cracked eggs, on the other dangled half a loaf of bread and a gallon of milk. Sliding them all onto the chipped linoleum counter, he flipped open the freezer door and flung out a squashed frozen orange juice, catching it in his other hand as though it were a basketball.

Still whistling that morning's hymn, "All Hail the Power of Jesus' Name," he twisted the dial on the stove to "medium-high," slid the frying pan from the shelf to the burner, daubed in a hunk of margarine, and began cracking the eggs into the soon-sizzling pan and tossing the shells into the sink in syncopation, so that the hymn sounded like the bridge to a rap song.

Brother Leon's eyes and hair were dark; his skin was a warm brown, the result of a happy marriage between a Puerto Rican and a Jamaican. He was short and wiry. Like the other friars of the community, he kept his head shaved Marine recruit style, but he wasn't able to match their full beards. As he scratched the itchy fuzz that was all the beard he had been able to grow, he discarded the last shell, chucking it over his shoulder from halfway across the kitchen as he went to get a lid. He knew, without looking, that he had made it. Years of basketball gave you that sort of intuition.

Speeding up the rhythm of his whistling, he scrambled the eggs till they were fluffy. Stove off. Lid on top. Pam! OJ in the pitcher, water on. Stir. Sloshing orange juice and water until the liquid deepened to a golden whirlpool, he ended the vigorous exercise with a tap of the wooden spoon on the counter and tossed it over his back into the sink. This time, his throw was off. He heard the spoon glance from the counter to the floor and sighed.

Shrugging, he headed for the refectory with the breakfast. From the corridor came the slap of bare feet and sandals and the vocalizations of six men hoping for coffee and eggs.

Coffee! Leon slapped himself on the forehead as he set down the food on the pine plywood refectory table. *Leon, how could you forget again?* Groaning, he turned back to the kitchen, only to see the ancient coffee maker sputtering out a stream of brown brew. Brother Matt, glass coffeepot in hand, was gathering the precious drops in a mug.

"What the—" Leon shook his head, bewildered. "I could have sworn I forgot to do that!"

"You did," Matt set the pot down calmly, smiling through his curly blond beard. "Typically, morning people like yourself who don't need a drug to wake them up forget about making coffee."

"Whew!" Leon heaved a sigh. "Well, thanks—you saved my skin. If I forget again, I'm sure Father Francis is going to write flogging back into the Franciscan constitutions!"

"Probably," Matt grinned, his blue eyes snapping. The head of the order was notably short-tempered where his coffee was concerned. "I have to admit there was a less charitable motive behind my making coffee for you."

"What's that?" Leon rummaged through the drawers, piling spoons, forks, knives, and plates into his arms.

"There are two kinds of religious brothers in the world, Leon. Those who can make coffee, and those who can't. I'm sorry to have to tell you which category you're in."

"Hey, I haven't attained my earthly perfection yet. That's why I'm here. But thanks all the same, Matt."

"Any time," Brother Matt looped his cord over his arm and carried the coffeepot and his own share out to the refectory where the other brothers were taking their seats.

Leon halted in the doorway as Father Bernard, the lithe dark-haired friar who was the resident mystic, murmured a blessing over the meal and the cook. After the fervent "Amens," Leon stepped forward and began hurriedly to pass out the plates and silverware.

"Sorry, there's no toast yet," he apologized. "It's coming."

"Who has the margarine?" Father Francis peered round the table over his coffee cup, his bushy grey brows twitching.

"Coming!" Leon quickly left and re-emerged with a plate piled high with toasted bread and the tub of cheap margarine. The eggs had already mostly vanished from the pan, and the toast quickly dispersed throughout the gray-robed crowd. Leon took one last look around and then pulled back his chair with a sigh. There was a sizable garbage bag on it.

"What's this?"

Brother Herman, a portly older friar who looked like Santa Claus on vacation, wrinkled his forehead. "I forgot. Clothes donation. I meant to bring it to storage last night. Here, I'll get it."

Despite the twitches of irritation that ran through his innards, Leon heaved the bag on to his shoulders. "Naah, I'll get it. I'm up." Sighing inwardly, he heaved the bag on to his shoulders and went out the door.

Religious life was filled with little frustrations like this one. You had to learn to live with the shortcomings of other men. *Besides*, he reflected as he ambled down the corridor, *this can be my penance for forgetting to make coffee again.*

Ah, who said that loving your neighbor was easy, anyhow? He swung into the small hallway that connected their house, an old rectory, with the church. The temporary clothes storage room was the vestibule of old St. Lawrence Church. It was packed with garbage bags stuffed with coats, shoes, socks, and underwear that generous families from six parishes had donated to the homeless. *Someone ought to organize this room*, Leon scowled as he looked around in the dim light for a bare place to stick the new bag. Well, at least someone had started to sort out the men's jackets into a pile on the floor.

Then Leon froze, his jaw dropping.

When he recovered, he spun on his heel, and darted back into the hallway. Luckily, Father Bernard had already left the table and was in the hall, talking quietly to Brother Matt. Leon caught Father's eye and motioned in bewilderment. Nodding to the other brother, the priest came down the hall, his gray habit billowing behind.

"What is it, Leon?" Father scrutinized Leon's face.

Leon led him into the storage room without a word and pointed.

Brother Charley was lumbering by, having come from answering the doorbell. Big, burly, and slow, he had led a wild life long enough to have a nose for trouble. He followed the other two friars into the storage room, towering over them. "What's up?" he asked, and then his eyes widened as he saw.

There's something about the atmosphere of a small friary that speeds up communication. As Brother Leon hurried up the passage to get Father Francis, he nearly bumped into Brother Herman, who was apparently seized by curiosity at the furtive movements of his brothers.

"Something going on?" the older friar asked confidentially.

"Just a crisis—in the storage room," Leon inched around him.

"Another rat colony?" Brother Herman's face wrinkled into a grimace as he glanced at Matt. "We'll have to get out the slingshots." The rats of the South Bronx were legendary in size, and the friars had been waging an unsuccessful war against them for possession of the church and friary.

"Uh—Father!" Leon waved at Father Francis, who was still nursing his coffee cup at the table.

A few moments later, Leon was leading Father Francis back to the storeroom. Charley was still there, squatting before the lump in the corner. Herman and Matt were trying to get a better view. In front of them, Father Bernard looked clearly lost. The whole community was gathered in the vestibule now—even reclusive Brother George had left his chores to peer around the doorjamb. The silence was almost funereal.

"All right, move aside. Who said we needed group support here?" Father Francis said, elbowing his fellow friars aside. Brother Leon saw Father Francis's bushy white brows shoot up his wrinkled forehead as he saw the object: a slim, white ankle nestled on the sleeve of a jacket. "Heaven help us," the community's founder muttered, and Leon knew they were both thinking the same thing—that someone had dumped a body in their friary. He could see the headlines now: BODY OF YOUNG WOMAN FOUND IN FRIARY. POLICE FILE MURDER CHARGES. "Just what we need," Leon murmured to himself, sweating slightly.

Brother Herman was frowning. He had edged closer to the pile of coats and was leaning his chubby frame over the body; turning his red, round face this way and that. Finally, he leaned back heavily with a sigh. "I think she's just sleeping," he said in a stage whisper to Father Francis.

There was an almost audible group sigh. "Well, that's something to be thankful for," said Father Francis briskly, in a soft voice. "But why should she be sleeping here?" His blue eyes traveled over the somber, bemused faces of his brothers. "Did anyone let her in?"

Six bearded friars shook their heads. Brother George's face was quite red.

"Well, I suppose we should wake her up," Father Francis straightened, and then, for once, looked uncertain. Nobody seemed inclined to disturb the owner of the white foot.

Leon, who had grown up with three sisters, swallowed and put out a hand to touch the coat-covered body. But before his hand touched the coats, the sleeper moved.

III

There are many beautiful churches in Italy, and even the tourists who walk in and out of them become pilgrims, of a sort. Bear tried to figure out, as he sat in the church of Santa Cecilia in Rome, whether he could classify himself as a particularly devout tourist or a rather casual pilgrim. He had been sitting there for a good forty-five minutes in the nave of the church lit by the natural light coming from the dome above. In the beginning, he had been consciously praying, but his stream of meditation had dissipated into random thoughts in the haven of the ancient stone structure. The last Sunday Mass had ended some time ago, his brother had gone back to the hotel, and now he was mostly alone, studying the ceiling structure and support pillars of the church, trying to picture how the building process had transpired. The thought of building a church like this one was fascinating to him.

Just across from him was the hallmark statue of Saint Cecilia. Despite the fact that he had now seen thousands of souvenir replicas of it on the street for sale, it had not lost its ability to move him. Father Raymond, his late mentor, had once told him the story. The statue had been carved in 1599, when Cecelia's tomb had been discovered, and her body found to be miraculously incorrupt. She had been the victim of a botched beheading around the third century.

The statue below the altar showed the slim body of a young girl lying face down on her side, her veil swept gracefully back, her head barely attached to her body. But despite the grisly detail, her form lay curled up as serenely as though asleep, her arms, carelessly thrown to one side. Her pose was deceptively accidental, for her fingers were curled in two deliberate symbols. On one hand, one finger points out, and on the other, three, proclaiming One God, Who is Father, Son and Spirit.

Despite his fascination with the architecture, Bear found his eyes drawn repeatedly to the smooth white form of the statue. It was mysterious to him. He wondered with bemusement what it could really mean. A girl. Death. Witness. Beauty. How they could all go together at once.

And as usual, his thoughts went from the statue of a girl to the real girl waiting for him on the other side of a stormy ocean, and he pondered again if it was time.

He had come to Europe to escape some problems and to find some answers. About a year ago, his life circumstances had changed drastically—he and his brother had been cleared of a crime they hadn't committed, and because of this, the substantial inheritance they had received when their mother had died had been restored to them, somewhat grudgingly, by their father. Bear's father had made it clear in his communications that he still wanted nothing more to do with his crazy religious sons, but the brothers' financial difficulties were taken care of, at least for the next few years.

But the sorting-out period had been difficult and prolonged, with legal proceedings and at least two court cases to get through before his life could be called "normal." After a while, Bear had felt the intense need to escape, and had arranged a long trip to Europe. He had spent most of his time wandering in and out of churches and other buildings like this one, looking at the bones of the architecture and wondering if he could become a stonemason or a sculptor. It had given him a long-needed rest after the stress, uncertainty, and danger of the past few years, but it had taken him away from her.

He thought of Blanche, a slender girl with white skin and black, black hair, long and shining like a dark wet rope down her shoulders. Blue eyes. Deep eyes, which said, even though she still might look like a child, she was almost a woman.

What did you do with a girl like that? Especially when she looked at you as though you were greater than you suspected you actually were, and you still didn't know who exactly you were.

Of course, as more worldly men knew, if you had a girl like that, you could look at her body and avoid her eyes, and thus avoid the whole question of who you were, or who you would be if you stayed with her. But he just couldn't do that.

Because of that, he didn't let himself touch her very often. Granted, that was difficult. Still, he didn't think it would be fair to her to do otherwise.

* * *

At the airport, he had asked her, just before he got onto the plane, "Does it bother you that I'm leaving?"

"Yes," she said at last, quietly.

"Do you want me to stay here?" he asked, worried.

"No," she said, and pushed back her black hair. One strand ran down her white cheek like a black ribbon. Her eyes were looking down. "I understand."

He didn't know what to say to her, and felt like a jerk, that he was leaving. Letting him go was a big thing for her to do. He was grateful.

He ran a finger down that black ribbon of hair. "I'll be back before you know it," he said.

"Will you?" she asked, looking up at him unexpectedly, and he saw then that she knew what he was thinking. That was the way Blanche was, almost preternaturally sensitive. Her intuition was very strong.

"As soon as I get things sorted out, I promise," was all he could say. Before he had gotten to this moment, he had thought about kissing her goodbye, but now it didn't seem right. Instead, he touched her fingers. As he shouldered his backpack and turned away onto the gray tube of the plane, he thought for a moment what it would have been like to kiss her, and even though he knew it wouldn't have been fair, that missed kiss hovered in the air before him. When he turned to look back at her, she was still watching him. She smiled at him.

And receiving that smile was as good as a kiss.

* * *

Now, in the church of fair Cecilia, the brave young girl of long ago, he studied the knuckles of his hands, knitted together. His hands were big, like Father Raymond's had been. And for the longest time, he had thought, when everything had sorted itself out, that he would become a priest.

Was that what Father Raymond would have wanted? Bear felt he knew his mentor's mind so well, but he had never been able to figure that out, when the man was alive. He remembered asking once, "Do you think I'm the sort of guy who would make a good priest?"

He could still remember the smile that creased Father's face. "So what are you trying to say, Arthur?" the priest had asked, and thrown the basketball over his head.

"I'm just wondering," was probably what he had replied, as he dodged to catch the ball. They were on the court, their usual routine after high school. Bear had never cared much for sports, but the priest, a tall, energetic man, shot hoops every day from 2:30 to 2:45 in the school gymnasium or the rectory parking lot. And Bear, who was called Arthur back then, and his brother had found it was the natural time to talk with Father, right after school let out. Sometimes the talks that began on the basketball court continued as the priest went on to his other tasks.

That day, they were in the rectory parking lot, and his brother wasn't with him, probably delayed in the library. "What makes a man a good priest—or a good husband—is being a real man. What distinguishes a real man is that he is able to give all of himself, without reservation, to the call. He doesn't just *want* to be able to give his whole self, but is actually able to, without holding anything back," Father Raymond had said, twisting the ball between his capable hands. "You need to be able to give your whole self."

Bear had thought about those words for a long time. Certainly he had felt that desire to give himself whole-heartedly to do a single thing. For example, when Father Raymond had been murdered, he had seen what he was supposed to do for the next few years. But once that was over, the free-floating fuzziness that had haunted him as a teenager returned.

Perhaps Blanche had sensed this. As the months went by, she had seemed to withdraw a bit, watching him, waiting for him to decide. It seemed to make sense to take some time off, go to Europe, remove himself from everything familiar for a while, in order to think and see if that call was really real, or just his imagination.

So he had traveled around Europe, sat in churches, tried to listen, tried to recover some sense of what it was that this mysterious God might expect of him. But he couldn't say the experiment had been a tremendous success. He did feel a little less restless, much less agitated, but he didn't feel any closer to knowing what his task was.

He had been writing to Blanche frequently. Always preferring the low-tech option, he had decided to use pen and paper to communicate with her instead of email. Besides, Blanche didn't have a computer in her home. He had sent her quite a few letters over the past few weeks. She hadn't sent him quite as many, although since he was moving around and she was remaining in the same place, it was natural that it would be harder for her letters to reach him than for his letters to reach her. He had tried to call regularly, since he usually enjoyed talking with her, as he always had.

Now it was the beginning of August, and he was starting to think about returning home. For one thing, the smell of the hot pavement in Rome reminded him awfully of the heat of New York City.

He had persuaded his brother to come over to Rome for vacation so they could do some sightseeing together before he returned home. Fish, as usual, was in total contrast to his older brother. He knew exactly what he wanted to do with his life: study history and literature. He had jumped into university studies with characteristic intensity, announcing his intention to finish his undergraduate degree in two years, to make up for lost time.

It had been hard to extricate Fish from his summer schedule of classes and papers, but in the end, Fish came to Italy. He reported that Blanche, who had offered to water the plants in their apartment while he was gone, seemed a bit stressed and anxious. But she was occupying herself with working and visiting old people in her spare time, and was going to be happy to see Bear again. Bear was glad, but he still did not yet know what he was going to say to Blanche when he saw her.

A letter had arrived that morning from Blanche, but Bear hadn't yet read it. Again, he wasn't quite sure why. Now he drew it out of his pocket and turned it over. Somehow he knew when she was sending him a "heavy" letter. Their last talk had been a bit heavy, too.

Chastising himself for delaying, he opened the card and read it quickly.

Bear,

I was thinking about our last conversation.

I don't know if I told you before that this summer at work I met a man who is dying, and I've been visiting him. He has no visitors except for me. Why? Because he won't forgive the people who hurt him, including his relatives and his sons. Now he's dying alone—well, practically alone. I'm the only visitor he has, and he doesn't seem to be well taken care of, so I've kept visiting him, even though it's sad to be around someone so bound by the past. It's very sad and so senseless. Even terrifying.

All I can think is that I don't want to see you become like this. I don't want to see you hardened, like this man is, by years of unforgiveness.

Not that I want to change you. But it seems that your past has a hold on you. Do you think that maybe you can't find peace and direction in your life because, on some level, you won't forgive?

I can only say this to you because you're my friend. Maybe seeing so much this summer has made me bolder. Or just more anxious that my friends and family don't end up like this man.

I'm sorry if this hurts you. But I thought you should know.

> *With love,*
> *Blanche*

He turned over the card in his hand, creasing it shut with a touch of resentment. He had to admit it wasn't altogether unexpected, given the tenor of their last talk, a week ago.

Thing is, Blanche had no idea how hard it had been. Well, he hadn't told her much, but she seemed to sense more than he was letting on, as usual. She wanted him to talk about it. He just wanted to put it behind him.

He rose and genuflected, a little distracted, before turning toward the door. As he did so, a curious disquiet came over him. Why did he suddenly feel as though he were running away?

All right, he thought, looking back at the white marble statue of the fallen girl and speaking to it as though she were Blanche. *All right. You want me to talk about it? We'll talk.*

Mentally he said a token farewell to St. Cecilia. Once out in the courtyard, he flinched at the heat of the afternoon day as he walked back to the hotel. It was siesta time by now—for everyone except the crazy Americans.

Up in his room, he quickly dialed Blanche's number, after calculating the time change. It would be six hours difference—after nine by now. But Blanche usually worked at her catering job till past midnight on Saturday nights, and now she would still be sleeping. *I should wait a few hours*, he told himself, reining in his sudden emotion.

Frustrated, he sighed and replaced the receiver. He unfolded the letter and read it again. She was only saying to him what Father Raymond had told him before. And he knew he should do it, but it was going to be difficult.

Something was odd about the letter, but at first he couldn't make out what it was. He studied it more closely.

Blanche's penmanship was usually precise and perfect, as good as calligraphy. She was a perfectionist that way. But this handwriting was more erratic, almost sloppy. If he hadn't known before opening it that the letter was from Blanche, he might not have recognized the writing as hers.

Something's really agitating her. Had she just been nervous about writing him the letter? Or was it something else? He picked up the phone again and pushed the numbers of the Briers' home number. He remembered that Blanche's mom and sister were on vacation, and that Blanche had been alone in the house for the week. All the more reason why he should call to make sure she was all right.

As the phone made the connection and started to ring, he tried to come up with something to say to Blanche, to explain this unusually timed phone call. *If something's really disturbing her, I'll hear it in her voice*, he told himself.

And if she *was* all right...? He wished he could say something groundbreaking to her, but he couldn't think of any way to begin except, "I got your letter..."

The phone rang, and rang, and rang, and rang. The answering machine came on. He hung up and dialed again.

And again.

And again.

There was no answer.

*"My name is Snow White," she said.
"How have you come to our house?" they
asked.
Grimm*

Chapter Two

*I felt a Funeral, in my Brain,
And Mourners to and fro
Kept treading, treading, till it seemed
That Sense was breaking through.*

*And when they all were seated,
A Service, like a Drum,
Kept beating, beating till I thought
My Mind was going numb.*

She was aware at once that she was no longer alone. Something had changed in the air—it was alive with breathing and stifled whispers. All of her muscles tensed, and she froze for a moment. *No. I have to face this.* Then, taking a deep breath, she sat up and turned, her hair sliding over her eyes.

She saw what seemed like half a dozen male faces peering down at her in the dim light. Two young faces stared at her from her feet. The rest looked over boxes and around bags. But there was something different about these faces. For a second, she thought it was an illusion, and then realized that it was real. But all of the faces had beards, and none of them seemed to have any hair on their heads.

The sight was so odd that she forgot to be afraid for a second, and she almost smiled. The men continued to look at her, and she realized that they must be as startled as she was.

"H—Hi," she said, recovering her voice.

"Uh—hi," said the Hispanic one nearest her. Above him, a round red face creased into a smile and waved a hand.

For a moment, there was an awkward silence. She was extremely conscious of being someplace she shouldn't be. She had thought that this church was still abandoned. But it clearly wasn't.

"Sleep well?" asked the round red face, embellished by a long white beard and round gold-rimmed spectacles, making him look like Santa Claus.

"Yes, thank you." She protectively pulled the coats around herself, even though she was fully dressed. Her heart was still beating fast.

"We were just surprised to find a guest in our vestibule. Sorry if we alarmed you," the older man went on, his white beard twitching as he talked.

"Oh—no, not really." She tried to smile, and the man beamed back at her.

"Relax," he said. "We're not skinheads. This is a friary."

"A friary?" she looked about her in bewilderment.

Muffled laughter erupted in several places around the room. "Yes. Believe it or not, this ruin is now a religious house. We just moved here," the Hispanic said.

"Oh!" she murmured, turning red. Of course. A friary was a sort of monastery, and that's what the church had been turned into. In her disoriented state, she had thought for an instant that a friary was some type of restaurant.

"Yeah, it sort of looks more like a Rent-A-Storage," the Hispanic one grinned at the others. "Not a bad idea for an apostolate. How about it, Father Francis?"

The oldest friar, who seemed to be Father Francis, smiled grimly as the others chuckled. "I'm Father Francis. This is the friary of St. Giles. We're Franciscan brothers in the Catholic Church."

"Oh!" she said. "I'm sorry—I really shouldn't be here," she murmured.

"How did you get in?" Father Francis asked her.

She gazed at him and swallowed. "I got lost last night. I was on the subway, and I—I got mugged." Her voice caught at the memory, but she went on relentlessly, steadying her voice. "They took my purse, and I ran. They chased me, and I came here. I knew this place, before, when it was empty. I had a key—"

"A key?" several voices asked at once. She put a hand to her neck and held the brass key on a gold chain, the one asset she had left.

"Yes—I happened to have the key—I'm sorry, it's a long story—" she said faintly. "I didn't know anyone would be here or I wouldn't have bothered you—"

Thoughts were whirling in her brain. *I'm in deep, deep trouble, and I don't want to get anyone else in trouble with me. Not my family. Not these monks who are being so kind…*

II

"You've had a very rough night, I can see," Father Francis's voice had lost its edge completely. "I'm sorry, but I'm glad you found your way here."

Brother Herman leaned down and gently touched her black head, his face all sorrow. "What's your name?"

She looked at his sympathetic face, and something flickered across her pale one—a spasm of shame or pain. Then she paused, and the edge of a smile touched her lips. "You can call me Nora."

"How about some breakfast, Nora?"

"Yes—thank you." Her voice recovered its stability and held onto it at last.

The brothers helped her up out of the coats, pushing back some of the piles. Brother Leon saw now that she was dressed nicely—or had been. Her dress was a thin yellow print of a good material. Her hair was cut short in a jagged way he supposed New Yorkers considered fashionable. There were faint traces of makeup on her face—not a lot, just the tasteful amount that girls who knew how to wear makeup put on. Everything about her—her poise, her watch, her small pearl drop earrings, her voice—said that this was a girl from the nicer side of town. Completely out of her element here.

"I'm sorry," she said apologetically. "But could you tell me your names?"

She was not so distraught that she couldn't be polite, Brother Leon thought. "I'm Brother Leon," he offered her his hand. She took it firmly, and smiled at him, a bit hesitantly. He returned it, liking her.

"I'm Brother Herman. Father Francis is the head of our little community," Brother Herman directed her gaze to the crusty old man. "Don't worry, he doesn't bite."

"Not visitors, at any rate," Father Francis shook her hand with a wry smile through his bushy white beard. "Novices, on the other hand, aren't as lucky." He shot a glance at Leon, who immediately tried to look pious and innocent. "Watch out for that one," Father Francis said, referring to Leon. "He forgets to make coffee." Nodding to her curtly, he made his way out of the room.

"This is Father Bernard," Brother Herman went on as the slim dark monk with an aristocratic black beard took her hand and shook it solemnly. His face was gaunt and dark-eyed, but his soft voice had a Long Island twang. "Very good to meet you, Nora. Let us know if there's any way we can help you."

"Thank you very much," she said, subdued by his deep, icon-like eyes.

"And that's Brother George," Brother Herman directed Nora to the scowling older man with bushy red hair who lifted a hand and vanished down the hallway, back to his dishes. "He's—a bit shy."

"Hi, I'm Brother Matt," the blond novice came over and shook her hand. "Hope you've recovered okay."

She looked at him in surprise. "Where are you from?"

"Indiana," he said, and laughed. His voice definitely had a drawl when contrasted to the sharp New York accents of the other friars. "I'm the first imported novice. All the other guys in the order are from the New York area. Father Francis gave a talk at my college and I came out to join." He grinned. "I made the coffee this morning, so don't worry, you won't be poisoned or anything."

She laughed a little, and found her hand enveloped in the clamp of two large hands. "Hi," a deep voice said above her. "I'm Charley."

She looked up at the brown-bearded face and green eyes. The accent was Brooklyn.

"Believe it or not, Brother Charley's in the seminary. Can you picture him a priest?" Matt said. "He used to be a Hell's Angel."

"Really?"

"Well, almost." Brother Charley flushed a little, and began to talk rapidly. "I sure spent a lot of my life trying to be one, but I never quite made it in. And then God caught up with me, and the rest is history, as they say."

"Was God driving a hot rod?" Brother Leon elbowed him. "Yeah, we're a new order, so we let in the riffraff."

The ex-biker said nothing, but smoothly put the smaller friar into a headlock and gave him a Dutch rub. Leon made choking noises and Charley released him with a smile.

"Come, sister, if we keep standing here, these fellows will keep talking until lunch time. I believe there's still some breakfast in the kitchen." Brother Herman steered her away from the three boisterous novices.

"I'll make more if there's not enough," Leon came up behind them as they walked down the friary corridor. "I haven't had my breakfast yet, either, Nora."

In a few minutes, he had set a plate of eggs—his portion—and toast before her at the refectory table. She started in hungrily. In the hallway, he could hear Matt and Charley joking with each other as they went upstairs to the bedrooms. Father Bernard passed by the dining room door, smiled kindly at the girl, and then vanished into the chapel.

Brother Herman settled his round Friar-Tuck bulk into a chair opposite the girl and chatted comfortably while she ate. When Leon came in with a plate of toast and a day-old bagel, he was telling her about their new foundation, their current ministry, and their plans for the buildings the archdiocese had just given them: the old church of St. Lawrence, the rectory, and an adjoining high school, St. Catherine's, which had been closed down by the diocese last year because of school consolidation.

"We're hoping to clean up the school, repaint it, and furnish it as apartments for the homeless, so that up to thirty homeless men can live there at one time." He looked wistful. "There's so much we could do—there's such a great need here in the South Bronx, you know. It will take a lot of work to clean the buildings before we can begin, but most of our time right now is taken up with distributing the food and clothing we get from the parish ministries around here. From time to time we get some laypeople to help us with the big cleaning work. All we've done so far is clear out some of the offices in the basement of the high school for our volunteers to use for bedrooms whenever they come down."

She nodded, eating. Brother Leon sat down beside her.

"So, Nora, where are you from?" Brother Leon helped himself to some toast.

She evaded his eyes. "Around here," she said quietly.

Brother Leon caught a slight warning in Brother Herman's eyes and reined in his curiosity. Apparently Brother Herman didn't think this was a good time for personal questions.

"I'm from the City myself. I'm sorry you had such a bad experience last night," he changed his tack.

"It was stupid of me," she murmured. "I got on the wrong train going towards Gun Hill Road, and I was trying to go back to Grand Central. I never should have been in this area so late at night. I really do know better than that."

Brother Herman nodded sympathetically. "Those things happen," he said, pausing a moment. "You didn't get hurt, did you?"

"No, just a little bruised. It happened so quickly—all they did was snatch my purse, really." She looked at her eggs, her cheeks turning red suddenly.

"Thank God that's all," Brother Herman said heartily. "It must have been a terrible experience for you."

"It was," she said, rubbing the back of her neck. "You've been very kind. And this food is very good." She looked at Brother Leon with a small smile.

"Thanks. Hey, do you want us to take you to the police station?" Brother Leon asked. "You could give a description of the guys—maybe they'll be able to find them. You never know."

She hesitated. "No, thank you," she said at last. "There wasn't anything really important in the purse. Just cash. And that will be gone forever."

Brother Leon dropped his eyes. She didn't want to go to the police. *Another strange thing.*

"Can we help you get back home?" Brother Herman asked.

"No, thank you," she said, and began blinking again. "I can't go home just now, and I don't know what to do next—"

Brother Herman offered, "If you need a place to stay, we do have those bedrooms in the basement of the high school that we mentioned," he said. "One of our ministries is offering lay people a place to stay and do service for the poor, as we do. Could you use something like that? Of course, I'll need to check with our superior, but I'd be happy to."

She raised her head, bewildered. "You would let me stay? Even though—I mean, do you let women work here?"

"Oh, yes. The bedrooms are in the building next door to us—it's completely separated. And no one's using them this week."

"That's very generous of you," she said with an effort. "But, I'm not sure you should. You don't know anything about me."

"What, are you a leper?" Brother Leon asked.

She looked at him, tears in her eyes, and was forced to smile at his expression. "Not yet," she said.

"Then at least wait and find out if it's okay." Brother Leon said casually. "It might be a temporary answer for you anyway."

"Well—I'd be glad to help clean up around here," she said, pushing back her hair. "But I'd like to get to Sunday Mass. Would you be having—?"

Brother Herman shook his head. "We already had our Sunday Mass at seven, but I'll check with the Fathers—that's Father Francis and Father Bernard—and see what they suggest. There might be a Mass nearby you could go to, but if not, I'm sure one of them would be glad to say Mass for you."

"That would be too much trouble," the girl objected.

"No, they consider it part of their duty. That's why they're priests."

"Thank you," she said quietly.

At least, she was Catholic and observant enough to want to keep her Sunday Mass obligation. Brother Leon got to his feet and said, "Hey, if you're done, give me your dishes, and I'll wash them for you." He had to finish cleanup. "Keep your coffee mug until you're finished with it. There's more in the kitchen."

"Thanks," she said, cupping her hands around it and looking past him out the refectory window. The sunlight made her eyes pale blue in her white face. Her thin, small eyebrows and thick lashes were black, but her eyes were still red from her tears.

He admitted to himself that she was quite beautiful, in a fragile, luminous way. But beneath that lovely surface he suspected lay some deep problems. Troubled, he scooped up the plates and went back to the kitchen.

III

...White Queen Blanche, like a queen of lilies,
With a voice like any mermaiden—

Nay, never ask this week, fair lord,
Where she has gone, nor yet this year,
Except with this for an overword—
But where are the snows of yester-year?

Where was Blanche?

Bear sat by the window in his hotel room and stared out unseeing at the dark, empty cobblestone streets of the Piazza Navona, pocked with pools of streetlight. The book of Dante Gabriel Rossetti's poetry he had been reading to distract himself had fallen to the floor, its lyrics having turned traitor on him. Once again he picked up the phone and dialed.

It was past midnight in Rome, but still daylight in New York City. Maybe Blanche was away for the weekend. Maybe the New York phone service was down. Maybe she was just at her summer job. But the feeling that something was wrong persisted.

He paused, and dialed her home phone again slowly, letting it ring on till the answering machine picked up the call. She still wasn't there.

Now he leaned back heavily in the upholstered chair, his six-foot broad-shouldered frame creaking the hotel furniture. He ran his large hands in his longish, and now thoroughly rumpled, black hair, and stared at the floor, unseeing.

He must have drifted off to sleep, because he was startled awake some hours later by his brother shaking him.

"I know—I need to go to bed," Bear murmured, half-asleep.

"Go to bed if you want," Fish said. "But it's morning now."

Startled, Bear looked around the hotel room, blinking at the morning sun coming through the windows. Rubbing his sore neck, he looked around the sitting area of their hotel suite.

"Rough night?" Fish said, half-smiling. He was dressed in a paisley lounging robe that, for some reason or other, always made Bear think that his brother was dressed up as Sherlock Holmes. Fish, as his brother was nicknamed (his real name was Benedict), certainly had that air of intellectual detachment, and like a fish, he was swift and hard to pin down. Younger by a year, he was in many ways a shorter, thinner, lighter-haired shadow of Bear, despite his sharper, more uneven features.

"Did anyone call?" Bear asked, trying to stretch the criks out of his spine.

"You were the one guarding the phone," his brother remarked, "But no. I take it you haven't gotten a hold of Blanche."

Bear shook his head, and Fish sank into the chair opposite thoughtfully. "Very strange," he said. "Not at all like her. Is there any chance she wouldn't be returning your calls for some reason?"

"Not that I can think of."

"I thought you said you two had a 'sort-of fight' last time you talked."

"It wasn't really a fight," Bear responded, defensive.

"I was quoting your exact words," Fish said blandly.

"It was really more of an intense conversation," Bear explained, toying with Blanche's card, which he had been using as a bookmark in his poetry book.

"Your story is changing," Fish remarked, picking up the book from the floor and turning the pages. "Who is this? Oh, Rossetti. Pre-Raphaelite poets again. You must be depressed. I'm sticking with your first explanation."

"I just don't know what to do," Bear said. "In a more specific sense than usual. Is this an emergency situation or not?"

"Why not call Mrs. Brier and check with her?"

"I already thought of that, but I have no idea where she and Rose are on vacation. I know they're in California, but I don't know what city. Now that I think of it, Blanche said they were going to be traveling around to different parts of the state, visiting different relatives."

"Call information and look for any Briers in California," Fish suggested.

Bear shook his head. "They're her mom's relatives," he said. "And I have no idea what Jean Brier's maiden name was."

"Well, that's bad luck," Fish remarked. "But I suppose if she's really missing, the Briers will probably notice it before you do and call you first."

"I don't want to risk that." Bear bit the edge of the card in his hand. "Fish, if I can't get a hold of her by morning—I think I should go back."

"Look, if you're that worried, call the police and see if they can check the house."

"Suppose they don't find anything there?"

"Then, obviously, we can all start worrying," Fish said calmly, ringing the bell for breakfast.

Groaning, Bear got up and went to his room to dress.

Reflections Banquet Hall, he thought as he fumbled with the buttons on his shirt. He had taken her there once for dinner, and she had ended up getting a summer job as a receptionist in the large restaurant/banquet hall on Long Island. Maybe they would have someone there who would answer the phone even at two in the morning. New York parties could run late. *I'll call and find out if she had been at work this weekend, and if she's scheduled to work on*

Monday morning, he thought. *Maybe she's even at work right now, still cleaning up after some party.*

Hurriedly he called information in the States, got the number for Reflections Restaurant and Banquet Hall, and was connected.

"Reflections." A deep woman's voice answered, sounding a tinge irate.

"Hi. I'm trying to get in touch with Blanche Brier, who works there, and I was wondering if you could tell me..."

The woman's voice came back after the transatlantic pause. "I'm sorry, but she doesn't work here any more."

"Excuse me?"

Pause. "She doesn't work here."

He fumbled for words. "She told me she was the receptionist there..."

"Yes, she was. But she doesn't work here any more."

"When did that happen? I mean, when did she stop working there?" his own voice had a slightly ghostly echo.

"I don't know."

"Could you check the schedule for me?" he asked, tinged with impatience.

"She's not on the schedule."

His words overlapped with hers. "When was the last time she worked?"

Pause. "I can ask someone."

"Yes, that would be great."

The phone was set down and the fuzz of static buzzed and rumbled in Bear's ear, like the sound of some electronic ocean.

A more cheerful voice came on the line. "You're looking for Blanche?"

"Yes."

"Hold on and let me see when she's working next," the voice said. There was a pause, and the voice returned. "Funny, I don't see her on the schedule at all for this week. Sorry."

"Listen," Bear said. "I know that. They said she doesn't work there any more."

"She doesn't? Oh, that's real strange."

"Could you tell me when the last time she worked was?"

"Sure thing. Lemme check."

Another thump and more static. Then the voice swam back towards him. "I saw her on Friday when I came on to my shift, but she might have done some weekend hours..." another pause. "Yeah, she got off work Saturday at midnight."

"And she didn't work Sunday?"

"The schedule goes from Saturday to Saturday, and she's not on this week's schedule. You say she's not working here any more?"

"That's what I was just told."

"Well, not everyone here knows what's going on. Maybe she's just on vacation this week. It's August, after all, and it's been real hot around here."

"Was she going on vacation?"

"Well, you know, she never mentioned it to me. But I don't really know for sure. You might want to call back in the morning. The day manager will be in then, and he'll have the full story for you."

"Thanks very much," Bear said.

"Hey, no problem. Have a good night."

Bear hung up the phone, his ears ringing.

After the turbulent transatlantic phone trip to past midnight in New York, he paced back to the sitting room and tried to mentally readjust to morning in Italy. Blanche wasn't working at the banquet hall any more. She wasn't there. She wasn't at home. Where was she?

Now, feeling acutely concerned, he phoned the Bronx police department and explained the situation—could they send someone by to check the house? They agreed to send a patrol car over, and he left his number so that they could call him back. Then he hung up the phone.

There was a knock and he opened the door. A hotel worker swept in with a breakfast tray, set it on the coffee table, and exited.

Fish, who had been reading in the chair, set down the poetry book and with mild irritation surveyed the Italian rolls, tea, and fruit. "Continental breakfast—a big name for 'not much,'" he muttered. "Is there any place around here to order eggs and bacon and pancakes at this hour?"

"I seriously doubt it," Bear said. He dialed the phone number for the airport and confirmed that there were available flights leaving for New York that afternoon. When he hung up, his brother was dumping several spoonfuls of sugar into his tea with a melancholy expression on his face.

"What's wrong?" Bear asked.

"I'm getting a feeling of my own. You're not going to find Blanche this morning, which means that we'll be flying back to New York this afternoon."

"Fish, I didn't ask you to come back with me. You should stay and finish your vacation," Bear said, surprised.

"No, no," Fish said, sounding like a martyr dying of slow suffocation as he spread jam on his roll. "I'll go with you. I don't have a girlfriend, but I still get to suffer the effects of having one."

Bear heaved a sigh. "Fish, I might go back and discover out that everything's fine—that Blanche just went away to a friend's house for the weekend or something. This time she just didn't tell me, that's all. You might be coming back for nothing."

"In that case, I'll just go back to taking my classes," Fish said wearily. "No, I'm coming. Knowing you, you'll walk right into some huge mess. And you'll need me to extricate you from it, again. So you called that place where Blanche works?"

"Yes. They said she wasn't on the schedule. I think that means she was let go. The girl I talked with sounded surprised herself."

"The mystery deepens." Fish tasted his tea and added a few more grains of sugar. "Especially as Blanche is not the type to get fired. She's quiet, she works hard, most likely shows up five minutes ahead of time every day—no reason to fire someone like that. Yet, apparently, she has been fired. And now she's missing. Even stranger." He started sipping his tea and looked at his brother keenly. "I think you're ready to go home now anyway, aren't you?"

"I'm still not sure," Bear confessed. "But I think I should."

Fish humphed but kept his thoughts to himself.

Once again Bear opened the card and studied her agitated handwriting. Perhaps Blanche had gone away for the weekend, which might be understandable, if she had lost her job. *But why hadn't she called him if she was in trouble?*

He came back to reality and realized Fish was saying again, "Are you going to eat your roll or can I have it?"

"I want it," Bear answered evenly.

Fish eyed it critically. "I'll fight you for it."

"Not a chance," Bear said, cracking a smile at his lightweight brother.

Fish sighed and reached for the hotel phone. "How do you say, 'Bring me steak and eggs or I'll slit your throat' in Italian?" he asked.

"Look it up in the phrase book," Bear said absently, and glanced out the window at the sky, whose clouds were streaked like white marble. *I've been gone for too long.*

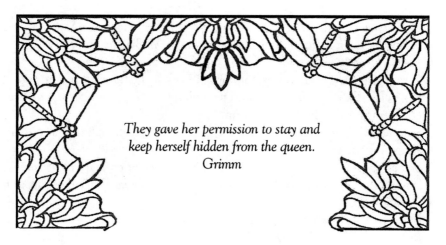

They gave her permission to stay and
keep herself hidden from the queen.
Grimm

Chapter Three

She woke up in a fright when the el train went by, roaring on its elevated tracks like an airborne dragon. And then she remembered where she was. In a ground floor room at the back of St. Catherine's High School, in what had formerly been a dismal office cubicle—as she had reason to know—but which had now been transformed with pale paint and soap into a room with a distinctly monastic air. There was nothing in the room but a cot and a chair and a small crucifix on the wall. For the first time in a long while, she felt safe.

Breathing deeply, she blinked at the glow of a streetlight coming in through the one window high up in the sturdy thick block wall. It was still night outside, and she could hear the screeching of tires and the thudding of boom boxes. It was perhaps twenty-four hours since her escape.

Eventually the rattle and screech of the metallic dragon passed, vanishing into the night. The subdued aftermath passed for silence, enough for her to think about sleeping again. At least it was cooler in this basement room.

It was a paradox. St. Catherine's was her old high school, the place she had dreaded going to for an entire wretched senior year and which she had sought refuge from, day after dreary, miserable day. And now, in a surprising reversal, it had become the place of refuge for her. Here, of all places, she now felt safe.

Everything in my life is turning into its mirror image. I'm not safe at home or with my family. I'm only safe in the dark and tangled woods of the City where no one I know can find me. I'm on the other side of the looking-glass...

Stop thinking, she told herself curtly. *Stop extrapolating. Stop drawing connections between things that aren't really connected. The whole point is, you're safe.*

Curling up on the hard but comfortable cot-bed, she tried to get herself to relax again. Safe. An ironic term. Particularly when part of the enemy was herself. Her intuition. Her imagination.

But there is a real enemy out there, she told herself. Hadn't last night confirmed just that?

You've been jumping at shadows and seeing threats in ordinary conversations all summer, the other side of her said sternly. *Calm down. Don't think about it now. Just let it go.*

But no, no, no! I'm not deranged! Someone really was *after me!*

But why? It makes no sense.

In an attempt to explain herself to herself, she tried to rebuild the events of the preceding days like a tenuous house of cards, trying to see if the structure would hold. It was still wavering.

Would you really be thinking that this was anything but a freak incident if you hadn't been working off the supposition that you were in danger in the first place?

That's not the point. The point is, I'm in trouble. All right, most *likely I'm in trouble. How can I escape?*

A partial answer emerged from her construction work, a face card balanced tremulously on two others. *I could go to him. I need to talk to someone, and he might understand, even though … it involves him.*

Rubbing the back of her head painfully, she sat up and looked around for a clock to check the time, and then realized there was none. She had no way of knowing what time it was. But even if she was crazy, she was rational enough to know that this time, the witching hour of the City, was no time to go outside alone. No matter how important it was for her to get help.

I'll wait until tomorrow morning, she thought. *I can slip out sometime tomorrow, and come back here if I need to. At least one more time, I've got to go and see him, and tell him everything that's happened.*

The realistic side of her concurred. *At the very least, you need to get a second opinion. Since you can't reach Mom or Rose, and Bear isn't here…*

It was ludicrous, ludicrous to think she could begin to handle this by herself, without her family or her friends. *But I'm alone,* both sides of her merged into agreement. *For better or for worse, this is my battle. For sanity. For my life.*

Mentally discarding the pack of cards and her efforts to reconstruct the past few days, she closed her eyes, wishing for sleep. She tried to think about something that had nothing to do with this situation, nothing to do with the cold black and red calculus of jacks, queens, kings, and aces.

Her hand on her heart, she tried to breathe deeply again. She could never remember dreaming, but perhaps she could escape into memories, memories of things that had been, that were wound up with wishes of how things might be—

Remember before this all happened, she told herself. *Back when you felt like you were a princess and that nothing terrible was going to happen to you ever again…*

* * *

Till it has loved, no man or woman can become itself… Emily Dickinson had said that, and it was true. At least, the girl felt it was true.

Holding his hand. Walking close to him, in the enclosed garden, shielded from the wind. They had been at a museum, and he had suggested they go outside and walk in the cloister gardens, even though it was the beginning of January.

"I love walking in gardens in the winter time," he had said abruptly, as they paced around the perimeter of the perfectly square garden, cut into four shapely but simple quadrants.

"Why?" she had asked, leaning against his dark brown overcoat.

"Because in the winter time, you can see them for what they really are. Their true shape. They say a truly well-designed garden is beautiful even in the winter, when to the eye, all its growth is barren and sleeping," he said. "Can't you tell?"

She looked around. It was not a particularly elaborate garden. At the center of its four quadrant beds was a font of water, drained at this time of year. There were a few trees, the winter remnants of plants and a lawn, and the arches of the medieval-style architecture surrounding the little space. The winter air made everything seem gray, black, and silver—the roof tiles, the pillars, the forked branches of the naked trees. "It's very simple."

"It doesn't need to be more complex," he said. "Does it?"

"No, you're right," she said with a sigh. "It's irreducible beauty."

She had been perfectly happy that day, wearing the white dress he had given her, still in that festive mood of the days that followed Christmas like trailing banners. Once again, she wondered how she, a very ordinary girl, had found herself in this situation. There was nothing particularly unusual about her. She didn't think she was extraordinarily beautiful or fascinatingly charming. For most of her life, she had been utterly typical—a rather shy, not noticeably talented person who did fairly but not unusually well in school, played the piano with average talent, a girl who was inclined to be bookish but certainly not a genius. And from time to time, she had odd senses about things, senses that were troubling, but usually accurate.

And yet somehow she had acquired a rather extraordinary boyfriend, and she still wasn't sure how that had happened.

"I still feel as though a unicorn has followed me home and wanted to be my friend, and I'm not sure what to do next," she murmured.

He had laughed at her analogy as he pushed back his dark unruly hair, shorn of its recent dreadlocks but already growing shaggy again. "Why a unicorn?" he asked, feeling his forehead. "Is it the horn?" They had just seen the Unicorn Tapestries a few minutes ago, so the image should have struck him as natural.

She laughed a little. "It's just that—I've always liked unicorns, but I've always been afraid of them at the same time." She felt silly, explaining. What she meant was that there was a mystery and a wonder about Bear, even now.

"I never believed in them before," she said truthfully after a moment. "I always thought they were myths. I never thought I'd find someone like you."

He had looked at her then, with his dark brown eyes, which always seemed to see more of her than she saw of herself. And as usual, she felt self-conscious, and a bit afraid, mixed with a generous amount of pleasure at being appreciated. To hide her feelings, she traced a finger around the cold edge of the empty stone font. It was astonishing how different it was to be close to a young man. She still hadn't gotten over how fundamentally unlike girls guys were.

"Do you know, I never believed that girls like you still existed either?" he said, running his own larger hand over the beveled rim of the bowl. "Not today. Not anymore."

She couldn't help smiling at him. "We were laboring under the mutual impression that our species were mythological."

He grinned. "Well, now that we have met each other, let's make a bargain. I'll believe in you if you believe in me. Is that fair?"

"That sounds fair to me."

"Should we shake on it?"

And so they did, shaking hands over the font. But he held onto her hand a bit longer than the handshake demanded, and searched her face. Again, she wondered, fleetingly, if this would be the moment they would kiss. He had never really kissed her before. Now as he looked at her, she felt her heart quicken, but for some reason, he seemed to be holding himself back. At last he squeezed and released her hand and turned slowly away.

"Unicorns can be dangerous companions," he had said, walking to a further quadrant of the garden, leaving her standing in the center. "I wouldn't want to hurt you, Blanche. After all, in some ways we are different species."

She had thought at first he was referring to the danger she had encountered when he was tracking down a ruthless criminal, but his last remark was cryptic. She waited, to see if he would explain.

He didn't. Gazing through the fork of one of the four trees, he looked over at her, a shadow of the old secretiveness about him still. "If I'm taking this slow, can you understand why?"

"I think I can," she said, in a small voice. She looked up at the peaked roofs around them, feeling a bit hurt nevertheless. She didn't understand why he seemed so unsure. Granted, it would probably be difficult for anyone to settle back into normal life after serving an unjust prison sentence, living on the streets, and engaging in a risky undercover investigation for a year or two. Being a witness in two criminal trials hadn't helped him either. She could appreciate why he was finding it hard, but his uncertainty hurt, even though she knew he wasn't trying to hurt her.

He paced around the perimeter of the garden in silence for a few minutes. She watched him from the center, and thought to herself that he was still like a creature of the wild in some respects. "You want to finish college, right?" he had said, apparently changing the subject.

She was quiet before she answered. "I don't know."

"Why not? I thought you said you wanted to become a nurse, like your mom."

She looked at the ground. "I'm not so sure anymore."

What she meant, but she couldn't say it, was that she had been wondering if she really wanted four years of school, only to take a job she wouldn't be working at very long, because what she really wanted was just to—

"I thought that if you went to college, maybe I might—try it out too, for a while," he said at last.

"Are you sure that college is something that you should just—try?" she asked.

"Well, it's not as though I can't afford it. I'm just not sure if I want to go yet."

She was quiet. Despite the fact that according to contemporary mores, there was no difference between men and women, she was realistic enough to realize that his not being sure if he should go to college had entirely different ramifications than her own uncertainty. For one thing, when he talked like this, she started to wonder if they should even be dating. It was frustrating, that her college decision was hanging on his. If he went, she wasn't sure she would go, but if he wouldn't go, and wouldn't engage in any kind of decision towards his life direction, she knew she probably should go ahead and make her life plans, regardless of him.

But yet, she had this inexplicable (and from the modern point of view, foolish and dangerous) urge to plan her whole life around his. She kept wondering if the modern point of view was ultimately the more practical one.

"I suppose it's one of the risks of getting involved with unicorns," she murmured to herself.

That fabulous monster paced towards her again, frowning. The wind rushed between them, stirring her white skirts around her ankles. She shivered inside her gray cloak.

"You know I have an errand to do in Europe," he said at last, kicking at a loose twig on the path.

"Donating Father Raymond's treasure to the Vatican Museums," she said softly.

"Yes. I'm going to bring them over personally. But once that's done with, I've been thinking of staying over there for a while. Would you mind that very much?" He wasn't looking at her, but at the twig.

"No," she had said, and realized that Bear extending his trip was not altogether unexpected. There had been a lot of tension building up in him over the last few months. Bear still couldn't talk about much that was troubling him, but she was beginning to see part of it. Maybe better than Bear could see it himself.

He ruminated, and then looked hopefully at her. "Maybe—if I stay till the summer—maybe you and Rose could come over and visit me. We could do some hiking together. That would be fun."

She had to smile at his sudden eagerness, but she dropped her eyes and shook her head. There was the whole issue of money, which hovered constantly between them. Bear was independently wealthy now, and her family had never been well off, particularly since her father had died. She couldn't afford to go to Europe—she couldn't even afford to go to community college without student loans—and she

didn't want to remind Bear of that, because it would
seem as though she were asking him to pay her way
to Europe. He would, in a heartbeat, but she didn't
want to ask. "I don't think I could," she said. "I've
got to work this summer if I'm going to keep taking
classes in the fall. Rose is going to be working too. It
just wouldn't be possible, Bear. I'm sorry."

"Well, at least you could keep it open as an
option," he said hesitantly. "I'll miss you."

"I'll   miss   you   too,"   she   said,   almost
automatically. Miss him! Of course she would miss
him. More accurately, she would struggle in the void
without him.

* * *

So in the middle of February, he had gone overseas to do his errand, and
remained in Europe traveling while she took classes at a community college,
finished her first year, and started looking for a summer job. He wrote to her
frequently, but still did not seem inclined to come back home.

When the summer began, he brought up the possibility of a European trip
again, a tantalizing possibility for her. Even if she had had the money, she
doubted the wisdom of going, without knowing where Bear was at. So she
stayed at home and worked. *Back to normality. Back to where I have always
been.*

But it wasn't normality, after all. Something fundamental had changed,
and she spent most of the summer trying to figure out what it was. Again, her
imagination mocked her. *You've gone through to the other side of the looking-
glass and everything is a chess game...*

*Perhaps it's a good thing you haven't seen Bear. Would he turn out to be
something different, on the other side of the mirror? A peril instead of a protector?*

In the black early hours of the new day in that unexpected shelter in the
City, she shivered.

II

On Monday Brother Leon had woken to the relative silence of the early
morning in the Bronx. It was not yet excruciatingly hot, probably the most
pleasant time of the day. He opened the window, which he had left closed
last night in order to sleep. Now there were no boom boxes growling in the
background, and he sighed, breathing in the smell of cooled-down concrete

and fumes from the cars snarling at each other during the A.M. rush on the Cross Bronx expressway. "New York," he said simply. It was home.

He slipped his heavy gray habit over his head (the outfit was comfortable now but he knew it would get hotter as the day wore on), wrapped a length of rope around his waist for a belt, kissed the cross of his rosary, which had been lying beside his bed mat, and looped the brown beads around the rope. Kneeling down, he fastened his sandals, and he was dressed.

Going downstairs, he slipped into the church, got to his knees and bent down, kissing the holy ground where the presence of the Lord resided. Getting up, he ambled over to his usual pew, genuflected and sat, pulling his hood deeply over his face to block out the view of the world, and began to focus his mind on his God.

He resisted the impulse to look up when he heard others coming into the church for the Office of Readings.

By the time prayer started, he was completely focused. After the Office was over, there was an hour of silent meditation, then Morning Prayer, then Mass. The friary prayer schedule was fairly rigorous. So it came as a total surprise to him, after prayer was over, to discover Nora sitting in the pew behind him. Not that he had forgotten about her, but he hadn't really expected to see her until about nine in the morning. It wasn't even eight.

She was still looking drained and apprehensive, but she smiled briefly at him in greeting, though she still seemed a bit uncertain. There was a prayer book on the seat of the pew beside her, and he wondered if she had been there for the entire two hours of prayer. Brother Herman came to her and leaned over to tell her something. Brother Leon guessed that he was inviting her to breakfast. She smiled and shook her head.

Apparently she didn't have much of an appetite, because she appeared at the refectory door only after they were finishing breakfast, a pale figure with her white skin and yellow dress.

"Good morning. Want something to eat?" Matt asked her after they had all said good morning, but she shook her head.

"I'm fine, thank you. I just came to find out when I could start helping with the cleaning."

"Not for about fifteen minutes. Would you like to change into some other clothes?" Brother Herman asked her.

Nora glanced down at her yellow dress, and half-smiled. "You're all wearing the same thing you wore yesterday. Isn't that the routine here?"

Several of the friars laughed. "If you'd like to help with the cleaning, perhaps you'd better change out of that nice dress. We do have quite a bit of donated clothing in the vestibule, as you probably saw," Brother Herman said. "You're welcome to help yourself. Most of it is men's clothing, but there might be some women's things or something you could wear."

"Thank you," Nora said. "I'll go take a quick look right now." She turned and vanished into the hallway like a ghost.

Leon was about to say something to Brother Matt—some sort of joke about having a yellow dress for a habit—when he caught a glimpse of Brother George's face. The older friar's blue eyes were sullen beneath his red hair. Catching Leon's eye, he scowled.

"I don't think we should have a woman living in such close quarters to us," he muttered. "This idea of giving mission opportunities to the laity is all very well, but I don't think we should have them popping in on us like this."

"Well, I guess the Fathers are still figuring out how this is going to work," Leon said flippantly, referring to the priests—Father Bernard and Father Francis—by their house nicknames.

"These are the sorts of things that should be settled on right away," Brother George said in a low voice. "Wasn't it St. Francis who said, 'The Lord sent me brothers but it may be the devil who has sent me sisters'?"

"Well, it turned out that the Lord sent him St. Clare," Leon felt obliged to say.

Brother George sniffed. "This girl doesn't seem like a potential nun to me."

Thinking that it was better to end the conversation here, Leon got up. "Can I take your plate?" he asked, and the older brother handed it to him. Leon took the two plates and silverware into the kitchen. "Where are we meeting for class?" he asked Father Bernard. As the friary was still being renovated, the rooms for the novices' classes changed occasionally.

"In the office," Father Bernard said, referring to the room where Father Francis paid bills and kept accounts. "We'll start in a few minutes."

Leon nodded and started to the chapel to get his notebook. On the way, he met Brother Herman coming from answering the door. "So what's up for this afternoon?" he asked Brother Herman, who was in charge of setting the work schedule.

"We're working in the high school again," Brother Herman said as they went down the passageway to the church. "I suppose Nora can help us out there. I should find something for her to work on now."

They saw Nora emerge from the vestibule holding some folded-up clothing, and Brother Herman said heartily, "Did you find anything?"

"I did, thank you," Nora said. She hesitated. "The vestibule—did you—could you use—well, *it* could use some straightening out."

"Yeah, to put it mildly," Leon said. "Looks like a truck sort of dumped it everywhere, doesn't it?"

"I could go through it for you," Nora said.

Brother Herman went into the vestibule. "It would be great if you could put them into different piles—shirts, coats, pants, that kind of thing. And all the women's and children's clothing in separate piles—we'll send them over to the women's shelter downtown. Eventually I'd like to get things sorted out by size."

"I could do that easily," Nora said. So they left her to her work, and Leon wondered if she wanted to be alone as he retrieved his notebook from his usual pew.

"Do you think there's more to her problems than just a mugging?" he asked Brother Herman abruptly as they walked away.

Before the older brother could reply, there was a banging at the front door of the friary. "The day is starting," Brother Herman said with a sigh. All day long, people knocked at the door of the friary, asking for food, money, clothing, or just because they needed someone to talk to.

"It's probably Fernando," Brother Herman muttered. "Father Bernard said he would be coming by to get some shoes. Why don't you sit with him while I find him some?"

Leon nodded. It was an unspoken rule that most visitors were not to be left alone in the friary, as too many of them would steal anything that wasn't nailed down.

As Brother Herman greeted the old man at the door with a smile and listened to that morning's list of woes, Leon let his mind wander. It occurred to him that they had left Nora alone in the vestibule, sorting clothes, and wondered if that was wise. *We don't know much about her,* Brother George had said. He admitted the older brother was right.

III

A girl with hair as black as night and skin as white as snow...

The airplane roared through the clouds over the Atlantic Ocean, and Bear, knowing he should be sleeping, but unable to force his stubborn body to comply with the change of time zones, drifted in a stupor of memories. He was seated by the window, and looking out at the billowing cloudscape below.

Drifting in a netherworld that was neither heaven nor earth, he hung suspended, not sure of where he was supposed to be. He couldn't do anything else until he got home, and the anxiety of wanting to do something and not being able to do anything put him into a coma of inaction that paralleled the larger inaction of his life.

He hoped, he prayed Blanche would be there at her mother's house when he got back, a little surprised to see him so soon, wondering if he had yet made up his mind. She had a right to know what to expect from him—

Princess, like a rose is her cheek,
And her eyes are as blue as the sky,

A fragment of a poem by Andrew Lang came back to him now. He had thought of it the first time he had ever seen her. That had been during his dark days, and rough living had made him rough. She hadn't known what to make of him when they first met, and couldn't figure out if he was a good person or a bad person. Being with her and her family had begun to civilize him again. He owed her a lot.

He thought about the contents of her letter. Maybe she was right. But he wasn't anxious to go digging into the squalid wastes of the past. Even after six months abroad, he wasn't ready.

Finally he broke from semi-sleep to realize that they were descending to New York City. The trip was over. He felt lassitude and resignation hanging all over him like weary and petulant children, and tried to shake the feelings off. His body thought it was seven o'clock in the evening, but on this side of the ocean, it was merely one in the afternoon. It was going to be a long day.

Fish closed the book he had been perusing and thrust it into his carryon. "Rats. I forgot to get Rose a postcard of something or other in Rome she wanted."

Bear smiled. Blanche's younger sister Rose had an unusual relationship with his brother. "What did she want?"

"Some sort of Sibyl from the Sistine Chapel." Fish took off his hat and rubbed his hair wearily. "You know she was going to be in some sort of play this summer?"

"Yes, Blanche told me. She got the lead in a summer stock production of *Through the Looking Glass.* She was playing Alice."

"Yes, that's it. Well, apparently it was critically important to her that I attend one of the performances. When she found out I was going to be out of the country and would miss the whole thing, she said I'd have to come back with a postcard of this Sistine Chapel Sibyl thing or—or something terrible would happen to me. Such as her never speaking to me again. And now I've forgotten the postcard altogether. So I suppose that's the end of my association with Miss Rose Brier."

"Well, allow me to be your savior," Bear said, feeling in his jacket pocket. "I got her one."

"You did?"

Bear held up the postcard of the Delphic Sibyl from the Sistine Chapel. "She asked me about it too. She said she had asked you but was sure you would forget."

"That redheaded girl knows me uncannily well," Fish muttered, taking the card and dropping his hat back on his head. "Thank you. I think."

They passed through the ordeal of customs and security with the usual hassles. After they reclaimed their luggage, Bear said, "Your car is back home, right? So I guess we need to call a taxi." He started looking around for a pay phone.

"I'll take care of it," Fish pulled out a cell phone, turned it on, and dialed. He glanced at Bear after he had made the call. "You really should have your own cell phone, you know. I don't know how I'd survive without one."

"I prefer to be low-tech," Bear said.

His brother rolled his eyes. "So our plan of attack is to drop off our luggage and get over to Blanche's house, right?"

"Yes," Bear said. "I have the keys to her house back at our apartment. Let me try her number again." He glanced around the airport terminal again, irrationally, as if he expected Blanche to be there, waiting for him. But of course, she wasn't.

There was no answer at the Briers' number, so the brothers went down to meet their taxi. Bear gave the driver his address and said, "Get us there as fast as you can."

He regretted his words soon, as the driver took this as free license to commit even more traffic violations than was usual for New York cabbies. As their taxi wove wildly in and out of traffic down the highway, Bear's anxiety over finding Blanche took on a faster tempo.

"Actually seems calmer here after the traffic in Rome," Fish said jokingly, holding onto the door and the back of the seat. "Why do you have the keys to Blanche's house?"

"Her mom gave me a set when I watched their house for them over New Year's, before I took off for Europe," Bear said. "Don't you remember?"

Fish shook his head. "I don't know why I'm surprised. I've seen that pile of metal you carry around in your pocket. Looks like you've kept every key that's ever passed through your hands."

"It's been useful," Bear said, feeling heaviness come over him again.

"I'd rather just stick with my set of skeleton keys," Fish said. He glanced at his brother, and attempted to change the subject. "Father Raymond said an international trip changes a person forever. So, do you feel changed?"

"I probably won't notice until this crisis is over." Trying to take his mind off the tension, Bear looked out the window at the passing buildings. "One thing for certain—most structures over here are pretty ugly by comparison with some of the old buildings I saw in Germany and France and Italy. Could you believe the beauty of some of that stonework in Venice?"

"Stonemasonry and stone carving is a dying craft in America, or so I'm told," Fish observed. "Even if we wanted to make buildings like those, we wouldn't know how."

"That's a shame," Bear said, and turned that thought over in his mind for the rest of the ride.

As they pulled up at their apartment building, Fish said suddenly, "Blanche was watering our plants for us. I wonder when the doorman saw her last."

"Nobody gets by Ahmed," Bear agreed. They had known the doorman since they had been children. "He notices everyone who comes into the building." He got out of the taxi while Fish paid the driver, and hurried inside to speak to the short Arabian man in his dark green doorman's uniform.

"Ahmed, have you seen Blanche Brier lately?" he asked, forgetting that the man would be surprised to see him after so long an absence.

The man started and dropped his eyes. "No," he said. "I have not seen her since Friday." He seemed distinctly uncomfortable.

"When you saw her, did she seem—upset or anything?" Bear asked, a bit awkwardly.

"No, she—well, she seemed as she usually is," the doorman said. "Excuse me. I must go speak to the manager."

Fish raised an eyebrow as the man hurried off. Bear was bewildered.

"Something's bothering him," Fish remarked, getting into the elevator, lugging his bag. "Not at all like him."

"I should have at least said hello first," Bear recollected his manners. "Maybe I just startled him."

"Humph."

The elevator reached the top floor, and Fish pulled out his own keys authoritatively. He unlocked and opened the cream-paneled door to their penthouse apartment and then paused, as though he was an animal who had caught a strange scent.

Bear passed him with barely a glance around. "Grab your car keys and let's go."

He hurried up the staircase that curved around the living room to the loft bedrooms at the top, tossed his luggage in his bedroom, and, rummaging around in his top dresser drawer, retrieved his key ring, which he had left here while he had been gone in Europe. As Fish had remarked, it was pretty heavy. One of these days, he should thin it out...

"Bear," Fish said from downstairs. "Something's wrong. Look around."

Struck by his voice, Bear walked to the staircase balcony and looked down at the beautifully furnished apartment that had been his mother's, now a significant part of their inheritance from her. It was a gracious living space, which his mother had designed herself and poured out her artistic talent into creating. Bear had been grateful that his father hadn't changed it during the time when it had been in his possession.

"What's wrong?" he asked in a low voice.

"I don't know—yet," Fish said, striding past the exquisite European Madonna panel hanging in the entranceway. He paused and looked around the living room as though he were afraid to go in, in case he tripped an unseen alarm. "My antennae are going crazy. Someone's been here since I left."

"Blanche has—" Bear said, and, spurred on by a sudden worry, he turned and searched through the bedrooms and bathrooms on the top floor, looking for what he dreaded finding—Blanche's body, wounded or even dead. But there was no sign of her.

He returned from his hurried search, telling himself to calm down, only to find his brother prowling through the rooms like a wary cat sniffing a strange dog.

"Something is wrong, but I don't know what," Fish was saying to himself again.

"Is something missing?" Bear asked, coming down the steps.

"If so, I haven't figured it out," Fish said. He stared at the rose-brocade antique sofa and suddenly crossed the oriental carpet and pointed.

"Someone's been under that sofa cushion," he said softly.

Bear looked at the seat cushion. It was slightly askew. Feeling odd, he looked at the ivory chaise lounge. The seat cushion there was also slightly lifted, as though it hadn't been put back correctly.

"Maybe Blanche was looking under the cushions for something she dropped," Bear suggested.

"The pillows," Fish pointed at the two dark velvet pillows thrown haphazardly on the floor next to the mosaic-inlaid coffee table. "What girl leaves sofa pillows like that?"

"Blanche was the last person who had access to this place, right?" Bear asked. "You haven't called in a housekeeper or anything?"

"Not since I left, no," Fish said. "No point in cleaning a house no one's living in, is there?" He glared around the room. "Someone's ransacked this place and put everything back," he said. "*But why?*"

"And how would they have gotten in?" Now on his guard, Bear stepped into the kitchen to see if anything was amiss. He looked at the herbs growing in the carved boxes arranged at the base of the kitchen's floor-to-ceiling windows. The ones Blanche had been watering. They looked slightly askew, as though someone had dug them out of their pots and dropped them back in without much care. "Look at these."

Fish fingered the plants gently, and then got up. "Check out that cabinet door," he pointed. The cabinet door over the refrigerator was slightly open. "Not shut right. And neither is that one over there," he said, pointing to another cabinet over the sink.

There was a knock on the door, and Fish and Bear instantly pivoted towards the door. Bear's heart pounded as he walked to the door and opened it.

"Arthur Denniston?" asked the tall, brown-haired man who stood there, pulling out a badge. There were two other men behind him, hands in their jackets, possibly covering their weapons.

"Yes," Bear nodded almost automatically.

"I'm Morris Tang, special agent with the Drug Enforcement Administration." He looked at Fish. "Are you Benedict Denniston?"

"That's correct," Fish folded his arms. "Is there a problem?"

The man gave a wry smile. "You are the owners of this apartment?"

"Joint owners, yes," Bear said. *It's either bad news, or trouble.* At first he had thought it was bad news—had Blanche been found dead? —But the sight of plainclothes policemen gave him an entirely different feeling. He had been here before.

"I'm here to advise you of the fact that federal agents found caches of controlled substances hidden in the cushions of your living room furniture this past Saturday, August the seventh," the man said. He pulled out a photograph, and Bear saw a picture of a man standing in front of their apartment door, holding up a plastic bag containing dozens of blue and pink pills.

"What the heck—" Bear said angrily. He glanced at his brother's face, and saw Fish had gone pale.

"Oh my God," Fish said quietly. "I didn't think it was this."

The agent looked at them carefully. "The pills in the photograph are metadylene-dioxymethamphetamine, or MDMA, otherwise known as Adam, or Ecstasy. MDMA is an illegal substance on the federal schedule. As the owners of the apartment, the government is holding you liable for the contents. I have arrest warrants here for both of you."

Bear felt a rush of strong emotion, which he crushed quickly and forcefully. "The drugs aren't ours," he said. "I'd like to call our lawyer. Someone's framed us."

Again.

So Snow White remained in the house of the seven little men and kept house for them.

Grimm

Chapter Four

aving fled down the labyrinthine ways, breathing hard, knowing it was a risk to come here, she hurried up to the house and knocked on the door.

A nurse came to the door, not—she noticed—the same nurse that had been there last time. His nurses had been changed again.

"Is Ms. Fairston in?" she asked cautiously.

"No ma'am," said the nurse, looking at her suspiciously.

"Can I see Mr. Fairston? Please? It's very important."

"He's not seeing anyone."

"Please. He told me to come and see him. Tell him Blanche is here."

"Just a moment."

Waiting, the girl unaccountably shivered in the summer's heat, praying that her chance would succeed.

In a few minutes, the nurse returned and said, "Come with me."

She followed the nurse across the black-and-white marble-tiled floor and up the steps.

"How is he?" she whispered.

"As well as can be expected for a man in his condition. I'm told he hasn't been out of bed in a month."

Then she's been told wrong, the girl said to herself. But as usual, she was silent.

She walked over the thick carpet of the hallway, trying to stop her hands from trembling. If only she still had her purse to hold onto. She had been fortunate to find a few subway tokens in her pocket for the ride over.

The nurse led her into the small bedroom at the back of the house where a television chattered, and left, shutting the door behind her. The girl noticed that she barely glanced at the frail figure on the bed. *Not good help,* the girl thought, leaning over to straighten the twisted pillows on the bed.

"Blanche. It really is you," Mr. Fairston said, blinking his left eye and twisting to sit up. Only one side of his face was active. The other side was frozen, motionless, a prefigurement of death. With his left hand, he turned off the television with his remote. "What happened to your hair?" He spoke with difficulty, but the girl was used to his accent by now, and had no trouble understanding him.

The girl tucked a stray strand behind her ear and tried to figure out how to answer. But the reality of what she had to tell him appeared to her now in all its ugliness, and she didn't know where to start. To put off the hard part, she checked the glass on his bed tray and found it was bone dry. She stepped to the small refrigerator in the corner to fill it from the pitcher she had suggested keeping there.

"Thank you—how did you know I wanted that?" the man asked gratefully, taking it with his left hand. His right was shrunken and lay useless by his side. One side of his body was paralyzed. His gray hair, as usual, was bushy and unruly.

She smiled as she gave him the water. "Those medications for your tumor make you thirsty. It says so on the labels."

He tilted his head to the left. "You're such a caregiver. How do you remember these things?"

She warmed at the compliment. "Perhaps it's in the genes. Remember, my mother's a nurse."

"That's right—I keep forgetting that."

"Plus, whenever I come to read to you, you always ask for something to drink, even though I'm the one doing the reading. Hasn't this nurse been making sure you're hydrated?"

Half the man's face grimaced in an expression the girl found comical. "She says I'd be better off getting water intravenously, but I can't stand IVs." He paused. "This isn't your usual day to come by, is it?"

The girl shook her head, and swallowed. "Actually, I am in a bit of trouble. I thought I'd, well, find someone to talk to..." She started to pick up the books and magazines that had dropped from the bed to the floor.

The concern that had been in the man's eyes returned, and his voice became lower. "My wife told me you had been arrested."

"What do you mean?" She turned back to him, her mind reeling.

Mr. Fairston convulsed in a cough. "She said you were caught with drugs at your workplace, and with thousands of dollars of stolen money."

Fortunately her hands were busy, and she managed to keep her voice calm. "Well, she's mistaken, isn't she? I admit things have been difficult the last few days, but I haven't been arrested. If I had, I wouldn't be here with you, would I?"

"Is that the truth, Blanche?"

"Yes." She sounded confident, but inside she was shaking.

The man rubbed his head with his good hand, and stared at her. "I'm sorry. I don't know why I should be so suspicious. I guess it's just that...I suppose I can blame the medication. Or the condition. You're going to think I'm paranoid."

"Well, sometimes it is hard to know what to believe these days." The girl finished tidying up the magazines and put them in a stack on a nearby shelf, using the time to collect herself. Now even this friendship was in jeopardy.

"But my wife seemed so sure," the man said wonderingly. "How could there be a mistake?"

"I don't know," the girl shrugged, glanced at the mirror on the wall, and saw that she was paler than ever. She quickly looked away. "How are you feeling?"

"Terrible," the man said with a half smile, trying to put aside the conversation, but she could see the doubt hovering in his eyes. "'Not going gently into that good night...'" he quoted Dylan Thomas again and sighed. "I guess it gets closer every day. The realization that there's not much time left for me. Before the tumor takes over and my brain goes blank. I—" he paused. "I was quite upset to hear this about you. But perhaps it was only a dream, after all. Some trick of my brain."

"Perhaps." She forced a smile.

"I don't like it when that happens," he said, his eyes looking up at the ceiling. "It's been happening more and more often lately. I don't like it when I can't trust reality any more. It scares me. I wish I could stop it. But—"

She was reminded of how it had been to lose her own father to cancer, realizing that the gentle giant of her childhood memory had shrunken into a weak, dying man—a man who had eventually become a corpse, and then a memory. Suddenly, being here was like losing her father all over again.

And he couldn't help her, after all. More alone than ever, she had to go beyond herself or risk cracking. "Would you mind if I prayed with you, Mr. Fairston?"

"Still berating me for being an agnostic?" he smiled at her wryly.

"Of course not. Just being myself."

He leaned back. "If you don't mind, I'll just listen. It's—peaceful."

She prayed, on the edge of that darkness and confusion. She prayed an entire decade of the rosary, feeling dry and barren within, hearing the faint reverberation of her voice on the walls in that cheerless sickroom. This was how it had been, for a long time now—comforting others, responding, smiling, going through the motions of her life, but inside feeling nothing but the echo of emptiness. The fear began to come upon her, and she struggled to keep her composure.

But as usual, the prayers seemed to soothe him. He stroked her hand as she finished. "You know, sometimes I think you're like the daughter I should have had, if I had had a daughter. I'm glad you came by, Blanche." His eyelids were growing heavy.

"I am too," she said, and this was sincere. She had always enjoyed visiting the elderly, but Mr. Fairston had become more than a work of mercy. He had become a friend.

> *If I can stop one heart from breaking*
> *I shall not live in vain*
> *If I can ease one life the aching*
> *Or heal one pain*
> *...I shall not live in vain.*

"You left your book on Emily Dickinson here again," he said, rousing himself and reaching shakily for the book on the bedside table. "I was looking at it while you were gone."

"Keep it," she said. "It's a gift."

"Are you sure?"

"I am. Keep it, until—"

There was a silence, the usual breaking-off of sentences. It was understood what the silence meant.

"I'm sure my wife will get it back to you. She's been saying I shouldn't see people, that it hastens my decline. But if you want to come, even if I'm not responding—I think I would like to hear you reading, still."

"I'll be back to read it to you," she said. "I promise."

He took her hand and squeezed something into it. "I know you will. In case you need it—" His voice grew faint, and she saw he was falling asleep.

Looking down at her hand briefly, she saw a door key.

"Thank you. I'll come back." She put it in her pocket—later on she would put it on her neck chain—and got to her feet, still stiff from her bruises. Gently she laid her hand on his forehead. His lips moved, but he didn't speak again. Her eyes traveled over the untidy and inexplicably dirty room, and she wished she felt safe enough to stay and clean it more thoroughly. How did the nurse stand it?

She got down on her hands and knees again and picked up the used tissues, bits of plastic wrappers, and paper scraps that littered the carpet, and put them into the overflowing wastebasket. She packed it down to keep it neater, and while doing so found a medicine bottle, white with its label missing. It wasn't empty—there were two ordinary looking white pills in it. At first she thought it had fallen from the cluttered bedside table, but as she looked at the medication and vitamins there, she could see this bottle was different from the others. Perhaps the white bottle was some sort of pain medication he had been taken off. After some hesitation, she thrust it into her pocket. *When I see my mom again, I'll ask her*, she thought fleetingly. Then, *Mom has no idea what's going on with me now.*

Quietly she let herself out of the room. Alone, she glanced around the dim hallway uneasily. She didn't like this house, as upscale as it was. At least she had managed to come during a time when Mr. Fairston was relatively alone. She didn't want to meet—

At the base of the staircase was a huge mirror, trimmed in stained glass flowers, and dragonflies. Its vast glassy surface had the smoky gray look of an antique. After coming down the steps, she couldn't help stopping to look at her reflection, and saw a girl with a pale face and unevenly-cut soot-black hair. Whose eyes were still red. *I look haunted*, she thought. *Not beautiful. Not any more. Surely no one would still think I was beautiful.*

"This has been a looking-glass summer," her sister had said flippantly, referring to the play she was in. "I feel like it's taken over my life."

Yes, that was how she felt—as though she had vanished through a looking-glass into a mirror-image world which seemed the same as normal life, but where everything was backwards. Where she wasn't even sure who she was any longer. She didn't even think she looked the same.

Blanche has been replaced by a fugitive from justice, a girl who's too scared to tell others her own name.

She paused, as though she had heard something close to her, and stared into the depths of the mirror. Once again, she felt it—the sense of a malignant presence studying her. As though the mirror were alive, with a personality—a—

Just another doorway into madness, she thought, and pulled her eyes away. Her imagination had become her enemy lately, and she hurried to the door and let herself out.

II

After the morning class was done, Leon had stopped by the vestibule to see Nora, but there was no sign of her.

"Hey, where's Nora?" he called to Brother Herman, who was busy planning the renovation and repairs on the church.

Brother Herman held up a piece of sketch paper to the light and said, "Hm? Nora? She left some time ago. She said she had an errand to run and would be back soon."

"Oh," Leon said, and shrugged aside his suspicions. *Why shouldn't she run an errand if she needs to?* he scolded himself. Brother George was sweeping the aisles with a broom, and looked over his shoulder at Leon. But seeing Leon's noncommittal expression, he turned away.

Leon's attention was distracted by a knock on the friary door. He started towards it, but Brother Matt, who was on porter duty, emerged from the refectory and got to the door first.

At the door was a tall, agitated black woman in a short denim skirt, holding a kid by each hand. Her scowl changed to relief when the friars opened the door, and she burst into a torrent of Jamaican *patois* mixed with English. Matt held up his hands with a confused smile.

"Hold on—let me get someone who can help you—Le—! Oh! Here you are," Matt started to bellow as Leon elbowed him aside.

"Yeah, you need the expert here—Aay, Marisol! *Wha a gwan?*" Leon queried, hitching up his rope belt. "Aay Donovan! Aay Jacky!" The kids grinned and started reaching for the dangling knots and the rosary beads.

Marisol yanked them back firmly with a sharp word. "*Nu bodda di priest! Dress back! Mi granmadda a visit, an shi need fi catch one flight tomorrow, but di taxi-man too tief! —*"

Leon listened attentively, "Her mom needs a ride to the airport," he relayed to Father Bernard, who had come out of the classroom. "They can't afford the taxi." The kids were reaching for his rosary again. "It's all right," he assured their mother, who barked, "*Mi seh no touch it!*"

"What time does she need to go?" Father Bernard asked, and looked at the woman.

"*Wha times yuh need fi leave ya?*" Brother Leon queried.

"Tomorrow. Two o'clock," she said.

"I think someone can do it," Father Bernard said, glancing at the novices. "How about you two take her tomorrow?"

"Sure," Brother Leon said, glancing at Matt, who hesitated.

"Yes," he said at last. Leon guessed Matt had something else planned, but as they were novices, they had to obey the novice master's orders.

Leon, who had his hands full with the kids, said to Marisol, "*Nuh worry.* And where do you live again?"

While the woman talked and gestured, Leon found his eye caught by a white car driving slowly along the streets. Nice cars driving in this area usually were either lost or belonged to drug dealers. But the dealers he knew of didn't drive white cars.

He focused in on what the woman was saying, and by the time he had gotten a sense of where she lived, the car had moved on.

"High school duty this afternoon," Father Bernard said, closing the door after they had said their farewells. "Let's go start Midday Prayer first."

After praying Midday Prayer, the friars who were in the friary gathered for lunch. Leon noticed that there wasn't much for lunch, just bean stew. And not much of it.

"We're almost out," Brother George said, scraping the last of the pan. "I think this was supposed to be dinner, too."

"God will provide for His poor," Father Bernard said easily. "Someone might send a food donation soon. And we can always fast."

After lunch, Leon helped Brother Herman gather cleaning supplies and mops and started over to the high school to continue the massive project of cleaning the abandoned building. To Leon's surprise, Nora emerged from the vestibule suddenly, wearing jeans and an oversized red shirt.

"Hey, there you are!" he exclaimed. "How'd your errand go?"

She seemed surprised at the question, and dropped her eyes. "As well as I could expect," she said. "I'm sorry I didn't get so far with the vestibule. Can I help you now?"

"Certainly. Follow the train," Brother Herman said, starting down the narrow hallway. "We're working in the high school today."

Leon gestured for Nora to go ahead of him. "You had lunch?" he queried as they walked down the aisle of the church.

"I'm fine. I had Danish and toast for breakfast in my room and I just had the rest for lunch," she said. "Father Francis sent them down to me last night."

"Day-old bread and pastries. We usually get tons of them from the bakeries," Brother Leon agreed. "Pretty much a staple around here. How are you feeling?"

"I'm fine," she said, a bit distantly.

"You look fine," he said, not believing her.

She glanced over at him. "I feel alone," she said flatly.

"Ah," Brother Leon said. "Well, give yourself a reality check. You're not alone."

That seemed to get through to her, and she said quietly, "I suppose you're right."

They followed Brother Herman out the back door of the sacristy, and walked down some steps into the courtyard linking the church, friary, and high school. Brother Herman unlocked the door to the high school.

"You said this was a new order?" Nora queried.

"We're part of a reform movement of the Franciscans," Leon explained. "I was in one of the established Franciscan orders before, as a novice. But when I heard about Father Francis and Father Bernard starting this new order, I left to join this one."

Brother Herman pulled open the creaking metal door, then stepped aside to let Leon, Matt, and Nora through. "We're cleaning out the classrooms so we can partition them into bedrooms. Let's start on the top floor and work our way down. That way, hopefully we'll be in the lower, cooler halls by the time it starts to really get hot."

"It's hot already," Matt pointed out.

The high school buildings had four stories, and just about all of them were in poor condition after a year of disuse. After they had trooped upstairs, Brother Herman looked around while Leon and Matt opened the windows to get some air circulating throughout the rooms. "Okay, I guess the first thing to do is get all the furniture into the hallways and stack it up. Then we'll mop."

For the next half hour, they worked at pushing all the school desks into the hallway and stacking them in piles. Soon Brother Charley came up to help them, setting the metal desks carefully into piles that towered up in the hallway. "Careful not to knock any of these over," he warned.

"Excellent!" Brother Herman said, wiping his brow as they finished clearing the room. "Now for cleaning the bathrooms."

The group moved into the third floor girls' bathrooms to start. Charley took the broom and started sweeping, and Matt and Leon took the mops. "What should I do?" Nora asked.

Brother Herman gave her a bottle of window cleaner and a rag. "How about you do the sills and panes? I'll do the radiators."

Leon was bursting with curiosity about where Nora had been and what had brought her here in the first place. Since Nora was looking pensive, he decided to try to draw her out of herself. *She's got to talk about what's bothering her*, he thought.

"So Nora, what do you think of our new order so far?" Leon asked, as he started on a tough spot on the gray and brown tiled floor.

"Well, I'll say one thing. You certainly are—different from what I thought friars would be like," she said, with a trace of a smile.

Brother Leon immediately put an enraptured look on his face and began to chant in Latin. Brother Herman didn't miss a beat and joined in.

Matt made a face. "Hasn't anyone told you Franciscans can't sing?" he groaned. "Don't even try."

Leon turned the chant into a rap beat and began to cut loose with the mop until Nora laughed, which was what he wanted. "You just haven't been around very many religious, that's all," he told her.

"Well," Nora said, wiping off her window, "I certainly didn't expect you to take me in. It's very generous of you to let me stay here."

"Well, we needed someone to test-drive our hospitality rooms to make sure they're shipshape," Leon said flippantly. "So we need you to tell us, on a scale of one to ten, how would you rate the vestibule storage room compared with the bedrooms in the basement in terms of comfort level? Otherwise the homeless and our volunteers will be sneaking around in the middle of the night to find our storage rooms. It could be a problem, you know."

She almost smiled, and said, considering, "Actually, they were both pretty comfortable."

"Glad to hear that. We'll send the data to our marketing department," Brother Herman said solemnly.

Leon had been hoping to follow up with a question about how she had come to their house in the first place, but Nora cut him off at the pass.

"Can I ask you something?" She stared down at the gray water dotted by white bubbles in Leon's bucket.

"Shoot," Brother Herman said easily, squirting another section of vent.

"Does it bother you if I don't tell you much about myself?"

She knew what I was about to ask, Leon thought. He glanced at Brother Herman.

"Sure it's all right," the older friar assured her. "Just tell us if you need any help."

"Thanks. I'd like to tell you more, but—I don't want to get anyone in trouble. I guess if you knew the circumstances, I keep thinking you might feel differently—" she pushed back a strand of ragged hair with the back of her hand. "It's a very odd situation." Leon noticed her hand was trembling.

"We don't have to know everything about your situation. If you want to tell us—if you feel it would help you—that's fine. But don't put yourself under pressure," Brother Herman said.

"Thanks," she said, wiping away something from her face, maybe just a bit of over-spray from the window cleaner.

III

The day of his transformation, there had been policemen at his high school....

...Arthur caught a glimpse of an officer in the principal's office as he passed, and a thin current of nervousness passed through him. He wondered why he should be nervous.

He was opening his personal locker when his backpack toppled out onto the floor, and smoothly, a plastic packet slid out of it. A white plastic packet. Frowning, he dropped to his knees to examine it. It was a clear plastic zip lock bag, with what looked like Styrofoam balls inside. Except they were heavy.

Picking it up, he stared at it, trying to remember if he had put it there, or what type of joke this could be. It was then that he noticed the feet of the policeman standing over him.

As they walked into the principal's office, he saw his fifteen-year-old younger brother Ben, who was fuming. "I've never seen this before in my life!" Ben snapped at the officer, tossing a bag on the table as Arthur came in. "This is ridiculous! Someone's set me up!"

"Like who? Who would put it in your desk?"

"I don't know—one of the other kids, I suppose." Ben rubbed the acne on his face and shook his head vigorously. "All I know is, it's not mine."

"Do you know anyone else who uses crack?"

"No. Not anyone that I know of. This is ludicrous. I've never even *seen* crack before. The officer who dragged me in here had to tell me what it was."

"You claim that you don't even recognize the substance in the packet?"

"It could be sugar balls for all I know. Do I sound like a user? Can I call my father's lawyer?"

The officer paused as his partner led Arthur into the principal's office.

"What's going on?" Arthur asked.

Ben rolled his eyes and glared at the officer. "What a mess," he murmured.

"Hold a minute while I take your brother into the other room," the officer said, putting a heavy hand on Ben's shoulder. Ben obeyed, although Arthur could see he was still steaming.

"Sit down," the officer said. He tossed the plastic packet on the desk in front of Arthur. "I'm going to inform you of your rights, and then perhaps you could tell me what's going on here."

Arthur stared at the pure white crystals. "I have no idea."

* * *

"Boy, this stinks," Fish murmured.

Bear was inclined to agree. They sat in the waiting area of the district courtroom, awaiting the magistrate who was going to hear the complaint against them. After that, they had been told that they would be sent to the jail for the next three days until the court decided whether or not to post bail. Bear was still trying to adjust to the idea that he couldn't just get up and walk out to Blanche's house to find her. He was under arrest.

"I knew something was eating Ahmed," Fish said softly, shifting position on the hard bench. "That's what was going on. The manager told him to look out for us. Poor guy."

"Just doing his job," Bear said. He looked at the agents who were flanking them. "Can't we have the cell phone back to make one phone call?"

The man shook his head gruffly.

"I thought we were allowed one phone call," Fish said pointedly.

"The timing of your one phone call is at the discretion of the Agency," the man said. "The magistrate will call you at any minute. When they bring you to the jail tonight, you'll be able to make as many phone calls as you please."

Bear persisted. "It's an emergency. It could very well have some bearing on our case. Can't you speak to someone—?"

The agent glared at him. "The timing of your phone call is at the discretion of the Agency," he repeated warningly.

"Calm down," Fish whispered to Bear, who was still bristling. "They've been about as friendly as we can expect."

"Friendly?"

"Well, at least they didn't handcuff us like they did last time," Fish said cheerfully.

"I guess we can be glad about that," Bear admitted. Even though the memory was five years old, it still made him wince.

* * *

Five years ago, he had become an outcast. Abruptly, with no forewarning. In his school sweater, uniform shirt and skewed tie, he struggled into the police car with difficulty because his hands were pinned behind his back and thought, *They've got to realize we didn't do this. We're innocent. They'll find fingerprints on our lockers that will show who really planted the drugs. They can't really believe we're drug dealers...*

He knew that almost everyone in the high school was looking on, and the humiliation was excruciating. As his grim-faced younger brother was pushed into the car beside him, he was trying to be optimistic. *Dad won't let them do this to us. Even if he doesn't care much about us, at least he'll be concerned about the family reputation, and he'll find out the truth. He's got to know we wouldn't do this.*

But his father had not listened to their explanations, and had refused to believe them. A coldness and fear had started to grow in him then, a realization that they were in serious danger and that no one of influence was going to be putting themselves to the trouble of finding out the truth of the situation…

* * *

"One thing is different now," Bear said to himself, and realized he had spoken aloud.

"What did you say?" Fish asked.

"Our dad disinherited us last time, but he gave us back our money from Mom's estate when we cleared our names. This time, we can pay our own bail."

"Yeah. Great. At least you're not paying for tuition like I am," Fish muttered. "You think they'll let us out on bail?"

"They will. They've got to," Bear said. "We have to find Blanche. I'm sure her disappearance has something to do with this mess."

Fish drummed his fingers on his knee. "No juvenile record this time. If we get convicted on this charge, we'll be living with the record for the rest of our lives. Let's call Charles Russell first. The sooner we talk to our lawyer, the happier I'll be."

"I wanted to call Mrs. Foster and ask her to go over to the Briers' house for us," Bear said.

"Not a bad idea," Fish said. He looked up as a brown-haired man holding a briefcase approached them. It was the same agent who had arrested them, Mr. Tang.

"While we're waiting, I'd like to present you with a few facts and in return, I'd like to ask you a few questions," the man said, sitting down and taking out a file folder.

"You can tell us whatever you like, but we're not going to answer any questions without our lawyer here," Fish said pleasantly.

As though he hadn't heard them, Mr. Tang took out a piece of paper. "The manager of your apartment building found the drugs hidden under the sofa cushions on Friday, and called the authorities. We obtained a search warrant, and when we searched the apartment, we found the drugs just as he described them. Do you have any idea of how the drugs got there?"

"Hold on—why was the manager of the building searching our place to begin with?" Fish demanded. "We're owners, not renters. Looking over the apartment while the owners are away for several weeks is one thing—but going through the cracks in the sofa? Come on! What possessed him to do that?"

"He told us he had an anonymous call," Mr. Tang said. "And he figured he'd take a look for himself."

"An anonymous call?" Bear repeated. "What sort of justification is that?"

The agent nodded. "I'm merely repeating what he told us. Can I ask you to verify your statement here that you've never seen these drugs before?"

"Again, we're not going to say anything without our lawyer," Bear said flatly.

"Can you verify that neither of you have been in the apartment for the past week?"

"No comment," Fish said. "Sorry, not until we talk with Charles."

Mr. Tang, nonplussed, turned over another piece of paper. "According to the anonymous call the manager got, the drugs were being delivered to your apartment by a courier who had been making several deposits over the course of the past week. Do you have any knowledge of such a person?"

"Again, how is the manager justified in making all these accusations based on anonymous information?" Fish persisted.

"We have been working with the security of your building to try to determine who has had access to your apartment over these past weeks, and they have identified a suspicious person, not a resident, who made several trips to your apartment over the past week. As it turns out, this person is a suspect in the embezzlement of several thousand dollars from a Long Island restaurant."

He removed a photograph from his folder and passed it over to the brothers. "Do you recognize her?"

It was a black-and-white image captured from their apartment building's security camera by the elevator. The girl was turning, looking past her backpack over her shoulder as though she sensed someone behind her and was afraid. Her black hair and pale skin were all too familiar. Blanche.

*So during the day, the girl cleaned
the house for them while the little
men went about their work.*
Grimm

Chapter Five

uesday morning. She pulled apart the plastic knot on a garbage bag
with relief and dumped its contents on the floor. In the stuffy little
room, the clothes smelled musty, and it was hot, but she didn't
mind. Working in the banquet hall this summer, she had been hot many
times in the winding back corridors, and had gotten used to it, sweating and
working. And folding clothes was like sorting out silverware, folding
napkins—repetitious work.

And despite her problem, it was good to be alone and working, instead of
talking to others, and trying to pretend that everything was normal inside
her. Solitude had usually been a comfort to her—

If I could only figure this out—what this all means—

Breathing deeply, she emptied out a garbage bag of assorted clothes onto
the floor and began to sort through them. Creating order out of chaos. It felt
therapeutic, giving her hope that the chaos of this summer would start to sort
itself out.

* * *

It began oddly, with a nagging sense of
vulnerability. The girl had heard of people having
dreams in which they forgot to get dressed, and
walked down the street in pajamas. She had never
had that dream, but she began to feel as though
something like it had meshed with her reality, and
that wherever she went, she was unconsciously

calling attention to herself. Telling the world that she was unprepared. And exposed.

After Bear had left, things that should have worked for her suddenly didn't. An instructor at her community college had practically promised her an internship at a nursing home, but at the last minute it had fallen through. She had searched for other work, but she couldn't find any. Her younger sister, in her usual good luck, landed a fun job working at a community theatre, and ended up starring in one of their plays. Rose loyally had tried to find her older sister a job there, selling tickets or painting scenery, but it hadn't worked out.

"Why don't you look for a waitress job—or catering?" her mother suggested. "What about Reflections?"

She balked at the proposition. "Not there."

"You've always said it was your favorite restaurant," Mother had said.

"But not to work at," the girl had said resentfully.

She felt it was unfair. Reflections, a lavish restaurant and banquet hall on Long Island, was a place you went when you were wearing your good clothes and wanted a celebration that felt bigger than yourself. She remembered eating there as a little girl, with her father and mother, at Christmastime and after special occasions, like going to a concert. Bear had taken her there on their last date. It was the place of festive elevation, where she and her family could pretend—at least for an evening—that they were royalty. Working there would dispel that illusion.

But dogged by unemployment and the prospect of not being able to go back to community college that fall, she gave in and applied, and was hired as catering-help in the banquet hall section.

In the barren desert of that hot, hot summer, she worked hard, carrying trays for numerous meaningless banquets, going from the heat of the kitchen to the chill of air conditioning, trying to look as though she were not sweating.

For a while, she kept the foreboding at bay. She had started visiting nursing homes, talking to the elderly, trying to discover what it would be like to be a nurse. Midway through the summer, she was made the receptionist for the banquet hall, which meant she had to be able to calculate, make some decisions such as which party sat where, handle money, and (most importantly) could wear a dress instead of the white shirt, black pants, and red bow tie of the caterer. It was odd, being promoted. Always having been the shy one in the family, in the shadow of a more flamboyant sister, she was surprised that someone had paid attention to her.

Then someone else had noticed her.

To be fair, she had noticed him first. It was at another banquet—more sumptuous than usual, for an upscale New York company. It had been a long evening, and she spent most of it on her feet, smiling and handing out programs to guests dressed in evening clothes. Most of them didn't even meet her eyes, but merely took the program and went on with their conversations, barely registering that she was there.

After the rush was over and the event inside the ballroom began, the girl set down her stack of programs and leaned against the wall. Someone (probably the event coordinator from the corporation) had removed the desk and chair that was usually there in order to better accommodate the flow of people, and now there was no place for her to sit down. The girl didn't want to break with the formality of the occasion and sit on the steps. She glanced around the foyer, wishing she could get off her feet and massage them. Through a clear pane in the stained-glass and brass doors, she could see the glittering crowd seated around tables. A flawless blonde lady stood at a podium, making a speech and basking in the applause, smiling. She wore a red satin evening gown designed to make her look as though she were emerging from the shining crinkled petals of a rose.

Scanning the program, the girl guessed that the woman must be the "Chief Executive Officer." The girl wondered what it must be like to be divinely beautiful, and apparently wealthy and powerful as well. *That's who I should want to be like,* she thought, *if I were a really modern girl. Up there in front of the crowd, fit and fashionably dressed, at the pinnacle of some career, not showing a sign of age or weakness.*

The girl smiled ironically. *With my small plans for the future, I never would be anyone's poster girl. I might even be a traitor, betraying the cause of women's empowerment...*

Then she had seen a man exiting the hall with a jerking gait, and she had hurried to open the heavy door for him.

He was leaning on a cane, gray-haired, his face gaunt, and his tuxedo looked a bit askew, as though he hadn't been quite competent enough to button it correctly.

"Can I help you with anything?" she asked in concern. His lips were blue.

"No, no, no," he eased his way down the steps. "Just going to get a breath of air. It's stuffy in there, even with the air conditioning."

She opened the street door and helped him out, despite his protests. As she did, she noticed that he wasn't favoring a hurt leg or swollen joints—the cane was, apparently, to help him keep his balance.

Fortunately, the night had cooled the City summer air, and the man took several deep breaths and looked more composed.

"Can I help you back inside?" she asked when he seemed to have recovered.

He glanced back wryly over his shoulder. He was not a particularly handsome man, but of course his features were more sharpened by his illness. His eyes were sunken and his skin wasn't a good color. "In there?" he asked, and shook his head. "No thanks. I'm an outsider now anyway."

"Are you?" she asked, still holding onto his elbow to steady him.

"Used to be vice president of the company, actually," he chuckled. "Maybe they still have my name on the rolls, but my word doesn't mean a thing there any more. Not much point in their paying attention to a dying man, is there?"

"Are you dying?" she asked. An odd question, but she was surprised at how normal her voice sounded.

"Not 'going gently into that good night,'" he grunted, sitting down on the flat stone balustrade beside the steps. "'Rage, rage against the dying—' oh, thank you. You're very kind," he said as she helped him sit down.

She had no doubt that he was speaking the truth. He was far more lightweight than a man his age and build should be. "Can I get you anything?"

"A cure for a brain tumor? You got anything like that on you?" he asked, his dark eyes lighting up, and he shook his head. "No, of course you don't. No one does. That's the problem. They haven't yet discovered a cure for death, have they?"

She paused, thinking momentarily of Christ and the empty tomb, but she didn't know how to bring it up without sounding pious. So instead she said, "A brain tumor?"

"Yes. Inoperable. Fortunately, it's not in the advanced stages yet. I have a bit of time. The doctors tell me I'll eventually lose control of my faculties and slip into a coma before I die." His eyes were dark, and his jaw thrust itself forward. "But I don't plan on letting myself get to that point, if I can help it. Like I said, 'not going gently—oh, pardon me. I already quoted that. You're going to think I'm a man of one poem." He laughed at his own joke, and coughed.

She had to laugh. There was something eclectic and independent about him, even in his frailty. But she was puzzled. He didn't seem properly groomed, particularly if he was really vice president of the company—

"Pardon me—" she ventured. "If you have a brain tumor, why are you having trouble breathing?"

He looked surprised. "I have a bit of a cold I can't shake off. Well, that's only to be expected, I guess." He fumbled in his shirt for something—medication, she supposed—but his eyes looked at her keenly. "You actually seem to know something about this sort of thing," he said. "Don't you?"

"Well, my mother's a nurse," she admitted. "I'm sort of interested in nursing."

"Is that right? You're a smart girl. What's your name? Can I ask you your name, or will it sound as though I'm trying to pick you up?"

"My name's Blanche Brier," she said, extending her hand.

"Jack Fairston," he said, squeezing it in a handshake that didn't have much power left to it. "So why is a pretty girl like you listening to an old codger like me?"

"Actually, I don't mind talking to older people at all. I'm thinking of majoring in geriatrics," she said.

"Geriatrics?" he grimaced. "Ouch. I can't get over the idea of being taken for one of those. Guess that doesn't make much sense. I should be happy to see the age of, say, seventy-five, which I'm obviously never going to see. Anyhow. Why do you want to work in geriatrics?"

"I—like old people, I guess," she said. "I like listening to them." Pondering it, she added, "And, I suppose it's partly because I don't have any old people in my own family."

"Is that so?"

She nodded, and glancing back at the banquet inside a bit guiltily—but there was nothing she should be doing—she resumed her explanation. "I never knew my dad's parents—my grandma died when I was just a baby. My mom's dad is dead, and my other grandmother lives in California. I just don't have a lot of family, at least not here in the City."

"Maybe most of us are looking for a sort of substitute family." He looked out at the darkness, which was mirrored in his own eyes. "I don't know. I suppose in a certain sense, I am. All I have left in the world now is my wife. She looks after me. I don't speak to my relatives, and now that my children are grown up, they don't speak to me either. My friends are uncomfortable around me, now that they know my condition. I don't even have any colleagues or employees left, now that I've been forcibly retired."

"That sounds rather awful," the girl said honestly.

"It is, rather. And ironic. For years, I've thought of myself as a very successful man. But for some reason I haven't succeeded in keeping many friends or family close to me." He stared at the ground, and for a moment, he looked truly sad. He coughed and looked up. An idea seemed to have occurred to him. "Tell you what, Blanche. I'm not going to be around much longer—I mean, getting around. I'm going to be bedridden soon. Since you say you like old people—and even though I'm not really old, I *am* really sick and could pass for being old—would you be willing to come and visit me?"

"I would," the girl said.

"Would you? That—that would be wonderful," the man said, his face quite changed. The girl had a momentary glimpse of how Mr. Fairston might have looked as a healthy man. He felt in his breast pocket and managed to extricate a card. "Here's where I am, or will be."

She took it. It read, "Alistair M. Fairston," and gave his home and his office address.

"I thought you said your name was Jack," she said, curious.

"It isn't," he said gloomily. "My real name is Alistair. I was named after one of my father's friends, unhappy man. You can see why I changed it. I kept saying one of these days I would have it legally changed, but I never got around to it and I suppose it's too late now. Everyone who knows me calls me Jack. Oh, and the office address isn't valid any more, like I told you," the man said. "Just in case you call it, and they don't recognize my name, so you don't think I'm scamming you."

She laughed again, and thought to herself, but *he could be scamming me. He might have picked up this card and be pretending to be vice-president of the company.* If he hadn't looked so ill—and she knew he was—she might have been more cautious. She might have held back.

But her doubts about his identity were pushed aside as the door to the hall opened, and a man came out. "Mr. Fairston?" he asked solicitously. "Your wife is looking for you."

"Why?" the man asked, a bit peevishly, then started and looked anxious. "Oh, have I forgotten something?"

"They want to present you with an award," the man said, taking his arm.

"An award? What for?"

"Well, this is your farewell banquet and you are the guest of honor," the man said, helping Mr. Fairston to his feet.

"Guest of honor?" he muttered as he fumbled with his cane. "Good grief, is that what all this is for?"

"Of course it is. Your wife arranged it."

Mr. Fairston grimaced. "I told her I didn't want a farewell banquet. They give me headaches. I don't want to have a farewell banquet with a headache. I'll get all cross and won't enjoy it."

"I don't think you have much choice," the man said with a smile. "Come on in now," and led him up the steps.

Mr. Fairston paused, and looked back at the girl. "You will come and visit me, won't you?"

"I will," she promised. "Thank you."

"Good night then," he said, and allowed himself to be escorted inside, where the blond woman in red came graciously to his side, kissed him on the cheek, and said something into the cordless microphone she still carried. There were cheers as the entire assembly got to its feet, clapping loudly.

Slightly moved, the girl watched the man hobble his way up to the stage amidst the applause. The blond goddess accompanying him looked over her shoulder, and met the girl's gaze. There was a coldness in her eyes that flashed like ice.

The girl stepped back into the night, surprised. For a long time she stood outside the door, holding onto the handle, listening to the screech and roar of the traffic behind her, rushing through the darkness.

* * *

II

As usual, Brother Leon had a difficult time concentrating on his Tuesday morning class on the Franciscan vows. He disliked sitting still, and shifted his feet and toyed with his pencil while Father Bernard lectured.

To make matters worse, they were in the room right next to the front door, and Leon was aware each time it was opened. He would catch snatches of conversation, get distracted, and have to forcibly turn his mind back to the explication of poverty, chastity, and obedience.

After a man had tried unsuccessfully to sell the friars a box of sugar packets "he just happened to find" outside a restaurant and Brother Herman had turned him away, Leon tried to pull his attention back to the Middle Ages and St. Francis. Then there was another knock at the door. Father Bernard sighed audibly, and looked at the door to the room, but as the office door was off its hinges, it was impossible to close it.

The knock came again, insistently, and Brother Leon wondered where the porter was. As the knocking continued, he stared at Father Bernard, wondering if his novice master would dispatch him to open it. The thought seemed to pass through the priest's mind, but just as he turned to Leon and started to speak, they all heard Father Francis emerge from the kitchen and hurry to the door, his sandals smacking on the floor.

"Hello," he said, his voice uncharacteristically cheerful, "And what can I do for you?"

There was a woman's voice, rasping and aged by time, saying something Leon couldn't catch.

"Well, we have food distribution on Thursdays. But come in, and I'll see if Brother Herman can give you something from the food pantry right now," Father Francis said at last.

"Oh, thank you!" the woman exclaimed. "That's so kind of you!"

"Herman!" Father Francis called, with the barest touch of irritation. Meaning, "Why weren't you here to get the door?"

"Coming!" came a frantic voice from upstairs, and the novices, who were all listening despite themselves, grinned at each other. They heard Brother Herman's bulk hurrying down the steps. *This is like listening to a sitcom,* Brother Leon thought.

"This is Bonnie. She just came to the neighborhood," Father Francis said, and for the next few minutes, the two older friars and the old woman chatted back and forth. Brother Leon heroically turned his attention back to the discussion of Sts. Dominic and Francis and their views on the vows. At last the conversation died away as Brother Herman led the visitor to the pantry, and Father Francis returned to his kitchen chores.

Then a few minutes later, Leon glanced up and saw someone standing in the doorway, inquisitively looking at the makeshift classroom. It was an old woman in a ragged black trench coat with bulging pockets, her shoulders stooped, her aged face covered by some kind of bright blue wool ski hat with a green visor covering her eyes. She wore incredible red high-topped shoes on her feet.

"Hi boys," she said in a cracked voice. "What you doin' in there?"

Of course, every eye in the room was on her.

"We're learning about Franciscan vows. These are our novices," Father Bernard said courteously, as though the bag lady were a visiting dignitary.

The woman fixed each of them with a gleaming eye. "Hi," she croaked again. "Well, carry on."

"We will," Father Bernard said as Brother Herman appeared in the doorway next to her, holding a bag of food.

"Here you are, Bonnie. Oh, I see you've found our novices. This is Father Bernard, Brother Charley, Brother Matt..." But the bag lady had already turned away and was heading down the corridor towards the refectory.

"We've met," came her cracked voice.

"Uh—excuse me!" Brother Herman hurried after her, his hands full of the sacks of food.

Brother Leon chuckled to himself and turned back to Father Bernard once again, but his attention was still partly aware of the bag lady at large in the friary. He could hear Brother Herman giving her an impromptu tour and ushering her back down the corridor.

"Interesting place," she was saying as he guided her back to the front door, now holding her bag of food. "Like those stained glass windows—Carry on."

At last the front door shut behind their visitor, and all the novices breathed a sigh of relief. Father Bernard turned the page of his book with a wry smile.

"According to the saints, the vow of poverty involves the surrender of our time," he said, a faint smile on his face. "St. Thérèse of Lisieux in particular believed 'a willingness to be interrupted' was necessary to the devout soul."

"Could you come up with any examples?" Brother Leon asked innocently, and Matt threw a pencil at him while the others chuckled.

III

* * *

Less than a month after being released from prison, circumstances had found Arthur standing on the streets of Manhattan at midnight, holding all his belongings in a pillowcase. He was still dealing with the realization that he and Ben had been disowned and thrown out of their father's house, and that there was no other home for them to go to. His brother, who had missed the entire scene with Dad, was shivering and coughing, having been woken out of a sound sleep to be informed that he was suddenly homeless.

"So, where are we going to go, since you've burned all our proverbial bridges?" he had asked, a bit peevishly. It was starting to snow.

"Let's go to St. Lawrence," Arthur had said at last.

"Father Raymond is dead," Ben had said flatly. "That new priest is never going to let us in."

"He doesn't have to know we're there," Arthur had said, and made himself walk, to push aside the feeling of desolation. "Come on."

Since they hadn't had any money and weren't yet streetwise enough to do otherwise, they had walked from upper Manhattan to the South Bronx. It took them hours in the cold wind and snow. When they reached St. Lawrence, Arthur had let himself in with the keys Father Raymond had once entrusted to him, and the two brothers had huddled in a corner of the vestibule.

"We have to get out before anyone comes—or they'll know we have keys—" his younger brother had mumbled before falling asleep. Simply glad to be out of the wind, Arthur slept.

They awoke early and quietly slipped out of the church onto the streets. A few moments later, a vision from their past life appeared in the form of their buddy Stephen Foster getting off of the subway, backpack on his shoulders, on his way to school. His dark brown face lit up when he saw them. "Hey Arthur! You got out, man! What gives?"

There wasn't much they wanted to say, but Stephen guessed more than they told him, because after he had heard their answers, he said, "You come home with me tonight. My mom won't mind."

And that was how the brothers first met Mrs. Foster.

* * *

So it was that when Bear found himself in trouble again, he had no problem with calling Stephen's mother. The heavyset black woman had accepted the boys as two more sons, and became a sturdy ally. He knew that she, shrewd but solidly certain of his character, would help him without doubting him. And she wouldn't ask any pointed questions until they were in private.

"My, you boys have a way of getting yourselves into trouble," was her understated reaction when he had called her from the jail last night and explained their situation. "I'll be right over to get the keys and go over to the Briers' house for you. Don't you fret, Arthur. God'll take care of your girl. You'll see."

The next morning, as soon as they were let out of their cells, Bear found the phones that the prisoners were allowed to use, and called Mrs. Foster back.

"What did you find?" he asked her, after they had exchanged greetings.

She paused. "Blanche is not there," she stated. "I don't think she's been there since Saturday. The mail hasn't been taken in and there was a Sunday paper in the slot."

By her voice, he gathered right away that she had more to tell him, but she wasn't going to tell him on this line.

"The good thing is that I found a phone number for Aunt Cindy on the calendar. The phone book says it's an area code for San Francisco. Think that might be the one where the Briers are staying?"

"Yes, it's a very good chance!" Bear said, with some relief. "We have to call them right away."

"Since you can only call collect, how about I call first and find out if Jean's really there? If she is, you want me to tell them everything?"

"No, just tell them I'm going to call. I want to be the one to break the bad news," Bear said. This wasn't strictly true, but he felt it was his responsibility.

"Can you stay by this phone?"

"I can call back in a half hour or so," he glanced around the phone room. There were a few other men waiting in line for the phone.

"Then call me back when you can. I'll see what I can do about calling those folks in San Francisco."

"Sounds good," he said with an effort. "Thanks for doing this."

"How you doing, Arthur?"

"I'm okay, but I'm worried about Blanche."

"How's Ben?"

"Oh, nothing gets him down. He says I've just gotten us in trouble again."

"You hang in there, Arthur. I know you must be going crazy in that place. God'll watch out for Blanche. And you. You'll see."

He walked back to his cell. For half an hour he paced around, waiting, wishing there was something else he could do.

"I wish you would stop," Fish said calmly, sitting on his bunk. "You're making me nervous."

Bear forced himself to stand still and rubbed his eyes. He hadn't slept well last night either. "Sorry."

"So we're in jail, and there's no sign of Blanche," Fish said to himself. "Well. I wonder if she's hiding because she knows the police want her?"

"I'm not going to assume that yet," Bear said doggedly. He couldn't get the picture of Blanche's frightened face in the photo out of his mind. "I wish I could know that she's even still alive."

"You're pacing again," Fish murmured.

Frustrated, Bear sat on his own bunk. After a minute of his mind running crazily along several trains of thought, he asked his brother, "Do you have any paper?"

"Not sure if I have anything. They took everything from me that could be possibly construed as a weapon." Fish turned out his pockets, looking for scrap paper. Finding the postcard of the Delphic Sibyl in his trench coat pocket, he said, "Well, there's this."

"That'll do," Bear said. He had a stub of pencil the prison guard had let him have, and started to make notes on the back of the postcard, writing small to save space. "I'm making a timeline. As far as I can tell, Blanche was last seen on Saturday, at the banquet hall where she worked. The police detective said that the management missed several thousand dollars that had been collected as part of a fundraiser that evening. Then someone found Blanche's backpack in the employee service room with a cache of Ecstasy pills in it."

Fish stared at the wall. "I don't envy you having to tell Mrs. Brier all this."

"Yeah. Me neither." His mouth went dry at the thought. A feeling came over him that he hadn't experienced in a while, but was still recognizable.

This was how he had felt towards Jean Brier over a year ago, when Blanche and Rose were just beginning to be friends with him. The guilty feeling that he was endangering her daughters by being friends with them, because he was in danger. He had been so relieved when that danger had passed.

But apparently, not all of it was over, after all.

Pushing aside the worry, he wrote some questions: *who would resent Blanche? Did she know something? Was she a danger to someone? Something fishy going on at the banquet hall?*

"Make sure you get that card back to me, or I'll face the grave displeasure of Rose," Fish murmured resignedly as Bear chewed the end of his pencil.

"You only get it back if you do me a favor."

"What?"

Bear ruminated as he carefully put the card in his shirt pocket and stood up. "Listen to Rose once in a while when she talks to you."

Fish blew out his breath. "Ah, one of the labors of Hercules."

"I didn't ask you to listen to her *all* the time. Just start by listening attentively every now and then. I think you'll find she has some good and interesting things to say."

His brother rubbed his brown hair. "Yes, she's a smart little kid. It's a pity she's so—sixteen."

"Actually, she's—"

"I know, she's seventeen, but it doesn't seem like it."

"Actually, she's eighteen."

"Is she?"

"Her birthday was this past November."

"Was it?"

"You were there. You even helped her blow out the birthday candles. Though apparently you didn't bother to count them."

His brother was staring, apparently making the mental adjustment. "How did I miss that?"

"You probably had a lot of English literature on your mind and missed it. So are you saying that being sixteen isn't an age, it's a state of mind?"

"For some people," Fish said, and paused. "Are you sure she's eighteen?"

"Yes, only a year younger than you, the mature nineteen-year-old that you are."

"I turned twenty in April, which *you've* apparently forgotten." Fish eyed his brother with his typical crooked smile. "Nevertheless, I'll try to start relating to her as a peer. *If* you stop pacing."

Sighing, Bear squatted on the floor again.

When he finally got to the phone again, Mrs. Foster gave him a new number and told him that Mrs. Brier was expecting his call. Thanking her and agreeing to call back later in the day, he dialed the number. Anxiously he listened to the phone ringing in far-off San Francisco, and swallowed.

Someone picked up the phone, and the electronic operator came on, indicating that there was a collect call from an inmate in a New York City jail for Jean Brier. Whoever picked up the phone pushed "1" to accept the call. Then suddenly Bear heard Jean's voice. "Bear? Is that you?"

"Hello, Jean," he said, and swallowed. "It's me."

"I got a call this morning from your friend Mrs. Foster. She said you were back from Europe—and in jail? What happened?"

"Uh, I'm afraid it's pretty complicated. Jean, let me tell you the most important part first. Have you heard from Blanche?"

Her voice changed abruptly. "No. I hadn't expected to. Rose and I have been out of touch with her for the past few days. We were up hiking on my uncle's property and we didn't have a phone. We got back yesterday and I called her then and left a message but haven't heard back. Is something wrong?"

"Blanche seems to be missing." He swallowed again. "I don't think she's been back at your house since Sunday. That's why I came back. We haven't found her."

"Have you called the police?"

"Yes, but—Jean, I'm afraid they're already looking for her. When Fish and I were gone, the DEA found drugs in our apartment. They think Blanche put them there."

Jean paused. He could tell she was taking this in. "So they arrested you?"

"Yes. Don't worry, we'll be getting bailed out soon. The important thing is to find Blanche. She was last seen at the banquet hall on Saturday night. She left her backpack there, and apparently they found drugs in her backpack too—"

Jean listened to his narrative in silence. When he finished, he tried to reassure her. "I'm going to do everything I can to find her as soon as they let us out. But I wanted to get a hold of you because I figured you should know right away."

"You're right. Thank you, Bear, for telling me," Jean said quietly. She was a rather stoic person, but he could tell she was on the verge of tears. "I don't know why I didn't see this coming."

"What do you mean? Has something been wrong with Blanche?"

Jean sighed before she answered. "I think so. She's gotten very solitary this summer, and very…preoccupied. I knew that she wasn't happy, but she couldn't seem to articulate what was wrong. Rose said—" she hesitated. "Rose said she was seeing things."

"What do you mean? Hallucinating?" A tremor went through Bear.

"I don't think so. Rose said she thought she was being watched wherever she went. She said she kept feeling an urge to run away and escape from them."

"What did she mean by that?"

"I don't know."

"Jean, I'm sure that these drugs were planted to frame her. Do you know anyone who might have something against her?"

"No, I don't. I'll think about it, certainly. But it doesn't seem likely."

"We can't rule out any options right now," Bear urged. "If there was actually someone watching her, we've got to find out who it was. Ask Rose to give you any details she can think of."

"I feel so irresponsible," Jean said, almost to herself. "We've been so caught up in the play that Rose was in, and work, and vacation plans—I can't believe I left her alone, knowing that she was feeling so nervous and afraid—I don't know why I didn't take her more seriously. I'm her mother, I should have known something was wrong. But she said she was keeping herself busy visiting Mr. Fairston and the nursing home and I didn't really think to press her for details—"

"Mr. Fairston?" Bear interrupted.

"Yes, a sick man she met at Reflections. He took a fancy to her, and she would go and read him poetry in the afternoons. She's been visiting nursing homes too. She just really clicks with old people."

"Er…That's great," Bear said with an effort, scribbling on the postcard: *check Reflections. Mr. Fairston. Check with all people Blanche visited. Who has something against Blanche?*

"But the problem was that between her visits and Rose doing the play and my working, I barely saw her this summer. She said she felt the need to be alone, but I'm sorry now that I gave her so much space. She's nineteen, but she's still so young…"

Bear wanted to comfort her but wasn't sure what to say except, "I wish I had been here."

"Well, you're back now," Jean said with a sigh. "I'm glad you are, and I'm very glad you called. Rose and I will get a plane home as soon as we can."

"Yes. Let me know if there's any trouble getting your tickets. I'll let you go now. I'll call if I have any more news," Bear said. "Goodbye."

"Goodbye, Bear."

He hung up the phone and stared at the cinderblock wall. It was as if a gulf had opened up between him and the Briers. *Blanche 'seeing' things. Blanche solitary and paranoid.* Images of girls hooked on drugs he had seen when he lived on the streets flashed before his eyes. A familiar voice full of class snobbery spoke derisively in his mind. *Her family's poor. You know that. How do you know she wasn't using you, after all? You gave her the keys to your apartment and left the country…how do you know she hasn't been taking things and pawning them all this time?…you always thought she was so good, so wholesome…Can you really believe in her?*

He tried to dismiss the thoughts immediately. He told himself that his vision was cloudy because of his stress, because of being in jail. But the picture of the princess in his mind as a girl with emotional problems who turned to drugs to fill some unspoken need tormented him, and he closed his eyes.

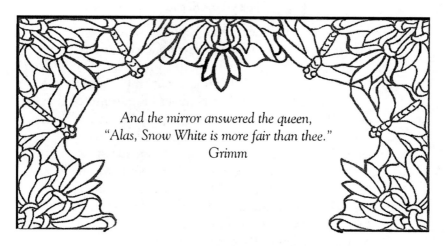

And the mirror answered the queen,
"Alas, Snow White is more fair than thee."
Grimm

Chapter Six

'Tis not that Dying hurts us so,
'Tis Living hurts us more
But Dying is a different way,
A Kind behind the Door

Simple work. Sorting clothing, restoring order. It seemed as though she had been sitting there for hours, surrounded by dust and clothes, working. At least the palpable sense of fear that had tormented her these past few weeks was receding.

An Emily Dickinson summer. She smiled to herself. Emily Dickinson, the pale poetess in white, who spoke of death and God beneath every other phrase—it had seemed a good idea to read her verses to a dying man.

At first, she had felt herself so remote from death. After all, it was summer, and although she was not completely happy, she was alive.

* * *

Not being sure of what she was going to do with her life had left her drifting. "I can't just wait around for my prince to come," she had lectured herself. But she knew it was no good. She *was* waiting. For Bear.

Day after day, she wrote to him. It was almost a mechanical process—taking an envelope, writing "Arthur Denniston" on it, then searching for his last letter to find out his current mailing address in

71

Europe—then writing, "Dear Bear" at the top of a sheet of paper. Then trying to figure out what to say.

She was not the sort of person who told about every detail of her day. Writing about work seemed dull compared to Bear's letters about his adventures hiking through Italy. Writing about her visits to Mr. Fairston and the people in the nursing home made her feel as though she were trying to broadcast her good deeds. So she restricted her topics to the weather and her reading. Necessarily, her letters to Bear were short. She wished she was like her sister Rose, who always seemed to find something to write about, whose letters were pages and pages long.

At first, it was a pleasant distraction to visit Mr. Fairston. She could talk to him—or at any rate, she could listen to him talk. Unfortunately, his health became worse and worse, and she felt sad as she watched his decline. At first he was only tired, but his coordination was becoming steadily worse. Soon he was confined to a wheelchair, and then to bed as he gradually lost control of the muscles on the right side of his body. A slow paralysis seemed to be coming over him. Fortunately he was an articulate person, and he found ways to talk even though one side of his face was inanimate. From time to time, things would confuse him, but mostly he still had clarity. She could tell he was appreciative of her visits.

When he still had the energy for long conversations, she listened to him talk about current events, about starting his company, about his wife. After a while, she sensed she was listening to an edited history, one that skipped over years of significant material. She guessed those missing years probably concerned people with whom he had broken off all contact. That was depressing.

It bothered her that Mr. Fairston, who, from the look of his house, was incredibly wealthy, couldn't afford to get a decent home nurse. Of course, there was a nursing shortage, but it didn't really explain why his nurses seemed even less competent than the ones in the crumbling nursing homes she visited.

His wife, whom Mr. Fairston constantly referred to, was seldom there. According to Mr. Fairston, she was very busy, with a company to run.

"My wife's quite a smart woman. Oh, she's a blond, and you know what they always say about blondes, but she's a smart one, I tell you. She got a hankering to buy this one corporation. I loaned her the money and said, go for it. And she did. Brought it into the Fortune 500 ranks, runs the whole thing herself. Brought me on to be vice-president, but it was more an honorary position than anything else. I told her to fly with it, so she wouldn't have to be indebted to me. She's doing quite well, quite well. Doesn't need me and my money any more. Which I have to say I don't mind." He chuckled, and coughed again.

That day, he had sounded particularly bad. The girl almost offered to get him some cold medication, but kept silent. After all, she didn't want to interfere.

The one or two times the girl and the wife met, the wife was friendly, coolly polite, or distracted, depending on her mood. One time she came in with a huge bouquet of red roses for her husband. Another time she marched in, woke him out of a doze, and demanded to know what was going on with the credit cards. She seemed to regard Blanche as part of the scenery, or, Blanche thought, like a maid who needed to be kept in her place.

But mostly, she was gone, and Blanche came and went from the Fairstons' richly-appointed house unmolested. She read Emily Dickinson, Caryll Houselander, and other poetry to Mr. Fairston. They talked about life, death, religion, and the possibility of his living until Christmas. Mr. Fairston was skeptical as to whether or not he would see it, and the girl tried to keep his spirits up.

"Things might happen before then," he said in an explanation the last time she had mentioned it, at the end of June.

"But if you look forward to it, you might just live to see it," the girl pointed out.

"I just don't look forward to Christmas," Mr. Fairston said. His right eye was half-lowered permanently now, and with his gloomy expression, the other eye matched it. "I haven't for years. After all, what is it except some kind of Winter Solstice celebration crossed with Madison Avenue Materialism?" He looked at her. "Of course you believe it's more than that, don't you?"

"You know that," she said. He often remarked on her Catholicism, and she had a feeling he wanted to talk about religion without really talking about religion.

"Almost all holidays are disappointing for me. Father's Day this Sunday," he murmured.

"Will you be hearing from your children?"

"Not unless some catastrophe befalls them and they're in trouble and need some of my money." He attempted a smile, but it was weak, and not just because of his poor motor skills. "I suppose it's better for me if they stay away. Talking to them only gets me upset. My wife's said it's not good for me. She's taken over relating with them since I've gotten sick, so I don't have the stress. I'm grateful to her for that."

The girl made a mental note to send Mr. Fairston a card for Father's Day, or perhaps to come by herself. After all, since her own dad was dead, her only plans for the day were to say some prayers for his soul, as she had promised him that she would. Checking her watch, she realized that she had to go.

"I'll be back soon," she promised, getting up and searching around. "I wonder where I left my purse."

"I don't think you brought it in," he said, looking around his messy bedroom. "Did you leave it in the hall downstairs?"

"I think I must have. Well, I'll see you next week." She pressed his hand and left.

As she walked down the steps, she couldn't help looking again at the huge smoky gray mirror trimmed with stained glass in the entranceway. She looked at her reflection with a trace of fascination. For some reason, her hair was looking unusually nice today.

She ran her hand down her long black hair, which reached down almost to her waist now.

Why is it that I'm looking good even though I'm not feeling happy? she wondered. Turning away, she saw her purse and backpack lying in the corner. She remembered now that she had put them there to help the nurse, who was bringing up a tea tray to Mr. Fairston.

Her purse seemed slightly disordered, and she wondered for a moment if someone had been going through it. But who would? The nurse might not be competent, but surely she was not so underpaid that she would be tempted to go through stray purses.

Caught by a strange sensation, she looked quickly through her purse. Her wallet, with five dollars in it, her makeup compact, her letter to Bear that needed airmail postage, and the usual odds and ends were all there. Puzzled, she closed the zipper of the purse and looked through her backpack, which had her work clothes inside, and closed that.

I'm being fearful, she thought to herself. She glanced at the mirror, and had the oddest sensation that it was laughing at her paranoia. Berating herself, she gathered her belongings and hurried out of the house.

* * *

II

Following his novice meeting with Father Bernard after lunch, Leon poked his head in the vestibule, curious as to what Nora had been up to. Already, the change was significant: she had piled up all the bags against the walls so that there was a clear path through the room. There were stacks and stacks of folded shirts, pants, and sweaters in neat rows along one wall.

"Awesome!" Brother Leon exclaimed. "Nora, you're a winner! I can't believe how fast you're sorting through this stuff!"

Nora, who looked hot and tired from her exertions, flushed rosy at the compliment. "Thanks," she said. "It looks like most of the clothes will be usable for your homeless men, but there were a few women's things. Like this dress," Nora made a face, holding up a huge shiny pink satin dress, which looked like it could fit an elephant.

"Could you use it?" Leon asked.

She chuckled. "No occasions where I could wear it comes to mind."

"Oh, almost forgot. Father Bernard said to tell you that he and Brother Herman are going out to do some work for the nearby parish, but they'll be back in about an hour. I guess the rest of us are clearing out too. We usually do some kind of missionary work in the afternoons."

"Should I answer the door or anything?"

"No. Actually, don't answer the door when we're away."

"I suppose it might look bad," Nora said, coloring again slightly.

"No, it's not that. It's just that we get all sorts of weird characters showing up here, and it's probably better, all things considered, that you don't answer the door when you're alone. Some of the people around here can be a little unstable. You probably shouldn't be alone with any of them either."

"Oh. Okay." She wiped her forehead.

"Anything wrong?" He could have sworn he saw her shaking.

"I'm just a bit hot and tired. I'll be fine." She spoke convincingly.

"Okay," Leon decided to take her word for it. "See you later, Nora."

The friars had decided to make their particular neighborhood their immediate concern. Every afternoon a pair of friars would go out and walk the streets, following a routine that was so ordinary it could be called "ministry" only loosely. They visited any of the elderly or ill that were shut up in their homes. They talked to whomever they passed, sitting on doorsteps or hanging out on street corners. They played with the kids. They listened to people, and found out what was going on. Who had gotten arrested, who had lost a job, who was in danger of being deported, who was having a hard time. It was too easy as a religious to get "spread thin"—doing very little for many people whom you barely knew. By grounding themselves in their particular neighborhood they hoped to guard against that kind of thing.

That afternoon, Charley and Leon had quite a few conversations on their walk. It was a hot, hot summer, and the only people not inside were those without air conditioners, and they were willing to talk to distract themselves from the heat.

As the friars turned back towards the friary for Evening Prayer, three kids shouting in Spanish waylaid them on their homeward walk.

Brother Leon answered them in Jamaican, which made them laugh, and Brother Charley, who was learning Spanish in seminary training, said with studied casualness, "*Hola, amigos. Comme'sta?*"

They horsed around with the kids for a few minutes, and then just as Brother Leon said, "Okay, *chicos*, we got to scoot," one girl held out a charm to them. "*Hermano* Leon, you need this."

Leon looked at it. He recognized it as a Santeria charm—the token of a superstitious religion widespread among parts of the New York ghettos. "Where'd you get that from, *hermana?*"

The little girl, who had dozens of black beaded braids sprouting over a blue headband, said solemnly in Spanish, "From my grandmother, to protect me. But you need it, because there's a scary witch in the neighborhood."

The kids all looked solemn, nodding. Brother Leon exchanged a brief glance with Brother Charley. The big friar looked quizzical. He wasn't following the conversation in Spanish.

Brother Leon squatted down in front of the little girl. "Hey, *pequeña hermana*, thank you for wanting me to be safe. But I don't need this. I belong to Jesus and Mary, and they keep me safe. But I will take it, just the same." He pocketed it.

"But the witch is driving around here."

"Who was the witch, *hermana?*"

"I didn't know her. But she looked like a witch."

"Ugly!" chimed in one of the boys.

"What, did you see her too?" Brother Leon asked the pudgy little boy in the oversized t-shirt, who nodded. "When did you see her?"

"Last night, on the streets, in a white car."

"That's why you need a charm, in case you meet her. We're all wearing them. She was scary. She might put curses on you." The little girl was worried.

Brother Leon patted her hand. "I'm not afraid of curses. Do you know a lady who is stronger than any witch?"

"Who?" the kids chorused.

"Mary. Because she is Jesus' mother. And Jesus is God." He crossed himself, and kissed his crossed thumb and finger. The kids all did the same, "Can I give you something special to protect you?" he asked, and they nodded eagerly.

He pulled out a silver medal with an image of the Virgin Mary on it. "This medal has a blessing on it. And the blessing will protect you, but what will protect you more is if you learn to love God with all your heart and soul, and love each other. Would you each like one of these medals?"

He distributed them to eager hands and the two friars said goodbye to the children, who scattered to their various homes.

"What were they talking about—a broohaha?" Brother Charley asked him.

"*Una bruja.* A witch. They said they saw a witch driving a white car on the streets last night. Angelita wanted to protect me—she gave me her charm."

He pulled it out and looked at it, murmuring a brief prayer as he did so. Having grown up in a Hispanic-Caribbean culture, he disliked Santeria, which often confused the ignorant by melding Catholic tradition with pagan and occult superstition. "It's a protection charm. She was pretty worried about me. You see, the protection charm is made for one particular person, and if you allow anyone else to touch the charm, the spell is supposedly broken. But it says a lot that she wanted me to have it. As they say, it's the thought that counts."

Brother Charley shook his head. "That stuff gives me the creeps."

"Likewise," Brother Leon put the charm back inside his pocket to dispose of later. "You heard of any *brujas feas*—ugly witches—in this neighborhood before?"

"No. Did she mean one of the Santeria people?"

"I doubt it. The kids know who the Santeria people are, but they didn't recognize this woman."

"Maybe they were making things up," Brother Charley suggested. "An ugly witch in a white car?"

"No, I saw a white car driving around this place too a few days ago. Something tells me they saw something strange—and described it the only way they knew how." Brother Leon mused. He didn't like the feeling he was getting.

III

"Mr. Denniston, and Mr. Denniston," the lawyer began, setting his briefcase on the table in the conference room of the jail.

Bear stared at Charles Russell, outlined against a barred window in a jail meeting room. The lawyer was a tall, aging man, whose smoothed-back hair remained remarkably red. The first time Bear had had substantial contact with him was at the age of seventeen, when the lawyer had been hired by his father to defend the brothers in court against the drug charges—unsuccessfully. They had been sentenced to juvenile prison for the maximum first-time offenders' sentence.

Bear suspected that Mr. Russell resented them for that fact—it was possibly the first case the high-paid lawyer had lost in years. He had been chewed out in front of the judge, too.

But he had been helping them through the reversal, once the drug charges were found, three years later, to be false. Now once again, he was here, at the prison, arranging for them to be bailed out of jail, a bit more grimly than last time.

"I am, of course, prepared to assist you in any way I can," the lawyer began, and paused, averting his eyes to his papers, "but there's a certain circumstance my firm and I need to be clear on. Up until now, I have been working for you because your father retained me. However, your father has made it clear to me on several occasions, and no doubt to you as well, that he would pay no legal fees for a second drug charge against you. In fact, he said he would cut off all monetary help or any posthumous share of his assets to you if there were a second charge. I wanted to make certain you were apprised of that."

Bear stared at him. "In other words, Dad's just been sitting around waiting for us to get charged again?" he said in disgust. "Guess he wasn't even convinced by Father Raymond's murderer admitting to framing us? That's just too—"

Fish shot a look at his brother that clearly said, *Calm down.* "Of course, Mr. Russell, we understand that," he said cordially. "If this is a matter of who's going to pay your fees, you can be assured that my brother and I will pay for this ourselves. Tell me what we're facing, Mr. Russell," he said.

Mr. Russell picked up his brief. "The US Attorney General is prosecuting you with criminal possession of a controlled substance according to tier one on the federal trafficking schedule," he said. "If they can prove trafficking, there's a mandatory five-year prison sentence in most cases."

Fish gave a low whistle, but his face was grim. "How soon until bail is determined?" he asked.

"Probably tomorrow," the lawyer said stiffly. "However, I should warn you that they might not let you out on bail."

"Why not?" Bear asked.

"Apparently, the DEA thinks you are a flight risk."

Bear absorbed this. "You mean, they think that if we're released before our trial, we'll just pick up and leave the country?"

"It's not unreasonable for them to think that," Mr. Russell said. "After all, you, Mr. Arthur Denniston, have been overseas for the past few months. From the financial information you provided them, they have easily deduced that both of you have the resources to leave and to live abroad if you so desired."

"Great," Fish breathed. "So what do we have to do to convince them that we're not going to try to escape our trial?"

"You have to demonstrate strong community ties," the attorney said. "Such as a job, attending school, family—"

"Well, I'm a student at NYU. Actually, I'm enrolled in several summer courses," Fish glanced at his watch. "I've actually missed two classes so far by sitting in jail. I had to get special permission to go on vacation in the midst of the course. I'd be happy to provide you with the letter from my instructor and the assignments I finished while I was on vacation."

"That will certainly help," Mr. Russell said. He turned to Bear. "And you?"

"I'm not enrolled in school," Bear murmured.

"Are you employed?"

"No."

"Any other family connections? Have you been visiting your father, for example? Could he vouch for you?"

"Haven't seen him in over a year," Bear said, resentful of his circumstances. "And no, he wouldn't vouch for me. I am close to my girlfriend and her family, though. And the Fosters."

"I see," the lawyer pursed his lips. "Well, we'll have to see if this judge will accept that. I have to say that the timing of these charges is fairly bad, since you just came back from overseas. MDMA is notoriously easy to obtain in Europe."

The lawyer picked up another case file. The two brothers watched him as he read over it. At last he spoke. "This girlfriend...she is the person mentioned here, as a suspect in the embezzlement at the restaurant?"

"Blanche Brier, yes," Bear said.

"And she was seen by security coming into your apartment, carrying a knapsack?"

"She was taking care of our plants. I gave her the keys."

Mr. Russell pointed to a copy of the photograph from the security camera. "And in this picture, she's carrying the same knapsack that her employers found drugs in?"

"Yes, so far as I can tell," Bear said.

"You have no idea where she is?"

"We don't. We were trying to find her when we got arrested."

Mr. Russell leaned back. "I could argue to the judge that it's clearly this Ms. Brier who is responsible for the drugs that were found in your apartment. After all, she had access to the apartment, you have both been out of the country, and since your juvenile record has been cleared, there's no reason for them to think that you would be the owners of the drugs. After all, there were no drugs found in your luggage."

More than slightly irritated, Bear shook his head. "I'm sorry, Mr. Russell, but that's not an acceptable defense."

"I agree," Fish said.

The lawyer leveled his gaze at Bear. "I realize that she's your girlfriend, but look at this objectively for a moment. Does she have financial need? Is it possible she might have been tempted to sell the drugs as a way of making money? Say, for college?"

For just a moment, Bear wavered, the image of Blanche's haunted face in his mind. Just suppose...? But suddenly, clearly, he heard his father's voice, touched with sarcasm. *And I'm supposed to believe that you wouldn't be doing drugs? You, a teenager who spends all his time doing who knows what?*

He knew what it was like to be falsely accused. He knew what it was like to be doubted, because you were lonely, and an outsider. He remembered standing by the dry fountain in the Cloister garden holding Blanche's hand, and saying, "*I'll believe in you if you believe in me.*"

"That's not an acceptable defense," Bear said again. "I don't care if I can't get out of jail: she's not the one behind this. In fact," he looked at the lawyer, "she's been set up. By the same person who set us up."

The lawyer shook his head. "I hate to say this, but a jury might think otherwise if the case comes to trial." He tapped the photograph. "You may think she's innocent, but you could have a tough time convincing others. That's not the face of a girl who has nothing to hide."

"Innocent until proven guilty," Bear said quietly, and knitted his fingers together in prayer. *I'm not going to turn against her. But God, if you can get me out of jail somehow, I would appreciate it. I need to find her.*

When the queen heard this, she turned yellow and green with jealousy, and her heart had no rest, so deeply did she hate the girl. And so she plotted.
Grimm

Chapter Seven

uesday night the heat broke, and the rain fell.

The girl heard it, late at night, and something inside her relaxed. She wasn't sure why the rain should make her feel relieved. But it did. For a while she stared up at the window of her room, watching the rain falling, dashes of silver through the cloud of dim darkness.

For some reason, she was feeling too furtive to turn on the light, and let someone know that she was awake. So she got out of bed in the dimness and dressed herself. There were no work dresses or skirts here for her to wear, only t-shirts and jeans. While feeling around for her sweater in the crate where she kept her clothes, she felt something hard among the folds of her yellow dress, and drew it out. The bottle she had taken from Mr. Fairston's house. She studied it again, worried. Another mystery.

After pulling on the black cardigan with unraveling cuffs, she ran her hand through her hair. It was too short. Once again, she felt sick inside.

Stepping outside into the torrent rain, she ran to the church's back door, tried her key in the lock, and pulled it open. It creaked shut behind her, and she stood inside, panting and dripping.

Like a shadow, she softly stepped into the sacristy, listening to the comforting thunder of the rain on the solid church roof. She looked around, the white bottle in her hand, seeking further solitude, hoping to avoid memories.

In the dusty sacristy that afternoon she had discovered a closet that opened upon a little room with a window, which was filled with old plaster statues, clearly stored there because they were in need of repair. The Blessed Mother had a chipped nose. St. Agnes had a broken hand and her lamb had only three feet.

Now she looked at the still and shabby dust-covered statues, and they seemed to invite her to join them. Some of them were as tall as she was, but others were more diminutive. Tentatively, she walked among them until she reached the largest one, who stood secluded in a corner, her glass eyes wise, her plaster harp chipped, her hand out, as though beckoning to her with three outstretched fingers. Who was she? An angel? But she was unwinged.

"Can you help me?" she whispered at the plaster woman, putting the medicine bottle in her open hand. It seemed to belong there. "I don't know where to turn—"

After a moment, she looked away, still torn inside. She put a finger on little St. Maria Goretti's shawl-covered shoulders and wiped off the dust. "Perhaps I should just go back, find out what happened, and risk being arrested," she murmured. "The police might find out the truth—"

But look what had happened to Bear, when he was in high school. Innocent people got convicted: what was to stop it from happening to her?

Looking around at the statues, she noticed there were quite a few women martyrs among them. Somehow, they had all found the courage to die for the faith, and she wondered about them. Had they always been strong, or were they ordinary girls in extraordinary situations? Was it genetics or grace? She hoped it was grace.

Otherwise, there's no hope for me...

II

Around midnight, a car alarm went off on their street, starting Brother Leon awake. He was so used to the obnoxious sound that usually he fell back to sleep within minutes. But tonight, for some reason, he couldn't. Maybe it was the heat.

For a few minutes he drifted in and out of consciousness, annoyed at the stupid alarm for stealing his rest. *Better than being woken by a rat bite, but not much better.* With a sigh, he began a litany of prayer again, naming the saints and intercessors in rhythm, asking for prayers for his family, the people who he had met that day, Nora ...

Usually, this line of defense brought him back into slumber fairly quickly. But now it failed, and he found himself becoming increasingly awake.

Irate, he sat up. *Okay, Lord. You behind this?*

Apparently someone out there needed prayer, big time. Stifling a yawn, he sat up on his sleeping bag on the floor, fumbled for his sandals and habit in the dark, and dressed. Trying to avoid the creaking parts of the floor for the sake of his brothers, he walked downstairs. Just as he reached the corridor to the church, it started raining hard, and he was pleased.

Once inside the church, he knelt down in the darkness gazing at the little light before the tabernacle. He crossed himself, yawned, (of course, *now* he was tired) and started in on the rosary.

He closed his eyes, but his spirit swept outwards, over the inhabitants of the friary, out on the streets, to the traffic passing by, to the people on the corners making drug deals, or in their apartments watching TV; huddled in the darkness of the night or the darkness of sin, their eyes reflecting the suffering, the barrenness, the world-weariness. His spirit, in thought, brushed over all of them, seeking Christ, looking for the tortured features of the Man of Sorrows in the empty eyes of the people of the night.

The mystery of the night was pierced through until it surrendered to the darker mystic night, the night of the soul in search for its God. In that night, Leon went wandering, and slowly his fingers moved over the beads, with longer and longer pauses, as his body inevitably succumbed to fatigue.

Then another sound, far quieter than the car alarm, but stranger, alerted him: metal hinges. Someone was opening the back door to the church. He saw through the open sacristy door a flash of dim nightfall and a girlish figure stepping inside, brushing the rain off her hair, then the door closed and the figure was enveloped in darkness. He recognized her.

Closing his eyes, he continued praying. After some time, the shape slipped out of the sacristy and started down the side aisle, straight towards the shadows where he was kneeling.

"Nora."

She jumped back with a cry, then clapped a hand to her mouth. "I'm sorry."

"Sorry if I startled you," he said softly.

She forced a laugh. "I was just going back to the vestibule."

"To sleep?"

Now she laughed in earnest. "No. To finish sorting clothes. I couldn't sleep."

He could make out tears on her face in the faint glow of streetlights coming through the stained glass windows. "You upset about something?"

She was silent.

"You want to talk about it?"

She breathed, wiped her eyes, and looked at him again. Then she sat down in a nearby pew. Picking the pew behind her, he sat down and leaned back.

"You'll think I'm crazy," she said at last.

"Maybe, maybe not."

She looked at him over her shoulder levelly. "I tried to tell my mother and my sister once, and they thought I was crazy," she said.

"Try me."

She glanced at him, and then looked away again. "I keep feeling," she said in a low voice, "a sense of death. A premonition. As though I'm in danger."

"From who?"

"I don't know. Isn't that paranoia?"

"Hard to tell," Brother Leon said. "But I can see it's upsetting you."

She looked up. "All my life, I've had these strange feelings about things, about things in the future. My dad, who's dead, used to say it was a gift. But lately, my intuition has been that I'm in danger. Of dying. And I don't know why."

"Is that what's bothering you?"

"That's part of it," she said in a low voice. "I keep thinking that someone's following me."

"Following you?"

She put her hands on her knee. "For a while, it seemed like every time I left my house, every time I went to work, every time I did an errand, I would see this man behind me in my peripheral vision. This big, tall man with a big head and broad shoulders, following me."

"This isn't the man who mugged you?"

She shook her head. "No. The guys who mugged me were young. This man has got to be about forty. And despite the fact that no one else has seen him, I'm sure I'm not imagining *him*. Although—I could be imagining that he's after me."

Leon scratched his chin. "Well, that does sound like something to be concerned about. Did you call the police?"

"I thought of that, but what could I tell them except that he was always in my vicinity? It's not as though he's ever tried to come up and talk to me. He's barely even looked at me."

"And you don't know who he is?"

"I have no idea."

"Just so I'm clear here—you're not telling me that you think this man is a spiritual manifestation of Death?"

She shook her head. "No. That's something separate. It's like this: all summer, I've been having this sense of being vulnerable. And then, a few weeks ago, I start noticing this man. Of course, this only makes me feel more and more paranoid. After a while, I had the sense that any random destructive force in my area was going to careen in my direction. Not that anything actually happened—well, not until the night I came here—but I've been feeling all along that something was *about* to happen. And frankly, it hasn't been—good for my sanity." She smiled wryly.

"You said you talked to your mom and sister about this?"

She hesitated. "Yes. Maybe it was just how I put it to them, but they didn't react at all well. I think my mom is starting to wonder if I've got some kind of emotional problem—just before she left on vacation, I overheard her asking a nurse friend of hers for the name of a reliable psychiatrist."

"Do they know you're here?"

She shook her head. "No. They're on a camping trip in California. I won't be able to reach them until next week. But at least they won't be worried about me."

Brother Leon thought. "Have you seen this man hanging around the friary?"

"No. It's kind of funny, but I'm relieved. Since the night of the mugging, it almost seems like I've escaped him by coming here. If he was really ever following me in the first place. Do I sound paranoid?"

"No, not at all," Leon said. "In fact, keep on looking over your shoulder for this guy. If you see him, tell us. Maybe we can find out what he's up to. Does that help?"

"Somewhat," she managed a smile. "I just wish I could understand what this means. It's as though my life has turned into a chess game, and I'm a pawn who has no idea what's going on. I just keep trying to go straight ahead and mind my own business."

"Well, you realize that if you're a pawn in a chess game and you keep walking the straight and narrow, you're going to invade enemy territory the further you go on," Brother Leon pointed out.

"That's what I feel like. Like I've crossed some sort of line, and now every piece I see is after me suddenly. But I don't know where the line was or when I crossed it."

"Nora, you crossed it by growing up," Leon said. "You know we're in a battle here, right?"

"You mean, a spiritual war between good and evil."

"Yeah. And you're on the good side, right?"

"Well, I hope so."

"When you grow up trying to do good, you tend to get better at it. And pretty soon, you might start being a threat. To the devil. See, God has a plan for you, and the devil knows it. Don't underestimate what God wants from you either. You might think you're just a pawn, but a pawn who reaches the other side of the board becomes a queen."

"I don't want to be a queen," Nora murmured, running her hands through her hair. "I just want to be left alone."

Leon chuckled. "Your only chance for peace is to put yourself in God's hands and trust Him."

She smiled ironically. "I'm sorry. I wish I could be sure 'the suffering had a loving side,' like Emily Dickinson said. Sometimes it's hard for me to think God finds me very lovable."

"Don't think that!" Leon said with vehemence, and she looked at him, startled. "I'm serious, Nora. You're not allowed to doubt God loves you. You can doubt everything else. Doubt the sacraments, doubt your sanity, doubt the existence of Saskatchewan or Siamese cats. But there's one thing you can't doubt, and that is God's love for you. No matter what happens to you, never doubt that He loves you. That has to be your foundation: He loves you. The universe might disintegrate around you, but that won't change."

She looked at him as though she had begun to understand something.

"'For the plans I have for you are good and not evil, life, and not death, to give you a future, and a hope.' Nora, c'mon, trust Him a little."

"Okay. I guess that's what Catholics are supposed to do." She sighed.

He rubbed his beard stubble again. "Look, you need to take your mind off some of this stuff. How about you give the vestibule a rest for now, and get out, for a change? Matt and I have got to drive someone to the airport today. Why don't you come along? Sound good?"

"Yes," she said, with a faint smile.

"Then do me a favor and go back to your room and try to get some sleep." He touched her shoulder lightly. "All right?"

"All right."

With a quiet smile she rose, left the pew and walked back out of the church as the rain hammered down on the roof. He closed his eyes and knelt.

Okay, Lord, so that's what you were up to. Now let me let her go, beautiful as she is, and give her to you. You take care of her. You'll do it better than I would, anyhow.

III

Wednesday. Still trapped in prison. At least it was raining. Bear rolled over in his jail bunk and blinked in the early morning light diffused through his plastic-screened window. He hadn't changed clothes since he had left Rome, and he was feeling increasingly grungy. Realizing he was awake, he buried his head in his hands and prayed. *God, please let me get out today. Or at least let me get some news about Blanche. Just to know that she's okay…*

There was a clang as the prison guards started to open the cell doors for the morning. Bear scrambled to his feet and ran his hands through his hair. He wanted to get to the phones and find out if there was any news. Fish sat up, yawning.

"Good Lord," he said. "Still here, are we? I keep hoping this is some sort of bad dream, and I'll wake up to find myself back in Italy."

Bear, his hands on the bars of their cell, cracked a smile. "I'd find that frustrating myself. At this point, I'm sorry that I ever went. If I hadn't gone, maybe none of this would have happened." He watched the guard anxiously as the man slowly came down the corridor towards them, opening doors as he went, taking his time.

"Then why did you go?" Fish asked wearily, as he lay back down. "It's obvious that you're in love with Blanche. I've always wondered why you didn't—propose marriage or something."

His brother's pointed question hurt. Bear swallowed, and said, "Because of how Dad treated Mom."

Fish rubbed his eyes. "Well, I know that they weren't happy together, but—what does that have to do with anything?"

"With them as my role models, how can I expect to have a good marriage myself?" Bear asked bluntly. "How can I be sure that Blanche and I won't end up just like Mom and Dad—cold and distant and talking around each other instead of to each other? It scares the heck out of me."

Fish stared at the ceiling. "You're not like Dad, Bear. You've got a lot more strength than he does. Definitely more than I do."

"Speak for yourself. You're the one who's got it all together."

Fish threw him a warning glance. "Only on the outside. You know that."

"Yeah, I know," Bear rubbed his head. "But Dad still influenced me. A lot."

"Dad's problem was that he never understood what marriage was all about in the first place. Mom said even she didn't know too much about marriage, until she started studying Catholicism. She said Dad just couldn't get it."

"It was more than just ignorance, though," Bear said, despite himself. "He—" He restrained himself. "Sorry, I shouldn't go into that."

Fish glanced at him. "I think I know what you're referring to," he said quietly. "You mean how Dad wasn't faithful to Mom."

"So you know about that?"

"By the time Mom died I had figured things out. When did you know?"

"By high school. Father Raymond knew too. Longer than I knew."

"Well, he was Mom's confessor as well as her friend. I suppose he must have known."

"I've always suspected that's why Dad wouldn't believe we were framed," Bear said, and rubbed his face with his shoulder. "Because—" he hesitated, remembering the scene too well. "Because of what happened when I found out."

"What, did you walk in on him kissing some woman or something?"

Bear nodded. "More than kissing. When I was fourteen."

"Yikes. What did you do?"

"Well, I was furious. I tried to leave without saying anything, but Dad wanted to act as though it wasn't a big deal, and called me back. I don't think he realized how mad I was. He told me I was old enough to know and said it was totally normal for men, then asked me what I thought. So, uh, I told him."

Fish was half-amused. "Seriously? What did you say?"

Bear blew out his breath. "I tried to give him the Father Raymond treatment. You know, I just told him the stuff Father Raymond used to tell us: about faithfulness, and manhood, and honoring vows. But I don't think I was particularly persuasive. I think I was mostly loud." He rubbed his face again. "I must have sounded like—He didn't take it well. Neither did she. It was embarrassing."

"Embarrassing all around, I'm sure," Fish said mildly.

There was silence between them, and the noise of the jail filled in the space for them. Bear felt the dull, aching sense of sickness in his mouth. He wiped his lips. "I'm sorry. I shouldn't have brought it up."

"Well, I didn't realize how long it had been going on, but I've known for a while that our family life was no bed of roses," Fish said humorously. He paused. "So Dad was mad at you because you made him feel guilty. So when we were framed, he pounced on the chance to believe that his Catholic sons were actually drug dealers, to justify his own behavior."

"Yeah, it seems that way to me," Bear said. "Father Raymond used to say the worst part of being bad is that you stop believing in being good. You think everyone else is just as bad as you are. And you look for ways to prove it to yourself, over and over."

"And Father Raymond was probably right, as he usually was," Fish ruminated. "At least you've had *him* as an example, Bear. Father Raymond was a faithful priest: he was married to the Church, and he kept his vows. Doesn't that help?"

"Yeah," Bear admitted. "It does."

At last the guard had reached their cell, and started to open it. Another guard came down the corridor. "Denniston and Denniston?" he said, "The magistrate's determining your bail this morning. Walk in front of me."

Thanking God, Bear waited as the first guard fiddled with the lock and at last opened the cell. Fish got off his bunk, and followed him out.

They were led to a blank gray room that resembled a miniature courtroom. Charles Russell was there on one side, and a lawyer from the DEA on the other side. Bear and Fish took their stand in the middle before the judge, who was only a few feet away from them behind a large bench, and the clerk of court opened their hearing.

For all of his previous annoyance with the man, Bear had to admit that Charles Russell was a good lawyer. He argued passionately against the DEA that, on the contrary, the plaintiffs Arthur and Benedict Denniston were not at risk for flight and had the legal right to be set free on personal recognizance.

It was difficult at times not to feel that he was at a tennis match as the DEA lawyer and Mr. Russell set their arguments and objections flying back and forth, being overruled or sustained by the judge. Fish looked back and forth from one to the other with interest, but Bear just stared at the floor and prayed. It was clear that the DEA considered him more of a risk than Fish, as Mr. Russell had warned that they would.

Bear was wondering if guards would be escorting him back to his cell when all of a sudden it was over. The judge set bail for five thousand dollars apiece, and Bear and Fish were turned over to the clerk to make their payments, which the lawyer had set up for them. After making their payments and recovering their personal belongings from the police, they were free to go.

Outside, it was still gloomy and raining, but Bear felt nearly happy. He took a deep breath, and managed to thank the lawyer as they stood on the steps of the jail.

"It seems like it worked out. I'm glad. Let's hope it goes so well at the trial." Mr. Russell warned him as he opened his umbrella. "This is only the beginning, you know. The first hearing is at the end of this month. Call me at my office today or tomorrow and we'll set up a conference about it."

"It's not going to come to conviction. The DEA is going to drop the charges, once we find out who did this," Bear said positively.

"I hope so," the lawyer said, still looking a bit uncertain. "Have you gotten any more news of your missing girlfriend?"

"Not yet, but we're going to start looking, now that we're out," Bear said.

"Remember you're restrained by certain limitations until you go to trial."

"Such as not leaving the country," Bear said, a bit annoyed. "I know."

"I certainly hope you find her," the lawyer said with what Bear guessed was professional compassion. "Good luck." He turned away and strode off to his car.

Fish walked quickly on Bear's heels as they walked to the corner where Bear signaled a taxi, which ignored him.

"Well, Charles came through, didn't he?" Fish said.

"I still don't know what to make of him," Bear blew out his breath as he looked at the cars tearing through the rainy streets. "But I'm sure the feeling's mutual. He probably has this nagging suspicion that we're just very clever con artists." He signaled once more for a taxi, again without result, and gritted his teeth. He and Fish didn't have umbrellas, and they were quickly getting soaked.

Lousy, lousy mess, he thought to himself, turning up his collar to keep the rain off his neck. As he did so, he saw a man turn his back on him. Bear looked swiftly at the man, who was standing about fifteen feet away with his back to him, looking out at the passing traffic as though he was also searching for a taxi. He was a big man, taller than Bear, with broad shoulders and a large head.

That man was watching us, Bear's senses told him, and he stiffened inside. He decided to walk over to the man on the pretense of looking for a taxi, and maybe get a look at his face. But before he could act, Fish leapt forward with a splash into the street yelling, "Taxi!" and a yellow cab pulled to a stop.

Fish opened the door. "Sometimes you need to be nearly suicidal to get these guys to stop." He ducked inside and gave the driver the address.

Bear tried to get a glimpse of the big man, but the stranger was striding in the opposite direction, his back towards them again.

The hunter led the girl into the darkness of the forest, but he could not bear to kill her. So he said, "Run away, child, and hide," thinking the wild beasts would devour her.
Grimm

Chapter Eight

he rain took the edge off the summer morning heat, and the conversation with Brother Leon had relieved some of the pressure on her mind. Despite her late night excursion, she woke up in time for the Office of Readings prayer on Wednesday morning and accepted Father Bernard's invitation to eat breakfast with them, since it was the feast of St. Clare, an important holy day for the friars.

She still felt uncomfortable with some of the friars. Father Francis seemed intimidating, and she had a feeling that Brother George, the red-haired brother, didn't like her very much. She had wondered a few times if it perhaps would be better for her to keep more to herself.

But the novices were friendly, and Brother Herman, the Santa Claus friar, was kind. And this morning, she actually felt very hungry. She settled down to eat her portion.

"Are you in college right now?" Brother Charley asked.

She shook her head. "I took a few nursing courses at the community college, but I'm not sure if I'm going to keep it up."

"Why not?" Brother Matt asked.

"She's trying to get an M.R.S. degree," Leon said in a loud whisper.

Indignant, she raised her eyebrows at him. "My mother did not raise me to be a fisher of men," she said.

The friars roared with laughter, including Leon, who was slightly embarrassed.

"She's got you there, Leon," Brother Charley grinned.

"Okay, okay," Leon said. "You ready for a big airport adventure this afternoon, Nora?"

"Sure am," she said, and actually felt more ready than would have seemed possible yesterday.

II

So that afternoon, Leon collected Nora and Matt, obtained the keys for the community's rusting old white painter's van, and got his entourage packed up to go to Marisol's apartment. Leon was in a happy mood. The rain had stopped and the sun was out. Matt had remembered that he had an appointment at four, but Leon expansively assured him that they would be back in time.

"I have a bad feeling about this," Matt muttered dubiously as they got out of the car. Nora had said she would stay and watch the van, which was double-parked.

"We're an hour early," Leon argued. "We'll have time." The kids were sitting on the stoop waiting for them. "Aay! *Wha a gwan?*"

"*Aay, Fadda Leon!*" they ran up to meet them.

"Nah man! *Brother* Leon!" he corrected them, laughing. "I'm no priest!"

The little boy threw himself at him, wanting to wrestle, and the sister shrieked and jumped into his arms. Swinging one under each arm, he carried them inside. "So your grandmother's going home? She ready?"

"*Nuh yet!*" the kids said happily.

They found Marisol and her grandmother packing. "Packing" in the loosest sense of the word—they were piling things into garbage bags. It was very disorganized.

Brother Matt looked at Leon. "We're going to be late," he warned.

"*We can elp yu?*" Brother Leon asked them after exchanging looks with Matt. "*Wha a go a di airport?*"

"*Dis and dis a goes,*" Marisol said. And she pointed at two Rottweilers with thick red collars lying down on the threadbare sofa. "*And dem a go too.*"

"The dogs?" Matt said doubtfully. "You think they'll let you bring the dogs on the plane? I thought you couldn't bring animals overseas."

"*A er daag dem,*" Marisol said firmly. "*Dem haffi go.*"

"All right," Leon said, trying to remain optimistic. He sized up the dogs, which, apparently realizing they were being spoken of, lifted their heads and looked at the new arrivals warily.

"Hey pooches," Matt said faintly, putting out his hand. "What are we going to carry them in?"

"*Yuh ave one crate fi dem?*" Leon said uncertainly.

Marisol pointed to a larger-sized cardboard box.

"They're *never* going to go in there," Matt said emphatically. "This is crazy."

"Maybe they traveled up here in one," Leon offered hopefully. He approached the dog. "*Aay, mongrels, unna want a ride to di airport? Good mongrel...*"

He looked at the grandmother, who said, "*Prince, Pouff-pouff, go inna di box!*" with a voice of some authority.

In answer, both dogs go to their feet and sprinted out of the apartment. Leon leapt and managed to grab the collar of one. Matt grabbed the other, lost his grip, and tumbled to the ground as the dog tore down the steps.

"I got him," Leon grunted, wrestling with the other thrashing dog. "Matt, help me—"

The grandmother was yelling, "*Prince, da no be baad daag!*"

With the efforts of Marisol, the grandmother, and the two friars, the dog was thrust into the cardboard box and the flaps were closed.

"He's not going to stay in there," Matt warned as the dog jabbed his nose through the crevice between the flaps over and over, barking furiously and skittering his claws on the box floor as he turned around in circles.

Leon was trying to keep the flaps shut and keep his hands out of range of the dog's teeth at the same time. "We need to get something else."

"*Prince! Shut yuh mout!*" the grandmother yelled over the deafening barks.

Marisol pushed a stack of newspapers and unfolded laundry off the card table in the living room, overturned it, and put it on top of the cardboard box, and started piling things on top of it to keep it shut. The box started to bow out slightly, but the dog finally settled down, snarling.

"Right," Brother Leon said. "Okay, let's get this other stuff down to the car and then we'll go look for the other dog."

III

After returning home for a quick shower and change, Bear and Fish picked up Fish's car at its garage, and drove, as agreed upon earlier, to the Briers' house to meet Mrs. Foster. There were no parking spaces on the Briers' street, so Fish told Bear to get out while he went to park further down. Bear opened the door, glad that the rain had stopped, and hurried up to Blanche's house.

The large black woman was standing on the stoop, leaning on her closed umbrella, and looking at the Briers' window boxes, which were lush with red and white roses. She immediately walked down the stairs to meet him on the sidewalk and hugged him.

"See? They let you out, didn't they, just like I prayed," she said. "God's taking care of you, boy."

"He is," Bear said, giving the woman a heartfelt squeeze in return. "Thanks for everything you've been doing, Mrs. Foster. You've been a lifesaver, again."

"It's no problem." Mrs. Foster glanced at the house and took his arm. "Before we go in, let's talk out here," she pursed her lips. Bear could tell from her expression that something had happened. His pulse began racing as they walked down the wet sidewalk.

"What is it?" he asked.

She lowered her voice. "I want to tell you this outside so that we don't speak about it inside. You never know what's going on with stuff like this these days." She whispered. "There are drugs in that house."

Bear started.

She turned around and pulled out the key. "I'll take you back now and show you what I found."

They walked up the steps and Mrs. Foster unlocked the door. The street door opened into the entranceway. Bear scanned the blue-and-white tiled floor quickly. A forgotten umbrella, a showering of mail and a rolled-up paper. "Saturday's mail is what I guess," Mrs. Foster said, unlocking the second door that led into the house.

Inside, the Brier's house was full of that sunny stillness, but with a pronounced echo of emptiness. Bear stood, looking around at the comfortably shabby couch, chairs, bookshelves and assorted knickknacks. The living room was straightened and neat. The kitchen was spotless, the teapot, cookie crock, and rows of mason jars gleaming on the laminate countertop in the dim light.

The door to the house opened again, and Fish walked inside, hands in the pockets of his trench coat.

"Looks very neat and clean in here," he said.

Bear had to smile. The Brier house was generally a touch more disorderly than it was now. "That's because Blanche was here alone. She's the tidy one in the family," he said.

"Ah," said Fish.

Bear knew Blanche was a highly visual person, and that it bothered her when things were messy. He remembered on many nights when he had come over, he would find Rose lying on the couch with a book and Blanche going back and forth, picking up things in the living room, or scrubbing stains off cabinets and counters in the kitchen. Once Bear had teased her about it, and she had said, "Things just bother me if they're out of place. I wish I were less aware of things sometimes. But I can't tune out a mess."

Bear privately guessed that the other reason was that housecleaning was Blanche's contribution to holding the family together, since her dad had died.

Jean had a full-time job as an emergency room nurse and didn't have much energy for cleaning. Rose was charming, but not very orderly.

Now the regularity of Blanche's habits—and surely, in the absence of her family, she would be even more regular in her solitude—was giving him important clues.

"She cleans the house in the evening," he said aloud.

Fish ran his finger on the coffee table. "Then why'd she miss that dust?"

"She must have left in the afternoon then," Mrs. Foster said.

"To go to work, where she was last seen on Saturday night," Bear said slowly. He scanned the room again. Fish walked into the kitchen, looking around. As Bear's eyes wandered over to the desk, he caught sight of a black and white photograph on it—a photograph of Blanche.

She was wearing a pale dress and was sitting on a chair, her long dark hair falling over her shoulders and down to the smooth white skin of her forearms. She was looking towards the left, and smiling calmly, her eyes, which he knew were blue, serene. It was a striking photograph. He knew he had never seen it before. Possibly from her high school graduation—but no, she had bought that dress just before he left for Rome, the yellow one. If it was the yellow one. It had to be recent.

He fingered the photograph, and turned it over. *Longbourne Studios* said a black stamp on the back.

Turning it back over, he checked the rest of the items on the desk. There was a neat stack of mail. They were all postmarked before August 7th, Friday's date. He tried to visualize this. Friday night she had come home, gathered and sorted the mail, cleaned up the kitchen, gone to bed. Possibly that photo had come in the mail, and she had left it on the desk. To frame it? To give it to her mother? Or to him?

After looking over the other contents of the desk, he turned back to Mrs. Foster and raised his eyebrows. She nodded and said, "Let's go upstairs."

They walked up the carpeted steps to the second floor of the town house. Gingerly, Bear pushed the door to the bedroom open. He had never been up here before, and looked around with some melancholic interest. The room Blanche shared with her sister Rose was pristine, the quilts on the bed smooth, the pillows fluffed, the stuffed animals perky and smiling. He surveyed the blue-painted desk—orderly—the scratched wooden dressers— cleaned and arranged. There were a few clothes tossed on a battered antique dining room chair. It looked like a girl's room.

He glanced at Mrs. Foster again, who pointed to the wooden jewelry box on Blanche's dresser. He lifted the carved lid. Inside were several compartments, with a few pieces of the simple gold and silver jewelry Blanche liked to wear. There didn't seem to be anything amiss.

Unconsciously, he put a hand to his neck and fingered the necklace that Blanche had given him, ages ago, it now seemed. A gold chain with a key on it. He was still wearing it.

He looked back at Mrs. Foster, who moved over to the box. Deftly she picked up the edges of one compartment with two thick brown fingers. It came out smoothly.

Below was a little satin-lined compartment. Inside it lay about six pastel pills, pink, green, and white, each stamped with the curlicue M that had been stamped on the pills the DEA had photographed in Bear's house.

Bear closed his eyes and prayed, feeling the lingering effect of the dark thoughts that had disturbed him in jail.

Mrs. Foster looked at him, her dark eyes sad, and replaced the little compartment. Then she turned to the ivory-painted bed with its carved knobs on each corner. She pulled out one of the knobs, and pointed inside.

Bear looked. Another M pill lay in the little hole.

Mrs. Foster pointed to all the other posts and nodded. Bear shook his head in disgust and bewilderment.

"Let's go back outside," he said at last.

Outside, Bear told Fish what Mrs. Foster had found.

"So we've got even more to tell the Briers when they come home," Bear said with a deep sigh.

Fish looked at Mrs. Foster keenly. "You put two and two together faster than I did. How did you know to look?"

She nodded. "When you told me they'd found things in her bags, and then that this had happened to you, I looked around real careful. I figured that whoever was smart enough to get inside your place wasn't going to have any trouble getting into this little brownstone and put stuff in her room."

"In the bedposts, too. Clever. How'd you know to check there?" Fish asked her.

She shrugged her broad shoulders. "I guessed. Plus some of the women in my neighborhood have kids on drugs, so I know where some of the usual hiding places are, sorry to say."

"Pretty sharp, Mrs. Foster."

Bear mused, "It was the same kind of Adam drug that was in our apartment. The mark on it was even the same. They may have come from the same cache."

"Yeah, I saw quite a few different kinds when we were doing our undercover work, but I've never seen an 'M' version." Fish paused. "Well, it's pretty clear that someone has been going to great lengths to set up Blanche. Someone must hate her pretty badly."

"Or someone wants to get her out of the way, just like Father Raymond's killer wanted us out of the way," Bear said.

"So how did she acquire a vicious enemy in the space of what—six months?" Fish queried.

"It doesn't take that long sometimes," Bear said. "What's puzzling is—what could Blanche do that would make her an enemy?"

"Beats me. I'm not a psychologist," Fish said. He pulled his hat out of his pocket and dropped it on his head. "So now what?"

"We go to the airport to pick up the Briers."

Fish shook his head with a sigh. "You just got bailed out of jail by the skin of your teeth, and one of the first things you do is run off to the nearest airport. This won't look good to the DEA, Bear."

"Too bad," Bear said.

*Thinking Snow White was gone
forever, the queen questioned her
mirror again.*
Grimm

Chapter Nine

he girl had remained in the van at her post, looking up and down
the streets a bit nervously. *I wish I could calm down,* she told herself.
*Brother Leon is right. I need to trust God more, and start...at least
giving Him the benefit of the doubt.*

She glanced at herself in the cracked rear-view mirror of the van, and felt
the pall creeping over her mood. She fingered the blunt edges of her hair,
feeling shaven of all her riches. *Not a princess...* Biting her lip, she pulled off
the red kerchief she had been wearing, tightened its knot, and put it on
again, trying again to feel less despondent.

Suddenly, the familiar feeling of being watched came over her, and she
turned quickly. But it was only the little Jamaican girl, leaning against the
door to the van with a winsome smile.

"*Aay,*" the child said, her black eyes crinkling into a smile. She couldn't
be older than three.

"Aay," the girl repeated, unsure. Normally she felt shy around children.

"*Yuh look suh nice,*" the child said.

The girl couldn't resist smiling back at the child's unconscious frankness.
"Thank you," she said. "What's your name?"

"*Jacky. Mi waan sit wid yuh.*" Jacky settled herself on the girl's lap, looked
at her with a half smile, and then cupped her small hands around the girl's
cheeks. "*Yuh skin suh white.*"

The girl guessed what she was saying. "So white?"

"*Yeh,*" Jacky smiled. "*Yuh face pretty.*"

The girl touched the child's smooth dark brown cheek. "*Yuh face pretty,*"
she said with deep sincerity.

Jacky giggled uncontrollably. " *Mi waan sit wid yuh when we go*," she said decisively.

Just then the girl's attention was diverted by a streak of brown as a dog raced out of the door of the apartment building and down the street. The little boy ran after him, shouting. "Pouff-Pouff *run weh!* Pouff-Pouff, *cum ya!*"

"Is that your dog?" the girl asked.

Jacky nodded. "*Is mi Granada daag.*"

A few minutes later, the two novice friars came breathlessly down the stairs.

"Did you see a dog—?" Leon panted.

Both Jacky and the girl pointed. "That way."

"Right. It's coming with us to the airport," Leon said. "Come on, Matt."

Thinking she should help, Blanche took her new little friend's hand and they followed them.

II

For the next twenty minutes, they searched up and down the streets and through alleys for the missing Rottweiler. "We are not making that two o'clock flight," Matt warned. "And those dogs are never going in that box."

"Hey," Leon said, as they passed a string of stores. "Let's check behind the grocery store. If we're lucky, we might find some wood packing crates."

"That sounds hopeful," Nora said, pushing her kerchief back, and Matt murmured that they might as well try.

So the two friars took turns jumping into dumpsters, and managed, wonder of wonders, to find two large packing crates. One had loose boards, but Matt found a hammer in the back of the van and banged them back in place.

Dragging the crates behind them, they returned to the apartment to find Marisol barely holding the returned Pouff-Pouff by the collar. Together, she and Leon managed to force the frantic dog into the crate and Matt banged another board over the top to keep him in. Nora and Leon wrestled the other crate upstairs. The dog started barking again as they returned.

"Okay," Leon said breathlessly, and called down behind him, "If you can give us a hand, Matt…"

But just at that moment, the cardboard box gave out and caved inwards, toppling the card table and the things on top of it and sending them crashing to the floor. The dog howled and emerged from the disaster, tore around the apartment frantically and swerved out the door and down to the street, knocking Matt over again.

The two friars and the women took off after the dog, but when they reached the street, there was no sign of him.

"*Prince! My poor daag run weh!*" the grandmother moaned in distress.

"*Mek im move and gweh!*" Marisol muttered blackly, and Leon was inclined to agree with her.

"Okay, let's get everything in the van and maybe we can drive around and see if we can find him," Leon attempted to be cheerful.

It was a good thing that the van happened to be mostly empty, because by the time they were done, it was packed full, what with the dog, the empty crate, and "luggage." Neighbors came from every direction to say goodbye and to watch the fun. Finally Leon and Matt got the grandmother into the car. The kids insisted on coming too. "All right, you can," Leon said wearily, and the little girl clambered happily onto Nora's lap.

"*Mi can sit wid Princess,*" she said, and Nora blushed.

The little boy commandeered Matt's lap, since there was no seating space left. To cries of "Goodbye! *Ave a good trip!*" they finally pulled out.

"What are we going to do about the other dog?" Matt asked from the back.

Suddenly the grandmother pointed. "*See im deh!*"

And there he was, trotting down a street, panting. Almost as though he had heard them, he looked in their direction, snarled, and took off down a street.

"Get him!" the kids yelled, and Brother Leon swerved the van around and followed him down the street.

"This is ridiculous! We're going to get killed!" Matt shouted.

"I'm gaining on him!" Leon said, swerving around a double-parked car in his lane.

"Go! Go!" the kids were shrieking.

"Saint Francis, lover of all animals, get this *stupid mongrel fi* to stop!" Leon breathed a prayer.

Panting, his tongue lolling out of his mouth, the dog skidded to a stop beside a trash bin blocking an alley, and Leon, tires screeching, double-parked and tumbled out of the truck with Matt groaning behind him. Valiantly, they pelted after the dog, which had taken off again, but this time, they managed to grab him by the collar. At last he was brought back, whining and growling, and was settled in the crate as the kids cheered.

Matt was looking at his watch as they got onto the expressway. "It's almost two o'clock now."

"If we hurry we might make it," Leon persisted as the dogs continued to bark themselves hoarse in the back.

Not ten minutes later, there was a shout from the boy in the back. "Brother Leon, *get di daag a chrow up!*"

"No," prayed Leon, but distinctive croaking noises from the crate in the back confirmed that the boy was correct. Leon pulled over to the side of the road.

The friars opened the back, and surveyed the mess, Matt holding his nose. The human passengers all tumbled out of the van, unable to stand the smell.

"He must have eaten something really gross," Matt said.

"*Kiss mi neck back!*" the boy said in awe.

"You got that right," Leon said grimly, rolling up his habit's sleeves. "Okay—guess we better unload, Matt."

By the side of the expressway, the friars unloaded the two dog crates and some of the luggage that had gotten thrown up on. Nora and the grandmother rummaged through the front luggage and managed to find towels and newspapers to clean up the mess. Not surprisingly, no one on the road stopped to help them.

Eventually they were on the road again. Matt muttered something about the time, but Leon was just praying that there would be another flight to Jamaica.

When they reached the airport, there was the difficulty in unloading the luggage and the dogs and parking the van. They had to pay for parking, and find a spot in one of the massive cement spiral parking garages. After much trouble, they made it to Terminal Four, where the grandmother's flight to Jamaica was departing.

They discovered that the grandmother was not alone in her luggage. Bundles of similarly-wrapped packages and garbage bags were piled around the terminal, and chickens squawked in crates. Even a billy goat was tethered to one side. Aroused by the new smells and sights, the two dogs rattled around in their rickety crates barking again.

Much to Leon's relief, there was another flight leaving for Jamaica, and, miracle of miracles, there was one seat left. Grandmother had her ticket transferred, and Leon helped her through the process, translating where necessary. Meanwhile, Matt tried to calm the dogs down, and Nora kept watch on the kids.

An airport attendant walked around the melee, roaring, "*Two undred pounds a di maximum luggage fuh dis flight!*"

"Two hundred pounds luggage?" Leon said to Matt. "This is never going to work."

When the grandmother's turn came, her luggage weighed over five hundred pounds. "Let *mi* pack it again," she urged.

"I don't think repacking is going to help much," Leon said, but obliged.

They ended up taking over half the luggage back to the van. "But at least the dogs are going," Leon thought to himself, and was looking forward to a considerably quieter ride home.

But the attendant shook his head when the friars pushed the crates up in the luggage cart. "*We cyaan tek di dog dem,*" the man said decisively. "*Win uh allow daag pan dis plane.* Too small."

"But they told her she could have the dogs on the plane before!" Leon objected, having checked this out with Marisol.

"That was for the last flight—this flight is a smaller plane. They won't take the dogs. There's just no room," another attendant explained.

Leon and the grandmother argued fruitlessly, and Matt ran his fingers over his rosary beads imploringly, but the official was unmoved. "No dogs," he said.

At last the grandmother turned, weeping, to the kids. "*Unnu can keep dem as a present,*" she said to them.

"I don't think Marisol will appreciate that kind of present," Leon said faintly, but was drowned out by the kids. "Yaaah!" they cheered. "*We get fi keep di dog dem!*"

"Right," Leon said mechanically as the grandmother tearfully made her way onto the plane. "Matt, well, we're loading the dogs back onto the van."

Matt closed his eyes. "Of course," he said. "I knew it. I knew it. I knew this was one of those days that was going to get me out of purgatory when I die."

"And put me in there for ten times longer," Leon said grimly. He knew he was never going to be able to explain this to Marisol adequately.

Glumly the friars pushed the luggage cart that had the dog crates on it back to the parking lot. This was a tricky business because if your hands were too close to the crate, the dogs would start snapping at them. Not wanting to lose a finger, Leon and Matt maneuvered the cart through the airport while Nora walked with the children, holding their hands.

They were trying to maneuver the luggage cart over the curbside. "Let's not risk tipping it," Matt urged. "Keep going until we find a ramp down."

"Fine," Leon said tonelessly. He was tired, and hungry, and not paying attention.

He glanced at Nora, who seemed to be a bit tense as well as tired. Suddenly he saw her startle and turn her head suddenly so that her hair and kerchief screened her face. Almost imperceptibly she moved to the far side of the baggage cart as though she were trying to hide. If he hadn't seen her flinch, he might never have noticed it.

Leon looked in the direction she had turned away from to see what was amiss. His eyes roved over the passing waves of people being dropped off or picked up. A bevy of Asian children, three male tourists with cameras, a couple of teenage girls yelling to their friends, a tall burly man in a dark jacket striding across the parking lot—

The man. There was a sudden bump and Leon's foot slipped and he stumbled off the side of the curb. Not wanting to fall, he unconsciously grabbed at the luggage cart and—

"No!" Matt yelled as the crates smashed to the ground. He pounced on one, and managed to hold it together, while its occupant yelped, but the other crate landed on its side, and two boards cracked. Leon grabbed for the dog's red collar but it was too late—

A howling Rottweiler took off across the parking lot like a fired torpedo and sprinted into the parking garage across the street.

Forgetting the man, Leon dashed after the dog up the ramp. "Nora, help me!" he shouted, leaving Matt to hold the other dog down.

"Stay with Brother Matt!" Nora ordered the kids. "I'm coming!" she yelled back, hurrying after Leon.

"Holy Mother St. Clare, you got to get that dog to stop," Leon moaned, trying to keep the dog in sight as he pounded up the cement ramp.

"What do you want me to do?" Nora panted, following him into the garage.

"I'll try—to head him off—and he'll run from me. How about—you take the elevator up—and see if you can—come down from the top and catch him?" Leon puffed.

"I'll give it my best shot," Nora called, and hurried into the elevator, which was providentially open.

The dog dove around the curve and vanished. There was a screech as an exiting car pulled to a stop. Leon pounded to a halt and let the car pass.

Gritting his teeth, Leon sprinted onwards to find the errant canine. He was not feeling the least bit of sympathy towards that creature at the moment. *If I'm lucky, he'll get run over and that'll be the end of him,* he thought to himself.

III

"Wretched mess," Fish opined as they waited at the airport.

Bear was inclined to agree. His stomach was in knots.

"Can't believe this is happening," he murmured, staring out through the windows at the landscape of the airport terminal, a strange country inhabited by fleets of white planes on one side and miles of ramps and spiral parking garages on the other side. "It's scarcely the way I'd hoped to see the Briers again. It's still not real to me."

"Well, I always told you not to get involved with the Briers, but you wouldn't listen," Fish said lightly.

"That's not funny," Bear said a bit sharply, and groaned.

But when the two familiar figures appeared at the gate, Bear found he could smile, despite the strain as he went up to meet Blanche's mother and younger sister.

Rose flew to him like a multi-colored bird. "Bear!" she cried.

He embraced her, and she held onto him a little longer than normal. The pause brought his apprehension to the forefront, and he found himself tearing up quickly.

"It's all right," Rose said in his ear. "We'll find her. I just know she's okay."

That was like Rose. She had faith. "Thanks," he said, in a quieter voice than he meant to use.

When he released Rose, he saw that her mother, Jean, was scanning the airport, as though hoping her oldest daughter would appear out of the crowd. He had done the same thing.

"How was your trip?" he asked, taking Jean's hand.

"Too long. Bear, I'm glad you're back. We've missed you," she said, hugging him. She was a tall woman with a tanned face, Blanche's blue eyes, and long brown-and-gray hair pinned back in a long braid. Right now her eyes were cloudy with tension, and she looked older than he remembered. Her eyes fell on Fish, and his brother smiled in greeting.

"Good to see you again, Mrs. Brier—Jean," he said.

"Thank you, Fish—it's good to see you too," she murmured. She didn't know him as well as she knew Bear, and Bear had always thought she was a bit uncomfortable with him. Then again, his brother was a difficult person to get to know. For everyone, maybe, except for the youngest member of the Brier family.

Rose had brightened right up at the sight of Fish. She had worn her red hair in a silky ponytail, and was sporting a new blue, green, and violet tie-dyed dress worn with a fluttering purple chiffon scarf.

"Fishy!" she said exuberantly, giving him an enthusiastic hug. Fish winced as he accepted the embrace with politeness.

"It's good to see you again, Rose," he said, unconsciously straightening his trench coat. Retreating slightly, he said to Bear in a low tone, "'Fishy?'"

"So—how are we going to find her?" Rose said, folding her arms in a suddenly business-like manner. She looked at the brothers expectantly, and Bear was touched by her confidence in them.

"We've got a lot to do," Bear said, recalling the new bad news he had to tell them. Not wanting to make a scene, he turned to his brother. "Fish," he said, "why don't you and Rose go get the luggage? I want to talk to Jean."

"Good, then Fish can fill me in on the details," Rose said, taking his brother's arm. "Tell me everything, Fish."

"Sure," Fish said, with only the barest trace of annoyance. With Rose on his arm, he stalked down the corridor towards the security checkpoint before the baggage claim.

"Shall we sit down?" Bear asked, but the older woman shook her head.

"I've been sitting down," Jean said, "this whole plane ride back. Is there any news?"

"Yes," Bear said soberly. He told her, as briefly as possible, what he and Mrs. Foster had found in the Brier house that morning.

Jean was bewildered. "What does this mean?"

"It's proof that someone went to great lengths to implicate her," Bear said with determination.

Jean had started pacing towards the windows overlooking the parking lot. She halted in the shadow cast by the nearby parking garage. "But who would have done such a thing to Blanche?" she asked. "Is this something that you were involved with, Bear? It almost sounds a bit like one of your undercover operations." She laughed shortly, but her eyes were despondent.

"I'm not sure how it's connected to me," Bear said heavily. "We've found drugs in three places where Blanche has been frequenting—my apartment, her workplace, and your home. I'm forced to conclude that someone is after her as well."

For a moment they stood in silence, watching a car on the third level pull out of a parking spot in the parking garage just across the street from them.

"Do we have any sign at this point that she's even still alive?" Jean whispered. "I haven't brought it up to Rose, but my mind is flying immediately to the worst possibilities. Kidnapping, or murder, or—now I'm wondering if she was actually seriously depressed after all. What if we find out that she's committed suicide?"

Again, Bear fought off the thoughts that crowded into his mind. "No," he said at last. "She wouldn't do that, no matter how depressed she was. Blanche might be fearful, and she might doubt, but at the bottom of her soul, she wouldn't despair."

"You sound very certain," Jean attempted to smile through her tears. "But you haven't seen her these past few months."

"But I know her," Bear said, and took a deep breath. "And I believe in her."

For a moment, Jean looked at him as though she were recognizing him for the first time. Then she wiped her eyes. "All right, Bear," she said. "I'll try to believe that we'll find her. That she's still out there, somewhere, and we can—"

Suddenly she pointed, her voice changed. "My God. Is that her?"

Bear looked out the window. Directly across from them was the fourth level of a parking garage. And inside the parking garage, a girl in a red kerchief was running after a dog. It was Blanche.

It was like a sudden vision from God, abrupt and positive and a bit odd. Although in a different building, she was no more than a hundred yards away from them. For a moment they both stood there, gazing stupidly at the picture of the black-haired girl in a red headscarf making a flying leap at the escaping canine, seizing him by his thick collar, and wrestling him around. She started to drag him coaxingly down the ramp towards the exit.

Then both of them sprang into action. Jean pounded the window and shrieked, "Blanche!"

Bear took off running down the terminal. "Stay there and watch her!" he yelled to Jean, who was jumping up and down and waving her arms, hoping to attract Blanche's attention. But the sunlight bouncing off the terminal windows was probably obscuring her motions.

As fast as he could, Bear tried to run to the parking lot exit. The number of people at JFK suddenly bloated in size as Bear tried to make his way down the terminal causeway. Obstacles flew at him from every direction as he ran. He dodged around departing and incoming passengers, leapt over a luggage cart, hurried down an 'up' escalator, and burst through the glass doors at the bottom.

There was a security checkpoint there, but Bear ignored it and rushed through. Two guards immediately jumped to their feet, shouting for him to stop. Suddenly Bear found his way blocked by two other guards who had appeared almost out of nowhere.

"Sorry sir, you need to go through the metal detector," they said, propelling him back by his shoulders.

"I need to find that girl out there," he pointed fruitlessly. "There's a girl out there in the parking garage, chasing a dog. I've been trying to find her— can't I go and get her first?"

"First you need to go through the metal detector," the guard said. "If it's really important, we'll send someone out to find her."

"It's really important," Bear said.

One of the guards started checking Bear for concealed weapons while the other one continued to stand in front of Bear, and began to explain about airport regulations. Bear wasn't listening, but was instead watching the ground floor of the parking garage, which he could glimpse through the windows behind the guard's shoulders. Bear became aware of how fast his own heart was pounding, and how fast he wasn't moving.

At last, the guard with the wand finished frisking him and let him go. Bear hurried outside to the parking garage and started scrutinizing the cars that were coming out. He didn't recognize any of them, or their drivers. The lady taking payments at the gate didn't recognize Blanche's description but promised to keep a look out. Frustrated, Bear turned to the windows of the airport terminal and tried to signal to Jean to come down.

Rose and Fish came running outside a few minutes later. Bear was steadfastly watching every car that exited the garage, but so far had only gotten odd looks from the drivers and had seen no sign of Blanche, or a dog.

"Are you sure it was her?" his brother queried.

"There was no mistake. Jean and I both saw her face," Bear said. "It was her."

"She's alive!" Rose said joyously.

"Fish, go and have her paged on the intercom. If I missed her somehow and she was going into the airport, she might still be in a place where she can hear the page. Rose, go inside the garage and look for her. See if anyone's seen her. I'll stay here."

"All right. Let's hope Blanche isn't here planning to fly out of the country," Fish said dismally, dialing his cell phone. "Or she'll be in even more trouble. Excuse me," he said into the phone. "Is this customer service at JFK? How can I find out if a person has a ticket on an outbound flight?"

"If she was flying anywhere, she was probably going out to California to find her mother," Bear argued, his eyes still scanning the passing cars and the exiting people, looking for anyone with a dog—why had Blanche been capturing someone's dog?

When Jean appeared, she was considerably happier, but could only say that Blanche had disappeared, dragging the dog down and around the ramp. She went into the garage to see if she could find Blanche. Bear remained at his post, asking guards and passing people if they had seen a girl with a dog. A few had seen a dog running away, but no one had seen where it had gone.

"Nothing to do but start searching the entire terminal to see if she's getting a flight," Fish said grimly when they gathered again. "Probably useless at this point. If she was here, she's probably gone by now."

But Bear's heart pounded with a new hope. Jean persisted, "We should at least try to find her here, even if it takes hours," she said. She smiled at Bear, who nodded.

Blanche is alive. She's alive.

At least they had that.

...when the queen heard Snow White
still lived, she bit her lip until
the blood ran down.
Grimm

Chapter Ten

She rose the next day to join the friars for two and a half hours of their routine: the Office of Readings, private meditation, Morning Prayer, and the Mass. It was difficult to wake up so early and pray so long, but unexpectedly sweet, a bit of manna in the wilderness. As she made her way through the still-confusing book of the Liturgy of the Hours, she thought briefly about becoming a nun. It was temptingly easy to consider. After all, becoming a nun meant marrying Christ. The only perfect Man.

She smiled to herself. Ah, yes, men, those imperfect mortals. Even the really amazing ones, like Bear, were imperfect. Heartbreakingly imperfect.

Suddenly she found herself blinking back tears. She hated to admit it, but yes, Bear had let her down.

If only Bear were different, if only he were from a happy family like her own, if only he didn't have to go off and figure out what to do with his life and leave her alone...then it would be so much easier to trust him again. But right now he certainly didn't seem likely to deliver any dreams of living happily ever after.

What was she supposed to do—hold staunchly onto her image of Bear as a flawless prince charming or admit that in some ways she had been deceived, or at least mistaken in him? There didn't seem to be any way out.

"Why spend money on what is not bread? Why spend money on what will not satisfy?" Isaiah asked in one of the readings of the day. She suddenly wondered if that meant that it was more sensible to spend yourself only on God, instead of placing yourself in the hands of anyone lesser.

But yet...She stared at the tabernacle. The answer to the riddle wasn't yet apparent to her.

After her solitary breakfast, she went to the vestibule but found her enthusiasm for finishing the job strangely lacking. Brother Herman came by.

"Good morning, Nora." He opened the vestibule door and sniffed the warm breeze of the summer morning. "Look at that sky. So blue, even here in the City. Lovely, isn't it?"

"It is," she said. But inside the stuffy vestibule with clothes piled up around her, it didn't seem like a blue-sky day.

"How are you doing?"

"Feeling unmotivated," she admitted with half a smile.

"But yet, responsibilities still call us," the bearded friar said with a smile and a sigh of his own and gently closed the door. "The people who come to our food pantry will start lining up outside soon," he said. "Can you come downstairs and help us get organized?"

"Sure," she said, squelching a sigh, and went.

II

Thursday morning was the day the friars handed out bags of donated food to any needy families in the neighborhood who wanted it. Around eight o'clock, a line of homeless men, bag ladies, and single mothers with kids started forming in front of the door to the basement of St. Lawrence Church. At nine, the friars opened the doors and started handing out bags they had prepared from donations given to them during the week: day-old bread from bakeries, dented cans of beans and boxes of macaroni, wilted vegetables, and other items collected from bakeries, groceries, and produce stands around the City.

Brother Leon walked among the visitors, joking with the men and greeting the kids, most of whom he knew from his neighborhood rounds. But there were a few newcomers. He recognized the fluorescent blue stocking hat and green visor of the old lady that had come to the friary the other day. She was someone you didn't forget quickly.

"Hey Bonnie! How's it going?"

Bonnie was going back and forth between two bags of groceries, taking out the things she apparently didn't like, and transferring them to another bag. "You got any tuna? Haven't had tuna in forty days and forty nights..."

"Same here," Brother Leon said, hitching up his rope belt. "I don't think we got any this time. Sorry. So where you from, Bonnie?"

"Queens," she muttered. "Just got up this way." She started shuffling off on one of her wandering rambles, and Leon, mindful of how Bonnie had meandered through the friary on her last visit, followed her, keeping up a stream of friendly banter. She didn't seem interested in him, though.

They wandered through the basement, Bonnie peering into any bags they passed, including bags already taken by others. Nora was talking to Marisol's little girl, who had come with her mother to get some groceries. He waved at her.

"Who's that?" Bonnie asked. "Your girlfriend?"

Leon grinned. "Nope. I'm already taken." He nodded to Nora. "She's a volunteer. She's been helping us out around the friary."

"Now isn't that sweet?" Bonnie fixed her eyes, dimmed by her green eyeshade, on Nora. "A pretty little beauty queen like that. What's her name?"

"Nora," Leon said reluctantly.

Bonnie started chuckling to herself as she puttered on her way, dragging her bags behind her. "Is that right? Nora, hey? A pretty little thing like that…" She paused, and looked at Leon. "You watch she doesn't try to hook you," she rasped. "You know that's what those kinds of girls do."

III

By the time they had exhausted the search of the airport, it was evening, and the Briers and the Denniston brothers had agreed to take a break from the search for Blanche until the next morning. Bear and Fish had dropped off Rose and Jean at their home, and had gone back to their apartment.

Once back at the apartment, the stress of the past several days combined with the time change had finally unleashed itself on Bear's body like a delayed wave crashing onto the beach. It immersed him in sleep that lasted until well into the next morning.

When he finally awoke, reality was still dim around him although it was just past ten. There was no sound but the soft whoosh of the air-conditioning. He rolled over in bed and looked out the window at the sun glaring over the tops of the buildings. The waves of heat enveloping the City didn't touch him, high in his tower.

He had fallen asleep in the bedroom that had been his mother's, a sanctuary of hushed and refined femininity. She had decorated it herself in tones of purple-gray and silver-white, and it was the room that most reminded him of her. The only alteration that Bear had made to the room was to hang up his mother's portrait. Now he looked over at the large image, painted in oils by one of her friends. Catherine Denniston had dark hair and blue eyes, fair skin—she had been a beautiful woman, before the cancer. Bear always felt a bit odd gazing at that portrait, which captured her expression from a time he barely remembered. Even then, though, her eyes had been sad. She had been a quiet, sensitive person, artistic, and long-suffering.

Feeling stiff from his long sleep, he sat up, touched his toes, and swung out of the bed. He remembered as a kid waking up here when he had crawled into his mom's bed after having a nightmare. After the darkness had passed the next morning, he had tumbled out of this bed to see the sun rising out of the windows overlooking the Hudson River and Central Park...

Long ago and far away, he thought to himself. Back then, he still thought he had a mother and a father who loved each other the way parents ought to, a whole life. Now he was acutely aware of how innocent he had been of the realities of the situation.

Getting dressed, he walked down the curving staircase that curled around the edge of the living room at the center of the house and went into the kitchen.

Fish was there, making himself some bacon in a frying pan. He glanced up at Bear. "You dressed? Good. We're meeting Mrs. Foster over at the Briers again. I recommend that we try to pick up Blanche's trail by going to her workplace, the banquet hall. But sometime today we've got to sit down with Jean and have a discussion."

"About what?"

"About what to do with the drugs we found in her house. It's one of those legal conundrums. If she does the right thing and turns them over to the police, she might be charged with possession the same way we were charged, or at least strengthen the case against Blanche. But if she doesn't turn them over, then she's breaking the law." He lifted a piece of bacon out of the pan and inspected it. "So there are some tough decisions to make there. You want some bacon?"

"No thanks." Dismally Bear opened the refrigerator and stared at the contents—mostly condiments. Obviously, neither of the brothers had been out shopping since they had gotten back. He checked the freezer, found a package of frozen potpies, and pulled two out.

"You can't microwave those," Fish said. "They take a half hour in the oven. And putting them under the broiler can really backfire. I speak from experience."

Without a word, Bear thrust the pies in the oven and turned on the timer.

Waiting again, he thought about Blanche, as he leaned against the central island. The search at the airport revealed that Blanche apparently hadn't taken a plane out. So she was still in the City. *What was she doing? Did she have any idea how worried everyone was about her?*

Quite possibly not, he realized. As far as Blanche knew, he was still in Europe and her mom and sister were in California. It was possible she had no idea what kind of turmoil everyone else was experiencing on her behalf. He wished again he had kept up better communication with her and not been so preoccupied with himself. Looking back over the past months, every time he had called her, it seemed as though they had talked about his problems, not about hers.

He stared out the window at the street far below at the currents of warm air snaking between the buildings. There were only a few pedestrians on the street at this hour. A man in a sports coat and sunglasses stood on the street corner, smoking, apparently waiting for a taxi. Bear had always wondered how people could smoke when it was so hot.

When they went downstairs to the lobby, Ahmed glanced at them, embarrassed.

"How you doing?" Bear said easily, trying to show there were no hard feelings.

The doorman nodded, and looked relieved.

Bear had no hard feelings against Ahmed, but seeing him reminded Bear that he was out on bail, and that unless he could prove his innocence soon, he might be returning to jail. Not only that, perhaps Blanche, when they found her, would also be charged and imprisoned. He didn't blame her for hiding.

The knot in his stomach returned as they walked onto the street. The heat of the street hit him like the blast of an oven. As he opened the door to Fish's car, he glanced around them. He noticed the man in sunglasses he had seen from the window was still smoking on the corner, apparently deep in the thrall of a tobacco addiction. From street level, Bear could see that the man's broad shoulders and large head looked ominously familiar. He had dark hair and a broad, flat nose, which looked as though it had been broken in a fight. Apparently perceiving that he was being watched, the man turned his back, tossed his cigarette into the trashcan, and walked away.

"Hey, shut the door—I've got the AC on," Fish said, checking his watch.

Bear obeyed and got into the car. *There's no coincidence here,* he told himself.

They picked up Mrs. Foster at the small apartment building that had once been their temporary home. "You sure I should come along?" she queried as she settled herself inside the car. "After all, Mrs. Brier doesn't know me at all."

"We'll just have to rectify that," Fish said easily.

When they reached the Briers' home, he took the lead in introducing Jean to Mrs. Foster.

"I've often heard Bear speak about you," Jean said. She was looking much better this morning.

"And I've heard him talk a lot about you," Mrs. Foster laughed.

"Would you like some tea? Coffee?"

"Coffee would be wonderful," Mrs. Foster said, and Fish concurred as well. Jean and Rose took tea. Bear accepted a cup, but drank it standing.

"I'd like to start by going to the banquet hall right away," he said. "Anyone else want to come?"

"I'll come," Rose volunteered.

"I think Bear and I should go alone," Fish contradicted his brother, and glanced perfunctorily at the redheaded girl. "Sorry, Rose."

"Rose, I'd rather you came with me anyhow," Jean said, seeing Rose's crestfallen face. "I'm going to the nursing home where Blanche volunteered to see if I can find anything out from the people that she visited. There are a lot of residents in that home, and if you help me, it will take less time."

"I could go with you too, if you want," Mrs. Foster said.

"That would be wonderful," Jean said. "Bear—my car's still in the shop. Could you give us a ride over?"

"Sure thing."

After dropping off the women at the nursing home, Bear and his brother crossed the Throg's Neck Bridge to get to Blanche's workplace. Reflections, Bear remembered, was a rather expensive banquet hall set on a choice piece of Long Island real estate. He had taken Blanche there once. They parked the car and approached the massive building, which had been built in the 1920's. They could see stained glass windows on the largest hall, which had turrets like a castle.

"I'd forgotten how much it resembles a church," Bear said.

"A place to worship food?" Fish asked.

Bear chuckled. "Who knows?"

They walked through the gated doors and into the reception area. There was no one at the receptionist's desk, but several waiters were chatting at a station further down the carpeted hall. Bear approached them, and a tall girl with a big frizzy ponytail came over to the desk.

"Can I help you?" she was Italian, and spoke with a characteristic Bronx accent.

Bear introduced himself and asked if he could speak to the manager.

"Mr. Scarlotti? Sure, I'll get him," the girl said, giving him a strange look, and disappeared through a side door. The other staff looked at them curiously, but didn't come over.

A woman in a caterer's uniform came into the reception area, wheeling a coat rack of costumes. All of them were black and white, and some of them were fantastical, sequined and bejeweled.

"What are those for?" Bear asked her as she stood, looking out the glass doors to the street.

"These? These were for a masquerade ball we had this past weekend," the woman said, and rolled her eyes slightly. She was about thirty, with a mop of curly black hair, thickly-mascaraed lashes, and wore pale purple lipstick.

"Looks like it was pretty fancy," Bear commented. Normally he wouldn't be this chatty, but he wanted to find out any information that he could about Blanche.

"They're a pretty fancy client," she said shortly, folding her arms.

"Are they rentals?" Fish indicated the costumes.

"Bought," the woman said flatly. "Just for this one event."

"Wow! Somebody must have money to burn."

"Their CEO doesn't spare much expense on their parties. They do a lot of their events here. It's good for us," she added positively.

"So what are they going to do with the costumes now?"

"They told us to pitch them. But I called one of the local theatres to see if they can use them. They're sending a guy to pick them up."

"I see," Bear paused. "Did you know Blanche Brier, who worked here?"

"Yeah, she was our receptionist," the woman said. "One of the more dependable ones." She looked at them a bit warily. "You friends of hers?"

"Yes," said Bear. "Actually, we're here looking for her. She's been missing since Saturday night. Her family is pretty concerned."

"Missing?" the woman repeated, her eyes suddenly widening. "For real?"

Bear nodded. The woman pursed her lips, opened her mouth, and then closed it again, apparently trying to decide whether or not to say more.

"I know she was fired," Bear said quietly. "And I heard from the police that they think she stole some money. But that just doesn't sound like the Blanche I know. So I want to find out what's going on."

"Did you ask a manager?" the woman asked.

Fish nodded. "We're waiting for him."

"You're not going to get much out of Scarlotti," she warned. "He's always watching out for the company reputation." She added, "My name's Assunta. I worked with Blanche. She was a good girl. Real nice to work with."

"Did you see her on Saturday?" Bear asked.

Assunta nodded. "She worked as the receptionist for the masquerade ball. This one." She jerked her heads towards the costumes. "For the Mirror Corporation. It was a fundraiser, though if you ask me, it was more of an excuse for a tax-deductible bash than to help anyone out."

"And there was money missing afterwards?"

She nodded. "I happen to know something about that. The guests had paid so much money per ticket in order to come. Fundraiser, you know. I think it was three hundred dollars or something. The corporation who was hosting the banquet had their staff count up the tickets during the dinner, and then the CEO of the corporation matched the donation in *cash*." She raised her eyebrows significantly.

"Cash," Bear repeated. "That's strange. Why would they do that? It's difficult to get a tax deduction on a cash donation, especially a large one."

"Fifteen thousand nine hundred dollars," the lady said positively. "The CEO had it up there, in hundred-dollar bills during the presentation ceremony. Like some kind of gangster stash."

"And how did it get stolen?"

Assunta rolled her eyes again. "They did the presentation halfway through the banquet, and the research foundation who was getting the donation wasn't exactly ready to keep track of a huge pile of hundred dollar bills. So they asked us to put it in our safe. And we did."

"And it was stolen from the safe?"

The woman nodded. "If it got there. Less than an hour afterwards the word went round that the cash was missing. The research corporation wants us to make up the difference now, and Mirror Corp. is being no help whatsoever."

Bear paused. "So how did Blanche turn up as a suspect?"

Assunta shook her head. "Apparently the CEO asked her to take it to the back because she was the receptionist. So there was a window of time where Blanche had access to it. And Blanche left work early. I saw her before she left, when the money went missing, and she said she had handed off the bag to Scarlotti just as she was told. She was going home early because she had a headache. But I don't believe she stole that money, not for a minute. Neither does most of the staff. But the management—the ones who have to come up with the lost sixteen thousand dollars to reimburse the research foundation—they're not so sure."

She looked over her shoulder as a short Italian man bustled into the room. Bear turned to meet him.

"Can I help you?" the manager asked, with a glance at Assunta that clearly implied privacy. Assunta turned away and looked out the doors of the hall.

"We're friends of Blanche Brier," Bear began.

"She was terminated on Saturday night," the manager said, his small eyes cool.

"She's also been missing since Saturday night," Bear said, with some warmth. "We've been trying to find out some trace of her whereabouts."

"That's not surprising she's missing, since the police have been looking for her as well," Scarlotti said a bit acidly. "But if you do find her, you can tell her that the search has been called off. They found the money yesterday."

Bear stared. "They found the money?"

"The Mirror Corporation gave the serial numbers of the bills to the police. Apparently the bills turned up in the hands of two young punks. They were surprisingly inexperienced, and ended up trying to pass the money off to an undercover cop. The hoodlums got away, but the police recovered the money. Highly unusual, but pretty fortunate."

"Does this mean that Blanche can get her job back?" Bear asked steadily.

The manager eyed him suspiciously and shrugged. "That will still have to be decided. It's still not clear how the money left this hall and got into the hands of the punks." He glanced at his watch. "It's a matter for the police to investigate. You should direct your questions to them. Have a nice day," With a nod, he turned and opened the door for them, only to have a young man with long hair pop in from outside.

"Hi, I'm from the Clothesline Theatre," he said brightly. "I'm here to pick up some costumes?"

"Oh, that's right," the manager looked about him, and Assunta stepped forward, indicating the rack.

"They're right here," she said.

"Fantastic! Listen, while I'm here, can I ask you to buy an ad in our upcoming winter program book?"

"That's his department," Assunta indicated Mr. Scarlotti, and she walked out the door into the parking lot. Bear and Fish followed her out, while the young man talked animatedly to the manager, thanking him profusely.

"Well!" she said, going around the shady side of the building and pulling out a pack of cigarettes. "That's good news! So maybe the police won't be looking for Blanche after all."

"Let's hope not," Bear said.

The woman shook her head as she lit her cigarette. "The research foundation won't care. They've got their money back. And I'm sure the management will just want the whole thing to blow over. They're probably just happy they don't have to shell out sixteen thousand dollars." She looked at the brothers. "Smoke?"

"No thanks. Listen, I heard that someone found drugs in Blanche's backpack," Bear said. "Do you know anything about that?"

She shook her head. "I hadn't heard that." She glanced around. "If you ask me, it's those *cetriolos*—sorry—who work at the Mirror Corporation who use drugs. You watch some of the people at their parties, dancing like maniacs, and you'd swear they were getting high. But I can't see Blanche doing that. She's just not the type."

"Another thing," Bear said. "Do you know if Blanche was being followed by anyone?"

The woman looked puzzled. "I don't know about that, either. But I didn't hang out with her much. Let me ask one of the younger girls." She held her cigarette out, and pulled open a door that was marked KITCHEN. "Rita!" she yelled.

"Yeah," the tall girl with the big ponytail whom Bear had talked to before came outside. "Hey. Ciggie break?" She glanced at Bear and Fish, and her eyes went back to Bear. "You know, I was going to tell you that you look familiar."

"Do I?" Bear exchanged looks with his brother. "I haven't been here in a while."

"You're Blanche's boyfriend, aren't you?"

Bear nodded, and she grinned.

"I saw your picture. Plus I served you that one time when you and her came here together. You don't remember. That's okay."

"She's missing," Assunta said soberly. "Since Saturday."

"You're joking," Rita said slowly. "Right?"

"I wish I were," Bear said.

Obviously shaken, Rita lit a cigarette and looked at Bear, her brow furrowed. Bear briefly told the two waitresses about seeing Blanche at the airport, and how she had vanished.

"He wants to know if anyone was following Blanche," Assunta said.

"The stalker, you mean?" Rita asked.

Bear's heart skipped. "You mean you saw him?"

"No, but I know who you're talking about. Blanche told me about him." Rita blew the smoke from her cigarette out of one side of her mouth politely. "The last few weeks, Blanche had been kind of jumpy when she was at work. She kept looking over her shoulder, makin' me nervous too, so I yelled at her. I said, 'So who's after you, Brier?' So she says to me, 'you ever see this guy following me when I come into work?' I hadn't, and I said, 'What's he look like?' She said he was a big tall guy, built like a bull. 'Might just be my imagination,' she said."

"You said you've never seen him?"

"No! But I sure as heck have been looking for him since she told me that. Especially when we left the hall together late at night. We'd both be looking over our shoulders until we got to the train station, and I would yell at her, 'Share the fear, why don't you?' She knew I was teasing. But I watched her back. I never saw the big guy, though."

Assunta was staring, her eyes were getting wider. "You said a big guy who looked like a bull?" she said slowly. "Oh man, this is too freaky."

"What?" everyone demanded.

She crushed out her cigarette and paused before she spoke. "I saw him in the banquet hall on Saturday night."

"Where?" Rita almost shrieked.

Assunta was low key now. "In the service hallway," she said. "Big tall guy. Bigger than you," she nodded to Bear. "With dark hair and a kind of flat nose. I was going back to the workroom to get my lighter, and I saw him. I thought he was one of the guests who'd gotten lost looking for the men's room or something. So I asked him if I could help. He wasn't too friendly. I sort of directed him back to the party area. But, you know, in those dark corridors, I wasn't going to exactly try to force him to go there if he didn't want to. I went into the workroom, got my stuff out, and when I came back, he was gone."

"Was that before or after Blanche left?" Bear asked.

Assunta put her head to one side. "I'm not sure. It was right around the time the money was missing, come to think of it. I shoulda mentioned that to someone. But Blanche's name was being floated right away as the one who snatched the money, so I forgot it. Besides, there were so many people there, and he was nowhere near the office where the safe was."

"You need to tell Scarlotti that," Rita insisted. "It's makin' me hyper-mad that they tried to stick this mess on her." She turned to Bear fearfully. "So you think that he got her?"

Bear shook his head, even though he winced at the thought. "No. We know she's still alive. Plus, I think I saw that man myself today. If he was looking to hurt Blanche in some way, and if he'd succeeded, he'd lie low. My guess is that he doesn't know where she is, so he's still looking for her."

Rita shook her head in disbelief. "Take me for a ride," she said. "This is freaky. You know, she said she thought that someone had been in her house, too."

"And she was right," Fish murmured. "She's been right about everything so far."

Another waitress put her head out the door and hissed, "Hey, you two. Scarlotti's looking for you. Get on back in here."

"Got to go," Assunta said, quickly stubbing out her cigarette. "Look, I'm telling the police what I know about this, okay?"

"That would be great," Bear said. "They need all the help they can get."

"Let me know if you need any more help. I'm always here. Just call. Good luck." She vanished inside.

"Same here," Rita said, pulling one last drag on her cigarette. "You want my phone number at home just in case?"

"Not a bad idea," Bear said, and scribbled it down on his calendar when she told it to him. He wrote down Fish's cell phone number on another sheet and handed it to her. "Here's my cell phone number if you need to call us. Thanks again, Rita."

"You mean, *my* cell phone number," Fish corrected him after the waitress had left. "You need to get your own phone."

"Yeah, maybe later on," Bear said distractedly.

Fish changed the subject as they walked back to the car. "So we've got a suspect. Not a very nice one, either."

"I can't believe no one took her more seriously," Bear said angrily, then fell silent. *If only I had been here, I would have.*

"Well, for whatever reason, she never elaborated on this to her mom and Rose or you," Fish said. "Fortunately for us, she mentioned it to her co-workers."

"We need to find out if she told anyone else," Bear said. "Maybe Jean and Rose can find that out from the nursing home folks she visited."

They got into the car, and Fish said brightly, "At least there's some good news. I'm going to make a guess that the older waitress is right—the police aren't going to pursue Blanche as a suspect in the burglary now that they've recovered the money."

Bear drummed his fingers on the dashboard. "Right. But that means that whoever was trying to set her up to be arrested is going to find that out soon, if they haven't already." His mind was on the big man.

"We're assuming, aren't we, that the same person who stole the money and planted the drugs in her backpack here also planted the drugs in our apartment to implicate us?" Fish asked as he drove out of the parking lot. "How do we even know that we were meant to be framed? What if it was just a botched attempt to frame Blanche?"

"That's what I'm thinking, despite how tricky it would have been to smuggle the drugs into our apartment," Bear said. "But if that's the case, it didn't work. The authorities arrested us instead of Blanche. And because Blanche wasn't around to be arrested here or at home, the case against her is dissipating. Maybe she's slipping out of the enemy's net." Tightness in him released. But only slightly.

Fish said grimly, "Wonderful. But that means her enemy will have to do something else to trap her."

Bear looked around them at the people passing by. There was no sight of the big man now, but he figured that he wasn't far away. "What we need to do is find the enemy before the enemy finds Blanche."

Chapter Eleven

own in the basement with the noise and clamor of the food line, the girl had started to feel overwhelmed. She felt it would never end.

As the passing out of food went on and on, she began to experience a strong desire to be alone, and when it seemed that the people were finally starting to disperse as lunchtime drew on, she slipped up the side steps and hurried back to her work in the vestibule.

Closing the door, she felt a wave of relief pass over her, even though it was hotter upstairs than it had been in the cellar. She wiped her forehead and looked around the vestibule, which, despite several bags of new donations, was starting to show signs of being finished, and she thought that perhaps she would sit in the church for a few minutes.

Sitting in the creaking wooden pew, she looked from the tabernacle to the stained glass windows, and started to feel her heart slow down.

Got to watch my heart, she told herself. She had a dysfunction in one of her valves, which meant that stress caused less oxygen to get to her lungs, and she had, on several memorable occasions, fainted. This summer, she had started taking medication, which had improved the condition, but of course, she hadn't taken any since she had come to the friary. It had been a background worry on top of everything else, but all she could do at the moment was to try and take things a bit easy.

Even so, she felt guilty for leaving the work downstairs. Had she run away from the people because they were unattractive and poor? Was she turning away someone who was in need?

Next time, I'll try harder. Sighing, she got up, genuflected, and walked back to the vestibule.

As she stepped into the little space, closing the door behind her, she saw she was not alone. The bag lady in the blue hat had followed her up the steps, and was sitting on a garbage bag, chewing on a lollipop and staring at the stained glass window above the door.

"Hello," the girl said.

"'Lo," the woman said, through her lollipop.

The girl hesitated. Brother Leon had warned her not to be alone with any of the visitors to the friary. "Shouldn't we go back downstairs?" she asked.

"Don't want to," the woman muttered. "Want to talk with you. You're such a pretty girl. And it's quiet up here."

The girl stood at the top of the steps and thought. *Yes, I shouldn't be alone with the woman, but according to the friary rules, I shouldn't leave the woman alone either... Well, I think I can handle one elderly woman, she decided at last. I can talk with her a few minutes and then hopefully I can persuade her to come downstairs with me.*

"What do you want to talk about?" she asked, sitting on another bag of clothes opposite the woman.

"I want to tell you how to do it," the lady said calmly, chewing on her lollipop. It was difficult to understand her.

"How—what?"

The lady didn't answer at first. She bit the candy off the stick, swallowed it, put the stick carefully into her left pocket, then pulled another lollipop out of her right pocket, methodically unwrapped it, and put it into her mouth. Only then did she resume speaking.

"How to get men to do things for you," she said.

The girl drew back. "I'm not interested," she said.

The old woman chuckled. "Don't look so shocked, honey. You're younger than I am." She heaved a sigh. "Not so young as I once was. Used to have men falling all over me. But then I got old, and other women, they started getting younger. When my husband started—but you don't want to hear about my problems." She waved the lollipop at the girl. "Let me give you some advice."

Old people were always giving advice, and the girl wasn't surprised to hear an old homeless lady offering to give her some. *Do I look as though I'm in dire need of assistance? Maybe I come off as helpless, she speculated as she resigned herself to listening.*

"You got to use yourself to your own advantage. That's your problem."

"I'm sorry?"

"No," the lady chuckled, coughed, and chuckled again. "No, you're not sorry."

Again the woman's mumbling confused the girl.

"What you need," the woman said finally, "is some better clothes. And some pretty things to catch the eye." She dug in her bags. "I've got something here you might like." She held up a gold chain necklace. "Only five dollars."

The girl had to smile. So that was what this was about. A sales pitch. She looked at the necklace, but it was clear that the catch on the chain was missing. It was something the woman had probably found while digging through a waste bin. "I'm sorry, I don't have five dollars."

"What about three? Two?" the lady persisted, but the girl shook her head, smiling.

"No, thank you."

"Hold on—what about this?" She scrabbled through her possessions again and produced a stretched-out elastic string of plastic beads, blue and orange. "Four dollars. It's vintage."

"No, thank you. I'm sorry."

"Then what about this?"

The girl paused as the lady held up a shining scarlet satin ribbon, with a delicate golden heart swinging on it. The heart was obviously not real gold, and was slightly dented.

"Three dollars," the lady said encouragingly.

The girl touched the ribbon with one finger but said, "I don't have three dollars."

"Two dollars? One dollar?"

It was pitiable to see how eager the lady was to make some kind of profit from the treasures she had scrounged from the trash. The girl put a hand into her jeans pocket. While sorting through clothes, she had occasionally found a coin or two in the pockets, which she had been storing up in her jeans. She was going to ask the friars later on what she should do with them. Now she pulled out her little findings and looked at them critically.

"How about thirty-three cents?"

"Done," the lady said eagerly, and put out her hand. The girl gave her the coins, and the woman counted them up several times, putting them in her right pocket. The girl saw dozens of other lollypops sticking up from her pocket. The friars had been giving them out downstairs, and this lady had apparently helped herself to the lot.

"Now, let me put it on for you," the woman got up and hobbled over to where the girl was sitting.

"Oh, I can do it myself," the girl said, but the old woman shook her head.

"Let me do it for you properly. The catch doesn't work."

So the girl, a bit uncertainly, sat still while the woman carefully lowered the red choker over her head and began to put it around her neck. The ribbon was smooth, and the girl ran a finger over it. She would let the old woman put it on her neck now, but she would take it off as soon as she got the lady downstairs. It was a bit showier than she would have liked. What she really wanted (and needed) was a ribbon to hold back her flopping black hair—

She swallowed as the necklace tightened against her neck and clicked shut.

"All right?"

"That's too tight," the girl said, feeling with her hand for the clasp.

"That's the way those things are," the old woman said, sitting down in front of her. She gestured. "That's why it's called a choker."

"It's rather uncomfortable," the girl said, swallowing again.

"But you look very pretty in it." The woman said, staring at her through the green eyeshade. "Yes, it suits you. Suits you well. Scarlet."

The girl tried to get a finger between her neck and the ribbon and couldn't. "Could you take it off?" she managed to say.

The old lady shook her head. "But you look so nice. Very very nice."

The girl tried to smile, and swallowed again.

"Have you ever heard of the scarlet ladies?"

The girl shook her head, and tried tugging at the collar to loosen it.

"I used to see them when I was a girl, in the dance halls, with their big flouncy skirts. They'd wear little ribbons round their necks. Black ribbons. They say it sets off the neck. Makes it look longer. Like a swan. Swans are white, with black eyes. But I saw one girl once, who wore a scarlet ribbon, just like that. And she'd move about in her flouncy skirt, and her eyes were like your eyes. Girls in scarlet, they know how to get things, how to use what they've got. They're not afraid to go down. You're like that, right? You're not afraid? Not afraid of going down?"

Right now the girl was more concerned about breathing. She fumbled behind her head with the clasp, trying to work it to the front so that she could undo it. But the ribbon wouldn't move. A bead of sweat rolled down her forehead.

"No, you're not afraid. You're a white girl with a little bit of red, just a touch of scarlet to get yourself what you want. That's what you are. You use your scarlet, your little bit of scarlet, and you get what you want, you do. You're not all scarlet, just a bit of scarlet. Just a bit. That's all you need to catch the eye, isn't it? And maybe you look better than the girls drenched in red because that's all you have, just one touch of red. But it's enough."

The girl worked and worked at the clasp, trying to figure out how to open it. It didn't seem like one she was used to. Holding her arms up in the air behind her head was awkward after a while. She was losing feeling in her hands, and lowered them hastily, wiping her forehead and swallowing again. Her mouth was going dry.

"Something wrong?"

"Can't breathe," she said huskily. "You have to get this off me—"

The old lady seemed to snap out of her rambling and came over to her. For a while, she tried fumbling around the back of the girl's neck while the girl waited, swallowing.

"My old hands just aren't good enough," she croaked, after groping for the clasp. "You need someone to help—You sit quiet while I—I would sit down if I were you—"

But the girl had already stood up in a panic, and that was the last thing she remembered.

II

"Where's Nora?" Leon looked around as they were ushering the last people out of the basement with their food.

"I haven't seen her in a while," Charley said. "Wasn't she with Marisol and her little girl?"

Leon was about to answer when he saw the blue ski cap lady opening the door to the vestibule steps. "Hey. Looks like Bonnie went AWOL again."

"Better check those bags she's carrying," Matt said in a low voice.

"Hey, Bonnie, you're not supposed to go up there," Leon said warningly. To his surprise, instead of scooting away, the old lady came up to him and tugged his rope.

"That pretty girl, she's sick."

"What do you mean, she's sick?"

"She got too hot. Upstairs. Better go help her."

"Charley, watch Bonnie." Leon hurried up the steps to the vestibule and yelled as he reached the top. Nora lay on the vestibule floor, sweating, eyes closed, her face white as salt. "Father Francis!" Leon yelled. "You guys! I need some help!"

The other novices came running up the stairs, and Father Francis, hearing the shouts, came in from the friary kitchen.

"Heaven help us," the older friar muttered, dropping to his knees and picking up Nora's hand, feeling her pulse and forehead. "She's having a seizure of some kind."

"Heat stroke?" Matt asked.

"I don't know," the older friar listened to her heart. "She's having trouble breathing."

Leon stared at the girl, and saw the red ribbon round her neck. He bent down and pulled at it, and was frightened at how tight it was. "Someone get this thing off of her," he said.

"You're right," Father Francis said, checking it. "Someone get me a scissors or a knife!"

Charley dashed into the kitchen for a knife and Matt into the office for a scissors. Charley returned first, and Father Francis, smoothing back his beard and biting his lip, slipped the knife blade between Nora's neck and the ribbon and sliced it through.

All at once, Nora started coughing, and Leon lifted her up by the shoulders, holding her head. Father Francis pushed on her diaphragm, and she coughed again, heaved, and started to breathe. After a minute or two, she opened her eyes woozily.

"What happened?" The words were barely audible.

"You passed out," Father Francis said grimly, holding up the scarlet ribbon. "This was on far too tightly to allow you to breathe."

"Where'd she get that from?" Brother Matt asked. "She wasn't wearing that before."

"I gave it to her," piped up a cracked voice from the back of the vestibule.

They had all forgotten about Bonnie. The homeless woman sat on a garbage bag, sucking on a lollypop.

"Did you put it on her?" Father Francis asked.

The woman nodded. "She looked so pretty in it." She paused, looking around through her green eyeshade. "What's wrong?"

"You put it on her too tight, and she couldn't breathe, apparently," Father Francis said, a bit curtly.

"I'm sorry," Bonnie said, blinking behind her eyeshade. "It was a present. She looked so pretty in it."

There was an awkward silence. Brother Matt caught Father Francis's eye and got up. "Bonnie, let me help you get your food."

"I was right to tell you, wasn't I?" Bonnie inquired, getting up. "I told you she was sick."

"Yes, it's very good that you told us," Father Francis said. "Thank you, Bonnie. That was the right thing to do."

In the silence that followed, Bonnie got up and shuffled down the steps accompanied by Brother Matt. The other friars looked at Nora, who was becoming more aware.

"Bonnie's not playing with a full deck, but at least she had enough perception to see something was wrong with Nora and come and get us," Brother Herman said.

"Someone let this Bonnie out of his sight," Father Francis said, glancing around with a beady eye. "Obviously, we shouldn't have let this happen."

Nora sighed. "I'm sorry. It's my fault. I should have stayed downstairs."

"Don't get up," Father Francis instructed. "Now, Nora, I don't know if anyone told you this, but it's really not good for you to be alone with any of the visitors to the friary."

"I know, I'm sorry," Nora murmured. "Brother Leon told me, but I—figured I'd just talk to her."

"Well, in the future, don't be talking to these people alone, and don't let them give you any fashion advice," Father Francis said, half-serious. "Some of them are harmless enough, but as you can see, someone like Bonnie can be a potential danger."

"I can see that," Nora said, blinking. "I'm sorry."

Father Francis put a hand on her forehead again. "You okay now?"

"I have this slight heart problem," Nora replied in a quiet voice. "It makes me prone to fainting under stress."

"And the heat probably didn't help," Father Francis said. "Okay. I think you're done with your work for today. Let us help you back to your bed. You need some rest."

With a mixture of sadness and worry, Leon watched the priest and Brother Charley help carry Nora back to her bedroom. He remembered Nora's words from their night conversation: *"After a while, it seemed as though any random destructive force was going to careen in my direction."*

Troubled, he took a few steps from the vestibule to the church, knelt down, and prayed.

III

"Did you find anything out?" Bear asked Jean as they picked them up at the nursing home slightly past noon.

"We learned something about Blanche," Rose said solemnly. "Those old people love her. A couple of them wanted to know why she hadn't come by this week. They couldn't say enough about her." She paused. "I used to think that Blanche was crazy for visiting nursing homes," she admitted. "To me, it's always been—well, boring. But Blanche was really committed to doing it. It makes me feel like I've wasted my summer, just starring in a play."

Jean rubbed her daughter's shoulder. "But Rose, you brought joy to a lot of children when you did it. Don't you remember how you just went on and on about those day camp kids you performed for?"

"True," Rose admitted. "I guess between the two of us, we take care of both ends of the spectrum, don't we? And I really enjoyed the kids' theatre."

Fish slapped himself on the forehead and pulled out the postcard from his trench coat pocket. "Which reminds me—here you are. But don't thank me—thank Bear. He remembered and I forgot. That *is* the correct Sibyl, isn't it?"

"It is," Rose said with some delight, examining the slightly battered postcard. "Isn't she beautiful? I wish I could look like her. Wise and innocent all at the same time."

Bear looked at his brother, who coughed and said, "You'll have to tell me all about your play. I regret that I missed it."

"So am I, Rose," Bear said. "Did you get any pictures?"

"We did," Jean said. "I'll have to bring them out. But first—what shall we do about lunch?"

"We'll take you out," Bear said. He wasn't hungry, but he could appreciate that the others might be. "Where's Mrs. Foster?"

"She had to go home," Rose said as they started out the door. "I like her. I'm glad she came with us."

"Yes, same here," Jean said. "She said she'd check in later."

Fish drove them to a local Italian bistro, and they had a quiet lunch. Bear picked at his food and made a show of eating. He had a feeling Jean was doing the same.

Afterwards in the car, Fish brought up the matter of the Ecstasy drugs that were still in Blanche's room.

"It's best to do something with them soon," Fish said, glancing at Jean who was sitting next to him in the front passenger seat. "If that anonymous source who tipped the DEA on to us is still operating, they're likely to do the same to you. Especially when they find out that Blanche might not be wanted by the police for embezzlement any longer."

"But what can I do with them?" Jean asked.

"Flush them down the toilet," Fish said.

"That wouldn't be right," Rose objected from the back seat. "We should turn them over to the police as evidence."

"But if you do that, you're liable for that evidence being used against you," Fish said calmly. "Or against Blanche."

"But still—"

"I don't feel comfortable with doing that myself," Jean said. "After all, if Blanche has been framed, wouldn't this be evidence that someone was trying to frame her? And if we destroy the evidence, mightn't we also be destroying things like fingerprints that might lead the police to the criminals?"

"Yes, you would be," Bear said with a sigh.

"The first question we should be asking is who put the drugs in our house? Who is trying to frame Blanche?" Rose asked, tapping her fingers on the seat. "And why?"

"That, my lady, is the ten million dollar question with the washing machine and the microwave thrown in," Fish said, switching lanes.

"We have to find someone who has a grudge against her for some reason," Bear said. "So far we haven't found one. The only thing we know about this person—or persons—is what they've done to frame Blanche."

"Well, let's go through the events. How would an intruder get the keys to your apartment?" Rose wanted to know.

"He could have either made a key, or he had a key. Any professional thief could do that. Getting by the doorman is what would be hard," Fish replied. "Ahmed has worked there for years, and it's his job to weed out actual visitors from potential burglars. He knows everyone who's ever lived in that building and would be sure to detain someone he didn't know."

"And how could someone get into our house?" Rose asked.

Bear shrugged. "Same way—make a key. Maybe someone even took the keys out of Blanche's purse while she was working, made a copy, and returned them before she realized they were missing."

"Blanche had the key to your house, right? So actually, if someone took her keys, they could have copied your key at the same time?" Rose queried.

"Ah. Also true," Fish said. "What we should do is go back to the banquet hall and try to get into that room where Blanche kept her belongings. I bet you it's not secure."

"But you said that the manager wasn't very helpful at all," Rose said.

"We'll just have to go back when he's not there," Fish said. "Maybe that girl Rita can help us out."

Because of his wary feelings, Bear had been periodically glancing in the rearview mirror since they left the bistro. "Don't anyone turn around," he said sharply. "Fish, keep an eye on that gray car back there. It's two cars behind us now."

"Think we're being followed?"

"I'm pretty sure. It's been making every turn we make."

Everyone in the car was silent, and Bear pressed his hands together, wishing again that he had never gotten the Briers involved with him and his brother.

"Look Jean," he said at last. "I want Fish to drop you two at your house. We need to talk more, but I don't like this kind of shadowing. We'll try to lose this guy and meet up with you later."

"That's fine," Jean said quietly.

"I don't like that idea," Fish said suddenly. "How do we know who this guy is tailing? Maybe he was tailing Blanche. You think he's tailing you and me. But suppose we drop the Briers off and he starts going after Jean and Rose?"

"You're right," Bear said. He waited until Fish got off the expressway, and kept his eyes on the rearview mirror. The gray car exited the expressway after them. Bear caught a fleeting glimpse of the driver. It was the big man.

"Fish, pull over on the next block and let me out," he said abruptly. "Let's see who he's really after. You drive the Briers home and stay with them. I'll get back there when I can."

Fish sighed and pulled out his cell phone. "Better take this with you. Don't do anything stupid."

Bear glanced at the Briers. "It'll be all right," he told them. "You two pray for me, okay?"

"I already am," Jean said with a half-smile, but her eyes were worried.

"Mom, he'll be okay. He's *Bear*, after all," Rose said confidently, and squeezed his arm. "See you soon, Bear."

"Right," he said. Fish pulled over, and Bear got out of the car onto the sidewalk, and shut the door behind him. Since he had picked the spot completely at random, he realized he was in a not-so-nice section of town. He told himself this was a good thing. Maybe it would encourage the man to keep shadowing him.

He started ambling off towards the north, the general direction of the Briers' house, keeping completely aware of his surroundings.

Up ahead of him, he saw the gray car turn off on a cross street and tensed. Fish and the Briers should have continued straight on this road for a while. Unless he was completely missing the mark, Bear guessed the car was after him and would show up again.

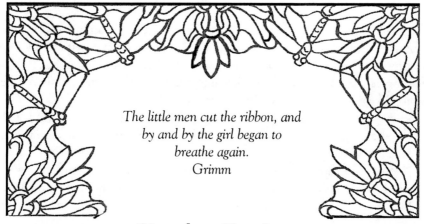

*The little men cut the ribbon, and
by and by the girl began to
breathe again.*
Grimm

Chapter Twelve

t had been a close call, almost too close. The girl couldn't stay in bed, despite her weariness. Not wanting to be alone again, she got up and slowly made her way back to the church. Perhaps if she sat for a while in the stillness, she would feel better.

She opened the sacristy door and walked through into the main body of the church. It was afternoon now, and the sun came in through the stained-glass windows, touching the pews with soft tones of purple, blue, green, and gold. Brother Leon was walking down the aisle towards her, holding a guitar. Seeing her, his black brows furrowed. "Hey, you're not trying to get back to work, are you?"

"No," she assured him, smiling at his concern. "I'm just going to sit."

"Good," he said. "That will help."

Just then she noticed Brother Herman sitting on a jury-rigged scaffold made of a board and two ladders before the statue of Mary. His bare feet dangled in the air as he drew on the top part of the niche behind the statue with chalk.

"What's he doing?" she asked, puzzled.

Leon glanced at Brother Herman and smiled. "He's getting ready to paint. It's his job to repair some of the cracked parts of the plaster and paint around here," he said. "Me, I can't even draw a straight line, but he's a real good artist. You'll see." Nodding, Leon loped away and vanished into the sacristy, guitar in hand.

Interested, the girl genuflected towards the tabernacle, and hesitantly made her way over to the homemade scaffold. She saw that the bearded friar was concentrating on transferring a sketch from the large piece of paper in his lap to the gray plaster of the niche.

He looked down as she drew near. "Go ahead and watch if you want. It doesn't bother me," he said heartily, and kept sketching out his planned painting with a thick stub of white chalk. The girl watched as beneath his deft fingers, slender curved lines became the long stems and petals of lilies, arching like a crown over the Mary altar.

Engaged, she sat down on the edge of the sanctuary, leaning against the marble altar rail. "That's lovely," she said when the friar stopped to look at his work.

"God's gift," Brother Herman said. "My vocation, and definitely my way of having fun." He glanced at her again. "How are you feeling?" he asked.

She smiled. "Much better, thank you." She watched him work for a few moments in silence.

"How did you know you wanted to become a monk?" she ventured.

"A friar?" he grinned down at her, and she realized her mistake and colored.

"Yes, a friar."

"'I went seeking Beauty, and Beauty, He found me,'" Brother Herman was apparently quoting something. "I went to art school, thinking I wanted to be a classical artist. Then on a trip to Greece, I encountered icon writers for the first time. In the Eastern churches, many icons are written—we would say painted—by monks. That first got me thinking of religious life. But in the end, I discovered that even though I enjoyed monastic life, I was more attracted to the Franciscan charism. So I ended up with the Capuchins, and when Father Francis started his order, I joined up."

"Hm," the girl said. "Can I ask you another question?—this may sound silly."

"I enjoy silly questions," Brother Herman said solemnly.

"Is it safer to be a monk?"

"A friar?" he teased her again.

"Yes, of course—I meant, a friar?"

"What do you mean by safe? Safety of the body or of the heart?"

He understood what she was asking, and she was relieved. "Of the heart, I guess." She hesitated, trying to find the words without sounding corny. Perhaps it was better to say it simply. "Last year I fell in love."

"That's wonderful," Brother Herman said, with feeling.

"But the guy I'm in love with has gone overseas and I'm not sure when he'll come back," she said. "And meanwhile, I'm having all these problems. I have this sense of danger hanging over me." She paused, hoping she wasn't bewildering the old friar. But he was nodding, and she guessed that he could see that her mugging and her recent attack today were enough to justify her feeling paranoid.

"What I really, really want is for him to just come back and make it all go away. But of course, even if he could just appear here today, it doesn't mean he could solve it all for me."

The friar nodded. "It doesn't really sound like it is something a human can save you from."

"That's what I'm starting to realize. So what I'm wondering is—have I made a mistake, loving him? I mean, if I had just focused on loving God somehow, then I wouldn't have these tremendous expectations of a very imperfect, very human guy."

"God can disappoint us too," the friar pointed out.

"Oh, I know," the girl bit her lip. "I think I first recognized that when my dad died. But on a percentage basis, God is going to disappoint you a lot less than human beings will. Isn't that true?"

Brother Herman cocked his head. "I suppose it is. But you don't choose whom to love on the basis of safety. Or because it's useful to you."

"I know. It's just—I keep wondering, if I wasn't in love, would it be this hard? If I weren't in love with a man, I wouldn't be expecting to be rescued. I'd just sort of be resigning myself and trying to tough it out. But because I let my heart become tender towards him, it's gotten so much harder for me and so much more disappointing. Isn't it better just to not depend so much on another person in that way at all?"

The friar was silent as he worked. The chalk made scraping noises on the wall. She looked over at the tabernacle again.

It's foolish to depend on unicorns. After all, what is a unicorn but a mythical beast that's always running away when you try to catch it? Maybe it's better to live your life without unicorns.

"Unicorns?"

She blushed, not realizing she had spoken aloud. "It's just an analogy."

"Have you ever seen the Unicorn Tapestries in the Cloisters? Beautiful," Brother Herman said.

She felt a sudden warmth. "Actually, we went to see them together, my boyfriend and I."

A smile creased Brother Herman's round red face. "You know, I had a deeply profound encounter with the Spirit of God when I first saw those tapestries, back when I was an art student, before I became a friar. It's a fascinating meditation on the Incarnation and death of Christ. You know the unicorn represents Christ?"

She hadn't read all the material in the museum, and shook her head.

"You know the famous final tapestry of the 'Unicorn in captivity?' Where the unicorn sits surrounded by a round fence, tethered to a tree, but looking peaceful and happy?"

"Of course. I saw it. It was lovely."

"That's an allegorical representation of Christ, who became a willing captive to the small circle of a woman's womb. Just as a unicorn gives up its wild freedom to lie in the arms of a virgin maid, Christ gave up his Godhead to sit in Mary's arms. And to become our Savior."

"Oh," she said. " I didn't know that."

"There are layers and layers to the story. Human love and marriage, men and women, God and the soul. On the exterior, the tapestries are about human beings hunting the unicorn. But if you scratch the surface, you find it's really a story about the unicorn hunting us, out of irresistible love. And when the unicorn finds you, your life is changed forever."

"Sometimes I wish I never met him," the girl said, her throat contracting suddenly. "I wish I'd never known what a unicorn was like. Then maybe—"

The friar held up a finger to his lips. He cocked his head, listening.

Pausing, the girl became aware of the sound of a guitar, and someone humming in a soft voice.

Brother Herman stroked his long beard, picked up his chalk, and struck out in a new direction on the plaster. "Listen to the words," he directed the girl in a whisper.

The girl strained, listening as the voice began to sing.

> *Sometimes, it amazes me*
> *How strong the power of love can be*
> *Sometimes it just takes my breath away.*
>
> *You watched my love grow like a child,*
> *Sometimes gentle and sometimes wild,*
> *Sometimes you just take my breath away.*
>
> *And it's too good to slip by,*
> *It's too good to lose,*
> *It's too good to be there just to use.*
> *I'm going to stand on a mountaintop and tell the good news*
> *That you take my breath away.*

Finished, Brother Herman climbed down from the ladder, and said in a confidential hush to the girl, "Let's go find him."

II

> *Your beauty is there in all I see*
> *And when I feel your eyes on me*
> *Sometimes you just take my breath away.*

Since my life is yours, my heart will be
Singing for you eternally
Sometimes you just take my breath away.

Leon missed a chord and swiftly tightened a peg. The old strings on Matt's guitar were giving out again. Sitting cross-legged in a corner of the sacristy closet, he regularized his picking again. The battered plaster statues of the saints stood around the little space, their graceful heads inclined towards him, as though they were listening. Closing his eyes, he sang softly,

And it's too good to slip by,
It's too good to lose,
It's too good to be there just to use.

I'm going to stand on a mountaintop and tell the good news
That you take my breath away.

At last he receded, and let his picking linger to a stop. When the last string had stopped vibrating and stillness filled the closet again, he looked up to find he had a live audience as well. Brother Herman and Nora were leaning against the wall of the sacristy, listening.

He was embarrassed. "Just giving a private concert to your invalids, Brother Herman," he said, nodding towards the statues that the artist friar was planning on repairing.

"Beautiful," Brother Herman said. He glanced at Nora, who still hadn't moved.

"Yes," she said at last. She took a deep breath. "Is that a religious song?"

"It's just a folk song from the 70's I learned growing up," Brother Leon said. "No, it's not really religious."

"But it's a true love song," Brother Herman said, patting Nora's shoulder. "And hence, deeply religious." He nodded his head towards the sanctuary. "Come and see?" he invited Leon.

A bit puzzled, Leon set down his guitar and followed them both out to the Mary altar. He looked up to see the dove's wings that now embraced the space over the statue of the Virgin Mary. Ten minutes ago, that space had been barren cracked plaster. Leon was silent, marveling at how Brother Herman's creations seemed to spring out of nowhere.

"Thanks for the inspiration, Leon," Brother Herman said. He glanced at Nora, and said softly,

"Better to see and desire than never to see!
Better to die from desire than never to see!"

Leon was not sure what he was talking about, but Nora apparently did. She nodded, wiped her cheek, and took another deep breath.

"You may be right," she whispered.

III

Bear kept on walking steadily, giving his tail—if it was a tail—a chance to locate and catch up with him. The sidewalk was dirty, the edges covered with trash blown by the wind and trapped in the crevices. Most of the stores he passed were boarded up or unoccupied. A dead section of town along a main road.

Making his way towards the Briers' house, he stopped and crossed the main road, heading west. After crossing the first lane of traffic, he stood on the median, looking from side to side, waiting for a chance to cross, and watching for his shadow.

Then he caught a glimpse of a broad-shouldered man coming up the street. It was him. Apparently he had left his car to follow his prey on foot. He stood a few blocks down from Bear, waiting to cross the street with a group of people. If Bear hadn't already been looking for him, he might never have noticed the man.

The old, once-too-familiar fear of being hunted came over him with a chill. *Who is he? A drug dealer from my past who found out I've got money now and stumbled onto Blanche as an easy way to get to me?* But he kept his pace steady.

Calculating the risks, Bear hurried across the traffic to the far side and started heading up the side street. He decided it was worth the risk to get a good look at this guy.

He walked for a few blocks, then took an abrupt turn down a promising alley and glanced around. There was a fire escape ladder hanging down on one side of the building, with a garage beyond it.

Bear moved fast. Using a garbage can as a way up, he clamped onto the lowest rung of the ladder, and wrestled himself up. Swiftly he climbed up to the balcony, then hurried to the corner of the building. If he was lucky, the man wouldn't look up—at least not right away. Climbing over the fire escape railing, he dropped onto the roof of the nearby garage and crouched down in the shadows.

He waited, holding his breath. From his viewpoint, he had a clear view of the alley and the street beyond. No one passed by. The minutes stretched on, and he was just wondering if he had been a fool after all, when there were casual footsteps and a man appeared at the corner of the alleyway and paused. He was wearing dark glasses and a light jacket, and something about the way he was standing made Bear guess that he was carrying a concealed weapon.

Come on, get closer, Bear internally urged, hoping to recognize the man.

But at this distance, it was still difficult to see him. The man checked the soles of his shoes as though he had stepped on something unpleasant, and Bear knew he was really trying to decide whether or not to pursue Bear down the alley.

Afraid of me? Or just not sure where I went?

He knew the man was more than his match in terms of build, and probably armed. *Chances are, he lost me*, Bear concluded, and wondered what would happen if he drew attention to himself. But an internal caution made him hold back. Unarmed on this rooftop, he was too much of a sitting duck if the man decided to shoot.

After an interval, the man adjusted the collar on his jacket and vanished, continuing up the street. Bear scrambled down the fire escape and crept down the alleyway as casually as possible. But when he reached the street, the man had vanished.

Bear started home, trying to calm his heart rate. *I think I almost met Blanche's possible stalker.* But the real question was still a mystery. What had Blanche done to make herself a target?

*The little men warned the girl,
"The queen will surely learn you
are still alive. Be on your guard
and let no one in if we
are not here with you."*
Grimm

Chapter Thirteen

*...Lord, open my lips.
...And my mouth will proclaim your praise.*

Standing at the lectern of the altar, catching the early morning sun, Father Francis read the antiphon for the Invitatory: "Come, let us give thanks to the Lord, for His great love is without end." And the opening psalm began.

Friday. Morning prayer again. She was getting used to the routine. It didn't seem quite so long. And she liked it. Now, standing in front of the Mary altar before Brother Herman's new design, she was once more experiencing nearly perfect content, despite the fact that her neck was still sore from yesterday's attack. *Ironic, isn't it? Now that something bad actually happened to me again, I almost feel free from the sense of impending doom.*

Father Francis began the hymn before the Office of Readings, and she joined with the other friars on the second verse:

> *To God the Father of the world,*
> *His Son through whom He made all things*
> *And Holy Spirit, bond of Love,*
> *All glad creation sings...*

She jumped as something ran over her foot. Brother Herman, in the pew behind her, also started. She turned around just in time to see Brother Charley leap into the aisle, grab a scaffolding plank leaning against the wall, and smash it on the ground with a tremendous crack.

Everyone in the church caught their breath. Father Francis looked up, his eyes wide.

Red-faced, Charley held up a dead rat by the tail. "Sorry. That wasn't very Franciscan, was it?"

Taking a deep breath and reverting to his characteristic dry humor, Father Francis made a sign of the cross towards him. "Absolved. Give him a decent burial after prayer."

Charley departed from the church with the dead rodent, and Father Francis, shaking his head, took up the Psalm again.

II

"Nora seems to be feeling better," Brother Matt remarked to Leon as they gathered their notebooks for the novices' class that morning.

"I'm not entirely sure that she should be," Leon said.

Matt looked at him. "What do you mean?"

"I don't know if I could explain it," Leon confessed. Not because he couldn't find the words, but because he didn't want to break Nora's confidence. She had told him about a sense of doom hanging over her a few nights ago, and he had been inclined at the time to brush it off as spiritual intuition gone haywire. But the fact that she had been assaulted, however randomly, bothered him. "She should be careful."

"After all, that's twice in the space of ten days that she's been attacked," Brother Charley spoke up, coming out of his bedroom. "You think she's just one of those perennial victims?"

"I think there's more to this than meets the eye," Leon said. "She hasn't told us everything that's happened to her."

"Brother George thinks she might be in trouble with the law," Matt said with some seriousness. "He thinks it's odd that she doesn't talk much about herself. 'She's too quiet,' he said to me."

For some reason, this irritated Leon. "Maybe she just isn't talking to *him*," he said. "And I don't blame her. I'm just hoping she'll talk to one of the priests about what's going on. *We* really don't need to know."

Brother Charley frowned. "So why are we talking about this?" he shouldered his backpack of books. "Let's go downstairs."

Feeling chastised, Leon tried to put thoughts of Nora's problems aside and concentrate on his *Catechism of the Catholic Church* class. Fortunately, it was apologetics-based, and he usually found the subject interesting.

But just as he was warming to the subject, there was another interruption. Brother Herman poked his head in the doorway. "Sorry, Bernard. Two things. Tonio is here, asking to see you. And the Knights of

Columbus are here with some food and other donations in a truck. Can I break up your class momentarily to get some help unloading?"

"That's fine—we're about due for a break anyhow," Father Bernard said. "I wonder what Tonio wants?"

"He said he wanted to go to confession," Brother Herman said. "He's out on the steps waiting."

"Praise God," Father Bernard said, and went to the front door. The novices followed, and went outside with Brother Herman while Father Bernard talked quietly to the homeless man who was standing at the door, hat in hand and a penitent look on his thin face. Outside the friary a large truck was parked, and Father Francis was talking to the driver.

The driver, Mr. Kane, was a Knight of Columbus who owned a discount store in the Bronx, and he was an occasional volunteer at the friary on the weekends. A white-haired, red-faced Irishman, he had already donated a used van, a furnace, and hundreds of cans of soup and beans to the friary, as well as any surplus merchandise from his stores. Today he had several boxes of groceries, which the novices unloaded gratefully, and something else.

"Utility garbage cans on wheels, from a janitorial supply liquidation," he said, pointing to stacks of gray plastic cylinders in the back of the truck. "I got them for a song but I don't think I'll sell too many at my store. So why don't you take 'em?"

"Thanks very much," Father Francis said. "Yes, I'm sure we can use them."

"Can you use twenty? If not, just take what you can use. I'll see if the Missionaries of Charity want the others."

"Ladies first," Brother Herman said.

Mr. Kane laughed. "Okay. But save me time driving. Why don't you take six of them, and I'll get the sisters more if they want?"

"Certainly," Brother Herman said, and looked at the novices. "Let's get them inside. Can you each take two?"

The novices wrestled the heavy-duty oversized trashcans out of the truck. But once they were turned right side up, the four revolving wheels on the bottom of the cans slid easily over the pavement to the basement steps. They thanked the Knight, who saluted and drove off to his next stop.

"These will be a real help to sort the donated groceries," Brother Herman said as they hauled them down the steps. "You know, cans in here, boxes in there... that will make it easier to put together the food bags."

"Plus they move easily," Leon said appreciatively. He pushed the can across the wide expanse of the basement floor. It clicked effortlessly along the linoleum, gaining momentum. Inspired, he quickened his pace, grabbed the sides, and leapt inside the trashcan. It hurtled across the floor and crashed into the opposite wall. "Durable too," he reported, checking the sides.

The other friars laughed. Grinning, Leon shoved himself off the wall and plunged towards them. Stepping forward, Charley grabbed the edges of Leon's can and hurled him across the floor again.

"Woo hoo!" Leon yelled. "Do it again, Charley!"

Not one to miss the fun, Brother Herman clambered into another can. He pushed himself off the table, and, finding that he wasn't going fast enough, grabbed the ends of Matt's rope belt. "Come on, Matt, run!" he urged. "Give me some momentum!" Matt obliged.

Seeing this, Leon grabbed Brother Charley's cord and took the reins in hand. "Race you, Claus!" The two teams of friars careened across the basement floor, the wheels of the cans spinning smoothly, a tremendously satisfying thunder.

"Will you look at these maniacs?" Father Francis stood in the doorway with Nora. "You'd think we were running an amusement park down here."

"Just test-driving the new garbage cans!" Leon called. "Hey, cut it out!" he exclaimed as Brother Charley started spinning him around.

"Come on and try them out, Francis!" Herman bellowed.

The novices immediately started up a chant. "Fa-ther Fran-cis, Fa-ther Fran-cis…"

"Good Lord," the older friar muttered, but his eyes glinted. Brother George came down the steps to see what was going on. The novices picked up their chant, slamming the walls and stomping.

Father Francis crossed to one of the trashcans and the novices cheered wildly. "How do you work these things?" he said. "George, give me a hand." George obliged, and pulled Father Francis across the floor in his can. With whoops, the other two trashcans took off after him. Nora sat on the steps of the basement and laughed and laughed.

Finding the rest of the friary deserted and wanting to investigate the din in the basement, Father Bernard came downstairs and paused, smiling at the sight.

"Am I going to get my novice class back or are you all becoming urban charioteers?" he asked.

Recollecting himself, Leon leapt out of the trashcan, hi-fived Charley and assisted Father Francis in getting out of his can.

"I say we keep a few of these for recreational use," the superior mused. "They're not bad. Good mileage, quick response time…"

"At the next chapter, maybe we'll write that into the norms," Father Bernard said. Together they all walked up the steps to the vestibule, and entered the church again.

"How did things go with Tonio?" Brother Herman asked after they had all genuflected in front of the tabernacle and were walking back into the friary.

"Odd. I went with him into the entranceway, and started to hear his confession. Then he started coughing and asked me for a drink of water. I went to get him one, but when I came back, he was gone." The friars reached the entranceway, and suddenly Father Bernard halted and pointed. They all looked. The spot above the doorway, where a large hand-carved crucifix had hung, was empty.

"So that was it," Father Bernard said quietly. "He didn't want the sacraments—he wanted to supplement his income." He sighed heavily. "Well, I didn't obey our own rule about not leaving visitors alone. Serves me right."

The rest of the friars were silent. "I'm sorry we were all fooling around downstairs," Leon said, deflated. "If we had been up here—"

"No, it was my own fault," Father Bernard rubbed his head, smiling wryly. "I was starting to think that my golden counsels were winning his soul. It's good for my humility, that's all."

Leon turned towards the door as he heard the sound of ominously familiar barking. There was a knock, and Father Francis pulled the door open to reveal a tight-lipped Marisol, straining against two yelping Rottweilers. As soon as the door was open, she released the leashes, and the dogs sped into the friary.

"*You keep dem,*" she said. "*Un present.*"

She turned on her heel and marched down the steps, ignoring Father Francis's protests, while Charley and George hurried to catch the dogs that were speeding through the church, still howling.

"I suppose this is another donation?" Father Francis said, shutting the door. "What on earth possessed her to give us these two devils?"

Brother Leon groaned. He knew too well why she had given the dogs to them, and he suspected he knew the Lord's reason too. "Purgatory," was all he said.

III

Bear sorted through the shiny pile of photographs and stopped at one picture of Blanche, standing in front of a backdrop of large chess pieces looming over her.

"That's from my play this summer," Rose said. "That was opening night."

Blanche wore a pale blue dress and a white sweater. Her long black hair, caught up in a white bow, fell down to her elbows. Bear searched her expression. To him, her smile seemed a bit forced. He wished it had been a close-up. He wanted a better idea of what had been going on behind her eyes.

He put the picture aside and looked at the next one. Rose stood next to her sister, dressed in a red little girl's dress with a black headband.

"That's me in my costume."

"You were Alice in Wonderland, weren't you?"

"Technically, no. I was Alice, but the play didn't take place in Wonderland. It took place on the other side of the Looking Glass," Rose explained, moving to a more comfortable position on the couch beside him. Fish was busy on the phone. Jean was out. Mrs. Foster was making lunch. It hadn't been a particularly productive day for searching thus far.

Rose pushed back her hair. "See, Lewis Carroll wrote two books—*Alice in Wonderland*, and *Through the Looking Glass*. Movies usually try to combine both of them into one story, but they're actually significantly different tales. Our director wanted to give the later book its due."

"And the differences are—? I never read them," Bear said. He looked through other pictures of Rose with various cast members dressed in odd costumes.

"*Alice in Wonderland* is about the White Rabbit, the Cheshire Cat, and the Queen of Hearts. Alice spends the whole time trying to get into this beautiful garden and growing bigger and smaller all the time," Rose explained. "*Through the Looking Glass* is less well known, but I almost like it better. For one thing, you can tell Alice is more grown up and independent. She makes her own decisions, even though they're not always the right ones. Looking-Glass Land is supposed to be the land on the other side of the mirror—everything is backwards. Alice discovers the world has become a giant chessboard and she chooses to take part in the game. Just like in the first book, she meets all sorts of strange characters. There's a snobbish Red Queen, and an old White Knight, who becomes an important figure for her. He and Alice are not exactly in love with each other, but they care for each other. The director said the White Knight is almost a substitute father for Alice—maybe an image of Lewis Carroll himself."

"You seem to have enjoyed it."

"Oh, I did," Rose said with a sigh. "I was so surprised that I got the part. It was for the Bronx Children's Theater. I wanted Blanche to try out too, so we could be in it together, but she said she wasn't an actress. I tried out for the part of the silly White Queen, but then the director had me read for Alice, and he picked me for the part. It sort of devoured our summer after that—my being the lead. Between the play practices and work, I barely saw Blanche after a while. But I kept telling myself I'd make it up to her when we went on vacation in California together. And then she decided not to go on vacation with us after all."

"Why was that?"

Rose paused. "Well, I think she was feeling—I don't know. Mom and I were worried about her, because she seemed so reclusive. But Blanche kept saying she just wanted to work more hours to make her tuition payment for college. I guess this summer she really grew up."

"Meaning?"

"We've always been a close family. Until now, Blanche's life sort of revolved around us. But this summer, she was off doing her own work, following her own activities. Like visiting Mr. Fairston and those folks in the nursing home. I didn't do that with her. And then I guess that things were going on inside her mind that she felt she couldn't talk about with us. It was hard to feel separated from her like that. I guess she was—well, becoming more of an adult. And less like a kid." She looked at Bear, smiling, but he could see a tear in her eye. "Sort of like Alice, I guess."

Bear thought about that. "She's been challenging me, too," he said quietly, thinking of her last letter and their last conversation.

"I wish we had made her come with us, but Mom said we needed to respect her decision," Rose said. She turned over the photos dismally. "She wanted to be alone, and Mom said we should let her be alone. I guess Blanche didn't want the struggle of having to explain to a lot of relatives we don't see too often about everything she was going through. They'd have understood even less than we have."

Bear was silent, picking at the edges of the photos. "Rose, I'm sorry," he said with difficulty.

"For what?"

"I'm sorry I didn't come back sooner. If I had, maybe I could have helped her sort through some of this. Maybe I should have been the one she was talking to."

"Well, maybe it was something she needed to face alone. If you had been here, you might have—I don't know, distracted each other. Who knows?" Rose said. "Maybe this is all happening for a good purpose."

"I hope so," Bear stood up. "I can't see that now, but I really hope you're right." Restlessly, he walked to the window to see who had just pulled up. There was no sign of the big man who had been following him, and Bear wondered where he fit into the puzzle.

To his surprise, Jean got out of the car and walked up the house steps. Tension was on her face, and Bear hurried to open the inside door for her. "Anything wrong?"

"I got my car back from the shop, at last, with a big bill," Jean said. "And on my way home, I stopped at the nursing home where Blanche visited to talk to the director. We once worked together, many years ago. I had a feeling yesterday when I spoke with her that she wasn't telling me everything. So, today I went back."

"Did she tell you anything more?"

Jean nodded.

Fish had hung up his cell phone, sensing that something was up, as Jean sat down on the couch next to Rose, who leaned against her mother protectively.

"The director was called by the DEA last week," Jean said quietly. "They told her that they had been given information about drug pickups that were occurring at the nursing home. She was told that the courier—the person transferring the drugs from one dealer to another—was reportedly leaving drugs somewhere in the nursing home. She had her staff do a search, and they found several packages of different drugs concealed in residents' rooms. The residents were all ones that Blanche had been visiting regularly."

"Where were the drugs? Did she say?" Fish asked.

"Behind dressers and under chairs. Sometimes the packages were inside women's purses that didn't belong to any of the residents. Apparently this is a regular trick used by girl couriers, who pretend to have lost a purse and come to 'find' it when they need to make a transfer. That's what the DEA told the director when she turned over the drugs to them." Jean's face was set. "What I want to know is—who hates my daughter so much that they've gone to such lengths to do this to her?"

There was silence. Mrs. Foster stood in the door of the kitchen, frowning. Bear looked at his hands.

Jean pushed back strands of gray hair that had fallen out of her braid. "I can see why Blanche was so paranoid. Someone's been tracking all her activities and changing all of her good, innocent deeds into criminal behavior."

"And somehow she knew it was going on," Rose said somberly. "She sensed it before she could have known. No wonder. No wonder."

Fish knelt down quickly and picked up a pencil. On a page of an open notebook, he drew a circle. "Blanche was watering our plants. Drugs left in our apartment." He drew another. "Blanche was alone in the house. Drugs left here." And another. "Blanche works at Reflections. Drugs left there." And another. "Blanche visits the sick and elderly. Drugs left there." He drew one last circle, then, pursing his lips, he connected the five. "Someone's trying to pull a net around her. In one of these circles Blanche is doing something that is making someone very, very angry."

"What's that last circle for?" Rose wanted to know.

"Is that for the attempts that we haven't found out about?" Bear asked.

"Could be. Or it could stand for the attempt that's yet to come." Fish tapped the pencil, frowning. "We have to find out who's behind this."

"Do you think it's an actual drug ring?" Jean asked. "Maybe Blanche knows something about them...?"

"I'd expect them to be a lot more violent," Bear said, and Mrs. Foster nodded.

"If it was a drug ring, she wouldn't be out at an airport chasing a dog. She'd be dead," Mrs. Foster predicted.

"Besides, if it was something like that, Blanche would go to the police," Bear said. "It has to be something that seems more ambiguous to her. So she's just gone into hiding."

Fish sat back with a sigh. "Plus, often drug gangs use violence because they don't have other weapons. I have a feeling we're dealing with someone who's certain that they don't have to bloody their hands to get rid of Blanche."

"I'd give a lot to know the identity of the anonymous source who called the manager of our apartment building," Bear said.

"Probably the same person is talking to the DEA and giving them all these tips," Fish said. "Anonymously, no doubt."

Bear pressed his hands together. "If only we could find her," he said. "She probably has the missing pieces. But we don't know what they are because we don't have her here with us."

"Well, if we can hold out, my guess is that if Blanche is still okay, she'll surface next week, when she's expecting you two to come home," Fish nodded to Rose and Jean. "As long as nothing happens until then…"

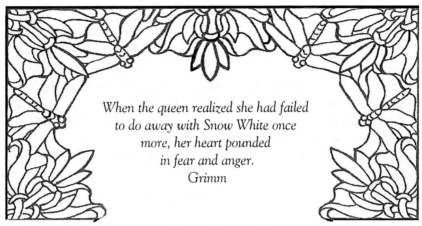

*When the queen realized she had failed
to do away with Snow White once
more, her heart pounded
in fear and anger.*
Grimm

Chapter Fourteen

it!" Brother Charley shouted.

The girl sat, and Leon chuckled. "Not you, Nora."

"I know," she grinned. "I just felt the need to obey."

The big novice was standing in the courtyard between the church, school, and friary, and the two Rottweilers were standing in front of him, eyeing him suspiciously. Matt and Leon were sitting on leftover cinderblocks, watching. The girl had heard the noise from the friary where she had been helping to finish the dinner dishes, and had come out to watch.

"Sit!" Brother Charley roared again, and the dogs looked at each other dubiously.

"They don't buy this dog psychology stuff," Leon called. "I told you this wasn't going to work. The Fathers are right: we should just send them to the pound."

"They can learn!" Brother Charley shook his head and planted his feet. "We just have to teach them their place. Back when I was a biker, I used to own a Doberman," he explained to the girl. "The key to working with these big high-energy dogs is to remember that they're pack animals. If you want them to obey you, you have to convince them that you are the Big Dog on the block." He pointed at the dogs. "You hear that? I am the Big Dog!" he snarled.

One dog perked up its ears, and wagged its tail slightly.

"Me!" bellowed Charley, pounding his chest. "I am the Big Dog!" He advanced on them and circled them, growling in a menacing manner. The dogs watched him, backing up as he stalked around them.

One of the dogs flattened his ears and started to wrinkle his nose to show his teeth, but Charley snarled back at him, and the dog backed up, wagging his tail.

When he felt that the dogs were significantly intimidated, Brother Charley put out his hands and said in a deep voice, "Come."

The dogs gingerly came forward, and licked his hands. He rubbed their heads, and they wagged their tails.

"Yeah, they'll obey you, but what about the rest of us?" Leon asked skeptically.

"We'll just have to stay on top of them until they figure out where their place is on the totem pole," Charley said.

"Yeah, at the way bottom, just above mice and rats," Leon said. "Good luck convincing Father Francis to keep them." He said to Nora, "I'm a cat person myself."

"I like dogs myself," Brother Matt said. "—the less energetic kind."

"I really don't care much for animals, believe it or not," the girl said.

"Ah, the Disney anti-heroine," Matt said. "They'll never cast you in one of their movies."

"Fine with me," the girl said.

"Sit!" Brother Charley ordered, and the dogs sat. One of them got up after a minute, and Brother Charley whirled on him. "I am the Big Dog!" he growled. Hastily the dog sat back down, wagging its tail.

"Maybe it's not a total waste of time. We could make this a public service announcement for the friary on the vow of obedience," Brother Leon said.

"Maybe New York City would be a better place if God would just come down here like Brother Charley and shout 'I am the Big Dog!'" Brother Matt said.

"At least me and all the other dyslexics would get it," Leon said, and the girl couldn't help laughing.

The problem is, she reflected as she got ready for bed that evening, *God doesn't come down like a giant to crush His enemies. He comes in human disguise. He comes in weakness.* She sighed, seeing the connection. "Just like men," she murmured. "Weakness."

"I get it now," she said aloud, and she shook her head wryly. "Not that this seems to solve any problems, but I get it now."

* * *

The last time she had talked to him was about ten days ago. She had called him, because her mother and sister were gone, and she was starting to feel lonely. But she hadn't wanted to call to tell him that, because she felt it would look as though she were trying to make him come home to protect her. She didn't want to do that. She wanted him to come home when he wanted to.

He had gotten her message and called her back at some unusual hour that was normal time for Italians but an odd time for Americans. He had seemed preoccupied and out of sorts. They had talked about this and that, and silence had overtaken them. For a moment, she wondered if they were really drifting apart.

"When are you coming back?" she asked finally.

"I don't know," he had said. "Maybe in September."

"Aren't you going to start college?"

"I don't know, Blanche. I just don't know."

She didn't want to sound like a mother, so she stopped asking questions. But Bear kept on talking.

"I just keep on feeling as though—I don't want to be pushed into anything. What keeps on striking me is the futility of it all. Frankly, it makes me angry. I just don't see why I should bother." There was a touch of fierceness in his voice.

"So what are you going to do if you don't go to school?"

"I don't know. Does it matter? I mean, now? I have enough money to last for quite some time. I could go off and be a shepherd. How about that?"

He was trying to be humorous. Her heart sank. It was difficult to see him being so—directionless.

"Bear. You said you were angry."

"Yes. I did." His voice was guarded.

"Why is that?"

"I don't want to talk about it."

"Do you know why you're angry?"

"I have some idea, yes."

"Something you haven't told me about."

"Blanche, I just said I don't want to talk about it."

She took a deep breath. "You don't have to."

"Good, because I don't want to."

"That's fine."

"Fine."

"Fine," she said softly, feeling her eyes well up with tears.

* * *

Now, in the darkness, she clasped her hands together on the bed. *I'm not giving up on him*, she thought. *Just because he's disillusioned and frustrated me doesn't mean I can give up on him altogether. Giving up on him would mean somehow—giving up on myself.* At last she attempted a prayer. "God," she whispered. "Please bring Bear home safely. And please help him see what he needs to see. And help me trust again."

II

The dogs set up a terrific howling during the beginning of morning prayer on Saturday, as the friars began their hymn. They kept up the sporadic accompaniment from their basement storage room all throughout the next two hours of prayer, making the times of silent meditation far from silent. Over breakfast, the Fathers discussed dropping them off at the humane society that afternoon, but no one could be spared.

"I suppose they can stay one more day," Father Francis concluded. "Well, Charley, it's good that you're training them. I suppose it might help them to have some sort of order in their lives."

Given this kind of beginning, Leon would have predicted that the dogs would be the main issue of the day. But the morning brought difficulties of a different kind. When the novices were cleaning up from breakfast, Brother Herman bustled into the kitchen with a worried, conspiratorial look on his face.

"What's up?" Leon asked.

"Jim Hornberg is here," Brother Herman said in a quiet voice.

There was an answering grimace from the novices.

"Brother Jim? Of all the people…What's he want?" Leon narrowed his eyes. Brother Jim had been his old novice master when Leon had first joined the Franciscans, before the new order had started. They had not gotten along, to put it mildly.

"Delivering a stipend from the diocese, on the surface. But his real motives are probably deeper, knowing Jim."

"He's come to pry and to spy and to sneer at the crazy drop-outs from the order," Leon said, a bit angrily, and Matt winced.

"You shouldn't say everything you think," Matt said, a minor reprimand.

Leon muttered an apology, and Brother Herman said, "We've got to make the best of the situation. Just be alert. The Fathers are going to be showing him around. They'll keep everything under control."

"What about Nora?" Brother George spoke up suddenly.

"What about her?" Leon asked, a bit sharply.

"She's just a volunteer," Matt said.

"Of course she is, but you think Jim's going to put that kind of spin on it when he goes back to the bishop's office?" Brother George returned. "She's been here far too long. It's going to look suspicious."

"How's he going to know how long she's been here if no one tells him?" Leon asked, staring hard at Brother George.

Matt said, feebly, "I can see George's point. Maybe we should have her lay low—send her out to the store or something."

Brother Herman looked undecided. "There's nothing wrong with having volunteers here. And our constitutions specifically talk about having good relationships with the laity."

"But you know what he might say—" Brother George warned.

"Phooey!" Charley spoke up for the first time. "Who are we trying to impress anyhow? Let him think what he wants to think."

"Well," Brother Herman heaved a sigh and continued in a hush tone. "We'll just have to put it in God's hands, as usual. He knows what He's doing."

Leon continued washing dishes with an internal growl, trying to squelch his strong impulse to punch Jim in the nose if he asked any stupid questions and wondering if it would be best for all concerned if he hid in the basement with the dogs until it was all over.

But just then, Father Bernard came in. "Leon, could you come with me?" he said authoritatively.

"Sure. What's up?" Leon said.

"I want you to come and greet Brother Jim," Father Bernard looked at him closely. "This will give you a chance to work on those bad feelings you and I discussed before."

Knowing exactly what his novice master meant, Leon internally mortified himself and, without a word, followed the priest to the chapel.

As Brother Herman had said, Fathers Francis and Bernard were doing their best to handle their unexpected visitor with as much charity as they could muster. Being older, they had gotten used to the inevitable politics of religious life.

Brother Jim was younger than they were, but a good fifteen years older than any of the novices. He was thick-lipped, paunchy, had fading blond hair, with a sharp nose and heavy eyelids over blue eyes. He smiled and smiled in his polo shirt and casual clothes as his former brothers gave him a tour of their new establishment. He expressed surprise that they had managed to get as much done as they had.

"No offense, Frank," he said, using Father Francis' nickname, which Leon knew the older friar detested. "But the opinion in most Church circles was that your new order wouldn't last a month." Brother Jim's perpetual smile broadened. "But you really seem to be almost thriving." He glanced at Leon, who was standing behind his novice master, but didn't acknowledge him.

"Much to everyone's delight, I'm sure," Father Francis muttered.

Father Bernard, the diplomat, smoothed between them. "Yes, we're actually surprised ourselves at how well the gamble has been going." He led the way up the stairs into the vestibule of St. Lawrence Church.

"Gamble? Oh, it was a gamble, all right. Most experienced religious wouldn't think of setting up a new order with no home, no permission from their superiors, particularly with no funding..." Brother Jim glanced up at the Mary altar, grimaced at the sketches of Brother Herman's master painting plan, and looked back at the others. "Well, you must enjoy proving everyone wrong."

Father Bernard seemed poised between two different answers, but Father Francis made no bones about his opinion. "Absolutely!"

Leon hid a smile. He caught a glimpse of Nora in the sacristy, gathering some cleaning materials.

"Humph. What an old-fashioned monstrosity the diocese has saddled you with," Brother Jim shook his head as they walked down the aisle of the church. He cast a sidelong glance at Father Bernard. "I suppose you'll be ripping out the altar rail and the fancy doodads on the ceiling, hmm?" He allowed himself a loud, long laugh.

Father Bernard attempted a smile. "Actually, we've been given some old statues and candlesticks—we plan to add to the existing interior substantially." He indicated Brother Herman's disassembled scaffold. "Herman is planning to redo the areas over the altars with original artwork."

"I should have guessed," Jim sighed regretfully. "I suppose he's still obsessed with Byzantine icons, eh? Poor old Herman. He should have switched rites long ago."

Father Francis's smile came across as baring teeth. "I *like* icons."

For an answer, Jim gave another long laugh as he paced up the aisle to the sanctuary. The other three followed him, a bit anxiously, genuflecting as they came to the tabernacle. Jim apparently did not notice, and made no respectful gesture himself. Instead he wiped his forehead. "Hot in here."

He examined the tiered marble altar with the air of a connoisseur. "Early twentieth century, very bad. Kind of reminds you of a wedding cake, doesn't it? Good thing there's not a lot of gold work on it. Or else you'd have to get this place burglar alarmed, with the neighborhood you live in."

"We keep the doors locked," Father Bernard acknowledged. "This church is kept pretty much for private use."

"And it's an oven. Personally I can't survive anywhere in August without air conditioning. Wow. Looks like you had some extensive floor damage repaired," Jim remarked, glancing around the sanctuary. His heavy eyelids swept over Nora, wearing jeans and red T-shirt, who was scrubbing the sacristy cabinets. "Hello there!" he said heartily.

"Hi," said Nora, brushing a lock of black hair out of her eyes and picking up her buckets, seeming a bit chary of the visitor. Brother Leon was not surprised when she slipped out the door into the courtyard a moment later. Jim surprised the other friars with a long, low wolf whistle. "My," he said. "Who's that?"

"A volunteer," Father Bernard said. "Nora...and several other lay people have been helping to renovate the men's residence we are planning here." His gaze was met by Father Francis, who frowned and shook his head wearily.

"Who gets you the volunteers? I should get them over to our place. All we get are old church ladies taking time off from 'Bingo.' Maybe you guys are doing something right, after all." Jim chuckled, then, seeing the joke was not acknowledged, chose to tease in a soft voice as they walked down the far aisle to the back. "I'm onto you now, Frank. I guess there were other reasons you wanted to get away from the mainstream, eh? Better watch yourself. Lawsuits are flying these days." He shook his head.

"We live our lives prudently, you can be assured of that," Father Bernard said, and then seemed to be struck with a sudden inspiration. He went on, "Surely you know of the community's long-term plans?"

"Plans?" said Jim and Father Francis together. Leon remained quiet.

"Why, the formation of a sister order of nuns," Father Bernard went on smoothly as they walked up the aisle towards the exit. "We hope to house them in the old grade school building if and when that becomes available. Of course, we're building the foundation for our future order now."

Brother Jim was open-mouthed, and Father Francis managed to suppress his stare behind a wry grin.

"Yes, it's possible that Nora may be our first postulant for the order," Father Francis forged ahead gruffly. Unsure, he raised a quizzical eyebrow to Leon, who gave his head a tiny shake, no. All of which went unobserved by Brother Jim. "All dependent on the leading of the Holy Spirit, of course," the head friar added.

"A convent of nuns?" the visiting brother was amazed. "So, Frank, Bernard wasn't kidding when he told us you had big plans."

"The Lord has big plans," Father Francis corrected him as they saw their visitor to the door. "The rest of us are just trying to figure out what He's got in mind."

III

When Bear and Fish arrived at the Briers' house on Saturday morning, they discovered Mrs. Foster was already there with Jean, and so was Charles Russell, who was looking distinctly ill at ease. The two women were sitting on the sofa, watching him sort through his papers. Rose was in the kitchen, setting up a tea tray.

"Charles, thanks so much for coming over," Fish said as he came in, and extended a hand to the lawyer. "I told Jean you'd be the best person to talk with about this situation."

"I'm not so sure of that," the lawyer said doubtfully. "Mrs. Brier tells me that she wants advice about turning over illegal substances that she found in her daughter's room. She says this has something to do with the case against you."

"That's correct," Bear said.

"Is her daughter still missing?" Mr. Russell looked questioningly at Rose, who gave a small smile as she set down the tea tray.

"Yes, she is. It's a week today," Bear said.

"I have to say straight off that it would be a conflict of interest for me or my firm to represent your daughter," Mr. Russell said to Jean with his usual courtesy. "As I explained before to my clients, if there's even a slight possibility a court might find your daughter guilty of incriminating the brothers, there would be a conflict of interest for me to represent her."

"I realized that," Fish said, sitting down on the edge of the couch. "However, this is a tricky situation, and I want to ask for your advice. I figured you'd be able to tell us how to proceed. And perhaps you could suggest someone who'd be willing to represent them in this matter."

The lawyer pulled out a legal pad with a suppressed sigh. "Well, perhaps you'd better fill me in on the details."

Bear and Fish related to the lawyer all they had found out so far, and the lawyer took notes, his brow furrowed. Then he questioned Jean, and then Mrs. Foster, who told about her discovery of the drugs. Mr. Russell went upstairs to see them, then came downstairs and made a confidential call to the city prosecutor's office, and explained the situation without giving names. Then he called a colleague of his who had experience with drug cases, and asked him to come over. The lawyer arrived after lunch, conferred with Jean and Rose, and agreed to represent Blanche *in absentia* until she was found. Then, after both lawyers had conferred and taken pictures of the drugs, they had Jean call the police. The police sent over a detective and his partner to investigate.

This all took hours, and after a while, Bear started to get antsy. "Do I have to stay around here for all of this?" he asked Fish in a low voice after the police had arrived and were listening to the explanations of Jean and Mrs. Foster. "Can't you handle this?"

Fish was intent on the proceedings. "I want to make sure that Jean and Rose don't incur any legal liability for what they're doing," he said. "Your presence is helpful in that regard."

So Bear sat and endured the legal talk for as long as he could, but his mind was elsewhere. To occupy himself, he began to massage the muscles in his upper arm. Last year he had taken a bullet in his arm, and although the wound had healed, it still ached from time to time, particularly when he was tense. He kept checking out the window periodically to see if he could catch any sight of the mysterious man, but the big shadow seemed to have stayed away today.

At last the police detective left, but the lawyers still had more to do. Jean was talking to the other lawyer, and Mr. Russell was talking to Fish.

Bear waited until his brother had paused in conversation. "Can I borrow your cell phone again?"

"No! Buy your own!" Contradicting his words with his actions, Fish slid a hand in his trench coat, handed him the phone, and resumed his conversation.

Bear went into the kitchen, and dialed the number he had gotten from Rita, the waitress.

"Hello, Bear," said Rita when she answered.

He was momentarily startled, and she said, laughing, "I have caller ID and I recognized the number."

"Oh. But how did you know to call me Bear?" He could have sworn he had first introduced himself to her as Arthur.

"That's what Blanche always called you. Hey, I was actually going to call you. I tried before but I guess you had your phone off or something. Your names came up at the hall yesterday."

"Did they?"

"Yes. Mr. Scarlotti—you met him last time—he's been telling all the shift managers that Blanche still isn't above suspicion."

"Why not?"

"Because the police recovered the money from two guys who were trying to pass off the bills, right? Well, Mr. Scarlotti decided that you and your brother must be the two guys."

Bear suppressed a snort. "That's a pretty big leap in logic."

"You're telling me. Anyhow, he's been saying the police were still investigating this matter, and no one from the staff is to talk to Blanche, or you two, if you come around again asking questions. He went on and on about how this might ruin our reputation, blah blah blah."

"Great," Bear sighed. "Well, then what I was going to ask you doesn't apply."

"Ask me anyhow."

"I was going to ask you if you could show me the room where the drugs were found."

"I think I can. Reflections is a pretty big place. I might be able to get you in without anyone noticing."

"Are you sure? That might cost you your job."

"Yeah. I figure I owe it to Blanche for not believing her. Besides, the summer's almost over anyhow."

Bear was grateful. "Thanks. When will you be at work?"

"Can you meet me there at one? There won't be so many people around, and maybe Scarlotti won't be in yet. The other manager is Mr. Carnazzo, but he wasn't around last time you guys came by, so maybe he won't recognize you."

Bear thanked her, hit the end button, and looked around. The police were gone. Mr. Russell, who was apparently finished with his inquiries, was packing up his briefcase. Mrs. Foster and Jean were talking together, looking over a list of phone numbers.

"They're going to make phone calls again." Rose looked at the brothers. "What are you two going to do?"

"I'm going back to the banquet hall," Bear said.

"Can I come with you?" Rose begged. "I just need to go out and do something to help find Blanche!"

Fish opened his mouth to object but Bear, knowing acutely how Rose felt, decided to overrule him. "Sure. Come along." He got to his feet.

Rose picked up a pink-fringed scarf and slung it around her neck. "Mom, I'm going out with Bear and Fish." Jean, on the phone, nodded and waved.

"Do you have Fish's cell number if you need to reach us?" Bear asked Mrs. Foster, who nodded.

"How can you wear a scarf in this heat?" Fish asked Rose as they walked outside.

"How can you wear that trench coat and hat?" Rose asked sweetly, putting on her silver-framed sunglasses.

"I think," said Fish, opening the rear car door for her and crossing around to the driver's side, "that the idea here is to be inconspicuously dressed." He turned on the air conditioner. "Which is not how I would describe your outfit." He glanced again at Rose's lively green summer dress that set off her red hair, and shook his head hopelessly.

"If you want to wait a few minutes, I can go upstairs and find something in gray and brown," she suggested. "I could even get my mom's raincoat. That way, I can look just like you."

Fish grumbled as he threw the car into gear and shot down the road. "The idea is not to imitate me, but to wear something subtle and unremarkable. No one ever looks at me twice, except possibly to notice how ugly I am. Fortunately, you won't ever be able to have that asset, so if you really want to be some kind of amateur sleuth, start by playing down your looks—and your fashion statement. Sensible suits and unattractive dark glasses might work. But then again, I wouldn't recommend that you even try to follow Nancy Drew's career path in the first place. I doubt you'd survive to star in even one further mystery novel, let alone three hundred and fifty."

"Fish," Rose said indignantly when he finally stopped talking. "You're not ugly. In fact, I've always found you rather winsome."

"See what I mean? You're hindered by poor judgment to begin with," Fish said, rubbing his face. "All right, pipe down, Trixie Belden. We need to figure out our plan of attack." He looked at Bear. "Is that Rita person supposed to be there now?"

"Yes," Bear said. "She'll show us around the place a bit."

"Good," Fish said. "Getting the lay of the land would be a help."

They drove up to the banqueting hall and parked. Rita, who was standing outside smoking, caught sight of them and hurried over to greet them. "Hi again," she said. "You're in luck. Scarlotti's gone for today. Only Carnazzo is here, and he's a stuffed shirt, but maybe we can get by him. I figure if they catch us, I'll just play dumb. We'll go in by the side door."

When they went inside, they could see caterers preparing one of the rooms for a dinner, laying out multicolored napkins and china place settings on dozens of tables in a room overhung with a massive chandelier festooned with colored glass beads. Assunta was among the waitresses, and she waved to them.

Rita led them down a hallway to a side staircase. "This is the banquet hall where Blanche was working last weekend, when we had the masquerade," she said as she led them upstairs, and opened the door at the top of the steps onto a vast room with high stained-glass windows decorated with grapes, flowers, and animals. The floor was parquet, buffed to a high gloss.

"Incredible," Fish murmured.

The architecture wasn't bad, Bear noted. He could tell the materials used to imitate a medieval Gothic structure were phony—painted wood instead of stone—but still, the effect was that of a rather noble theatre. A fitting scene for a drama.

"What a spectacular party place," Rose said.

Rita made a face. "Yeah, except that at night, you can't see the colors in the stained glass. They look black, and then, with the brown walls, it's *really* dark in here. I like some of the other halls better."

Bear looked around, picturing the hall full of glittering costumed guests. And in the midst of it, a figure in white, alone, but erect. Blanche.

Just then, someone called, "Rita!"

Rita turned and the others glanced to see who was calling her. They saw a fat Italian man in shirtsleeves puffing towards them, his face red with the exercise.

"Who's up there with you?" he demanded.

"What's wrong, Mr. Carnazzo?" Rita asked, glancing helplessly at Bear.

*And Snow White saw no harm in the old
woman, and let her in. The old woman said,
"What a fright you are! Let me help you
comb your hair properly—for once."*
Grimm

Chapter Fifteen

he vestibule was as clean and as organized as it could get, until the
friars received more donations. The girl looked around with a sigh,
and closed the door behind her.

That morning, none of the friars seemed to be around. She had guessed
that the novices didn't have classes, but no one had told her what the
Saturday schedule might be like. *I'll just start looking for something to do,* she
thought, and wandered into the sacristy. After some investigation, she
decided she would start by cleaning the high cabinets, which were full of dust.
That way, she could be near the statues of the saints in the closet, which she
had dubbed The Sisterhood.

She was well into her work when she heard voices. Glancing out into the
main church, she saw the two priests and Brother Leon talking in the
sanctuary. There was a pudgy blond man in a polo shirt with them, and he
hailed her with a hearty, "Hello there!"

For some reason, she didn't quite like how that man was looking at her.
Returning the greeting, she pushed back her drooping hair again, feeling on
edge. Her hair was really annoying her, and she decided to use that as an
excuse to return to her bedroom and hunt for her red bandana, which she
hadn't been able to find.

She hurried across the courtyard, fiddling in her pocket for the key to the
high school that Father Bernard had given her.

Once inside her room, she took a deep breath. It was a pristine, peaceful
little place that actually felt homey, despite its sparseness. She had added a
wildflower wreath and hung a picture on the wall, which made it cozier.

Kneeling beside the crate where she kept her few articles of clothing, she
started to look for her bandana. It had been missing for a couple days now.

This morning, she had checked to see if she had left it in the bathroom. Now she was wondering if she had left it in a pocket somewhere.

There was a knock at the high school door. Perhaps the friars were done with whatever it was that they had been doing. Hopefully, she went down the hall and pushed the heavy metal door open. A hunched-over figure in a blue hat with a green eyeshade. Bonnie.

"Hello," she said cautiously.

"Hello," said the lady in her crackly voice, fixing on her with eyes that were dim beneath the green shade. "I got something for you."

"I'm sorry—I really shouldn't take anything else from you," the girl apologized. "I'm not supposed to let anyone in."

The woman's eyes were lowered to a plastic bag she was twisting back and forth in her hands. "Don't want to come in. Just felt bad—you got sick before. My fault. Came to see how you were." She coughed.

"I'm doing well, thank you."

"I was wrong about you." The lady swayed from side to side as she repetitively turned her bag. "You don't need to be a scarlet girl to get what you want. These monks, they have their Mary, right?"

"Yes," the girl said. The woman was rambling again, and the girl pushed aside her eerie feelings.

The woman nodded. "Pale and cold and white and above and beyond them. That's what they like. That's how you are, right? So transparent and clear, like a pane of crystal glass, no fingerprints on it. Untouchable." The woman fiddled with her bag rhythmically again. "You don't mind hearing old Bonnie talk, do you? No one listens to old Bonnie."

"I'm listening," the girl said.

The lady hacked at her cough again. "Some water—you got a drink of water in there?"

"Sure. Just a minute."

She turned, but before she knew it, the old lady had followed her into the high school. The girl paused. Once again, she remembered. *"Don't let anyone in."*

All right, so I've got to get her back out.

"What a sweet room," the old lady said, pausing at the door of her room. "Is this yours?"

"Yes."

The old lady took a step in, touched the sketch of the Virgin Mary, discarded by Brother Herman, which the girl had found and hung on the wall. "So pretty in here." Her eyes beneath the green shade traveled over the bed, the flowers in the little bottle on the windowsill, the spiky crown of dried flowers hanging from the side of the bed. "You've got a touch, you have."

It was nice to have another woman appreciate these things. Missing her mother and sister suddenly, the girl said, "Thank you."

The old lady lowered herself onto the battered wooden chair as if it were made of china and looked from side to side, silent, not moving. Her hands were still: her tic had stopped. She seemed to have forgotten about the drink of water.

"We really, really should go back outside," the girl said politely, after a moment.

"I want to talk to you, dearie."

"We can talk outside."

"You've taught me, about being beautiful. You don't have to be scarlet. You're a white maiden, white as snow, aren't you? Pure as the driven snow. That's what they want. Someone who's untouchable. Beauty above them like a star." She leaned forward. "I've seen a lot in my time, dearie."

"I'm sure you have," the girl said.

"I've had my wild days, I'll tell you, when I was a scarlet girl, and I'll tell you: you Christians are right about things between men and women. Sex." The woman nodded sagaciously. "Wicked, that's what it is. It's disgusting. No, you have it right. None of that for you. You stay above and beyond the men. You can still get what you want. You be a snow maiden, and they'll serve you like a queen so long as they believe you're above it all." She nodded. "Stay untouchable. Never give yourself away. That's how it's done."

But sex isn't wicked, in and of itself, the girl mentally objected, but the old woman was drawing something out of her bag. "See? I made a poem about it for you." It was a silver hair comb, and affixed to the top was a silver star flower, made of rhinestones, obviously an antique.

"I can't buy anything," the girl said regretfully. "I shouldn't, it's—"

"It's a gift," the old woman said, putting it into her hand.

The girl blinked, and thought to herself swiftly, *but I need something for my hair.*

Carefully she combed back the side of her hair that had been flopping over her face all morning, and pushed the comb in. It held her hair perfectly. Wishing again she had a mirror, she put up her hand to feel it.

"That's right," the old lady said. "Never say old Bonnie never gave you anything." She drew something else out of her bag. "Here. Smell this."

It was a perfume bottle of a clear liquid. Taking off the stopper, she smelled it, and felt a blast of cold, chilly air sweep through her until her breath froze inside her. The stars shone over her in a black, still night.

II

After Brother Jim had seen the whole friary, he took his leave, saying that he had a lunch meeting. For the first time, he seemed to notice Leon.

"Oh, it's you. Didn't recognize you at first with the beard and haircut. Still here?" he said in feigned surprise.

Leon nodded. "Sure am. How's the chancery?"

"So busy, as you can imagine. It's been nonstop since I was hired," Brother Jim said. "How's your novitiate going?"

"Pretty good," Leon said. "I'm happy to be here."

"So far," Brother Jim said with a small smile. "Well, I've stayed long enough. Stay cool, you guys! And keep your burglar alarms on!" He chuckled as he walked down the steps to his car, and walked around it carefully before he got inside and turned on the engine.

"Making sure he still has all his hubcaps," Father Francis muttered. "Bernard, I'm not at all sorry we left."

The novice master shook his head. "God have mercy on him."

"Working at the chancery...Thank God he's not a priest or I'd be afraid someone would make him a bishop," Father Francis said as he shut the door.

"It won't happen," Father Bernard predicted with confidence. "They'll make you one first."

"Ha!" Father Francis snorted.

Leon went to the chapel to recollect himself for a few moments. Oddly enough, as he prayed for Brother Jim and the Franciscan order, Nora kept on coming to mind. As usual, he tried to turn his distractions into prayers, but the sense kept nagging at him that something was wrong. He finally looked up and saw that she wasn't in the church. He couldn't hear any sounds from the vestibule, or from the sacristy, where he had last seen her.

He got to his feet, reproaching himself. *Are you sure she's not on your mind because you're becoming too attached to her?* But despite his inner rebuke, he went to the vestibule anyway.

No sign of her. Frowning, he went to the sacristy, opened the back door of the church and looked out into the courtyard. It was deserted, but he saw a figure hurrying away down the alley. A figure in a blue ski cap.

He remembered the last time he had seen Bonnie—*and beside her, Nora lying unconscious on the vestibule floor.* Now concerned, he dashed back to the friary and called the others.

"What's up?" Matt was the first to appear, with Charley behind him, trailed by the dogs.

"Anyone know where Nora is?"

"Haven't seen her. Is she back in her room?"

"Haven't checked there yet. Charley, see if she's in the basement," Leon sprinted across the courtyard with Matt following and banged on the door. "Nora! Are you in there?" he called.

There was no answer. "It's locked," Matt said, pulling at the handle.

"I'll go get the keys," Leon said, and ran back inside the friary.

He quickly located Brother Herman talking with the Fathers and asked for the keys. Brother Herman followed him out to the high school. The dogs were running around the courtyard, barking. When Brother Leon opened the door to the high school, the dogs dashed inside and went straight to Nora's room, pushing open the door as they went.

Leon stepped inside, saying, "Nora?" He noticed the clothes in her crate were scattered on the floor in front of the door. At once, he saw her on the bed. The dogs were nosing her hand. He might have thought she was sleeping, but her face was oddly still. One of her hands slid over the side of the bed and dangled there.

"Is she okay?" Brother Herman pushed past him. He felt her forehead. "She's out cold."

Bonnie. Leon tore outside, the dogs at his heels.

He ran down the alleyway where he had seen the old woman disappearing, and, reaching the sidewalk, looked up and down the street. The dogs ran in circles, their noses to the ground.

"Come on, you dumb dogs, be useful," he begged them. At last one of them perked up his ears and ran off to the right, followed by the other. Praying this was an actual trail and not a distracting piece of meat, he hurried after them.

Looking in both directions, he saw a lady sitting on her stoop, with her grandchildren playing on the sidewalk. "Hey, Mrs. Santos, you seen Bonnie? That old lady with the blue hat."

The lady nodded and pointed. "She was going that way. Towards the train."

Leon thanked her and jogged on, the dogs loping beside him. Across a vacant lot, a side street, a median strip littered with cans. Beneath the massive iron trunks of the el train, he hurried through the criss-cross of shadows. Then far ahead, he saw a figure in a blue hat climbing the tall steps to the train. There was no mistaking her.

Double-timing his pace, he crossed the street just in front of several oncoming cars, rounded the corner, and banged his way up the metal steps. His heart was pounding as he reached the turnstiles blocking his way, and he realized he didn't have a token, or any money.

Quickly he turned around and saw a group of black teenagers climbing up the steps behind him. He put out his hand. "Can anyone give me the fare for the subway?" he asked.

His ears reddened. When he was in the old order, money had almost always been provided. Here, it was different.

The teenagers stared at him, in his medieval gray robe and rope belt. Again he repeated politely, "Please. Could any one of you give me the fare for the subway, for the love of God?"

Several of them passed, giving him wide berth, but one kid dug in his pocket and tossed him a token. "Thank you!" Leon said gratefully. "God bless you." An el train clattered and roared as it came into the station beyond them. The dogs drew back in deference, but Leon hurried to the platform.

As he pushed his way through the turnstile, he murmured prayers for his unexpected benefactor and looked around. There was no sign of Bonnie.

The train hissed impatiently, and feeling the prompt of his guardian angel, he got on and grabbed onto one of the poles as the doors slammed shut.

The teenagers were on this car, and they looked at him quizzically as he scanned around, looking for Bonnie.

"Are you some kinda priest?" one of them said at last.

"No, I'm a Franciscan brother," he said, putting aside his quest for the moment. "Thanks for the help," he said.

"No problem," said the boy who had helped him. "Do you like, beg for a living?"

"In our community, we take a vow of poverty," he said. "We only live on what others give us."

The kids were curious, and Leon answered their questions and tried not to be distracted. When the train roared to a stop, he stepped out of the train and watched to see who got out. No one resembling Bonnie did, so he figured he should keep on riding.

III

Mr. Carnazzo stopped in front of Bear and Fish and scrutinized them distrustfully. "I'm sorry, but as manager of this establishment, I'm going to have to ask you to leave," he said stiffly.

Bear stared at the manager. "We're just—" he said. Fish put up his hand and stepped forward authoritatively, cutting his brother off.

"Leave?" he repeated. "Isn't this hall available?" he asked, pulling out an appointment calendar. "I'm interested in renting your facility for an event I'm having."

"What kind of an event?" the manager said suspiciously.

Bear looked at Rose. "A wedding," he blurted. Rose, immediately picking up the cue, moved closer to Fish and took his arm possessively.

"Yes, that's right, a wedding," Fish gritted his teeth in a smile at his brother. "So can I rent this place? We were just looking it over and it seems adequate."

"Well—" The manager hedged. "I'll have to check with someone first."

Fish heaved a deep sigh, took Rose by the arm, and flipped open his calendar. "The date's December eighteenth, and I want the best hall you have to offer. How about the one downstairs with the drippy things on the chandelier?" He started to trail the manager, who was retreating in the direction he had come.

"But honey, are you sure it's big enough?" Rose queried, putting on her sunglasses. "We have five hundred guests coming."

"Five hundred? Who said we were inviting your side of the family?" Fish glanced over his shoulder at Bear and grimaced, meaning, "Hurry up and look. I can't keep this up forever."

Bear looked back at Rita. "Better show me that room quick."

Stifling a grin, Rita opened a side door and led him down a twisting narrow hallway lined with doors. "This is where Blanche and I were working the night of the masquerade. They had us tying ribbons on balloons in one of the back rooms. We left our stuff on the floor near where we were working. That's where they found the drugs too."

She opened a door to a small low-ceilinged room. The room was carpeted in a dark pattern. Inside were a worktable and several banquet chairs that were in disrepair—one was missing a back, another tilted crazily to one side. A cheap oil painting with a big gash in it leaned against one wall.

"What happened to that?" Bear asked curiously.

"Someone put their fist through it at our last event," Rita said dismissively. "That masquerade ball for Mirror Corp was a really wild party. Those people get out of hand sometimes. If you ask me, some of them are doing drugs."

Bear looked around further. A pot with cigarette butts lying in it stood in one corner near the window. Small pieces of black and silver ribbon still littered the ground. Bear saw something gleaming on the ground beneath the table near the wall: a pair of shiny silver-colored scissors. He stooped to pick them up.

"We were using those to cut the ribbons for the balloons," Rita said. "That one must have gotten left behind."

The scissors were heavy, and sharp. Then he noticed something else on the floor, almost invisible in the shadows, and picked up a few.

"What's that?" Rita asked.

"It looks like hair," he said. A few other shorter strands lay strewn about.

"Freaky," Rita breathed. "Blanche's hair?"

"That's what I'm guessing," he said. Yes, the strands were long enough. An eerie feeling came over him.

Assunta came inside furtively and closed the door. "Find anything?"

"A bit," Rita said. She explained to Assunta while Bear looked around the room further, aware that he didn't have much time.

There were two windows in the room. An air conditioner unit blocked one window, but the other was slightly open.

Bear crossed to the window and put a hand on the sash. It moved up and down easily. He pushed the window open and looked outside. They were on the second floor of the building. The heavy branch of an oak tree hung outside the window, providing some needed cool shade on the building.

"Anyone could climb up the tree to get to this window," he observed.

"Or get out the window and climb down," Rita pointed out. She smiled. "I think it's been known to happen. Girls on shift sometimes have their boyfriends meet them here and do the Romeo-and-Juliet thing."

Bear paused, staring out at the waving green leaves. The riddles forming in his mind were still incomprehensible to him.

Through the leaves, he saw a figure standing on the far side of the street, smoking. A big man in a black jacket, wearing sunglasses.

He motioned to the waitress. "Assunta," he said. "Is that the man?"

Assunta squinted out the window at the man. "Yes. That's him," she said positively. "I recognize the nose. He's the one I saw in the hallway the night of the party."

"No mistake then," Bear said grimly, putting a leg out of the window. "I've had enough of it."

"Are you going after him?" Rita gasped.

"Only thing I can do at this point to find out who he is." He grabbed the tree branch easily—he could almost crawl onto it—and looked back at the two waitresses. "Can you find my brother and tell him where I've gone?"

"Sure," Assunta said, and Rita nodded.

"Tell him I'll be in touch by cell phone. Thanks for showing me around, Rita."

"No prob. Man, you're a babe."

Shaking his head, he shimmied down rapidly. Once he reached a good height, he dropped to the ground and started to approach the man.

The man saw Bear coming, and paused for a moment to put out his cigarette. Tossing it into a trashcan, he turned and walked away. *Now that he knows I've seen him, he's going to try to disappear,* Bear thought. *But I can't let him go.* He turned back, as though he were returning to the banquet hall, but once the man had gone around a corner, he retraced his steps and started following him.

Bear had shadowed people before, and was familiar with the method. As he followed the man, he kept out of sight as much as he could, without drawing attention to himself. The man walked for several blocks and reached the train station on the Long Island Railroad. Bear had to stop to buy a ticket, but the man apparently had one. He walked right through the turnstiles onto the platform and waited for a train to come. Fortunately, Bear joined the crowd on the platform and hooked his sight on the man before the next train arrived.

The train took him to Penn Station in Times Square. Once they reached Penn Station, the man got off immediately, and Bear kept tailing him as the man bought a paper, then abruptly hurried to the shuttle train to Grand Central. Knowing that the shuttle had only one destination, Bear felt confident enough to let him out of sight.

When the shuttle halted in Grand Central, Bear made sure he was the first one out of the cab and sat down on a bench to watch the rest of the passengers emerge. The man got off last, and headed into Grand Central. Eyes fixed on his quarry, Bear followed, praying that this chance would work out in his favor.

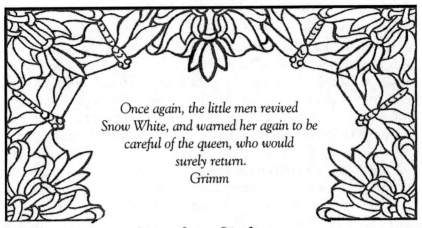

Chapter Sixteen

he woke up to find Father Francis taking her pulse and feeling her forehead.

"What happened?" she asked weakly.

"I'm afraid you'll have to tell us that," Father Francis said wryly. "We just got in here and you were passed out on the bed. Is your heart bothering you again?"

There was a thick, sour taste in her mouth. "I don't think so," she said feebly. "I think she gave me—ether or something."

"Who?"

"Bonnie. She was here again. It was my fault—I let her in. She asked me to smell some perfume, and…"

"…And that's the last thing you remember," Father Francis said, shaking his head. She could see the other friars standing in the door to her room. Charley, Matt, Father Bernard, and the cross one, Brother George. Brother Herman was sitting at the foot of her bed.

"Where's the perfume?" George asked with some skepticism, looking around. But it seemed to have vanished.

"I think she took it with her," the girl said, feeling a bit fuzzy, as though she had imagined the whole thing.

"What color was it? Did it smell sweet?"

"Clear, and I think it was sweet, at first."

"Chloroform," George muttered.

"Nora," Father Francis said quietly. "Was this another random attack, do you think?"

She shook her head.

"Do you know why Bonnie would be targeting you?"

Aside from the fact that everyone malicious seems to be after me, no, she almost said. "Please," she said faintly. "Please let me think about it a little more before I tell you anything."

Father Francis kept his keen gaze upon her. "You need some rest," he said at last and got to his feet. He looked around the room. "Did she take anything?"

"Seems to me like she was looking for something," Brother Herman said, looking at the crate of the girl's clothing, whose contents were scattered and disheveled.

The girl put her hand to her hair, but the antique star comb was gone. Of course. Fingerprints. Her gaze traveled around the ransacked room. "I can't imagine what she would have taken," she managed to say. "I'll look over everything later."

"Fair enough." Father Francis put a hand on her head. "Thank God you're all right." He prayed a short prayer for healing and all the friars joined in the Hail Mary at the end. She prayed with them.

"Thank you," she said, grateful for the prayer and grateful that they were letting her be.

After they had gone, she lay on the bed, staring at the white wall, but everything she saw before her was blackness. Once more, she felt utterly, completely alone, and her doom, which she felt she had escaped, was hanging over her again...

* * *

"What's wrong?" Mr. Fairston asked when she paused in reading to rub her hands.

"Oh, I have a slight heart ailment and I get tired easily under stress, that's all," she said, feeling scraped thin. Bear was still gone. Her mother and Rose had left on vacation. Fish had gone to Europe. All day she went from one place to another, where no one really knew her, and where she was alone, even when she was in a crowd.

"You should be more careful of yourself," Mr. Fairston chided her, turning his head restlessly on his pillow. "I have a brain tumor, and even I don't look as pale as you do."

"Well, I'm always pretty white, even in the summer." But when she glanced in the mirror beside the bed, she saw she did look more pale than usual.

"You've got to start taking better care of yourself," he said, his left eye creasing in worry. "Is something wrong?"

"I felt a funeral," she murmured. "Like in the poem."

"Your own funeral?" he asked. "Or mine?"

"I'm not sure. Do you know what I mean?"

"Of course I do," he stared at the wall with one eye. "I'm living with that every day. But why should you be feeling it?"

"I don't know."

"Well," Mr. Fairston tried to make a joke in the silence. "Don't you go and die before I do. That's not fair."

Not exactly a comforting thought, she thought as she went outside into the heavy evening heat to the night shift at work. In the crowds near the subway, she caught a glimpse of broad shoulders and a large chin beneath a flat nose, and sunglasses. Quickly she turned her head forward again. *He's here. He's here.*

She had been sensing him at the back of her mind for some time: the large ominous figure. And now he was right behind her. But what could she do but go on?

When she stopped to cross the street and looked around again under the pretense of watching for cars, there was no sign of him. His absence mocked her.

She crossed crack after numerous crack on the endless sidewalk, drawing closer and closer to the train that would take her to work, and sensed at the same time she was heading into danger, not out of it. *But there's nothing,* she told herself again in frustration. *Just my paranoid intuition*—her intuition that was so strong and so severe she wished she could ignore it. It seemed at times that every possible danger in the world presented itself to her in her mind. Why? Was it truly God, trying to warn her, or the devil trying to torment her? Most of the time she had to assume the latter, just to find an excuse to ignore it and go on.

The sense of foreboding was persistent. On the train, she looked over her shoulder a few times. But the man in black was gone, and no one else around her seemed a likely candidate. She tried to concentrate on the novel she had brought along— Jane Austen's *Northanger Abbey*. Not exactly the most comforting thing to read when you were nervous…

"Hey, you're not wearing black and white!" Rita exclaimed when the girl walked into the workroom, which was crowded by a flock of black and white balloons netted in bags.

The girl, startled, looked down at her dress and realized her mistake. Tonight's ball was a black-and-white masquerade, and all the servers had been asked to come in black-and-white dress. She had been so preoccupied with protecting herself that she had completely forgotten and worn her yellow summer dress.

"Well, it's almost white," she said, half an excuse.

"At least you look nice and that long braid is plenty black." Rita admitted. The waitress was wearing a white sequined top and shiny black pants, with a black-and-white polka-dot seventies-style jacket. "I thought I'd come as a disco dancer."

"Looks good," the girl said, and tried to get business-like. "What do we have to do with these balloons?"

"Put ribbons on them and bring them out to the hall. Mirror wants them all over the ceiling. Mr. Carnazzo is having a hissy fit about it, because he hates having stray balloons hanging up there for days on end. But it's for our biggest client. They always get their way."

"If we put really long ribbons on them, that might help," the girl said, picking up the scissors.

Being around other people doing her usual job had dispelled her fear, but she was still haunted by the lingering feeling of being under surveillance, the steady beat of another's heart walking in sync with hers.

"You seeing things again?" Rita asked her when she looked over her shoulder for the fifth time as they set out napkins. "You're worse than usual today."

"Sorry," she said. But she knew, somehow, that her feeling was more than imagination.

As the event began, she tried to distract herself by enjoying the costumes people came in— everything from panda bears to playing cards—and ignore the sense of unreality that was growing around her.

Then it happened—the first scent of real fear passed by her. She went rigid, and didn't quite know why. She had just handed a program to a man in an executioner's mask, and he had taken it without even glancing at her. Now she realized that the large broad shoulders disappearing into the crowd were too familiar.

Her heart began beating fast and her palms began to sweat as she passed out more programs and tried to work her way back to normality. Somehow.

* * *

II

Leon was still riding the train, praying that his guardian angel would alert him when Bonnie got off, as he kept talking with the teenagers and looking out the windows when the train stopped. So far no one.

The teenagers finally got off at the Grand Concourse, and Leon recollected himself and wondered if he had broken his vow of obedience by coming out this far, and furthermore, was Bonnie even still on this train? By now the el train had dived underground, and had crossed the river to Manhattan Island.

Praying a general rosary for Nora, for Bonnie, and the teenagers he had just talked to, he stood poised by the door as the train grudgingly slowed its speed to stop at 96th Street. Again, he watched the leaving passengers, more anxiously, because the crowds were larger downtown. Out of the corner of his eye, he saw a bright blue something bobbing through the crowds exiting from the very first car.

He dodged after it. But just as he was closing in, he realized his mistake. This hat was worn by a twelve-year-old boy. He halted, deflated, scanned the crowds and saw, unambiguously this time, the fluorescent blue stocking hat and black trench coat quickly hurrying up the steps aboveground.

Now he pushed through the turnstiles, sprinted to the steps and hurried up, apologizing to the people he pushed ahead of. But by the time he reached the street, the crowds were massive, even on a hot Saturday afternoon. For a while he turned one way and then the other, but there was no sign of the old lady.

It took him some time to beg for another token and get on the subway back home to the friary. All the way home, he felt slightly foolish. He was somewhat gratified to find the two dogs sitting by the el train station waiting for him.

"Sorry, I couldn't find her," he said, rubbing their heads. "Come on, better get back to our home."

By the time he got back, it was past lunch, but apparently no one had eaten. He was told that Nora was fine, but resting. The rest of the community was gathered in the library of the friary. Brother George was fixing one of the bookshelves, which had suddenly cracked in two under the weight of an ancient copy of *The Encyclopedia of Franciscan History*. Matt was holding up one end for him. Brother Herman and Father Bernard sat on the battered couch, and Father Francis pontificated from a creaking rocking chair.

Leon went straight to Father Bernard, knelt down, and asked forgiveness for leaving the friary without permission. Then he explained why, as the rest of the community listened.

"Well, this is a puzzle now," Father Bernard said, after forgiving Leon. "Apparently one of our volunteers is being stalked by a homeless lady."

"If she is a homeless lady," Matt said. "I'm having my doubts."

"Well, she can move quick enough when she wants to," Leon said. "And apparently she has enough money to take the train too."

"Nora herself is a mystery," Father Bernard said, stroking his beard. "Has she told any of you anything about herself? About her family?"

"A bit of a mystery? She's a complete unknown!" Brother George snorted, banging irritably on the end of the bookshelf. "Even if she does dress nice, she landed on our doorstep with about as much background as any one of our homeless guests!"

"But she is a hard worker," Brother Herman said. "She's been a tremendous help this past week."

"What do you think, Father Francis?" Matt asked.

"I think," Father Francis raised his bushy eyebrows as he looked at his little community, "that we should invite her up to join us for a late lunch. Since we happen to all be here today."

All the others stared at him.

"She'll tell us when she's ready," Father Francis said calmly. "Right now, I think she needs to get her mind off of things. And I think we should expend some energy towards helping her do that."

One by one, the others nodded.

Father Bernard went down to Nora with the invitation, and Brother Herman served up the pea soup that he had been cooking that morning, while the others set the table and got things ready.

Nora came up to join them a bit uneasily, wearing her yellow dress again. But the company quickly put her at ease as they shared the meal together.

"So all the work we've been piling on you hasn't driven you away yet, eh?" Father Francis said to her.

"No, not at all. It's refreshing. I feel like a farm girl again," she confessed.

"What, did you grow up on a farm?" Brother Matt asked with interest. He alone among the friars had grown up in the country, in the Midwest.

"Well, a small one. My mom and dad had one in upstate New Jersey, a small town called Warwick. We had chickens and a garden. I guess we liked to think of it as a farm."

There! Background information. Brother Leon nodded at Brother George, who nevertheless was still eating his soup with a dismal frown.

"And now here you are, in the big city," Father Bernard shook his head. "Quite different!"

"Yes. Oh, we'd always had connections with the City—my mom grew up here, and when my dad died, we moved back. But I'm glad I didn't have my childhood here."

Brother Leon considered this, glancing around at the others. "Ah, it's not so bad. I grew up in Harlem myself."

"Wasn't that rough?"

"I guess you kind of get used to it," Brother Leon admitted. "You got to play in wide open fields. My cousins and I played on trash heaps. We never knew what we were missing."

Brother Charley nodded sagely. "Lots of city kids are that way. I had a friend who moved to Arkansas. After three weeks she came back to Yonkers. She said the quiet just drove her nuts. And she was terrified of the snakes and the bugs."

Nora chuckled. "She'd rather deal with muggers and boom boxes?"

Brother Charley shared her amusement. "Yep. That was what she knew. People can learn to live with just about anything."

"Including a lot of things they should never have to live with in the first place," Father Francis said.

Everyone nodded their heads. The results of the evil of societal breakdown were all around them, and too many—especially children—grew up accepting that the kind of abuse they lived with was normal.

"Well, that's why the Lord sent us here," Father Francis said briskly after a moment. "Blessed be His name. Speaking of which, how are plans going for the Feast of the Assumption tomorrow?" He turned to Father Bernard.

"We're having a party for the neighborhood people," Father Bernard explained to Nora, and cleared his throat. "At noon, we'll have a procession with the Blessed Sacrament around the block, and pray the rosary when we return to the church. Then, refreshments in the courtyard. Brother Charley has been stockpiling Danishes and doughnuts from the local bakeries. I think we've managed to get some juice—Brother Matt is picking it up tomorrow from the Knights of Columbus. That's about it."

"What about something for the kids?" Brother Leon asked. "I mean, they'll love the procession and the doughnuts, but isn't there something we can do for them?"

"I haven't had any brilliant ideas," confessed Father Bernard. "I mean, it's not like it's Christmas and we can have the novices put on Santa Claus costumes and clown around. It's a bit more serious."

"What about a play?" Brother Matt asked, suddenly inspired. "We could put on a short play on the church steps, like they did in the Middle Ages."

"All right, you novices come up with something," Father Bernard said. "Something about Mary would be good."

"And which of them is going to be Mary?" Father Francis asked, sipping his coffee with his eyebrows raised.

"Nora!" the three novices chorused, and Nora looked up from her soup bowl to find all eyes on her.

"That is, if you want to," Matt said, embarrassed.

She paused, and swallowed the food in her mouth. "I'm not an actress."

"That's fine. None of us are actors," Leon assured her.

"Wait, but what are we going to do? Act out Mary's Assumption?" Brother Charley scratched his head. "Uh, that might be a bit complicated."

"No problem!" Leon said expansively. "We'll hook up a pulley to Brother Herman's scaffold and have Nora raised up into the heavens...how does that sound, Nora?"

"Perhaps something a little less ambitious," Nora said softly as the others chuckled.

"I've got it," Father Francis said suddenly. "Why not the story of Our Lady of Guadalupe? There are a lot of Hispanics in this neighborhood. They'll love it."

"Fantastic! That way, all you have to do is appear, Nora, and hand Juan Diego a bunch of roses." Matt pointed to an image on the wall. "Can you dress up like the image that appeared on Juan Diego's tilma?" he asked.

They all turned to look at the picture of Mary, dressed in a cloak covered with stars, standing on a crescent moon, rays of the sun coming out all around her.

"She's dressed as an Aztec princess," Brother Leon said. He had always loved that picture, especially Mary's mild face.

"I can do the narration," said Matt. "Charley, you be the bishop. And Leon can be Juan Diego."

"We don't have to be too fancy with costumes, but I can do some things. Nora, what do you have in the storeroom?" Brother Herman asked. "If you get me a sheet for a poncho, I can sketch Our Lady on it. Leon, you can wear it inside out until the scene with the bishop. Then you can step offstage and reverse it. Then when you come on to see the bishop, you can empty out the roses at his feet and voila!" he gestured.

"That would be great!" Leon enthused.

"And if you can find me something like a blue sheet, I could paint stars on it, and that would work for a mantle for you, Nora," Brother Herman went on.

"I think there is a pale blue sheet there, actually," Nora nodded, still looking unsure.

"*Hermano* Herman, you could use the canvas from your drop cloths for a poncho," Brother Leon suggested.

"What about that monstrous pink dress?" Nora asked suddenly, turning to Leon. "That might make a good robe for Our Lady. I think it'll fit me—it's huge, but I could belt it."

"With a purple or black sash," Brother Herman said.

"There's a bunch of old neckties—I can use one of those," Nora said. She sighed. "All right, you win. I'll do it."

"Hurray!" the novices cheered.

They were such an odd company—a half dozen or so bearded men in gray and one black and white girl, seated round a rough table in a squalid kitchen. But from the roars of unchecked laughter that engulfed them, it was evident that there was a unique bond melding. A ring of plain metal set with the jewel of a girl.

Yes, it was unusual, Brother Leon reflected. It would not last—there was little practical way Nora could remain with them. But the image was a lasting one, and he tucked it away in his store of memory as an unusual glint of light from the Kingdom of Heaven, God's odd reflection.

"Well, thank you for lunch. Let me see if I can find the dress," Nora said after they had prayed grace after meals.

"And the blue sheet," said Brother Herman.

Brother Leon followed them out to the vestibule, and halted in admiration at the neat stacks of folded trousers and shirts, and the rows of coats hanging from pipes fitted into the niches on the sides.

"This looks great!" he said. "It must have been a lot of work."

"I was happy to do it," Nora said, sorting through a handful of ties that were hanging from a wire hanger bent into a loop. "Here's a blue one—and a purple one."

"Where's that sheet?" Brother Herman asked.

"Over there with the dresses," Nora said. "I threw everything that wasn't men's clothing over here." Brother Herman began to dig through a pile that represented the last bit of the former chaos.

Leon was still shaking his head. "It's neat to see how your hours of work have paid off—" he was saying, when suddenly Brother Herman stopped with a puzzled look. He fished in the pile and pulled out a crumpled brown paper bag. "What's this?"

"Oh, that's just some junk jewelry and loose buttons I found among the other things," Nora said dismissively. But when Brother Herman emptied some of the contents into his hand, she paused. Leon stared. Inside the bag were dozens of pink, green, and white pills.

III

In the crisscrossing madness of Grand Central, Bear almost lost the man, but he caught a glimpse of him strolling down the ramps to the Metro North trains. On this lazy Saturday afternoon, the commuter rails were nearly deserted, so Bear had to be more careful. He slowed his steps and paused by a bank of ticket machines, keeping his eyes on the man. His target meandered up and down several terminals before choosing the Harlem line.

Bear slipped down to the platform when the man's back was turned, and waited behind a pillar, wondering if he should just go up and speak to the man in this public place. But before he could act, a train pulled up, and the man got in the first car, which was empty. A crowd of day-camp kids surged down to the platforms, their counselors shouting, "Hurry! Everyone stay together!" Bear joined their melee as they piled into the second car of the train. No one else got on.

The camp kids shouted and ran around the car as the counselors tried to get them to sit down. Making his way through them, Bear walked to the front of the car and squinted through the Plexiglas windows of the barrel doors at the front of the car. He couldn't see much, but he could see the broad-shouldered shape of the man. It looked like he was sitting down, reading a paper.

A conductor walked through the car and Bear bought a ticket for White Plains. As the train started with a burst of air that sounded like a dragon gasping, Bear sat down, giving one last look at the man's black cloth-covered shoulders. Only New Yorkers would wear black in this heat.

Emerging into the artificial daylight of the Harlem station, the train deposited the day camp kids. The big man didn't move. Neither did Bear. Now the train was empty, except for himself and the man. Bear wondered if the man knew he was being followed.

Through the darkness of the underground the train surged, and Bear looked out the window next to him. His eyes focused on his own reflection upon black. No other reality was present, just the man in black and himself on a train speeding out of the underbelly of the City. The phantom of Blanche, the white and black girl he was seeking, hovered in his thoughts. Maybe they were both seeking her.

The cell phone rang, and he answered it automatically. "Fish?"

"Where are you? Where is my phone? I'm still at the banquet hall, reduced to asking to use their phone. Rita said you left."

"I'm following the man on a train heading North to Hartsdale."

His brother groaned. "I *knew* something like this would happen if we split up. Okay, what's your position?"

"Uh, we're getting towards Melrose, I think," Bear said, glancing at a train map he had picked up.

"All right. I'll get Rose off to her house, and then I'll drive up that way as soon as I can."

"Right." Bear hung up, and focused again on his quarry as the train emerged from the tunnel into daylight. A sun boiled somewhere in the haze in the vaguely western end of the City. They were coming to a station.

The big shoulders stood up and started to move. Like the shadow that he was, Bear watched him go, and then followed.

The man hurried down the steps of the train platform to the parking lot, his paper rolled in his hand like a truncheon. But as Bear walked down the steps, he saw the man pounding up the staircase that led to the other side of the platform as a southbound train pulled into the station. The big man was doubling back on his trail.

Slowly Bear crossed to the staircase as the man vanished over the top. Tense, he waited at the base of the steps, listening as the train screeched to a stop. Then he slowly climbed up the steps until he could look over the edge of the platform. There he got a glimpse of the man getting onto the train. The third car.

Bear took a deep breath and waited. The conductor made his last call for passengers, signaled the engineer, and the four-car train started to leave. Bear hurried up the steps as the train began to pull away, and sprinting, grabbed the door handle and leapt onto the last car just as it cleared the platform.

"You shouldn't do that!" the conductor reprimanded him. "Very dangerous!"

"Sorry," Bear said, pulling out his wallet and buying another ticket.

He knew he had better call Fish again and tell him he was now heading in the opposite direction, but first he wanted to locate his quarry. Moving through the empty car in the same direction as the train, Bear opened the barrel door in the front of the train and stepped onto the small platform between the cars. A rubber diaphragm kept him from falling between the cars to the tracks, which clattered beneath his feet. The yellowed plastic of the next car's window was too opaque to see through, so Bear cracked the door. The car was empty, except for his prey.

Then the train roared into the tunnel again and all was black.

He cracked the door again as they rushed deeper into the tunnel. The man was moving. He was walking forward to the front of the car and yanking something red. For a moment, Bear wondered what he was doing, but then there was a long wheeze of compressed air and the cars clanked together harshly beneath Bear's feet. Grabbing the safety handles on the back of the car, he realized the train was coming quickly to a halt. The emergency break had been pulled and the train was stopping...

The train was several hundred yards into the twilight of the tunnel entrance. Bear could make out arches beside the track, running by swiftly but more and more slowly as the train ground to a halt. He looked back at the man, and saw he was pulling the door handle to open the door. Then he was gone.

Bear immediately guessed what had happened. The man knew he was still being tailed, and was trying to lose his pursuer in a most unconventional manner.

And most people, Bear thought, would give up the chase at this point. He didn't like the look of the tunnel himself. *But there was Blanche—*

With a bare pause, he crashed through the barrel door into the car, yanked open the back door and jumped out into the hot roar of the dragon's cave.

The noise outside the train was horrendous, and Bear got away from it as fast as he could. He went with his instincts: that the man was switching directions again and running towards the tunnel entrance.

Black on black is nearly impossible to see, but Bear tried to orient himself. He made out the third rail, a metal cable to his left running parallel to the tracks, with the words DANGER 700 VOLTS spray painted on it at regular intervals. He could make out the light from the north end of the tunnel, a barely-seen glow, and started towards it, giving the cable a wide berth. The row of archways was to his right, and beyond them were two other train tracks with more pillars and arches in between. The tunnel must be some kind of merge point for several rail lines.

He caught sight of a figure against the light running down the tracks, and started after him, ducking from pillar to pillar so that he couldn't be seen, if the man turned around. The ground was made up of fist-sized rocks, which made it difficult to keep his footing.

Eventually the train they had left behind started again and was gone in a streak of rattling thunder.

Now Bear paused behind a pillar, listening in the sudden vacuum of deafness, which turned into the silence of an echo. The man had vanished. But after a moment Bear had regained his hearing enough to hear rapid, jumping footsteps to his right. He had crossed over to another set of tracks. Reeling himself in towards the sound, Bear dodged around the pillars, zigzagging back and forth towards his prey.

The next time he paused, he realized he had lost it. He froze and edged behind a pillar of concrete, feeling around the edges in the dark and peering towards the late afternoon light at the end of the tunnel, about two hundred yards ahead. The rest of the tunnel was thick with shadows, but nothing moved.

He waited. Waited. Waited for the man to make the first move.

Then he heard the footsteps again, from a dark area to his left. He shot a brief glance around the pillar but saw nothing and retreated. The man was making his way from pillar to pillar just as Bear had done. And the steps were growing closer.

I can wait, he thought to himself. *I can wait.*

He heard breathing. The man must be very close now, and Bear was aware, now that he was close to him, of just how big the man actually was. He swallowed silently.

Just at that moment a high ringing noise started in his jacket pocket. The cell phone. Bear reached to silence it, and was grabbed by the shoulders. He was pulled around the side of the pillar and pinned against it by his neck.

Recovering with a curse at the timing of the phone, Bear swung back at his assailant's face with his right fist, but the man easily blocked it with an elbow. Ludicrously, the phone continued to ring.

Bear then yanked his left hand from his pocket and rammed it into his assailant's gut. The man tried to knee Bear in the stomach, but Bear blocked him and, crossing his wrists, broke the man's hold on his neck. The man stumbled backwards, and Bear, freed, charged him, throwing his weight against the man's waist and shoving him to the right to avoid the third line. If either of them hit that, they would both be dead.

But the man wasn't thrown. Instead, both of his fists came down hard on Bear's back. Gasping, off-balance, Bear let go of him, rolled over, barely avoiding the live line, and scrambled to his feet, breathing hard.

This guy knows something about street fighting, Bear thought. He shifted to the side of the tracks furthest from the cable but kept his eyes on the man, waiting for the telltale motion that meant the man was reaching for a concealed weapon. If that happened, Bear only had an instant to rush the man before the scales tipped decidedly in the assailant's favor.

The man leapt forward with a jab, and Bear batted it and lunged with his right. The man dodged, but Bear nicked him on the right side of the face, and heard the man curse. The man punched Bear in the ribs, and Bear rammed his elbows down onto the man's back.

The man slid behind him, tripped up Bear's legs, and drove his elbow into Bear's face. Feeling himself falling, Bear grabbed the man's sleeve under his arm and yanked him over as he fell. He landed on his back in the gravel, and heard the man land next to him. Instinctively they both rolled away from the third line.

No time to lose. Bear scrambled to his feet, slipping on the oily rocks, searching once again for his enemy. He saw the man make the signal motion inside his jacket—he *did* have a weapon—

No time. Bear lunged for the man's right arm, yanking it downward hard. The man's hand was empty—Bear had stopped him from grabbing his weapon—but the empty hand became a fist that rammed hard against Bear's stomach, shoving him against a pillar. Caught off guard by the force of the man's drive, Bear's lungs froze inside him. He felt a sharp blow to his face, and his head flew back to smash against the concrete behind him.

Stunned, Bear felt his body crumpling to the ground. He fought off unconsciousness, but the fight itself turned into a paralysis. He felt himself being frisked. Then the man stooped over him, yanked his hands backwards, and handcuffed him. The touch of the cold metal made Bear stiffen, and he fought back, even though his head still swirled in the blackness.

The man grabbed him by the scruff of the neck and shoved his head to the ground on the train tracks. His ear pressed to the cement of the railroad tie, Bear could see the live cable a few inches away from him.

The man's voice was deep. "Listen, punk, you better explain yourself quick before the next train gets here and interrupts you."

Chapter Seventeen

 he girl stared at the pills, and the whole purpose that the bag lady had served suddenly came into focus. *I thought I'd eluded her,* she thought.
But actually she was just biding her time…

* * *

It was a wild party, and the energy crept beyond the guests in their black-and-white costumes and spread to the servers. Rita snapped her fingers as she leaned against the wall, waiting for people to come by her table for more desserts, and even the staff in the heat of the kitchen seemed a bit more animated by the music.

The girl felt she was the only one who was a stranger here. She didn't care for the atmosphere or the music, which was a wild, tumultuous jazz without boundaries that was echoed in the almost spastic movements of the people who danced on the floor and chattered at the tables. Strobe lights flickered on and off against the gothic ceiling of the hall, turning the floor below into a world flashing alternately from black to white. The girl, the only one in a colored outfit, felt more out of place in this world, although her dress was now effectively white.

At last it occurred to her that, as all the guests had arrived and the tickets had been tallied, she could probably leave her place at the door. After all, the dinner was over and there was only dancing on the schedule. She had noticed other receptionists usually left after the last guests arrived, but it had been her practice to remain loyally at her post in case she was needed before the event ended. But tonight, she decided she was going to leave.

Edging along the wall between the tables and assorted guests, she tried to make her way to the door that led back to the workroom, where the servers could rest between shifts. It was not a place she enjoyed staying, but right now it seemed like a sanctuary.

Just then a hand grabbed hers. "Hey, wanna dance?" a male voice said, and she found herself looking into the face of a toucan. Actually, a man dressed in a tuxedo with an oversized toucan's mask.

She didn't want to dance, but any protest she could have made was deafened in that crowd. The man flung her forward into a reeling juggling match that was one part dance and three parts craziness. At first she tried to keep up with him, to be polite, wondering if she would get in more trouble for dancing or for stopping. But when he started trying to pull her closer, she seized a chance and dove beneath the arms of two swinging salt-and-pepper shakers and away from him.

By now she was in the middle of the sea of dancers, and she tried to fight her way out as quickly as she could. Then she saw him.

The big man, still wearing his black hood, was leaning against the wall. When her eyes fixed on him, he seemed to look straight at her. He leaned forward and started walking in her direction.

Numbly, feeling the fear, she turned and ran through the dancers. *Why am I running?* she thought to herself. But having walked the fine line of sanity and fear for days, she wasn't going to stop because of an unanswered question. Suddenly she reached the edge of the head table, and without thinking, ducked underneath the floor-length tablecloth.

In the darkness beneath the table, she tried to recollect herself. *He's coming for me.* It was running through her mind. *He's coming for me.*

I have to get out of here now.

Crouching on her hands and knees, she scuttled down the long length of table, avoiding the occasional leg, heading towards the narrow door in the back wall that led to the prep rooms. She reached the door, looked in both directions, and still ducking down, slipped through it.

Once the door was closed behind her, muffling the deafening beat, she got to her feet, taking a deep breath, and tried to brush back the strands of hair that had escaped from her long braid. *Now even I am starting to act strange, not just think strange...*

"Blanche!" Assunta, one of the servers, called her name and she pivoted around, startled.

"Yes?"

"Have you seen the cash bag? The one with the donations?"

The girl shook her head. "Not since I handed it off to Mr. Scarlotti a half hour ago."

"So you don't know where it is?"

"Ask Mr. Scarlotti. He took it from me," she said helplessly. Her head was throbbing. "I've got a headache. I'm going home."

"Okay. See you later." The server disappeared into the kitchen corridor.

Rubbing her temples, the girl made her way towards the workroom, hoping it was still open and that she could just slip out and go home.

When she opened the door, she was surprised to find someone in the room. Mr. Fairston's wife, head of the Mirror Corporation. Standing near the corner where the girl's purse and backpack were.

"Is something wrong?" the girl asked tentatively.

The blond woman was dressed in a black dress with white diamonds on it, and wore long white gloves. Earlier in the evening, the girl remembered that she had been wearing a tall white crown. Now, her golden hair falling in tendrils around her neck, she turned towards the girl, a set look on her face. "Yes. There is."

She walked over and sat on the edge of the table, surrounded by scraps of black and white ribbon. "I want to talk to you."

"All right," the girl said, and waited.

But the woman said nothing. Instead, she picked up a tumbler of dark soda that had been sitting near her, put something in her mouth in a quick dabbing motion, and downed it with the drink. She licked her lips, staring at the wall.

"Are you all right?" the girl asked.

"I have a headache," the woman said.

"I'm sorry," the girl said. *So do I*, she almost added, but remained quiet.

There was a long silence, while the woman drank the rest of the soda and stared at the wall.

"I want to talk to you about Jack," the wife said at last.

The girl waited.

"He wants to die, you know." She wiped her mouth and licked her lips again. "He doesn't want to wait until he's feeble and incapacitated. We planned it together. Our last night together. Then he's going to go. We had it all planned out. It's in his will."

"You mean, he's going to commit suicide?"

The woman nodded. "It was his idea. It took me a while to get used to it, but that's what he wants. The problem is," she looked at the girl sideways. "Now he's afraid to do it, because he thinks you won't approve."

"Approve? Of course I don't approve," the girl said, her mind racing. "Are you saying he's changed his mind?"

"He's confused," the woman said flatly. "He's upset. It's disorienting him." She turned around. Her eyes bored into the girl's. "I need you to support his decision to end his life."

The girl took a deep breath. "I can't. I don't believe it's right."

The woman slammed her fist into the table with vehemence. "I knew this would happen. I knew it, as soon as you started visiting him." Suddenly she glared at the girl with virulent hatred and growled in a deep, strange voice. "I'm sick of your games. I'm sick of it!"

Sweat was standing out on the woman's forehead. The girl knew instinctively that something was wrong with her, very wrong, and tried to run for the door. But the woman lunged at her shoulders, threw her down on the table, snatched up the scissors, and held them to the girl's throat like a dagger.

Pinned down, gazing at the shining silver blades, the girl struggled to stay calm as her heart painfully skipped. The woman leaned over her, hissing, her pupils large, dark holes of emptiness. "I'm so tired of your games, your lies, your little—"

"Let go of me," the girl tried to speak calmly. "Let go of me, Mrs. Fairston, you're not well."

For an answer, the older woman shoved her to one side, and the girl fought out of her grasp and tried to move away. But the woman snarled and pinned the side of her head down to the table.

"I'll teach you to try to steal my husband," she breathed, and drove down with the scissors open.

There was a horrible *smack* right next to her head, cold steel against the back of her neck, and the girl screamed into the woman's gloved hand. With a tremendous effort, she rolled away and fell off the edge of the table on the floor, light-headed and dizzy.

"Stay away from my husband!" the woman rasped. "Not so beautiful now, are you? What are you, but a conniving little tramp—"

It took a moment for the girl to realize what had happened, and that was only when she saw her braid spilling onto the floor from the table. Her hair was gone. Mrs. Fairston had cut off her hair. The black rope tumbled to the floor like a dead thing.

The woman stood over her, breathing hard, her eyes glazed over, her jaw twitching. The girl became aware of a nasty sound. Mrs. Fairston was grinding her teeth, over and over again. The girl's spine shriveled at the noise.

Suddenly the woman moaned and buried her head in her hands. She looked down at the scissors and then at the girl, and seemed to recollect herself.

Sinking to the ground, the woman crawled to her, seized her head, and patted it frantically. "I'm sorry. I didn't mean to do that—I don't know what came over me—This has been so hard on me—all this with Jack—I've said things I didn't mean to say—it's the stress—it's crushing me—"

She drew Blanche to her feet, picked up Blanche's purse, and pushed it into the girl's hands, all the while gazing into her eyes. "But Blanche, stay away. Stay away."

Trembling, the girl got to her feet, her cut hair disheveled and falling over her face, but not taking her eyes off the older woman, who had started to smile again at something that wasn't there. The grinding sound began again. The beautiful woman was staring at the fluorescent lights of the ceiling and grinding her teeth with a horrible smile on her face.

The girl's hands grasped the door, opened it, and she fled down the shadowy corridor, like a rabbit running from a mad dog.

She turned a corner and tumbled into his arms. He caught her by the shoulders and she found herself looking up at him. The big man. The stalker.

"Please, let me go," she whispered, struggling and realizing that she was immobilized. "Please. I need to go home. Please."

It was the oddest thing in the world. Something changed on his face and he released her with a mumbled, "Excuse me." She didn't know why. Maybe he didn't recognize her, with her hair short, in the dark corridor.

For whatever reason, he let her go and she shot away, not trusting for a second chance. Even though she realized she had forgotten her backpack, she wasn't going back to get it now. Her only refuge was the night.

Through the night she darted, her feet pounding the sidewalk, to the train home.

It was only when she had left the train and gotten on the subway that she opened her purse and discovered the bills hidden in the bottom. Thousands of dollars in her purse. At first she wondered if it was a bribe. And then she realized what had just happened. Her actions had transformed her into a criminal. She was trapped on the other side of the looking-glass.

* * *

II

"That's Ecstasy," Leon said, touching the pills.

"And quite a bit of it," Brother Herman said. "How—?"

Nora sank to the ground, a defeated look on her face. "Are you going to turn me in?" she whispered.

"Hold on!" Leon said, pulling her to her feet. "Nora, what's going on here? What do you mean?"

Nora gave a shaky laugh that turned into a sob. "I'm not sure I can explain. I don't know if I understand it myself. First it was the money. I mean someone planted thousands of dollars in my purse—that's what was stolen on the subway. Now, it looks like I'm being framed for drug possession." She took a deep breath. "That's why Bonnie knocked me out with the choker. She was planting the drugs here. I bet she put them in my room too."

"Why would she do that?" Leon asked.

Nora avoided his eyes. "I don't know exactly why, but she's been trying to ruin me. She must be connected to the money thing, too, somehow."

"So she wasn't here to take something—she was here to leave something," Brother Herman said.

Nora looked from one to the other. "Do you believe me?" she asked, almost incredulously.

Leon understood what she was asking. After all, she was a stranger in the wilderness of the City where it was normal to lie, cheat, and steal. He took a deep breath. "I believe you, Nora," he said simply.

"I don't know if you should. I could be a con artist. I could be tricking you all—" Nora rubbed her eyes. "Oh, this is irony. I used to be the one who didn't trust anyone. If I were you, I would throw me out right now."

Brother Herman laughed. "We specialize in foolishness around here," he said, and patted her shoulder. "We believe you."

"And, of course, we still want you to be Mary in the play for the Assumption celebration tomorrow," Brother Leon added, folding his arms. He couldn't resist teasing. "If this was all a stunt you pulled to get out of the part—"

She had to laugh. "No, no, it's not." Then she burst into tears and she sobbed. "Thank you. Thank you so much. You're going to think this is silly but—you all have saved my life."

III

Bear tried to thrash himself backwards, but the man had him pressed down against the rocks by the neck.

"You going to talk?"

"Maybe if you let me go," Bear managed to say.

The man released his neck, and Bear, aching from the fight, twisted around in the handcuffs. He could see the man was pointing a heavy revolver at him. "Who are you?" Bear demanded.

"If I wanted you to know, I'd have worn a name tag," the man leered at him. "Heard about you. You call yourself the Bear, right? Going down for two counts of drug possession. Caught red-handed in your apartment. Stupid of you, kid."

"How did you know that?"

"I've got my sources. So why are you following me, Teddy-Bear?"

The anger inside Bear welled up dangerously and he leaned forward. "Where is Blanche Brier?"

The man was momentarily thrown. "Who?"

"Don't fool with me. You've been stalking her. Admit it." Bear demanded.

"I don't know what you're talking about," the man said derisively.

Bear was mad enough now to not care. "Yeah sure you don't, liar. You've been following her. And she's missing. What did you do with her?"

"Who you calling a liar?" the man squeezed Bear's face. "Listen, freak, you better not accuse me of stalking. I don't mess with girls that way. Especially not girls like that—"

"You do know her, don't you?" Bear said quietly. "Why were you following her? If your motives were honorable, you shouldn't have a problem telling me that."

The man's face was still unreadable, but he paused. Then he pulled Bear off the tracks away from the live cable and rolled him backwards against the base of the archway dividing the tracks. Bear kicked at the rocky ground to shove himself upright and fixed his eyes on the man's face.

The man said briefly, "She's a drug courier."

"Then you're an undercover cop," Bear said. "Or else, why would you care?"

"Oh! Smart kid. I used to be an undercover cop, but my work was a bit too creative for the NYPD."

"You're a private investigator?"

"Close, Ted. Let's say I'm a freelancer."

"Why do you think Blanche is a drug courier?" Bear asked.

"You should know that better than me, freak," he said. "Heard you were the supplier for the drug ring at the banquet hall and you were using her for delivery work."

Bear asked scornfully, "I suppose an anonymous source told you that, right?"

"So?" he returned. "We get anonymous tips all the time."

"So you've been stalking Blanche—oh, pardon me, *shadowing* Blanche— to find out if she was delivering drugs for me. You found lots of evidence, right? A girl who spends her spare time visiting nursing homes? Come on. If you're really an old hand at this, you can't tell me she fits your profile."

The man was unmoved. "They did find drugs in her backpack, and at other drop-off points."

"Did you ever see her actually handling or dropping off the drugs? Anyone could have put them there. Did it ever occur to you she would be a terrific fall girl for a real criminal to use?"

"Yes, actually, it has occurred to me," the man conceded grudgingly.

"Well, you scared her pretty badly. She told her co-worker she was being followed and then, not long after, she just vanished the night of the masquerade ball. Then you showed up on my tail, and her co-workers fingered you as the guy who had been following her around, and who they saw in the corridors the night of the ball."

"My source said she was going to be picking up a large shipment that night. I was going to intercept her."

"Oh, so did you? Did you catch her making a transaction?"

"No. But the police found the drugs. Same as last time."

"But you didn't actually see her doing anything with them?"

"No."

Bear could not keep the sarcasm out of his voice. "So why are you spending so much time investigating a pretty unpromising rumor? Or are you new to this job after all?"

The man put his face close to Bear's. "For your information, the next time the source called, I told them not to waste my time."

"You mean you were starting to think that maybe Blanche was innocent, and that someone was trying to set her up?"

"Yeah. The whole thing was just a bit strange," the man said. "Besides, I got new orders to keep an eye on you, as we were told that you might bolt town. That's what I was doing when you started getting too nosy."

A rumble turned into a roar as a train sped by in the tracks to the far left. The man clapped his hands to his ears, and Bear huddled against the pillar, trying to shield himself from the noise. Moments later, the train was gone.

The man shook his head, and pulled Bear to his feet. "Okay, start walking. The name's J.D. Hunter. I work for the Drug Enforcement Administration and I'm taking you in."

"In? For what?"

"For assault."

Bear snorted. "Oh, sure, like *I* assaulted you. As I recall, you started it."

Hunter gave him a hard look. "You were sneaking up on me in a dark tunnel. I was finding out what you were up to."

"I didn't understand your curiosity," Bear said evenly. "I was just defending myself."

"When you hit back, I was sure you were armed," Hunter said reflectively. "But then you didn't have a weapon. You either have a lot of guts or a lack of brains to fight that way."

"It's the way I learned in prison," Bear said. "We didn't have weapons there."

"Oh! Prison!" the man said. "Didn't see that on your record. Juvenile record?"

"It was wiped clean. I was locked up on false charges," Bear said. "History lesson. You don't have time to hear it now."

Hunter looked him over again. "Some history. You just go looking for trouble?"

"Not unless I have to. But you were my lead to find Blanche. I didn't know if I'd have another chance to find out where she is," Bear said. "Her family and I have been searching for her for almost a week."

The man paused. "Look, I told you I didn't feel right about the allegations against the girl. You—I still don't know about you. But you're right—the girl just isn't the type. I'm willing to let this pass, for now, despite the charge against you. But I warn you, it's more because of her than because of you."

"I understand," Bear said.

Hunter undid the handcuffs, and Bear rubbed his wrists. "You better not make me regret this, kid," the agent warned.

"I won't," Bear said.

"And some professional advice: next time you follow someone into a dark tunnel with no weapon on you," Hunter paused before he started to walk away, "turn off your cell phone."

Bear felt his face grow hot, but he nodded. "Yeah. Thanks for the tip."

Hunter made his way out of the tunnel, but Bear, too embarrassed to see the man in daylight, pulled out the offending phone and called Fish.

"Snow White shall die!"
cried the queen, "even if
it should cost me my life!"
Grimm

Chapter Eighteen

He will have pity on the weak
And save the lives of the poor.

She knows where I am, the girl thought to herself, as she toyed with the faded red ribbon on the prayer book as the friars intoned Evening Prayer. *So why doesn't she just call the police and have me arrested?*

She must be afraid to, because she thinks I know too much.

So what is it that I know?

After prayer, she tentatively made her way down the aisle, step by step, to the sacristy. There she leaned against the closet door and looked at the Sisterhood, standing quietly in the sunset-colored light.

What should I do?

Again, she walked among the statues, feeling a surge of affection for the dilapidated images. In this place where she had no female friends, they took the place of womanly comrades. She remembered how Brother Leon had been singing to the statues, and pondered that. From the back corner, the woman with the lyre beckoned to her with outstretched palm, and Nora went up to her and looked in her frank glass eyes. On the plaster hand lay the white medicine bottle that the girl had taken from Mr. Fairston's room.

Perplexed, the girl picked it up again, remembering that she had put it there the night she had come to the church during the rainstorm and talked to Brother Leon. She looked at the bottle again. No label, and two white pills inside. *If I had more nursing experience, maybe I'd understand what this is,* she thought to herself. Sighing, she put it back in the hand of the saint's image. *Hold onto it for me just a bit longer, St. Cecelia. Thanks.*

193

Frustrated, she put her hands in the pockets of her jeans and felt around for her door key.

It was gone.

Worried, she checked the chain on her neck, but there were only two keys on it, the key Bear had given her to St. Lawrence and the key to the Fairston home. No, she was sure she had put the door key right back in her pocket last time she had used it, right before she had encountered Bonnie...

....So she did take something after all.

That means she's planning to come back.

II

"Nora, you have got to be even more careful," Leon said to her when she told him as they were going into dinner. "Have the dogs sleep in front of your door, okay?"

"Okay, I will."

He felt frustrated with her, that she wouldn't tell them more about what her situation was. She had told them some of her story, but clearly, not everything. *Now I have to take my own advice,* he said to himself. *Trust.*

It was Saturday night, and according to the Church's liturgical calendar, Sunday had begun. It was also the eve of the Assumption, and an air of festive solemnity reigned. After dinner in the refectory, the community gathered in the library together. Father Francis gave Nora a seat on the rocking chair, and the others sat around in various places. Brother Herman passed out cups of tea and the inevitable day-old baked goods.

"Nora," Father Francis said, "would you consider going to the police about this whole matter?"

"Believe me, I've been wondering that again and again," Nora admitted, pushing back her hair. "But I think I need to wait."

"What are you waiting for, if it's not too much to ask?" Father Francis queried, putting down his tea.

"Well, for one thing, my family should be home from vacation on Tuesday. But more than that even, I'm waiting for someone," she said steadily. "My boyfriend. He should be back from Europe soon, and I'm pretty sure that he'll know what to do. He's kind of been in this situation before." She looked at Brother Herman. "And I've decided to believe in him." The white-bearded artist friar smiled.

"All right," Father Francis said, and lifted his cup back up to his lips. "You tell us if you need any help before then."

"Can I ask you all for your opinion on something?" Nora said abruptly, staring at her teacup. "I've been debating about whether or not to finish college. Because—well, I guess I'm thinking about that M.R.S. degree," she admitted, blushing. "I know everyone says I'll regret it if I don't finish, but I just don't know if it's—my path."

"Then continue to pray about it," Father Francis said. "I can't tell you what's right for you in this matter. But both going to college and getting married are huge decisions you shouldn't let yourself drift into, or choose out of fear or impatience. Take your time. Think deeply about what you want and what God is asking you." He took another sip from his tea. "I *can* tell you that it is not impossible that God is calling you to take this step. He often calls us to take steps that seem foolish to the world. But you have to pray and choose carefully."

"And don't just go because all your friends are," Leon said. "I wasted two or three years in college because I didn't know what I wanted to do with my life. And by the time I figured out that I wanted to join a religious order, I had student loans to pay off first."

"Well, it's not really a decision I can make right now," Nora said with a sigh. "It's all theoretical until the man I want to marry proposes. And unless *he* figures out what he's doing with his life, I'm sort of in limbo." She rubbed the back of her neck. "So what degree did you end up with?" she asked, as usual directing the conversation away from herself.

"I barely got a B.A.—in mental health and human services," Leon said. "I was going to be a counselor."

"But when he realized they don't allow the incurably insane to be counselors, he gave it up," Matt put in.

"Ha ha ha," Leon said easily. He had been hearing that joke for a while.

"And what about you?" Nora looked at Brother Charley. "Did you go to college?"

The big novice nodded. "I was an auto mechanic and biker first. Then I decided to get a degree in business. Never thought when I went back to college that I'd end up a friar and a seminarian."

Nora looked at Matt, who was sitting next to Charley. The blond novice shrugged. "I'm probably the most average one," Matt said. "I was majoring in theology and philosophy because I knew in grade school that I wanted to become a religious. For me it was a matter of finding the right order."

"What about you?" Nora asked Father Bernard. The black-haired friar smiled.

"To tell the truth, I thought I was going to sell carpet, like my folks did," Father Bernard said. "But I just wasn't meant to be in flooring."

He looked at Father Francis, who drained his teacup and set it down. "I was a sociologist, and am a psychologist," Father Francis said. "I got my doctoral degree after I became a religious."

Nora turned to Brother George, who had sat, silent and surly, sipping a cup of hot water during this whole exchange. "What were you in your past life—I mean, before you became a monk?"

Brother George said in clipped tones, "I was a pharmacist. Before I became a *friar*. Not a monk. Haven't you paid attention to anything since you've gotten here?"

Leon winced at Brother George's rudeness. Nora turned away suddenly, her hair whipping over her face, and got up.

"Nora, hey, are you all right?" Matt started to ask anxiously.

"Excuse me—I have to go get something," she said, and turned and fled down the hallway.

Leon turned on the older friar. "There was no need for that!" he exclaimed. "You've been trying to make her uncomfortable ever since she came here!"

George's face registered shame, but he became defensive. "I never wanted her to be here. She's been a disruption to regular religious life ever since she got here. And now it looks as though our order is going to get involved in a police case because we let her in!"

"Our whole life is a disruption of regular religious life!" Leon retorted. "It's one crisis after another anyhow!"

"But that doesn't mean we should go looking for trouble! It shouldn't be like this!"

"Shouldn't it?" Father Francis cut in coolly, jostling his teacup. "What is it you want, George? A monastery? Maybe you're in the wrong place."

"Maybe you should go off and become a *monk*," Leon interjected. "Maybe you should join the Benedictines and make fruitcake."

"Leon," Father Francis said sharply, and Leon knew he had gone too far. He pulled himself up short, and tried to calm down.

"We're not here," Father Francis said in his roughest Brooklyn accent, "to put down the Benedictines, or the lay people, or anyone else for that matter. We're here to 'put down' ourselves, aren't we? And I may be a dim bulb, but I don't see that happening right here between you two brothers."

"I'm sorry, George," Leon said, attempting a genuine mortification of his pride.

"I'm sorry too, Leon," George said, and although Leon knew it was not deliberate, George's voice had a tint of superciliousness that made Leon's streetwise pride go crazy. He thrust out his jaw and sat down.

"Well, well. As Christ said, 'Where two or three are gathered in My Name, there's bound to be problems,'" Father Francis opined dryly. "Let's get ready for night prayer, shall we?"

Leon tried to put it aside as he finished his tea. It didn't make it easier for him when Matt started (unintentionally or not) humming the tune of "And They'll Know We Are Christians By Our Love" as he got to his feet.

As Brother Charley opened the door to the library, the dogs trotted in, tails wagging, then abruptly paused, staring at the sofa, where Brother Herman and Father Bernard were still sitting.

"Hey pooch," Father Bernard put out a hand. "What's wrong?"

Snarls broke forth from the dogs, and they approached the sofa sniffing. Brother Herman hastily got to his feet, but Father Bernard, perplexed, said, "Good pooches...?"

Suddenly the dogs' growls turned into full-fledged barks as they leapt onto the sofa, scrambling over Father Bernard's lap, sending his tea and the cushions flying.

"Holy Saints Francis and Clare!" the priest gave a yelp as Leon and Charley tried to grab the dogs. Then all at once, rats seemed to explode from every crevice of the sofa. Over a dozen furry gray whip-tailed cones darted out from under the cushions and beneath the tattered skirt, squeaking and making beelines for the doorway. Howling, the dogs pivoted and leapt after the rats, barreling into each other as they went. The friars all flattened themselves against the wall to avoid the rodent-and-canine avalanche.

The dogs vanished into the depths of the friary but they could be heard, snarling and snapping at their prey. When the friars finally located them in the basement stairwell, the two were engaged in a massive tug-of-war over a large rat carcass. The remains of several others were scattered on the steps.

Father Bernard shuddered, "I'm never sitting on that couch again."

"Those were big ones," Leon said in awe.

"Well, well, so these devil dogs are useful after all," Father Francis said.

"I'd say they're less devils than exorcists," Father Bernard corrected him.

"What do you say we call them 'Cappu' and 'Shin?'" Leon asked.

"Sounds like a plan," Father Francis said, and blessed them.

III

His brother was not noted for his sensitivity or tact, but when he picked Bear up and heard his story, Fish seemed to be possessed by an incredible discretion, at least for the moment.

"What's Jean's number?" he queried, as a weary and sore Bear tumbled into the back seat of the car.

Bear told him the number, and Fish, who had taken his cell phone back with a comment about Bear's lack of technological savvy, punched in the number. "Jean?" Bear heard Fish talking. "It's me again. Bear and I were wondering if we could come back over to your place for a while...You're having a late supper? No, I'm sure we wouldn't mind that at all. Bear, do you object to food? No? No, of course he doesn't. Can we pick up anything on the way? No? All right, then. We'll go change and be over there soon."

He glanced over at Bear. "You need some R&R after that episode. More than pizza in a foodless apartment."

"Thanks, Fish," Bear murmured, his eyes closed.

Bear had rarely been so glad to see the Brier home, and it was an added bonus to find Mrs. Foster there again, too. Apparently she and Jean had really hit it off. After a few minutes among his close friends, he felt more relaxed than he had for the past few days since he discovered Blanche was missing. Jean looked over his injuries from his fight, and pronounced them not serious—mostly bruises—which he was glad to hear, as he was already stiff and sore.

During dinner, Jean suggested they avoid talking about the crisis. So Mrs. Foster told them about the girl her son Stephen was dating. Bear asked the Briers about their trip to California, and Rose embarked on an extended narrative of their adventures. Then she asked him about his European adventure, and he told them a few stories. There was a lull in the conversation, and Bear noticed that everyone else was still eating. He tried to think of something else to talk about.

"So what are your plans for the fall?" Jean asked, beating him to the punch.

"Actually," Bear said slowly, "I've been thinking about starting a company specializing in the restoration of old buildings, particularly churches. Maybe concentrating on stonework."

"Stonework?" the women said.

He rubbed his chin. "Over in Europe, the buildings are so incredible, particularly the churches. We've lost a lot of those skills—masonry, stone carving. I'd like to start a company to bring some of those skills back, a company that could also do restorations of old churches and historical buildings, or create new ones in the old style. I was thinking of looking around for a master whom I could hire and then make myself his apprentice. Maybe later on I could take on some of these street kids without job skills, make them apprentices, and teach them, like they do at the Episcopalian cathedral in the City. I had a few ideas when I was over in Rome, and I've got to develop them, but in the fall, I think I'll start pursuing that." He outlined a few ideas he had about how to proceed, and noticed that even Fish was listening with interest and approval.

"That is so cool," Rose breathed as he finished. "I hope it works out."

Bear let himself smile, as he took his last bite. "Yeah, I guess the time in Europe was productive for me, after all." He stretched. "Of course, serving a mandatory federal prison sentence of five years for drug possession would postpone those plans a bit, so, Fish, why don't you and I get back to business?"

"Just what I was thinking myself," his brother said. "Jean, would you mind if Bear and I talked privately for a few minutes?"

"Not at all," Jean said. "Rose and I were going to make some cookies."

"How about I do the dishes?" Mrs. Foster said, getting to her feet.

Jean also got up, "You two boys can go sit out in the living room and talk. Can we get you tea?"

"Yes, please. In order to think clearly after a dinner that good, I require tea," Fish said, and Bear nodded, and eased himself onto the couch. His body began the process of shutting down almost instantly.

"Did you find out anything more at the banquet hall?" Bear murmured, forcing himself to ask. Truthfully, he just wanted to sleep.

"Just that they charge an enormous price for rental, that they are able to get napkins in peacock blue, if necessary, and that they contract with the same bakery who created the wedding cake for Frank Sinatra's granddaughter. Amazing how Miss Brier can be so charming. She had Mr. Carnazzo eating out of her hand by the time we were done. Oh, and if she ever does get married, she told me she'd rather have a wedding reception in an old barn with square dancing. That was after we left."

He sat up, perceiving that Bear was dozing. "Now, first tell me what you found out when Rita showed you around."

Bear stifled a yawn and detailed the story.

"Hmph. More strangeness but no real progress. As difficult as it was for you, you probably learned more from that Hunter guy. More proof that whoever is behind this has been going to great lengths to set up Blanche. I wonder. Are they trying to get at Blanche through us or get to us through Blanche?"

"They could be trying to get both of us," Bear said, touching the back of his head where a large bruise was spreading out. "Or at least me in particular. I feel singled out for some special attention."

"Not that you haven't gone looking for it," Fish pointed out. Bear guessed Fish was irked that Bear had gone off on his own after Hunter without consultation.

"Well, I found out one good thing: Blanche wasn't being stalked. An agent was watching her, and he was becoming convinced that she was innocent. I'm relieved about that." Bear yawned, and covered his mouth.

"I'm going to put in a call to the DEA and find out if this Hunter guy is really an agent of theirs, since you didn't bother to ask to see his ID," Fish said.

"I was handcuffed and under his gun in a dark tunnel when he said that," Bear objected.

"Excuses, excuses. Well, I'll find out the truth. So, anyhow, it looks like Blanche was spooked by this agent following her around and took off someplace for a few days. At least we know he didn't do her in, although if she doesn't watch herself, she'll end up framed for drug possession like we were," Fish said reflectively.

"Yes, that's the question: framed by who?" Bear asked, feeling as though someone were shuffling cards endlessly in his brain.

"Whoever is doing it is not terribly creative. They've planted drugs in Blanche's house. Then they send a tip to an agent to watch her. They plant drugs in our apartment and send a tip to the manager. That's their mode of operation."

"But who are 'they'?"

"Well, to start with, they must know a lot about Blanche. And by deduction, us."

"No kidding," Bear said.

"They might know us personally as well which would mean we know them."

"Great. When we find out who they are, I'll take them off my Christmas card list," Bear said.

"Who are you taking off your Christmas card list?" Rose asked as she came from the kitchen doorway with the tea tray.

"Ah, thank you for the tea, Rose. Now...run away and play for a while," Fish said.

Rose made a face, set down the tea tray on the table, and sat down on the couch firmly. "It's my sister who's missing," she informed Fish. "I don't see why you should keep trying to exclude me."

"It's hardly personal," Fish said, taking a teacup with a sigh and preparing it in his usual manner. "If we don't include you, it's only because we don't want to see you get yourself killed."

"I won't get killed," Rose protested.

"Is that a promise?" Fish asked dryly, stirring his tea. "If you break your word, I'll never believe you again."

Rose shook her head at him. "How can you even taste your tea if you put that much sugar in it?"

"Don't change the subject. I don't want to be the person responsible for depriving the world of Rose Brier. Under no circumstances are you allowed to help us do anything more dangerous than...changing the oil on my car."

Rose looked at him disdainfully. "I know how to do that already. My dad showed me how."

"Really? That's stupendous. Why don't you go outside and do it for me now? There's a good girl." Fish got to his feet and pulled Rose to hers. "While you're at it, check all the fuses. I think some of them are blown."

"Rose? Let the boys alone for a while," Jean called from the kitchen.

Rose glowered. Bear met her eyes and nodded his head in his brother's direction. *Be patient with him,* Bear's wry expression said.

Barely mollified, she got up. "Yes, Mom, I'll leave the *boys* alone," and with a toss of her red hair, left the room.

"I wouldn't have minded if she stayed, Fish," Bear said quietly.

"Sorry. I am a strictly two-man strategist. Trying to involve more than one other person in this will make my head ache." Fish slumped down in his seat. "Winsome," he muttered to himself. "Where in the world did she come up with that?"

Bear grinned. "Taken in by your endearing personality, obviously. I've always thought you were rather winsome, myself."

"The fact that I was so charming had escaped me until just now." Looking over at Bear, Fish relented. "All right, if you want to invite them all to talk with us, go ahead. I'll try to be cordial."

"Okay, Mr. Winsome." Bear raised himself painfully to his feet and went out into the kitchen. Mrs. Foster was up to her elbows in dish suds. Jean was dabbing chocolate chip cookie batter onto a baking sheet. She looked at him with raised eyebrows and he nodded his head. "How are things going?" he asked her.

"Fine. You said you had some fairly good news about Blanche?" She opened the oven and slid the tray in.

He told her and Rose what he had learned from Hunter. Rose and her mother and Mrs. Foster listened avidly. When the cookies came from the oven, they all stood around listening and eating them from the hot tray until Jean said, "Let's be civilized and sit down at the coffee table, shall we?"

So they trooped into the living room again, where Fish offered to help serve the tea.

Bear rubbed his forehead, still trying to wake up. "Jean, I forgot to ask you, in all the excitement, if you and Mrs. Foster found out anything more today. You were talking to the old people Blanche made home visits to?"

"Well, I think we've covered just about all her nursing home patients. They're not all old. Some of them are just invalids," Jean said. But she shook her head. "Actually, there's still one person I haven't been able to track down. Her friend Mr. Fairston."

"Who?"

"I mentioned him before. He's the sick man Blanche used to read poetry to. I've never met him, but I know Blanche was worried about him. She described him as a lonely old man with relatives who seemed to be neglecting him." She looked up, and Bear saw that she was crying. They all needed some sort of let up to the stress and suspense. Rose rubbed her mother's shoulders.

"I know visiting him and trying to encourage him was very important to Blanche."

"But you can't find this man?"

"No," Jean sighed. "All I know is that he was at a banquet Blanche worked this summer. His number's not in the phone book, and I can't track down his address either, so I'm at a dead end."

They were all quiet for a few moments before Bear said, "Maybe tomorrow we can go over the details with you and see if we can track him down." He suddenly felt weary all over again and irritably massaged his sore arm.

There was a pause. Rose picked up a cookie and pointed at Fish with it. "Before Mom brought up Mr. Fairston, I was trying to figure out if this was connected with jealousy, somehow. I mean, you know, Blanche is very pretty, and I keep on wondering if there's a rival here who wanted to get her out of the way..."

"Just like a romantic," Fish muttered, drinking his tea. "I grant you, she *is* very pretty, but it would have to be a fairly extreme case of jealousy for someone to go to the lengths they have. And that's not very likely, is it?"

Bear suddenly looked at Fish, blinking. The next moment, he had gotten to his feet, shaking all the china on the table.

"Are you all right?" Jean said, taken aback.

His mind was racing as he walked over to the desk. "Jean, do you still have that photo of Blanche?" he asked. "It was here with the mail when we first came to your house before you got back."

"Yes, it's right there in the slot with the envelopes. I was wondering about it too," Jean said, rising and following him. "It's such a good photo of her."

Bear found the photo as Fish and Rose came over. Fish, who hadn't noticed it before, whistled when he saw it. "Great picture," he said.

But Bear had already turned it over. He grabbed the nearby phone book and started turning pages.

The other four watched him, mystified.

"What are you looking for?" Rose asked finally.

"Longbourne Studios," Mrs. Foster had caught on at once, pointing to the photographer's mark on the back.

Longbourne Studios didn't advertise in the yellow pages, but Bear found their name in the white pages. He dialed the number.

A phone picked up, and a perky female voice said, "Good evening! Longbourne Studios."

Bear cleared his throat. "Hi. I have a question about a photograph from your studio. It's very important."

"That's probably something you'll have to talk about with our photographer, and I'm afraid he's gone for the evening."

"Is there any way I can reach him over the weekend? Like I said, it's very important."

"Oh, he'll be in tomorrow."

"Sunday?"

"Yes. He said he'd be in at noon to get his equipment. Would you like to see him then?"

"That would be wonderful."

"Super! Then I'll leave a note to tell him that you'll be in." She took his name and number, cheerily thanked him for calling, and hung up.

Bear hung up the phone and turned to find four sets of eyes staring at him.

"Bear?" Fish asked tentatively, after a few moments of silence.

"Just a hunch. Just a hunch," Bear murmured.

"Is it going to be dangerous?" Rose asked.

"Most likely not," Bear said.

"You *are* taking me with you," Rose said.

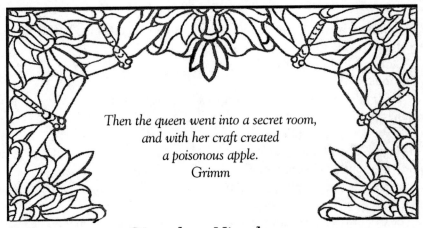

Then the queen went into a secret room,
and with her craft created
a poisonous apple.
Grimm

Chapter Nineteen

unday, August 15th, dawned bright and hazy, and the night-ridden City seemed to blink stupidly in the bright sunlight, unsure of what to do with it. The heat continued to expand, making the smell of tar rise from the pavements, and air conditioners and fans pumped out tiny breezes in small compartments all over the City. But in between the buildings was sandwiched nothing but hot air, stirred slightly only by the never-ending metal bodies of cars whisking over the black streets.

After the usual discipline of prayer, Mass, and breakfast, the friars spent the morning getting ready for the Assumption party. The girl worked around the friars' complex, doing whatever needed to be done, but feeling disconnected from it when she stopped paying attention to the immediate moment.

She and the novices rehearsed the Our Lady of Guadalupe skit, and she was relieved to find out that it wasn't a very big part, although she was still nervous at the thought of so many eyes being on her. At least she didn't have to say anything.

After the rehearsal, she tried on the shiny pink dress. It would work fairly well for Mary, she thought. The glossy patterned fabric that was tremendously gaudy in a street dress was subdued enough for a stage costume. And it was a modest dress, although meant for a much larger person than she was. She suspected it would be hot wearing it, but she decided to make the sacrifice. During a lull in the preparations, she sat in the vestibule on a stack of trash bags, ripped elastic out of a pair of shorts, and, using a sewing kit borrowed from Brother Herman, sewed the elastic into the waist of the dress to gather it in to fit her figure.

She looked up to find her new ally among the friars standing in the doorway. "Hard at work?" he asked.

"Yes. Did you find out anything?"

"Well, it's not in a prescription bottle. It looks more like a supply bottle that doctors or pharmacies would keep on hand for dispensing medications. It's either something your friend got directly from his doctor or else..."

"Or else what?"

"He got it illegally. Is that possible?"

"It's not impossible," she smiled, feeling a bit faint.

"When I get a chance, I'm going to make a few phone calls. Then I might be able to tell you more."

"I appreciate it."

"I will say this: chances are, you were right to be suspicious."

Her hand holding the needle trembled and she jabbed herself accidentally. A drop of blood appeared on the side of her hand, and she put it to her mouth. "Thank you."

II

Even though the Assumption party wasn't supposed to start until three, kids started arriving shortly after noon. Leon and the novices kept them occupied in various ways, while Nora and the older friars continued their preparations.

Nora was sorting out good Danishes from stale Danishes for the kids' treats in the kitchen of the basement. Brother Leon paused beside her on his way to carry out a load of trash, and noticed that she looked pale again.

She looked up and saw him watching her. "Something wrong?"

"I was just going to ask *you* that."

"The only thing that's wrong is the same thing that's been wrong the entire time I've been with you," she said with a half smile. "But, if it's any consolation," she added, "I do feel slightly better about the situation than I did before."

"Glad to hear it," he said lightly. And then, "Are you sure there's nothing else we can do for you?"

"Pray." She looked down for a moment. Changing the subject, she said, "I'm done with my costume."

"Great! Last time I checked on Brother Herman, he was working on your mantle of stars. You might want to go up and try it on."

"Thanks," Nora said, and gave him a small smile. She turned back to her work.

Leon fingered his rosary. He felt a need to get himself back on track, to figure out why he was suddenly feeling so apprehensive. Ascertaining that he wasn't needed to do any more party prep for a while, he went upstairs for some quiet time with the Purpose in his life.

Finally the party began, and the neighborhood folks started arriving, as well as other weekend volunteers. Nora passed out the Danish and doughnuts, and smiled at the kids. Marisol came up to him, in a slightly better mood than she had been last time. "How are the dogs?" she asked Brother Leon.

He grinned at Cappu and Shin, who were racing around the courtyard, wagging their tails. "Best rat catchers we've ever seen."

The sun was baking the asphalt as the party trickled out into the street to see the playlet performed on the steps of the church. In costume, Brother Leon stood in the doorway of the church looking out at the crowd, heard a step behind him, and knew Nora was there.

When he turned to look at her, she was resplendent in her shimmering pink gown, her head draped in a blue mantle, painted with Brother Herman's silver stars. She was, put purely, lovely.

"How do I look?" she asked, pushing back her black hair behind her ears.

"You really look the part," he told her, grinning.

"I can't say that I feel like the Immaculate Conception," she murmured nervously, catching sight of the crowd.

"That's okay," he said, patting her shoulder. Feeling a wave of premonition pass over him, he said, "You make sure you stay close to us. Look, I know it's hard for you, but please don't go off on your own."

"Why are you saying that?"

"You know how you keep saying you have a bad feeling? Well, now I have a bad feeling. So keep your wits about you, and don't go off anyplace. Especially with any friendly bag ladies. Promise me?"

She gave in to him and smiled. "All right."

Brother Charley, holding a bent pipe with a cross taped to it for a bishop's staff, came into the vestibule. "All set?" he said gruffly to Brother Leon. His eyes fell on Nora. "My lady," he said simply, inclining his head and bowing low.

Nora flushed, and made a rather graceful curtsy. Squelching the sudden trepidation that had risen up in him, Brother Leon leaned out the door, and gave thumbs up to Matt, who picked up his guitar and stepped forward and addressed the crowd in English and in Spanish. When he introduced the play with a flourish of steel strings, there were cheers.

Leon stepped out and began his lines. A natural ham, he threw himself into his part, improvising as he described to the audience his devotion to our Lady and his desire to hurry on the long road to daily Mass.

When the central doors of the church opened and Nora appeared at the center of the church steps, the children in the audience all gasped.

"*Encantadora*," he heard one say. Nora unassumingly took a step down and gestured to him.

Matt explained to the audience that the Lady had asked Juan Diego to ask the bishop to build a church for her. Leon hurriedly acceded to her request, and hurried off the stage as Nora retreated gracefully back into the church.

Next was the scene with the bishop. Charley and Leon took the opportunity to play up the comedy in the scene, with Charley looking at "Juan Diego" with exaggerated disbelief, and Leon insisting on his vision. Charley showed him to the door, pushed him out with his staff, and Leon sat dejected on the steps.

Then Our Lady appeared again, and gestured to Juan Diego that he should keep on trying. So Juan Diego promised to go again the next day.

But the next day, Juan Diego's uncle, played by an ailing Brother Herman, was sick, and Juan Diego had to go fetch the doctor. He was halfway there when he recalled his appointment with Our Lady. Instead of going to meet her, he decided to sneak away. Leon explained this to the audience in a whisper, and started to pussyfoot off the stage when the doors opened and Nora appeared again, this time with a slightly severe expression. When she touched him on the shoulder, startling him, and he leapt up in the air in shock, the audience convulsed with laughter. Brother Matt made a face at Leon. "Okay, tone it down," he murmured.

Penitent, Leon knelt before the Lady and explained with his usual exaggeration his uncle's poor state of health. Restraining a smile, Nora gestured, and Matt explained that she promised to heal his uncle, and send a sign to the unbelieving bishop. She pointed to the side door, where Charley obligingly shoved out a bucket with several artificial roses in it, indicating to Juan Diego that he should go and pick them. Leon climbed up the steps, and with great joy picked the roses and triumphantly brought them to the Lady. Nora solemnly arranged the roses in his tilma and sent him on his way.

Now Charley came onstage, and a few moments later, after surreptitiously turning his poncho around, Leon returned once more. He begged with the bishop, who was even more pronounced in his skepticism than before. At last, in despair, Leon announced that he had a sign from the Lady. He undid his knotted poncho and let the roses spill out. A gasp went up from the audience as they saw the image of Our Lady. And indeed, Brother Herman had painted an image that was not only like the Guadalupe image, but one that resembled Nora as well, with her fair skin and black hair. A few of the kids in the audience began to clap, and soon the friars had a standing ovation on their hands.

As the play ended, the audience cheered, and, enthusiasm being what it was, when Father Bernard invited them to join the procession with the

Blessed Sacrament around the neighborhood, men, women, teenagers, and children all followed the friars appreciatively. The procession began, with hymns in Latin and Spanish sung with gusto. After the procession and Benediction, the audience poured into the basement for the party. Nora, who had tried to slip away to change, was firmly caught by the children and made to stay. They even begged her not to take off her costume, and she relented.

It was a good party, and it lasted longer than it probably should have. By the time it was over, the sun was starting towards the west and the friars were behind in their nightly schedule.

"Are you coming over for supper?" Leon asked Nora as they swept up the hallway after seeing the last of the children out.

Nora shook her head. "I don't think I can swallow a bite—I'm pretty tired," she said.

"Something worrying you?" he asked.

"Well, you know how it is when you're waiting for something," she said.

"Like what are you waiting for?"

She half-smiled again. "I hope I'll be able to tell you more, soon."

Again, he felt that current of warning. "Look, just make sure you take the dogs with you when you go back into the high school tonight, okay?"

"Okay."

"And don't open—"

She finished for him, "—the door for anyone. I know. I promise."

"And if you see anything suspicious, just run, okay?"

"All right. I'll try. I know, I'm a total weakling and I need your protection." A touch resentful, she picked up a big tray of Danish crumbs and carried it off to the kitchen.

Leon watched her, and then turned away as Matt came up to sweep up the dust pile he had gathered.

"Leon, are you sure you're not spending too much time with her?" he asked in a low voice.

Reddening slightly, Leon winced. But he knew what Matt was asking. "I'm trying to keep myself detached," he said, attempting not to sound defensive.

"It's just—we're supposed to relate to the volunteers like sisters, but we have to be careful."

"Yeah. I'm being careful. Thanks for asking."

Leon put away his broom, looked around the basement, and seeing he was done, decided not to linger around. The other friars and Nora could finish the job. He went back upstairs to the chapel to prepare for evening prayer.

III

The photographer of Longbourne Studios kept erratic hours. After attending early Mass, Bear, Fish, and Rose had showed up at noon at the posh little Manhattan studio only to be told that the photographer, Mr. Vincent Van Seuss, had arrived at seven a.m., collected his equipment, and sped off somewhere. Even the chic blond receptionist, "Renee," had no idea where he had gone.

Rose and Bear had occupied themselves with looking at the extensive portfolio of Mr. Van Seuss that was available for the public, while Fish had settled into a comfortable chair for a nap. Huge examples of the photographer's work hung lavishly from the high ceiling to the floor, mostly bold black and white renditions of gorgeous blond ladies strolling down Fifth Avenue or swimmers sunning themselves on the decks of yachts, or small children playing naked by the seashore.

After waiting for some time with no success, Bear and Fish had finally taken Rose out to a late lunch downtown, leaving the receptionist the cell phone number. Although they dallied over their meal, talking about novels to pass the time, there was no sign of the photographer when they finally returned. "You would think he'd dropped off the face of the earth!" the receptionist had exclaimed. But Bear noted she didn't look too concerned. Apparently this was the way that Mr. Van Seuss ran his business.

There didn't seem to be anything else they could do but wait. At least it was Sunday, a day of rest, so Bear let Rose talk them into going for a walk to relieve some of their stress. They had walked downtown, and Rose had just persuaded them to go into a hat store so she could try on a particularly intriguing hat, when Fish's cell phone rang. It was, wonder of wonders, Renee the receptionist.

"I just heard from him, and he said he'd be back at the studio at seven to talk with you," she informed them proudly.

This was somewhat of a letdown after an entire day of waiting.

"Too late for me," Fish had said after he had hung up the phone. "There's a required lecture at the University tonight. Since I'm here, I feel in all conscience I should go."

"Are you sure you can't skip it?" Rose had asked, toying with the hat.

Fish had looked at her, mildly disgusted. "Miss Brier, a college education is a privilege not to be taken lightly."

"Oh," Rose had said solemnly. "I didn't know."

"Of course you wouldn't," Fish had said. "No, I don't think I can afford to miss this lecture. It's an Austrian professor speaking on the minor poets of the Romantic revival, and she's about the only decent authority left on the subject. Bear, be a good big brother and drop me off, will you?"

"We'll call you on your cell phone if we discover anything really important," Rose promised.

Fish looked at her and rolled his eyes. "Unless it's Blanche herself, or a culprit ready to confess before a jury, it can wait until I'm done with the lecture," he said. Bear had steadily refused to discuss his hunch with either of them, so Fish had expressed doubt that this meeting would turn up anything worthwhile.

Thus at seven o'clock Bear and Rose found themselves waiting for Mr. Vincent Van Seuss, the photographer, while Fish attended his lecture. By 7:30, there was still no sign of Mr. Van Seuss.

Renee, who had not recognized Blanche's photo, had helpfully loaned them several additional books of portraits Mr. Van Seuss had made over the past few years. Rose scanned every single page, but, as Bear had guessed, there were no pictures of Blanche among them.

Now they sat on white wood chairs with black leather cushions, staring at the charcoal-colored carpet, Renee's empty desk, and the red walls with their rows of faces and bodies.

"What a nice position she has," Rose indicated the absent Renee. Bear had guessed that Renee was in the back room painting her nails, not wanting her boss's clients to see how idle she was. "She seems to have nothing to do but sit around in this classy office just in case someone happens to come in."

"I wouldn't want her job," Bear said.

He wondered again about his stonework idea. It was a little extraordinary, he knew, but he had a feeling he could make something of it. *If only everything else works out,* he thought. *If only Blanche...*

Rose nudged him. "Someone's coming," she whispered, and Bear got to his feet as the studio door opened and a tall, harried-looking man in a tweed suit and a silk shirt with a handsome profile entered the room, carrying several bulky black leather bags. Seeing them, he brightened up.

"Welcome, welcome," he said, taking each of their hands, speaking with the barest trace of an accent. "I am so very sorry for keeping you waiting so long."

He chatted with them as he divested himself of the camera equipment, mentioning the fine weather and a bit of what had kept him so long—an attempt to photograph a flock of pigeons flying away from the pier. "It's not as easy as you might think. Pigeons are not the type of bird you can hurry," he explained. "You must forgive me for detaining you."

His easy charm made Bear and Rose feel rewarded for waiting so long. With this personality, it was no wonder Mr. Van Seuss could keep such an unpredictable schedule without frustrating his clients.

He ushered them into his office, which was a bit more disheveled but far more comfortable, with large, soft, black leather chairs. Coffee? A drink?

Rose said yes to a soda. He took one himself and then leaned forward on his black wood desk, saying, "Now, how can I make myself of assistance?"

Bear pulled out the photograph of Blanche, and Mr. Van Seuss' eyes brightened.

"You would want to know if I took this photograph?" he queried.

Bear said he would.

"Yes, I did. Such a lovely girl, isn't she?" His eyes traveled to Rose. "And you must be related to her."

Rose admitted that the girl was her older sister.

"Wonderful. A most bewitching family. How else may I help you?"

Bear asked how he had come to take the portrait.

"That is both simple and not as simple to tell. I was asked to go to a home to take a photograph of a man and his wife about two weeks ago. Of course I do not give out my clients' names. But I will tell you what I can. The man, you see, is very ill, and his wife wanted a last portrait of them together. That portrait did not turn out so well. The man is very ill. He does not look his best. I did what I could. It is very sad.

"Now, as a photographer, I have learned one must be spontaneous in the search for art. Such as today—I have to photograph pigeons, but the pigeons will not cooperate. But while I am waiting for the pigeons, I find incredible puddles along the dockside, with the wind making ripples. So I photograph the puddles and the reflections of the clouds. Just the same thing with this shoot I was telling you of. The beautiful black-haired girl—your sister—she is there. She is visiting the sick man. She is enchanting. So I ask her, may I take your photograph? She does not mind.

"I take the photo, but it is not exactly as I want. So I take some more. Not what I want. So I ask her to sit down for me. She sits on the chair as you see, here, and I photograph her. But her beauty is playing games with me. I cannot capture her as I want. So I move the chair, I play with the light. She is very patient, she smiles, and she has this wonderful ironic smile, like the Lady with a Secret. I try her in a number of poses until I use the whole roll. So much that the lady of the house—whose husband I came to photograph—I think she is becoming annoyed with me. And as I said, that photograph of her and her husband does not turn out so well. But as for these pictures— miraculously beautiful!"

Bear wondered aloud how Blanche came to have the picture.

"Oh, well, of course, when I come back with the photographs for the couple to choose, I bring a few of the girl as well, in case I see her. I should admit I was hoping to see her again. She is so very lovely and with such a gracious manner. One enjoys talking to a girl of that sort, especially when one is my age. And I was happy to find her there. She is so dedicated in visiting the sick man. He says it means the world to him, and I, seeing her, can understand. I showed the girl the pictures, and she is surprised and happy at how they look. She asks me if she may purchase this for her mother, and if she may come to look at the others later on. I gave her the one. Then, you see, the lady of the house—who does not seem to enjoy having such a beautiful young thing so near to her husband—comes in and is cross with me because she does not care for the pictures I took of her husband and herself. So the visit does not end well, but that is not the girl's fault."

Mr. Van Seuss rose. "Would you care to see the other pictures I took of her?"

Rose and Bear said they would. Despite what Mr. Van Seuss had said about not giving out his clients' names, Bear was hoping that he might tell them more.

Mr. Van Seuss sorted through his pictures, each set in its own thick white envelope of textured paper marked with his red and white trademark symbol. Not finding anything, he checked his calendar for the day and consulted with Renee, then re-emerged brandishing another envelope.

"They were in my second-best briefcase!" he exclaimed. He took out a stack of glossy black and whites and smoothed them out on the burgundy leather cover of the desk with a professional hand.

Blanche's features, white and black, gazed up at Bear from the table. Mr. Van Seuss had indeed managed to capture Blanche's elusive expressions of quiet allure. Each one was a little better than the previous one, although none was as stunning as the one Blanche had chosen for her mother. Bear wondered to himself that Blanche hadn't mentioned the photographs to him. Perhaps she had intended to surprise him with one.

He was pulled out of his reverie. "Who is this?" Rose asked, pointing to another photograph that had slid from the envelope.

Bear stared at the black and white image, and felt a tremor run through him as though he had been swiftly and silently rammed by a truck.

"That is the couple whose picture I went to take, as I told you," Mr. Van Seuss said apologetically. "As I said, it was not a very successful venture."

The man in the picture looked frail, very frail. But the woman stood beside him, tall and tanned and beautiful, and as archetypal as all the blond beauties lounging on the yachts in the waiting room outside.

He should have known. It had been there all along.

"Thank you very much, Mr. Van Seuss," Bear heard himself saying as he got to his feet, so unexpectedly that Rose was startled. She said something in a questioning tone to him, but he barely heard what she was saying. It was time to go.

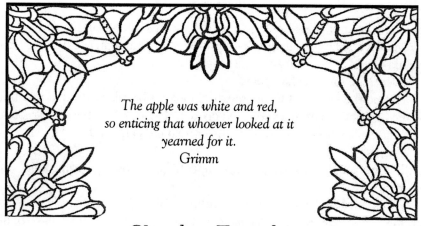

The apple was white and red,
so enticing that whoever looked at it
yearned for it.
Grimm

Chapter Twenty

erhaps they think I look like her, but inside I'm not the least bit like the Blessed Mother, she thought to herself, walking back to the high school, swept suddenly again by the feeling of self-consciousness she had lost while serving the friars' neighbors. *But of course, nobody could really be like the Blessed Mother. All of us are sinful, or at least terribly inadequate—*

"Nora!"

She halted, and looked at the door to the friary kitchen. Brother George hurried down the steps to her and handed her a piece of paper and the bottle. "I had one of my old colleagues look up the serial numbers on the pills. Here's what it is."

She read the unfamiliar ingredients, and looked up at him quizzically.

"Does your friend have heart problems?" the friar asked.

"No, not at all. He said he was lucky that way."

"Well, then I'm not sure why he'd have a bottle of these pills. This is heart medication."

"Heart medication."

The friar nodded. "It would introduce a subtle toxicity into the patient's system that over time could cause dizziness, confusion, even hallucinations. He'd be very sick. Not exactly what someone with a brain tumor would need."

"Would it kill him?"

"It's hard to say, but it might. It's not a poison, but it could start heart problems that could kill him or put him into a coma if not used properly." He paused. "Now, I'm not a doctor, so I don't know if there might be some other problem he's having that would require this medication. But I'm going to make an educated guess here. The bottle you gave me was a supply bottle. It may be that he obtained it without a prescription, and didn't realize the effect it would have."

"I see," she said mechanically.

"But on the surface, I would say, he shouldn't be taking this. Not without specific instructions from a very good doctor." He looked at her. "This sounds like a bigger situation than a nineteen-year-old girl can handle."

"It is," she said.

"I hope you'll consider getting some help," Brother George said with concern.

She nodded and took a deep breath. "I will. Maybe Father Francis can help me…First I've got to get changed. Then I can think about it—Thanks very much, Brother George," she called over her shoulder as she hurried on.

"You're welcome," Brother George turned to go back up the steps.

Her heart beating faster, she opened the door with the replacement key Father Bernard had given her. "Cappu! Shin!" she called, remembering her promise to Brother Leon to not go off alone. There were no answering barks.

She glanced around the courtyard, but the dogs were not in evidence. Perhaps they were tracking down a rat somewhere.

Well, I can at least go inside and get changed, she thought. *Then I have to go and see what can be done…*

As she opened the door to her room, pulling the bobby pins out of her veil, she heard a faint noise. A rat? She dropped the hood of the veil and looked into the shadows in the corridor beyond. A creeping sensation came over her. Someone was inside the building.

"Who's there?" she called, in case it was one of the friars.

There was a footstep, and a figure came around the edge of the corner. She could see the green eyeshade.

Run. She turned, gathered her skirts, ready to run back towards the door. "Blanche."

She knew that voice. It was similar to Bonnie's voice, but deeper, richer. Younger.

"That is your real name, isn't it? Don't go yet. I just want to talk to you."

Go. She started towards the door again.

"Is there any harm in listening to me? Just stay by the door and listen. Did they really say you couldn't even speak to me?"

Hand on the door, poised to run, she looked warily over her shoulder at the figure in black.

"That's right," the woman said, shuffling closer and halting about ten feet away. She wasn't wearing her blue hat, and lank black hair hung around her wrinkled face, still covered with the green visor. "But now you call yourself Nora: the dark girl. That's what you want to be, right? You don't want to be a silly young thing needing to obey orders to be kept safe. You've grown, you've learned how to survive in the night."

"What do you want?" the girl asked brusquely, feeling a chill on the back of her neck. *I can still run if I need to*, the girl told herself. *I can still run.*

For an answer, the old lady bent down, opened one of her bags, and pulled out an apple. She bit into it, and munched, looking at the girl meditatively.

"You're not running away from me now, are you? That's because you want to know. You don't want to be a pawn of monks, or men. You want to be independent. You want to be free. A girl of the night, a lady of the dark. Just like me, Nora. Just like me." She dabbed a hand into her bag again and held something out. An apple lay in her palm, round and red and shiny. "Would you like one? They're fresh."

The girl shook her head, no. *I'm not that stupid.*

The woman laughed. "So you're a better girl than Eve?" she chuckled. "Smarter than that unlucky lady, are you? Or are you just afraid to know? Would you rather trust in some man, or in some patriarchal God who's never been in your shoes?" She paused. "What's that in your hand?"

The girl covered the bottle with her long sleeves and looked at the old woman guardedly.

"So you *do* know what's going on, don't you? It's silly to have pretenses any longer. Don't you want to know the other side of the story? Her story, instead of his story?"

"I'm sure you have some way of justifying yourself," the girl said at last.

"I've been wondering why you're doing this for him. Do you even know what you're doing? Is it for the money? Or are you just in love with him?"

The girl faced the old woman stolidly. "I'm not in love with your husband." She pushed her hand on the door to leave.

"I'm not talking about my husband."

The girl froze, and looked around.

Seeing she had made an impact, the woman sucked in her breath. "You don't know as much as you think you do, do you? It can be dangerous to meddle in matters that are too big for you."

Suddenly the woman darted forward and pulled her away from the door, spinning her around. Now she was between the girl and the door. She made a grab for the bottle, but the girl held it away from her and screamed. They struggled as the woman yanked at the girl's arm, but the girl wrapped the bottle tightly in both hands. Breathing hard, the woman pinched the nerves at the base of the girl's neck. Black spots swelled up before the girl's eyes.

The woman's voice whispered mockingly in her ear. "Sleep, sleep, black night girl, snow white girl, and dream of your phony prince…"

II

"Has anyone seen the dogs?" Charley asked, pausing in the doorway of the refectory.

"I haven't seen them," Brother Herman said, and the other friars around the table shook their heads.

"I think they escaped again," Charley groaned. "Shin's the worst. He'll sneak out when I'm not looking all the time."

"Needs more discipline," Brother Matt said.

"Well, I guess they'll be back when they're hungry." Charley sat down at the table with resignation. "I've got to get busy building a pen before they get lost for good."

"You'll build it tomorrow," Father Francis said, pointing at him to indicate that Charley was under obedience. "Remember—I am the Big Dog."

Charley panted and inclined his head. The others chuckled.

Leon put down the plate of steamed cabbage leaves he was serving. "Aren't the dogs with Nora in the high school?"

Brother George cocked his head. "I'm not sure, but I heard her calling them when she went back to her room."

Leon reminded himself not to be too preoccupied with Nora, and focused his attention on meal prayer. But after the blessing was prayed, he got up. "Father Bernard, can I go check to see if the dogs are in the high school with Nora? She shouldn't be there by herself."

"You may," Father Bernard said, handing him the key, while Matt raised his eyebrows slightly.

Leon paid no attention to him, but hurried out to the high school, crossing the courtyard in the dim light. The sun was almost down.

Anxious despite himself, he banged on the door. "Nora?" he called as he pushed the key into the door and turned it without waiting for an answer.

The door creaked open, and he flicked on the hallway light. Nora lay on the ground, and someone stood over her. The light glinted on a green eyeshade. Seeing Brother Leon, she turned and fled down the corridor.

In an instant, Leon was at Nora's side. She was groggy, but aware.

"Are you okay? Can you get up?"

Nora glanced down at her empty hands. "She took the bottle."

"What bottle?"

She stumbled to her feet. "That's what she wanted, all this time."

"Are you sure you're okay?"

She nodded. "I have to—"

"—Go get help." He could hear the intruder racing up the steps of the high school to the second floor. Plunging into the shadows, he followed her up.

Up and up the steps he ran, past the locked door to the first floor, the second floor, up to the third floor door, which he knew was unlocked. The echoes of his coming distorted sound, and when he reached the top of the steps, he couldn't hear where the intruder had gone. He listened, his heart beating, praying for guidance. The doors at the far end of this floor were locked, so he guessed that Nora's assailant was still on this floor.

Carefully he looked through the window of the door at the top of the steps into the shadowy hallway. Nothing moved.

He pushed the door open silently and stepped into the corridor. It was still lit with the late summer evening sun, peering through the glass doors of the classrooms. Along the sides of the hallway were the stacked-up desks, movable blackboards, chairs, and other furniture they had moved out of the classrooms. Any of these obstacles could provide a place to hide.

Step by step, he moved down the corridor through the stacks of furniture, scanning for movement, listening intently. Fortunately the classrooms were mostly open and bare. A quick look inside each told him they were empty.

At last he was coming towards the double doors at the far end of the corridor. He knew they were chained shut. As he moved closer, a dark figure suddenly rose up from the ground before the doors.

"Don't make a sound or I'll shoot you!"

It was Bonnie's voice. She was standing in front of the doors in her battered black trench coat, brandishing a gun, a streak of sunset red hitting the muzzle. The green eyeshade still covered most of her face, but the hat was gone. No longer hunched down over her bags, she was taller than she usually seemed, taller than Leon himself. And clearly not an old woman.

Help would be coming soon, Leon knew. He raised his hands, grateful that she hadn't fired first.

"Where's the closest exit?" she demanded, tossing her head so that the long black and gray hair flew to one side, making it suddenly obvious that it was a wig.

Leon nodded his head back over his shoulder. "Behind me."

"You're going to walk me there without calling attention to yourself," she directed, training the gun on him.

In answer, Leon leaned against the wall of the corridor. "First you tell me who you are, and what you want with Nora," he suggested.

Bonnie snickered. "Can't you figure it out for yourself?"

"I'm kinda dumb that way. You tell me."

"Why, drugs of course," the woman drew in her breath. "Didn't you find her cache? She took off about a week ago with a stash, and didn't pay the cartel. So they sent me to recover the goods."

"So she's a small-time drug dealer and you're the woman above her on the totem pole?"

"That's how you could put it."

"Liar," Leon said flatly. "Liar. This isn't some drug cartel payback. This is character assassination. Maybe starting to go beyond just character."

The woman snorted. "So she's been working her charms on you too, huh? I can imagine what kind of story she told you. Are you going to start moving or do I have to get nasty? I've got hollow point bullets in this gun, and they'll rip your insides to shreds if I shoot you. It's a bad way to die."

Brother Leon scrutinized her, standing his ground. Despite her threats, he was fairly certain that the lady wasn't going to fire that gun, which would alert everyone to their position. "What's with the eyeshade?" he said easily. "You're a little too eccentric, even for a bag lady."

Not bothering to answer his question, she brandished the gun once more and said, "Move!"

Brother Leon went on the offensive again. *Keep her talking.* "Funny, I know quite a few drug dealers, and I find your story hard to believe. If you want to get rid of her, why the disguise and the fooling around with choker necklaces and perfume? Why not just take her out? In fact, why don't you just take me out instead of letting me talk your ear off?"

"I was just asking myself that," the woman said.

"I'll tell you why," Leon said, pointing at her. "Because you're not a drug dealer any more than Nora is. You're some high-class uptown lady and you're trying to ruin this girl's reputation for some reason of your own. And you're trying to do it carefully so that you don't get any stain on your own name." He spread his hands. "I'm right. Aren't I?"

"If I were you, I would be worrying about the consequences your run-down monastery will be suffering for harboring a criminal."

"First of all, we're a friary, not a monastery," Brother Leon said, folding his arms. "Second of all, who is Nora that she's such a threat to you?"

"None of your business."

"Oh, if my brothers are going to be getting in trouble with the police for sheltering her, I think it's our business."

"And she's your particular concern, isn't she? And you're just another man who's fallen in love with her."

Brother Leon stared at her, taken aback by the change in gears, but seeing the trap. "Well, you're wrong," he said. "I haven't." He was glad he had been reading his own heart on this subject, and he knew, as he said it, that it was true.

"So blind, so blind!" Bonnie purred. "Don't you know what beautiful women do?"

"Manipulate men, you mean?"

"But of course. That's how the game is played. The great war game between the sexes."

"It's no war, and it's no game," Brother Leon said. He was watching her carefully, and listening. She couldn't get out without getting past him. He wondered if he dared to tackle her with the gun, but he didn't quite trust that he would be quick enough.

"Then perhaps you've met very few really lovely women. Perhaps that's why you're in a monastery in the first place," the lady hissed.

"Friary," Brother Leon automatically corrected her as he gauged himself. With a quick prayer, he seized a nearby desk and half-shoved, half-threw it toward Bonnie, ducking as he did so. As he had guessed, she didn't fire the gun, just dodged. Then she got behind a stack of metal school desks jutting out from the wall and shoved them towards him with vehemence. The stack teetered.

Ho boy, Mother Mary... were his last thoughts as the metal pile came crashing down on him. He had just enough time to throw up his arms to shield his head from the onslaught. The noise of ten desks hitting the floor in three seconds was deafening.

III

"You want me to drop you off here?" Rose sounded puzzled as Bear pulled over to the side of the curb.

"Yes." Bear turned off the car and tossed the keys to Rose. "Go and get Fish out of his lecture. Tell him it's very important and to meet me back here." He grabbed the suit jacket he had worn to Mass and got out of the car into the sweaty heat of the New York evening. Darkness was coming on fast.

"Okay," Rose tried to sound cheerful as she slid into the driver's seat and fumbled around for the seat adjustment. "Are you sure you can't tell me what this is all about?"

"I probably can later on, but there is someone I need to speak to first," Bear said. "Sorry I can't be more specific." He didn't want to talk about this until he had actually done it.

"That's okay," Rose said. She slid the seat forward several inches until she could reach the pedals. "Boy, are you tall!" She pulled away, leaving him on the sidewalk to stare at the great house, alone.

This was where Blanche had been making her visits, and he had never known. Why hadn't he persisted in asking her more about it? Did she know? How could she not know?

Somehow or other he made his way up the steps to the regal front door. But once there, he stood, looking from side to side, unsure as to whether or not he should go further.

Hardened with a new resolve, he rang the doorbell. He hadn't been here for a long time—a year? Two years? No, he realized now it had been almost four years. That had been back when...He swallowed and stopped the memory by ringing the bell again.

No one was coming to the door. He glanced upwards and saw a light on in one of the upstairs rooms.

When another two minutes had gone by without an answer to the doorbell, he pulled out his key ring and carefully picked through it. He never threw away keys, but all the same, it had been so long ago that he might have gotten rid of this key, since he had been sure he would never come back here again. The situation had seemed so hopeless. He found the key.

Still, they might have changed the lock. Sliding it into the door, he turned it and heard a click. The outer door opened.

He stepped inside the long narrow entranceway that led to the internal door of the house—an oversized black door with a stained glass window, a golden coil snaking through huge red poppies. Through the clear glass surrounding the flowers, he could see the staircase and hallway beyond. There was no sign of life within. He walked down the short corridor to the door, wondering as he did whether he was tripping burglar alarms. He didn't care.

Below the door window was a long brass plate that read THE FAIRSTONS.

For a moment, he paused, taken aback. Was this the right house? Then he figured it out: Fairston. His father must have amalgamated his name with that of his second wife's, something Bear supposed was a trendy New York thing to do. Instead of Fairchild-Denniston, just Fairston.

No wonder Blanche hadn't made the connection—nor had he or Fish. He knocked on this door, just in case. Once again, no answer.

He took out the matching door key and unlocked the door. "Hello?" he called cautiously.

Inside, the air conditioning made the house frigid after the warm oven outside, and he shivered and shrugged on the jacket. Only the overhead chandelier lit the cold darkness, three stained-glass lotus-shaped flowers dripping orange glass tendrils over his head. He looked around at the staircase, the door leading into the downstairs office, and then met his own eyes in a huge mirror to his left.

That hadn't been there before. He stared at the vast mirror, festooned with stained-glass ornaments of dragonflies and red fire flowers. It was nearly ten feet high, and its shiny surface reflected mainly the shadows of the rest of the dim interior, the reflection of the lotus lamp blending into the mirror's other adornments. His father's second wife had always had a thing for stained glass, he remembered now, though she hadn't cared for churches at all.

"Hello?" he called again, and paused, listening. There was only the faint murmur of the air conditioning. Quickly, he walked down the passageway to the kitchen. There was a light on over the stove, but the rest of the kitchen was dark. He could see that someone had had a meal recently—dirty dishes on a tray sat beside the sink. Fresh yellow bananas sat on the counter, and an apple peel was left on the kitchen table. He guessed the servants still came in every morning, to clean up. His dad never cleaned house, and Bear couldn't imagine his second wife doing so.

He opened the door to the garage and peered inside. Two cars sat in the garage, with space for a third. The garage doors opening on the back alley were tightly shut. No sign of life.

Shutting the door, he paced down the hallway towards the light at the other end, past several doors into a little sitting room that opened into the dark living room. There was a reading light on, and a fashion magazine was overturned on a coffee table.

It was a small room, but with marble tables, angular statues, sculptured metal lamps, lots of hard metal surfaces, more impressive than comfortable. His mother had never lived here—this had been the home his father had purchased after their separation. Painful memories welled up too quickly.

He had to see his father, but he didn't like this place. It was almost as if there was a peculiar smell in the place that made him queasy. Unfortunately, it was all too familiar—that unpleasant feeling in his stomach.

But your past has a hold on you. Blanche had told him in her last letter. *Do you think that maybe you can't find peace because, on some level, you won't forgive?* Though she might not have made her observations in a way that motivated him to change, she had been right about this.

"Hello?" he called once more, loudly, this time.

He listened hard, for the sound of the television, anything. There was silence, except for the usual vibrations of the City beyond the well-insulated walls that shielded the dwellings of the wealthy from the outside clamor. Now he became uneasy. Didn't anyone hear him? Why wasn't someone coming? Was there no one here, after all?

Finally, he stepped through an archway into the adjoining living room, and began prowling through the darkness, searching for light, for sound. He made his way to the windows and tried to look out, but couldn't figure out the drapes. Giving up, he looked back at the lighted sitting room. All was stillness.

His eyes began to adjust to the darkness of the living room. The shelves on the walls had once held books, he remembered, but now he saw the outlines of various objects d'art, probably of the woman's choosing. They had certainly remodeled this house since he had last been there. No surprise.

He moved toward a second wide archway. Before, this room adjoining the living room had been the music room. Cautiously he stepped inside the deeper darkness.

There had once been a piano here, and he had spent some of his lonely hours in this unbearable house here, working on piano lessons. Playing music had been a distraction with some satisfaction, an excuse to numb his outer senses to concentrate on those fascinating patterns of notes and bars. Bear put out a hand and touched smooth wood. The piano was still here. He caught a whiff of the smell of ivory and dusty innards, and lemon oil, and memories closed around him swiftly, inexorably. It made him want to run, but he stood his ground stolidly. He had hated it, hated the long corridors and stuffy interiors of this house, where everything was silence and secrecy and lies.

* * *

Trying to put his life together again, after prison. Sitting next to his brother on the couch in the living room behind him. His father, tight-lipped, standing before him, lecturing his sons about probation and accountability and curfews. "If you're going to live in this house, I am going to expect high standards of behavior from both of you." Arthur had listened, rather sarcastically thinking what a paragon of morality his father had suddenly become.

That had been his first day home from prison, also the day he discovered that the same blond woman he had caught with his father was now living with him. Although they were still not married, she had become a fixture in his life. She had begun to take possession of the house, rearranging things. Talking about plans for extensive renovations. Returning home blissfully from shopping with his father's credit cards.

Arthur couldn't figure out if it was moral for him and his brother to live with them. His father's affair was about as interesting to him as one of the sordid soap operas the blond woman followed with professional interest, having once been an actress in television and off-Broadway plays. His father was fascinated with her. She wanted to start an investment firm, like the one his dad owned, but more "cutting edge." She and his father discussed marketing strategies constantly. Arthur and his brother tried to tune it out as much as they could.

They were preoccupied with far more visceral matters.

His last afternoon at the house, he had had a fever. His brother had been at a GED class, and his father was at work. Arthur had been playing the piano, but the melody he had been attempting to recreate had faltered into dull silence, and he was leaning on the piano lid, staring at nothing. His health hadn't been great since his mother had died. The grief had become an ache that surfaced in bouts with the flu, and resulted in a sort of mental paralysis, where he would sit for long periods, doing nothing, half dozing, half aware.

His motionlessness must have made him invisible, because he had woken up to hear the blond woman in the next room, talking on the phone. He could see her long curving leg bouncing on her knee as she chattered, sitting on a cushioned chair. He buried his head in his arms to escape looking at her, though he could still hear her voice.

"Yes, it's finally about to happen. I'm about to become a sinfully wealthy woman."

The sluggishness of gloom was still infecting his mind, and he hadn't quite understood.

"… Now that his wife's really out of the picture, things are finally moving. Yes, it's been almost a year. That annoying little woman. She kept hanging on forever, too. Fortunately for me there's no cure for cancer."

She laughed, apparently at someone else's joking response. Her voice made his skin crawl.

"Yes, as soon as he makes the vows, I'm getting the company up and going. Yes, he's promised to fund everything. I can't wait."

When the woman hung up the phone and rose from the chair, he didn't want to move and let her know that he had heard. Anger surged through him, followed swiftly by a wave of hopelessness. Part of him cynically said *if Dad wants to marry a fortune hunter, let him.* But part of him grieved for the father he had once believed in and insisted that he not keep silent.

All this time, he was straining his ears, trying to figure out where the woman had gone. In the insulated silence of that house, it was difficult to know if she was still in the living room or if she had left.

At last, he had slowly lifted his head, to see her standing in the doorway watching him. A smile flitted around her red lips when she saw his expression.

...“Go ahead and tell him. Your father's never going to believe you,” she had taunted.

That night, his father had called Arthur into his home office and confronted him with the marijuana he had found in his son's room. His face was taut. “I see I still can't trust you.”

Arthur set his jaw, knowing that it was useless. After all, his father hadn't believed him the first time. But he said it anyway. “It's not mine.”

His father raised his eyebrows. He was turning red, which told Arthur that his father was dangerously angry, even though his tone was civil. “Just like the crack in your locker was not yours.”

“Yes.”

His father fumed. “Young man, tomorrow, I am checking you into rehab.”

I'm not going,” he said obstinately. “I'm not a user.”

“Oh really? Then how do you explain these joints?”

And just as before, his father hadn't listened to his explanations. Now he started interrupting and talking back to his son, as though he were another teenager. “So why are you trying to blame all of this on Elaine, Arthur? Trying to spread the guilt around? You pretend to be so religious, and all I see is sneaking and lies.”

Something snapped inside Arthur, and he turned on his dad. “You only see what you want to see! You didn't want to see how you were hurting Mom. You don't want me on your conscience, so you pretend you don't know me. You won't see your sin, so you won't see anything.”

"Shut up!" his father barked. "I've had enough of your dramatics!"

There was silence while his dad ran his hands through his silvered hair in frustration, and Arthur threw himself back down in his chair.

At last his father got up, walked over to him and looked him in the face, his eyes cold. "I will tell you this, son. You are not getting one single penny from me from this moment forth unless you go to rehab. You can't stay in this house until you decide that you will. I am freezing all your bank accounts, I am taking away your checkbook, you are getting zip, nothing from me. Nada. You understand?"

He looked back at his dad. "You can't take away the money I got from Mom," he said, and regretted it as soon as he had said it.

"I most certainly can. I have control of those assets until you're twenty-one." His father walked away, then swung around and added, "And that goes for Ben too. You two might as well be the same person—he does everything you do."

"That's not fair! Ben has nothing to do with this!" Arthur exclaimed.

"A jury found you both guilty," his father shot back.

"He's just as innocent as I am."

"Then you've just deprived him of his money as well," his father said unreasonably. He sat down at his desk and turned on his computer, indicating that the conversation was closed.

Arthur rose, furious but unable to speak. After a long moment, he spoke, fighting to keep his voice calm. "Dad. What would I have to do to prove I'm telling the truth?"

His father hesitated, not looking at his son. "I don't know. I don't know if I can ever trust you again."

"Then it's pointless for me to even try, isn't it?" Arthur said bitterly. "I might as well go out and start doing drugs right now, for all the difference it would make to you."

His father gritted his teeth and turned back to face him. "If you were to bring me back a legal document stating that the charges you were imprisoned for were found to be false, I would give you back your mother's money and your share of my assets when I'm gone. Isn't that fair?"

"It would be, if this were only about money, Dad," he retorted. "But it's not." And he stormed out of the room to his bedroom and slammed the door.

...Only to find the blond woman there, smiling triumphantly.

"Get out of my room," he had said evenly, not sure why he suddenly felt afraid.

She took a step forward, hands on her hips. "It's not your room any more, is it?"

* * *

Standing again beside the piano, Bear realized, by comparison, that prison hadn't been as repugnant to him, nor those dangerous years on the streets, as living in this house had been.

Now the interior was so structurally changed that it more resembled a nightmare about the house than the actual house he had once lived in. He took a step further into the darkness, and caught a glimpse of an orange glow. He turned, and saw the entranceway where he had come in, with the lotus chandelier.

Disoriented, he paused. How had he come back to this place? Mentally he traced his steps backward to the sitting room and down the corridors—but suddenly his attention was distracted. The front door was opening as a slender figure stepped inside.

His heart rushed upwards as though through dark waters towards the light. It was Blanche.

*Snow White longed for the apple
and soon she could not resist.*
Grimm

Chapter Twenty-One

ursued by darkness, she had plunged into the subway tunnel once again with a sense of being caught in a repetitive cycle of time.

Always running, always her heart beating with this painful intensity, always pursued, always surrounded by nothing but the mechanical roar of the dragon's belly—deeper and deeper into the shadow . . .

Poisoned. He's being poisoned. Is he even still alive? And if he is, will he believe me?

When the serpentine train had halted, she had hurried upward, above ground, back into the tangle of streets and buildings. In that vast concrete forest, she was nothing but a single soul moving frantically among so many other souls, effectively invisible until she came at last to the house again, pulled out the key, and let herself in.

Journey's end. She faced the mirror again, and took a deep breath, gazing at the silver surface and the smoke behind the glass.

You couldn't stop me. I'm here.

II

"Leon, are you all right?"

It seemed only a few minutes later that someone was calling him. Leon groaned and struggled against the pile of metal desks that covered him as Matt and Charley quickly pulled them off.

"What happened to you?" The Midwestern friar's voice was anxious.

Leon wrestled himself from the ground, shoving desks aside as he tried to stand up. "Bonnie was here—after Nora."

227

"Where is she now?"

"Bonnie? She took off. Where's Nora?"

"She just came and got us," Matt said, looking back over his shoulder as he moved a last chair. "I thought she was right behind me."

"Where'd Bonnie go?" Charley asked, pushing desks back against the wall.

"Uh, I was a bit preoccupied and missed that part." Leon rose and stumbled towards Charley. "We've got to get after them. Bonnie—whoever she is—wants Nora for some reason of her own. I had a chance to talk with her about it—on the wrong end of a gun, unfortunately."

Charley caught him by the shoulders. "Whoa! Steady there, little brother. Looks like she roughed you up a bit."

"Yeah. With some help from the desks, as I'm sure you can tell." He rubbed his sore forehead. "Come on, let's go."

As Leon had suspected, there was no sign of Nora in the courtyard. Down on the streets, the novices looked around. "I asked our neighbors if they saw anything. Mrs. Himina saw an old lady going down the alleyway, but didn't see much else," Matt said. "She said the old lady got into a white car and drove off, real fast."

The white car. The ugly witch. It made sense now. Leon's foreboding was growing stronger. "I'm going to ask the Fathers for permission to go to look for Nora."

"Not without us, you're not," Charley said, and the other two novices fell into step beside Leon.

III

Blanche was here.

He both recognized her and didn't recognize her. She was swathed in some sort of flowing gown that shone in the cloudy lamplight, yet her petite figure was unmistakable. But her hair, her long curtain of dark hair was gone. Cut short.

He had barely time to think of this, because he started towards her as soon as he saw her, reaching out his hands in the darkness. She stood in the muted yellow haze in the distance, looking around, apparently unaware of his presence. Just as he seemed about to reach her, an invisible wall sprang up against his hands and face with a thunderclap. Glass.

He was trapped behind the mirror. She startled, and glanced quickly at the mirror, right at him, seeing no one but herself. Stupefied, he stood, disoriented, his hands on the glass wall, as she flew quickly past the mirror and onto the stairs. "Blanche!" he called.

At the sound, she barely halted for a moment, a question on her face, then hurried up around the curve in the staircase, away from him. He rapped the glass now and called her again, but he seemed to be invisible, or far away. She had vanished into the darkness.

Blindly he turned and fought his way through to the living room, then rushed through the sitting room back down the corridor. What had once been the doorway into the music room, was now blocked with a sheet of one-way glass, framed to look like a huge mirror. Why? And why was Blanche here at this hour? It didn't matter—she was here. He had to find her.

At last he found himself back in the entranceway, rushed up the steps into the darkness, then halted, and looked up and down the passageways to the left and to the right. No one.

She had vanished once again. If he hadn't been so sure that he had seen her, he might have thought she was a phantom, a trick of the light in a house of mirrors. Gritting his teeth, he strained his ears for any sound, looking for any motion.

At last he thought he heard a murmur of voices to his left. Tense, he stepped softly down the passage, his footsteps muffled to nothing by the thick dark carpet. The voices were near impossible to locate, but after going up and down the passage twice, he finally placed the sound and halted in front of a closed door. He noticed a thin bar of light coming from the crack at the bottom of the door, and put his ear to the door. The voices were coming from within, and one of them was Blanche's. The other was fainter, a weak male voice. Blanche and his father, talking.

He put a hand on the doorknob, and turned it slowly. It opened without a sound. The voices grew louder.

Inside he saw a luxurious white desk, and above it, a flat-paneled computer monitor flickering on an empty room. The voices were coming over the computer's speakers, and on the screen, he saw the video images of two people talking. The colors were off, and the outlines were tinged with green. A menu tag at the bottom of the screen read "cam 6."

Incredulous, he stepped into the private office suite, then fixed his eyes on the monitor again. It showed an image of a bedroom with pale lime-green walls and a white bed and black furniture. There was a sick man lying in the bed, and a girl sitting on a stool beside the bed. The colors in the picture were bad, but he could see the girl, her face washed out to white, her hair black and choppy, her eyes dark smudges.

He studied the two figures. The girl was Blanche, and she was sitting on the stool, leaning towards the man, nodding her head. The man was speaking haltingly, with difficulty in a shallow, rasping voice that Bear slowly recognized despite the speech impediments. His father. But the figure in the bed bore little resemblance to the tall, urbane figure he remembered. His ruddy face was now pale and shrunken, his cheeks hollowed out, his hair limp and lifeless. One side of his face was clearly not operating the way it should be. And his eyes looked larger than Bear remembered, and drained of energy.

He made out his father's words: "...of course I'm always glad to see you, but why are you here so late?"

The microphone thinned the girl's voice out. She was tense, her hands on her knees as she sat. "I had to," she said. "I talked with a pharmacist, and found out about one of the medications you've been getting. It's not what you should be taking. You have to stop taking it until you check with another doctor."

"Well, actually I already know it's not what's normally prescribed," the man said, one half of his face looking clearly uncomfortable, the other half slack and motionless. "It's something Elaine was able to get for me." He fumbled with the bedspread with his left hand, picked up a remote control, and clumsily punched a button. A large television in the corner blinked off, and a buzz in the video monitor fell into silence while the picture on the computer screen became a bit sharper. "There are places you can get these kinds of things, if you know the right people, like Elaine does. It does seem to help the pain."

Bear smiled grimly at the irony. *So Dad has been using drugs—illegal prescription drugs.*

There was a pause. The girl said timidly, "But my friend told me that this drug could put you into a coma."

"But I'm probably going into a coma anyway," the man said. "Don't worry. I know about the side effects, Blanche. I'm very careful about how much I take. I limit myself to one dosage a day. So there's nothing to worry about." He smiled with half his face. "You're very sweet to be so concerned for me. But I very much doubt that Elaine would be doing anything that would harm me."

That last line was typical of his father, Bear knew. No matter how outrageously Elaine might behave, he was blind to it.

"But you said you were...afraid," the girl seemed to have difficulty finding words.

The man tilted his face, in an attempt to shake his head. "You have to understand, Blanche, that my disease affects my moods, and my judgment. I know I might have said something to you that might have made you feel that I was more worried than I actually should have been. Elaine is a temperamental person. She's difficult to live with at times. People have found it hard to understand why I would stay with her, but Blanche, at my age, you crave stability. All my life, people have come and gone, and I need someone who's going to stay with me. People say she stays with me because of the money. Well, Elaine has plenty of assets of her own—the Mirror Corporation.

I know she doesn't need me, but she chooses to stay with me. So I can put up with some of the things she does because—well, because I'm grateful that she's stuck with me. Which is more than I've done for other people." He looked at her. There was silence. Blanche seemed to be embarrassed.

"You look like you're starving." With one hand, he pushed a tea tray towards her that was hovering over his chest, suspended on a black metal swinging arm. "Elaine made me dessert, but I couldn't touch it. Are you hungry?"

"I am, thank you." The girl took the plate from the tray and began to eat something off the plate that looked to Bear like strudel. "It's delicious."

"Yes, some family recipe. I forget where she said she got the fruit from, but I know she orders a crate of apples around this time of year from our friends in New England. There's tea in the pot."

The girl murmured something in appreciation. She turned over a teacup from the tray, picked up a small lime green teapot, and poured herself a cup of tea. Bear noticed a red rose lying on the tray beside the teapot, a spot of dark blood on the wavering screen, like a stage prop.

"By the way," the man said, and paused, lifting up his chin so that Bear could see his familiar profile. "Elaine said that you're dating my son."

IV

"Your son?" she asked, a bit stupidly, jerked from her own parallel reverie and eating the dessert. She had fallen silent, feeling sillier and sillier for coming all the way out here, daring the darkness, only to find out that there had been nothing to worry about all along. So his question threw her for a loop.

"My son, Arthur Denniston."

She blinked, trying to match the mental image she had created of Mr. Fairston's selfish, distant children with Bear and Fish. "He's your son?"

"Yes. By my first wife, Catherine. Who died of cancer."

She stared at the sick man. Of course that's why Mr. Fairston seemed so familiar. Now she saw the family resemblance beneath the marks of age and illness.

He squeezed a corner of the blanket with his good hand. "Elaine told me Arthur and Ben were just arrested again for drug possession. She showed me the notice about it in the paper. So I know it's true."

She hadn't moved, even though her heart was racing, probably faster than was good for her heart. It was silly, completely irrational, but when she heard the bad news about Bear's arrest, the only thing she could think was, *He's back. He's come back.*

V

"Did you see a white girl with short black hair come through here recently?" Brother Leon asked the man at the token counter on the subway. It was a chance in a million. He didn't know if Blanche had taken the subway. And even if she had, she might have either had a token or gotten one from the machines.

"I have no idea if I did or I didn't!" the man said, looking up at him with a perplexed smile.

"Thanks anyway," Leon reddened, and retreated.

"So what do we do now?" Charley asked. He and Matt looked at him soberly.

"Um—I'm not sure," he said.

He looked around as they walked back down the stairs, and spotted a homeless man stretched out in the shade of the staircase. He was surrounded by three mangy dogs on leashes that wagged their tails when they saw the friars.

"Brother Leon!" the man said, sitting up, and Leon recognized him from his neighborhood rounds.

"Hey Robbie, how are you?" he asked, reaching out to touch the man's hand.

"Doin' fine," the man rasped, shaking his hand.

"How's the pooches?" Brother Leon tousled the head of the nearest dog, which licked his hand appreciatively. The other dogs were already checking out Matt and Charley.

"That one got himself kicked by a jerk who came through here last night at midnight. Poor Molly was just being friendly, and he kicked her. Lookit!" The man indicated the smaller dog, which was holding its leg up as it stood, in a half-hearted attempt not to put any weight on it.

"That's too bad," Leon said, examining the dog. "Look, you come by the friary and I'll have Brother George take a look at it, okay? He knows a lot about animals."

"He does? Thanks. Maybe I will."

"Robbie, have you seen a young white girl with short kinda ragged black hair down this way anytime this evening?"

Robbie looked around meditatively. "Well, there was a girl—a pretty one—who came through looking like that. Bout half hour to an hour ago?"

"Yeah, I'd say so."

"Indian girl? With one of those scarf and nightgown things?"

Brother Leon squatted down. "What? You mean in a sari or something?"

"Yeah, all pink and blue with stars. Kind of wild."

Of course—she had been wearing her Guadalupe costume! Leon reddened to think he had forgotten that. "Yes, that sounds like her."

"Yeah, I saw her when I was up there, afore the man kicked me and my dogs out. She got on the train."

"Did you see which way she went?"

"Towards Manhattan, I'm pretty sure."

Brother Leon's heart skipped a beat. "Thanks, Robbie, thanks a lot." He hurried up the steps to the train, with the other novices following close behind.

VI

Bear had moved further into the windowless office, watching the computer monitor with its spy video camera capturing every word that Blanche said, every move she made.

On the screen, Bear's father looked at the girl warily. "I hope you're not going to try and tell me that he's innocent? I can tell you I've heard that story, many times before, from Arthur."

"I know he's innocent," the girl said firmly. For some reason she was smiling as she pushed back her chopped hair.

"Blanche, you know, it bothers me that you never told me you two were dating."

"I didn't know." She half-laughed and got to her feet. "I mean, I didn't know he was your son. All I knew was that he wasn't on good terms with his father, and…" she turned away, putting a hand to her hair to push it back behind her ear. It was a familiar gesture, but the hair was now so short it didn't stay. *And she cut her hair…?* he distractedly thought to himself.

The girl crossed to the bedside table, her face away from the hidden microphone, so Bear missed her words. Then she turned back towards the bed, and he heard her saying, "…but mostly he just never talked much about you. And, the name Fairston, well, he never mentioned that you had changed your name."

"Maybe he didn't know about that, though I was sure Elaine had told him and Ben," the man said slowly.

The girl set down the bottle of medication. "I'm sorry—I don't mean to change the subject—but there is another reason I came over here. I—I saw Elaine. And she said you were planning on committing suicide."

The man put his head to one side. "Did she? That's odd. Well, I told her a few days ago that I'd changed my mind."

"You did?"

The man seemed embarrassed and raised his good hand to his straggling hair to try to smooth it. "Well, the more I thought about it, the more it seemed to me that I was depressed. You told me that once, remember? It sort of stuck in my mind, and I kept wondering if—well, I thought perhaps I should talk to a counselor first. Consult a professional."

"Why not a priest? It would cost you a lot less," the girl said, almost teasingly as she sat down again. Bear winced, but his father only chuckled.

"I knew you would say that. Blanche, I just don't know. I'm one of those people who's had bad experiences with priests."

"Well, I've met a few good ones," the girl said. Then she paused. "Did you know Father Michael Raymond?"

"Blanche, don't even go there. I'm sorry, I can't discuss this, even with you. It's a shame he got killed, but I had one too many conversations with him. Plus, I heard a whole lot more about him than I ever wanted to hear from my sons, believe me. And—well, from Catherine, too." The man sank back into the pillows, his face looking hollow. His good eye closed, but the other remained half-suspended between sleep and waking.

There was silence, and the microphone instantly sucked up the lack of sound into feedback.

The man spoke again, and the microphone rapidly adjusted, cutting off his first words. "—thing that bothers me—if you are dating Arthur, do you know why he won't speak to me? You'd think that if he knew I was dying, he would show a little bit of concern."

"I don't think he knows," the girl said.

"That's impossible. Elaine told me she'd—"

The girl leaned forward. "I don't think you should believe..." Then she rose. "Look. I've been in nursing homes this summer, Mr. Fairston, and you aren't being cared for properly. Even the low-income homes make sure that..." Blanche had turned away from the microphone, and her last words were cut off.

Getting closer so he could hear, Bear took a step forward towards the monitor, bumping the settee that stood against the wall and putting a hand on one of its corner knobs to steady himself. It wobbled beneath his touch.

He looked down at it.

Acting on an impulse, he pulled the round knob out of the post and looked into the hole. Lying stacked one on top of the other in the small hole were several pastel pills. He could just make out the curlicue M of the one on top.

Suddenly, he caught a movement out of the corner of his eye and, before he could react, something was clamped over his nose and mouth. A sweet smell overpowered him and he dropped out of consciousness.

*No sooner had Snow White eaten
the apple than she fell down,
still as death.*
Grimm

Chapter Twenty-Two

At last she had a chance to tell him everything she had been seeing that was wrong—the attitude of the nurses, the neglect of what should be basic hygiene…she rattled off her concerns, and ended, "I regularly visit a publicly-funded home where conditions aren't the best, but you would be getting better care there than what I've seen here."

Shaken by her diatribe, she sat down, her hands shaking uncontrollably. She rubbed them, and noticed, oddly, that they seemed to be rather numb. *Being this upset is not good for my heart*, she thought automatically, and took a deep breath, trying to relax.

Mr. Fairston was visibly thrown. He almost looked frightened, because only one side of his face could show the shock. "If you noticed this, why didn't you say anything before?" he managed to say.

"I don't know," she said miserably, and wearily brushed back her hair. "I suppose I thought it wasn't my business…I didn't want to question your judgment…or Elaine's. After all, Elaine and I barely know each other."

"But sometimes someone coming in from outside can see things we can't see ourselves," Mr. Fairston said, his expression calming. "I know that wasn't easy for you to bring up."

"Just bringing it up's not much good unless it will make a difference," Blanche rubbed her hands again, and tried not to be worried about their coldness. "You need to get better care, and the sooner, the better. I just don't know if—" The sheer persistence of Elaine in tracking down that medicine bottle told her that something was still very wrong. She wondered why Elaine hadn't yet returned. *Perhaps the friars managed to grab her*, she thought hopefully. *Perhaps it's over. And Bear is back...but is he in jail? I really hope not. In any case, I should get going before Elaine returns...*

"Are you feeling all right?" Mr. Fairston asked her, tilting his head to one side, which she recognized was his way of gesturing.

"Oh, yes." She picked up the teacup with both hands, hoping the warm cup would heat her hands, and took a sip. But she could barely feel its heat.

"That's funny, because I was just thinking you were looking worse."

A wave of nausea passed over her, and she put a hand to her stomach. *It's just because I haven't eaten much all day,* she told herself. *And my heart hasn't been beating normally. Probably that sweet desert was the last thing my system needed after those pastries we had at the party.*

She managed to take a long drink of tea, and the nausea passed, but a strange heaviness, like exhaustion, had started to hit her. It must have been her run from the friary to the subway, then running from the subway to here, all the while terrified of the specter she had left behind her. "I'm just tired, that's all." She could tell that Mr. Fairston was getting tired, too. She should let him sleep.

"How's work been going? Have you been getting up too early?"

"I haven't been going to work," she said, yawning. "Actually..."

But she decided that she didn't want to go into it right now. Brother Leon would be mad enough with her for leaving after she had promised to stay. "I'm sorry, I'm just so tired. I should get going."

II

"How the heck are we going to find out which stop she got off?" Brother Matt asked as they stood on the subway train, having begged some tokens from passersby.

"I'm going to make a guess that she's going to get off on 96th Street," Leon said, scanning the subway map.

"You mean where Bonnie got off last time you followed her?"

"Yeah. After all, Nora went to the subway just like Bonnie did. How much do you want to bet they're going to the same place?"

"And where are we going to go from there?"

"Uh—we could just—walk around until we find her, I guess."

"This is crazy," Matt rubbed the stubble on his blond head.

"But it's all we have to go on," Charley rumbled.

Leon just prayed.

III

The dull taste on his tongue became unbearable, and he swallowed. There was a smell around him of carpet, plastic, perfume, and dust. Someone had rolled him onto his stomach, and his face was pressed into the floor. Bear rolled his head to the side and opened his eyes, blinking in the light, to see a spreading plain of orange and blue triangles on a nubby carpet. He was still in the office.

When he tried to get up, his muscles kinked in agony around his hands. He attempted to wrench them apart and winced at the pain. A smooth, thin plastic cord was bound tightly around his wrists and pulled into his skin. Turning his head, he saw the bun feet and dusty belly of the settee. His ankles were tied together and bound to one of its legs, which were wrapped with lamp cord. He saw that a small table lamp lay a few feet away on the carpet, its cord sliced off, and two small decorative speakers from the computer lay skewed beyond them, also cordless. He jerked his wrists apart again, trying to slip the knot, and realized he was only cutting himself. The slender cord had no give, and the knots were rock hard.

Foreboding swept over him. He twisted his head up and looked at the computer. The monitor flickered, as before, on the scene of his father and Blanche, though now without sound.

Slowly he looked over his shoulder. Above him, seated on the curved back of the settee, feet planted on the seat cushions, was a figure in a battered black trench coat with a witch's face.

Withered cheeks were covered by a green eyeshade, and a wig of stringy black and silver served for hair. Perched upon the back of the couch as though seated on an exotic throne, its pose was so still, so bizarre that for a few seconds he thought it was a dummy someone had propped there. The eyes were glassy and empty, the limbs motionless.

He fought to master himself in this swelling horror and forced himself to fix his eyes on the dead eyes of the mannequin.

"Elaine," he said, and compelled himself to end the word with certainty.

There was a dead silence, filled by the whirring of the computer. He felt suffocated, suspended between reality and some dreadful insanity, but made himself wait, his cut wrists throbbing.

At last there was a faint rustle, and the figure on the back of the couch stiffly raised an arm, and removed its eyeshade. Then it touched its neck, lifted a corner of the mask, and pulled it away, taking off the wig with it. Rumpled golden hair cascaded out around a smooth ivory face with unusually bright blue eyes.

And the voice, very rich and full, spoke.

"Arthur," it said, and the word was savored.

She was as beautiful as she had ever been, but he could tell she was older. Her looks were growing tired, sharper with age. Now she crossed her legs, and he could see that beneath the trench coat, she was wearing a black tank top and tight black pants. She tossed the clipped plug of the electric cord down at his chest, and despite himself, he flinched.

"So, Arthur, I wasn't expecting to find you sneaking around my home office at this time of night, but as you can see, I was prepared to deal with you. Lucky for me I even had chloroform handy. Are you going to tell me why you're here, or should I just call the police?"

"I came to see my father," Bear shifted to ease the pinch against his wrists.

"Oh, really? This late at night? And after not contacting him for—let's see—eighteen months? And instead of going to his bedroom, you wind up in my office. Hmm. Ulterior motives, anyone?"

She looked down at him spitefully. He tried to keep eye contact with her, but it was difficult, particularly as she wasn't looking at his face. Feeling his vulnerability acutely, he managed to work himself up onto his elbows and inch further away from her.

"You've grown up, Arthur. You know, I always thought you had quite a bit of potential. Despite the fact that you were such a prig when we last met."

"What do you want with me?" he demanded, his face reddening.

She chuckled. "Since you're in my house, I should ask you questions, shouldn't I? You and your girlfriend." She said the last word with undisguised disdain. "If that's what she really is, and not just some pawn in your master plan."

The submerged fear, the same fear that had first appeared in the church of the martyred virgin, crashed over him now like a tide. "What do you have against Blanche?"

Now Elaine laughed softly as she stepped over him with a kick and crossed to a bar in the corner of the office. She poured herself a glass of soda, put something in her mouth, and swallowed it with the cola. "Oh, come on, Arthur. Can you really think I'm such a fool?" She squatted next to him on the floor, toying with her glass. "Let's not play with each other this way. You lie. I'll lie. Let's be frank with one another."

He didn't like her being this close, and shrank back against the sofa. There was something about her—there had always been something about her—that made his hair stand on end.

"We know what this is really about, don't we?" she lowered her chin and looked him in the eyes. "It's a chess game. And you know what the goal of a chess game is, don't you?"

He forced himself to talk, to keep the intellectual give and take going. "To take the king."

"Right." She kept looking at him steadily, a smile playing on her face. "That's what this has always been about. From day one. But in all your calculations, you've forgotten the most powerful piece on the board."

"The queen."

"That's right," her voice dropped to a whisper. Now her chin hung swaying over his face.

"Elaine, get away from me."

Her lips smiled, but she didn't withdraw. "So the young upstart king went away and found himself another queen."

"Another queen?"

"To replace your mother. And I'm sure you planned it that way. Why else would your father form such a quick, strong attachment to a girl he didn't know anything about?"

Her red lips were still smiling, but the blue eyes were hard. "I underestimated you, long ago, Art. You're just as calculating as I am. I knocked your mother out of the contest once, and cancer took her out of the match completely. Things looked set for an easy win. But now, late in my game, you send in another queen. You picked a pawn, put a crown on her head, and then you sent her in because *she looks just like your mother.*"

The coincidence was striking. He couldn't deny that he had been raised by a beautiful, quiet woman with dark hair and fair skin, and now he was dating a girl with the same features and a similar personality. Some men tended to marry women who resembled their mothers, didn't they? How could he argue that it wasn't by design—at least not by his design—that Blanche had found herself in the midst of this deadly family battle? He had tried to shield her from it completely, but through some crazy chance the man she had befriended was his own father.

The blue eyes were sparking with anger now. "So you see, Arthur, I know what you've been up to. But these sorts of games—'who is the fairest in the land' games don't always end up so nicely."

"And you really think I *planned* it all?" Bear returned in disbelief.

She sat back on her heels and drained her glass. "You knew I owned the Mirror Corporation. After all, I started it back when you were still living with us. Your father was vice-president. And you must have known that we always used Reflections for our functions. It must have been too convenient to have your princess connive her way into a job and meet your father. I admit I was taken in, especially since she always used a cute nickname to refer to you. Until I saw the letter in her purse addressed to you, I had no idea who she really was. But I'm pretty quick on the uptake."

So Elaine planted the drugs in my apartment to get rid of me, and Fish, and Blanche. He suddenly remembered Mr. Russell's words that Dad "...would cut off all monetary help or any posthumous share of his assets to you if there were a second drug charge."

"Elaine," he said quietly. "When did you plant the Ecstasy pills in our apartment? Before Blanche started visiting Dad, or afterwards?"

"Ecstasy? I've no idea what you're talking about," she said airily, tossing her golden hair. "I haven't been in that apartment in years. Though of course I used to go over all the time when your father still owned it."

And of course she would have passed beneath Ahmed's radar because of that. She had used pills from the same cache she was concealing here—but of course, it would be difficult for him to prove that now, and she knew it.

She leaned her elbows on his chest as she watched him, apparently amused at finding out how little he had known. "Do you expect me to believe that you're just the clueless victim of circumstances? Poor Arthur. And I have you just where I want you, and there's no way out. But you know I've always had a soft spot for you. We could replay that scene from four years ago, if you want."

Four years ago, she had refused to leave his room, and had whispered an offer, "*Kiss me, and I'll make your dad give you your money back...*"

"No," he said evenly, and tried again to push himself out of her reach. But he couldn't move any further from her and they both knew it.

"But this time you can't run away from me, can you, young king?" she whispered, leaning closer. Her breath was stale, and terrifying.

He somehow managed to press himself further back without moving down, but he couldn't go very far. The cord was biting into his wrists with a vengeance.

"Elaine, cut it out. Leave me alone!" he jerked away unsuccessfully as she took his face in her hands.

She laughed and stroked his cheek with her fingers. "Why are you so nervous? Can't we be friends? This is a perfect opportunity to get reacquainted while we wait for Blanche to finish in there." Her eyes flickering to the screen, he saw the jealousy burning there. "This queen of yours is a piece of work." Now her face dropped closer once again. "Do you really love her, or is it just an act?"

He ducked his head sharply and hit her chin so that her teeth clacked together. She swore, and slapped him across the face.

"Don't fool with me, Arthur. I don't have the patience I once had," she warned. "You're still my delinquent stepson, just a few steps away from the police and a five-year prison sentence. If you can use her to play chess games with your dad, you can certainly play chess games with me."

"It's not a game," he whispered, his face stinging. "It never was."

Her eyes sparked. "Then how about I go and get Blanche and have her join us?"

No. He tried to keep his face blank, but she had already caught sight of his expression.

She grinned. "Sounds like a plan. I wonder what she'd think to see her prince now? And I'm dying to see how she behaves once she's in your position." Elaine got to her feet, pulled out a pair of scissors from her pocket, and traced the silver blades with her fingers, an odd smile on her face. "I believe this could be fun. And informative. I might not have to call the police after all."

Setting the scissors down, Elaine pulled a dark handkerchief and a baggie out of her pocket and a perfume bottle. Pulling out the stopper, she doused the cloth with liquid, folded it, and stuffed the wad into the baggie and back into her pocket. Then she picked up another lamp, unplugged it, and sliced off its cord. All this time her jaw was working itself back and forth, and he realized she was grinding her teeth. He knew what it was. Ecstasy.

At last she thrust the scissors back in her pocket and leaned over him. "Too bad you couldn't learn to play the game better, young king," she said with a strange smile, rumpling his hair. "It's time to take out your queen. Be back soon."

The door closed behind her quick footsteps. Bear tried again to jerk his hands free of the wires, and looked helplessly at the computer screen. He prayed that Blanche would sense evil coming, and escape again. *Even if I can't.*

IV

The girl blinked. The walls felt as though they were closing in on her. A throbbing began in her head. An echo of footsteps.

I felt a funeral in my brain...

"Blanche, are you sure you're all right?" Mr. Fairston asked.

She got up, and grabbed the back of the chair to steady herself. "Yes," she assured him. "But I think I should go now." She licked her lips, her throat swelling in fear. *It was coming. Closer.*

The door opened, and the wife stood there.

"Well, hello. This is certainly a late night visit, isn't it?" Her voice was chilly. She had an electrical cord bunched up in her hand, and the girl wondered why. But she felt as though it almost didn't matter to her. *The footsteps were coming...*

And then Sense broke through. She went down, and, like Alice, fell a long way into the dark, absurdly, disjointedly. She felt herself sinking, and yet the floor never rose up to meet her. She just fell, through oceans and past planets, spinning head over heels, slowly, ominously.

There was a terrified rattle of voices above her, and she still knew what they were saying. The wife's voice came shrilly, "Are you all right? What's wrong?" And Mr. Fairston saying, "Oh God! Oh God!" as though he really were speaking to God for once.

And she finished knowing, then—

V

Bear, his throat dry, fixed his eyes on the monitor. Blanche was slumped over the chair—barely conscious. Had something happened to her because of her heart condition...?

But no, it was something worse than that. Far worse. He had seen it.

He saw Elaine shaking her shoulders, slapping her face, a look of panic crawling over her features. There was no response. Blanche's head lolled to the side, her black hair falling sideways over her face.

Elaine said something to his father, and the man twisted forward and seemed about to argue. But instead, he just jerked his head in a nod. Apparently he believed whatever she had said. Putting an arm under Blanche, Elaine half-carried, half-dragged her from the room.

Bear twisted towards the door, listening. But the suffocating carpet deadened all sound of footsteps. He could not hear if they had gone. He could not hear them returning.

He struggled once again to see if he could loosen the cord on his hands, but all he did was give it the chance to gnaw deeper into his skin. Giving up, he studied the wire that tied his feet to the thick leg of the couch. He braced himself against the settee, curled his knees to his chest as far as he could, stretched his legs out again, and yanked them back with a ferocious jerk that wrenched his ankle joints painfully. The settee moved, but the cord didn't break. No good.

He glanced at the monitor again. His father had rolled over, and was staring at the wall. Nothing moved. He wondered if his dad, lying weakly in his bed, knew what was going on, and if so, could he have done anything about it. There was no phone in his room. No way for his father to get help for Blanche...his father was in a trap, shut off from the world, unable to get out, bound by his disease and the insane control of his second wife...

And Blanche had walked into that trap. *And may not come out alive,* he thought bleakly.

And unless something happened, neither would he.

There was a tremor in the air. The door swung open silently and he realized that he was still desperately caught.

Elaine stood in the doorway. Alone. Her face was blank, expressionless. She shut the door behind her, walked over to him, and looked down.

"You tried to take the king," he said steadily.

The blue eyes stared at him, and the red lips twisted but made no reply.

"What was in that stuff Blanche ate? It was meant for my dad, wasn't it?"

"I don't know what you mean." Elaine's voice seemed to come from far away.

"You tried to murder him."

"No, I didn't!" she snapped, suddenly vicious. "It's not murder to put someone into a coma. Your father is dying already. The doctor says he'll be in a coma any day now, and when that happens, he'll die within the month."

His wrists were numb, and he struggled to stay upright. "Blanche wasn't dying."

"Chess games can get ugly. I warned you. I warned her. I warned you both. But she just had to interfere—if she had just stayed away—"

"—Then Dad would be dead. I'm sure his suicide would have been convenient for you," he cut back.

She turned on him. "You don't know a thing about your father, Arthur. He wanted to commit suicide—he even wrote it out in his will. Why should you be concerned if I was going to help him to die a swift, merciful death? You don't know how lonely and tormented he's been all these months, feeling abandoned by his sons. You got the money from him and went right to Europe, not even bothering to come by and see him. All these months he's been alone."

Bear felt the stabs of guilt thrust through him, silencing his accusations. "I didn't know he was dying," was all he could say.

"Just like you didn't know that Blanche looked like your mother," sneered Elaine. "You're so full of it." She punched a button on the computer and the screen faded to black.

He tried once more to brace himself as she walked into the corner of the room. "What did you do with Blanche?"

She yanked up a corner of the carpet and pulled out a wooden box that was set into the floor. Taking out a key, she unlocked it, and took out a small white envelope. "I put her body in my car. To dispose of later."

"Is she dead?"

"She's as good as dead."

"Elaine, it's not too late. Take her to the hospital."

"They couldn't do anything for her."

He knew what she was doing. And what she was not saying. Setting his jaw, he waited.

"Still," Elaine seemed to be rethinking her works as she pulled on a pair of gloves. "I suppose I could let her live. So long as she's not found anywhere near this house and so long as she stays in a coma, she's no threat to me. If that's your idea of mercy—eternal sleep and living death."

He didn't answer her sneer but watched her movements steadily.

She smiled at him faintly. "You want to come down to the car with me, Arthur? If you come along quietly, you can even pick out the place where I'll drop Blanche off."

This was a feeble attempt to get him to walk to the place of his execution. He shook his head. "You'll have to drag me," he said softly. "I'd fight you tooth and nail." At least a struggle would leave evidence.

"Just as you like." Her eyes flickered, and she took out a syringe and sifted the powder from the envelope into it. He watched her as she took out another packet, and emptied that into the syringe as well. And another.

She went to the bar and poured a glass of water. Then she drew some of it up into the syringe and shook it methodically.

Now she gazed at the swirling white powder in the syringe.

"I'm curious," she said absently. "You always said you never did drugs. Was that true?"

"Yes," he said, swallowing.

"So you've never done heroin?"

"No."

"I'm told it's not a bad way to go," she said, setting down the needle and pulling a scarlet scarf out of the box. "It will make sense to the police, too. You were high on drugs, and you broke into my house, and I was forced to restrain you, but you had overdosed, and you died while I was getting the police."

He saw the abyss she was sliding towards, and for her sake as much as his own, he said, "You don't want to commit murder, Elaine. You said you didn't."

"It's too late, Arthur," she said, fiddling with the scarlet scarf and twisting it into a rope.

"It's *not*," he found himself saying, trying not to be distracted by the scarf.

She needed to tie his arm in order to get to the vein. "I'm going to have to send you flying to the stars. There's the black and the white. The checkmate. You're going to win, and I can't let you. It's all black and white, Arthur. There are no switching sides or switching colors in chess."

"This isn't chess. This is life. Everyone has a chance to change sides, even at the last moment of their lives," he was trying to reach her with his eyes, while being aware of her every movement.

"Even to a bad girl like me?" She laughed softly as she came forward, sliding her hand into her pocket. "'From a woman came sin, and so we all must die.' We're the ones who began it all."

He tried with all his might not to flinch, trying to meet her gaze even as he carefully shifted his position. "But," he said, "there was the woman who was full of grace, who said, 'yes.' And that's how the end of sin began."

He thought he saw a gleam in her eyes. She held out the scarf, but started to pull her hand out of her pocket, the pocket with the chloroform. "Full of grace," she murmured, "White as snow."

As she darted forward he ducked his head and hurled himself into her. They collided with such force that she reeled backwards, hit her head against the wall, and crumbled down in a black heap, dropping the chloroform and the red scarf. Immediately he curled into a ball and rolled himself back to a wobbly sitting position again, tense, watching for her next move.

Stunned, she crawled forward, her bright blue eyes glittering at him in wrath.

"So," she said savagely, "this is how you treat a woman?"

He could tell she had not been prepared for such a show of physical force, and she wasn't anxious to take him on again.

"I'm going to take your queen," she spat at him, "and drop her body on the figure eight ramp to the Henry Hudson parkway. And then I'm just going to go round and round on that figure eight until there's nothing left but a bloody pulp."

She stumbled to her feet, snatched up her mask, wig, and visor, and tore out of the room, slamming the door behind her.

His heart was racing. He had bought himself some time—*but at what cost?*

Blanche, he shouted in his mind, *What have I done to you?*

When the little men found Snow White
lying as if dead, they called her name,
combed her hair, washed her with water and
wine, to no avail. She would not wake.
Grimm

Chapter Twenty-Three

She was sliding in and out of consciousness, scenes coming upon her in bursts like flashes of light, followed by silent darkness.

The darkness had her, and she felt as though she had been running from it all summer, running from it this entire past year, running from it all her life. And all this time it had been gaining ground steadily and was now overtaking her.

A flash, and then Bonnie was there again, the empty green eyes hovering over her in darkness. "It's too late," she said in a dull voice. "If only you had stayed away, this wouldn't have happened—"

The black pupils of her eyes seemed to grow out of the bag lady's face until they consumed her. Consumed everything.

And that was all. It was over.

The last thing she sensed was the sound of someone starting a car.

II

"Leon, where are you all?" Father Francis's voice on the phone was tinged with exasperation.

"Uh...on the corner of Broadway and 96th," Leon said. "It's our educated guess that Nora took the subway down here. But we can't seem to find out where she went from here."

"Is Brother George with you?"

"No, he's not."

"All right. I'm sending Father Bernard with the van to help. He'll be there in about a half hour, okay?"

"Okay."

"Leon, God will take care of her."

"Keep praying," Leon said, and hung up the pay phone.

"Where to, Big-Little-Dog?" Charley asked again.

"Uh, Charley you stake out this corner and wait for Father Bernard. Let him know what we're doing; Matt, you and I'll split up and circle round the block again. We should be able to spot Nora if she comes back to this station. Let's meet back here in about fifteen minutes, okay?"

All nodded and split up. They had been doing this for the past hour. He was glad no one had complained.

It was late at night now. He walked through the thinning crowds, the hot wind flapping his habit against his legs. The worst part was the blind searching, not really knowing where to look.

At last he stopped and forced himself to stand quiet for a moment, looking towards the Henry Hudson Parkway, where an occasional car drove leisurely by, exiting and entering on the figure-eight cloverleaf ramps. Beyond the parkway, the lights of New Jersey glimmered across the river. Inwardly Leon reached out, to trust, to hope...

As he was turning around, he saw a white car screeching around a corner. It was being driven by a woman with a green eyeshade.

As though an electric current had run through him, he jumped forward, running hard, his sandals banging the pavement. *Come on, come on*, he thought to himself. The car was speeding towards the ramps leading to the Parkway.

He caught a glimpse of Matt and shouted, "Matt! It's Bonnie!"

Matt turned and followed, but Leon had a hundred yard lead.

There was no way they were going to be able to outrun a car. Still, there was a chance she would have to stop at the light first to get to the cloverleaf ramp. *Let's hope she's going south*, he thought, and raced for the lower loop of the cloverleaf.

He saw the white car starting up the ramp and was close enough to hear its engine churning to a stop. It halted, then jerked forward again with a screech and got onto the Parkway. Leon climbed over the concrete barrier, and looked in the shadows of the darkest part of the ramp where the car had paused. A body lay sprawled on the road, a jumble of blue and pink sheets with black hair. Nora.

Shouting, Leon ran to her, seized her and tried to drag her out of the roadway, or at least into the light. She was still warm, but unresponsive, her body a dead weight.

He had been trying to follow the sound of the car. When he heard the whine of its engine, he figured that the owner of the car had gotten directly off the Parkway and was coming around again for another circuit.

Hurriedly he threw Nora's arm over his shoulder, pulled her into a fireman's carry, and raced for his life down the ramp and off to the side. He saw the headlights and they blinded him momentarily. The car wasn't stopping. It was speeding towards him in fury.

He reached the bottom of the ramp and scrambled over the concrete barrier, tumbling onto the ground three feet below with Nora on top of him. The white car screamed past him with rage, but couldn't touch him.

Stumbling to his feet, he stooped to pick up Nora again, hoping against hope that the fall hadn't hurt her worse. "Matt?" he shouted. Now he was on the road beneath the parkway, even less traveled, where similar dangers awaited him.

Shouldering Nora, he tried to figure out the quickest way to safety. He heard the whine of the white car once again, and staggered in the opposite direction. Bonnie would be making another circuit of the cloverleaf, looking for a way to get off and crush him. And this back road would be an ideal place to do it.

He started back towards busier town streets, lurching beneath his burden. Tires squealed. He had unwittingly stepped out into traffic. *Careful!* he said to himself, and hurried unsteadily across the road, making another car shriek to a stop to avoid him. He heard what he was certain was the sound of an illegal U-turn. There was a blinding sweep of headlights.

Then the car swerved aside and pulled to a stop beside him. It was white. He blinked, and recognized a familiar battered Toyota. Inside were Brother George and Matt.

"Get inside, quick!" the older brother rasped.

Leon tumbled Nora inside the car, Matt grabbing her shoulders and pulling her in. Leon squeezed in and slammed the door. The Toyota roared to life and sped away from the deadly cloverleaf.

"You okay, Leon?" Brother George asked. "What happened to Nora?"

Leon was too winded to reply. For a few minutes he looked this way and that way, trying to see if the white car was following them.

But it wasn't. He didn't see it again.

III

God, help me, Bear begged. *Please help Blanche. Please protect her.* He worked feverishly at his bonds, until his wrists were hot, wet, and stinging, but to no avail. At last he realized it was useless. He thought of shouting for help, but who would hear him? Fish and Rose might have come to the house, but they would be locked outside on the street, unable to get in. Did Fish have a key? Bear doubted it—his brother didn't hold onto things like old keys. They might be standing outside the house right now, trying to decide what to do. They might even suppose he had just gone home and leave. Bear's heart sank.

There was only his father—could he possibly hear him? And if he heard, could he come? Would he come?

As desperate as his situation was, he balked at the thought of doing it. But what other choice did he have? He gritted his teeth and made himself move, yanking his ankles upwards, gritting his teeth against the pain. The settee was heavy, but he could pull it inch by inch from the wall. Jerking and dragging this burden bit by bit behind him, he forced himself across the carpet over to the door. At last he put his mouth down to the crack. Swallowing and wetting his lips, he barked hoarsely, "Dad! Dad! Help!"

There was no answer. He roared with all his might, "Dad!"

Dizzy with the effort, he leaned his head back, feeling desolation overwhelm him. Elaine would come back, and he would die here, in this suffocating nightmare of a house, unheard. Unseen. Would his dad even know his son had been here?

"Dad!" he screamed again, and closed his eyes with the pain that heaved up in his chest. *I'm like a kid, a crying, sobbing little baby, crying out for his dad,* he thought. And it was probably just a pointless prelude to despair.

As he waited, the minutes passing, he thought for a moment that he heard a noise.

A faint, scrabbling scraping noise. Like a mouse creeping over the carpet.

He lifted his head and tried to hear through the ringing in his ears. Minutes went by.

There it was again. "Dad?" he tried again, and his voice was more like a croak than a human sound.

"Arthur? Is that you?" a voice came outside the door, as though from far away.

"Yes," Bear whispered. Then he cleared his throat. "Yes," he said again, hardly believing what he was hearing.

"I heard you calling."

"I need your help," Bear hesitated over what to say had happened. A fear suddenly rose up in him, of what Elaine might have told his father. He could imagine her going to the bedroom with some lie before she left. "Your oldest son was here, robbing our home. I had to call the police to come and get him."

And Dad would believe her. He had always believed her.

Yet, Dad was outside the door right now.

"Are you all right? Why are you here?" his dad was saying.

Bear was fast fighting more and more despair welling up in him. *He'll never believe you. You'll never get him to trust you again. Especially not after you've neglected him for so long...*After all, a man as intelligent and sophisticated as his father couldn't even accept that Elaine was responsible for his shoddy medical care. How much less likely was he to believe this twisted stratagem of Elaine's? He had lived years under her spell.

"Dad, I—" he started, and then heard himself saying, "We need to help Blanche. She's in trouble."

There was a pause. Then his dad spoke. "Where did Elaine take her?"

"To the highway. She said she was going to run over her." Bear's words slowed as he felt anew the crushing weight of all the previous times he had accused Elaine to no avail. Years of pain and hopelessness welled up inside him as he remembered the humiliation of his father incredulously refusing to believe that Elaine would try to seduce a high school boy. Now the stakes had only gotten higher. Who was his dad going to side with—Blanche or Elaine?

Bear waited for his answer, his heart numb.

"Okay. I haven't been doing too well lately, but I'll try to get the door open."

"Thanks, Dad," he said, swallowing again. He heard more soft scraping noises. Then he added, "It might be locked."

"I think I can get it," said his father.

Bear heard hands fumbling with the lock, heard a knob turn, a click, and the door swung open.

He had expected to look up and see his father looking down at him, but to his amazement, his father was crouched on the floor, holding onto the doorjamb with one hand, while the other hung lifelessly down, both hands creviced like a skeleton's. His skin was translucent, and his eyes hollowed. There was no way a man in his condition could stand upright. Bear realized that his father must have crawled down the hallway to get to him.

"Arthur," his father said, his voice husky. "Who did this to you?"

Bear shifted onto his side and blinked. "Elaine," he finally managed to say.

IV

It was night.

Night, inevitable night, had come upon her.

Even as she succumbed, falling through deeper and deeper layers of unconsciousness, she struggled to understand what had happened. *How it had happened.*

Another flash, this time more like delirium. She was with the old lady, back in the corridor of her old high school. It was red outside the windows.

The hallway was spinning around her as she tried to get to her feet.

"Where are you going to run to, Blanche? The enemy's inside you now. You can't escape."

Blanche staggered down the hallway, and Elaine followed, laughing. The sound began to melt away into music that sounded like one of Bear's piano pieces played backwards. There were ants climbing all over her leg. Blanche's hands were shaking, but she tried to brush them off.

Then all of a sudden she came upon the corpse of what looked like the body of a dead horse, lying in its own blood. Elaine was standing on it, wearing red high-heeled shoes and grinding her teeth. There was something in her hands, something long, white, sharp, and twisted. Her voice spoke again. "I've got one last message for you, Blanche. It's a life lesson, and I never want you to forget it. You can wait forever, and the prince will never show up. He's not coming, Blanche. He never does. Your trust was in vain. You were better off alone."

She was smiling at Blanche, but then her smile slithered off her face and down her arm, a red worm. It was coming towards Blanche. It stretched itself around her bare leg and began to suck. Elaine began floating up to the ceiling in a dance, waving her arms, her shoes shrieking. The unicorn's horn fell and shattered to the floor. The windows began to slide down the walls. Blanche tried again to walk, but Elaine was everywhere, blocking her wherever she tried to go. "I'm going to make you into a lamppost," Elaine said to her, and began to twist her around and around, and Blanche felt herself becoming stiffer and colder, like iron. Then slowly the world began to crystallize around her, like glass.

I'm turning into glass, Blanche thought, and then sank into silence. Only the sirens outside kept screaming. Or was it still Elaine's shoes, screaming as she ran, ran away?

Who could find her now, in this darkness?

V

After circling around to leave word with Charley for Father Bernard, Brother George had driven back to the Bronx to take the unconscious girl to the Catholic hospital nearest the friars.

As soon as he and Matt had laid her down on the hospital gurney, the nurses had swarmed around her, taking her pulse, checking her vital signs, and hooking up an IV. A nurse came with a clipboard, and Leon gave her as much information as he could.

"Do you know why she's unconscious?" one nurse asked.

"I know she has a heart problem of some kind," Leon said hesitantly.

"Check for digoxin in her system," Brother George cut in suddenly. "I have an idea that she might have been dosed with it."

The medical people immediately pulled the gurney into a curtained-off cubicle to hook her up to a heart monitor. Waiting and praying, the three friars stood outside.

After some time, a doctor came out. He recognized the friars and came over to them at once. "She's having life-threatening arrhythmia," he said, and explained, "Her heartbeat's abnormal, and, combined with low blood pressure, it doesn't look as though her brain's getting enough oxygen and glucose. It seems like she's gone into a coma."

"Are you checking for digoxin?" Brother George asked.

The doctor nodded. "Normally we'd try cardioversion—electrical shocking—in this case, but because of the possibility of digoxin, we're putting her on heart-protective meds instead. Her life is in danger. Do you know why she was taking digoxin?"

Brother George shook his head. "All I know is that this afternoon she gave me a bottle that contained digoxin pills. She said she thought someone she knew was being poisoned with them. A man with a brain tumor. When I said it might make him sick, make him go into a coma, she was upset and hurried off. I warned her to get help, but—" he paused, and his voice dropped. "I don't know what happened after she left."

"Is that why you went looking for her?" Leon asked, after the doctor had made some notes and hurried on his way.

The older brother nodded. "I asked Father Francis if I could take the car and go looking for her. Just like you, I was driving around the 96th Street station."

"Then I saw him, flagged him down and sent him after you," Matt said.

"George, this sick friend of hers with the brain tumor—did she tell you his name?" Leon pressed.

Brother George shook his head. "I don't even know Nora's last name. Do you?"

The two novices each shook their heads. "We don't know a lot about her, do we?"

Leon looked at the curtain behind him, where he could see the shadows of the medical personnel still working on the comatose girl. "Nora, I wish you had told us more," he whispered.

VI

It took Bear's father a long time to cut the knots on Bear's wrists, which had gotten tighter during his exertions. It was an excruciating process, and his dad only had one hand with which to use Elaine's desk knife. By the time his dad had tugged the last cord free, Bear's clenched jaw ached from the effort not to cry out. He had thought at times that his father would wear out or give up, but apparently the state of Bear's wrists was so terrible that his father's anger kept him going. "What kind of monster did this to you?" he said over and over again as he worked at the knots.

Bear kept repeating, rather lamely, "I did most of it myself, trying to get free." His father didn't seem to register the fact that Elaine could have done such a thing, which didn't surprise Bear.

When his hands were free, Bear had to admit that they looked pretty awful—the skin all around both wrists was lacerated and bleeding.

"Thanks, Dad," he said.

His dad was pale, but his one working eye was concerned as he tilted his head over his son's hands, "We need to get something for those cuts, Arthur."

"We need to find Blanche first. And we need to call the police," Bear said, starting to untie his legs from the couch.

"Right." But his father sounded bewildered. "I knew Elaine was jealous of Blanche. Still it's hard to believe..."

"Dad, don't worry about it right now. We'll work it out somehow." The cords came free and Bear turned anxiously to his fragile father. "Let me help you back to bed."

"No, I won't go back to that bedroom," his father sounded surprisingly vehement. "Help me downstairs."

Bear shouldered his father's good arm, frightened at how light his father was. "Dad, what's happened to you?" he asked as he helped him down the stairs.

"Don't you know? Brain tumor," his dad said, the working side of his face tense as though he were holding in pain. "The doctor said I'll probably go into a coma soon, most likely for good."

"I'm sorry I didn't know," Bear fumbled for the words as they reached the first landing.

"I wrote to you—didn't you get the letter?" his father queried, tilting his head at him.

"No, I never got anything," Bear said.

"I gave the letter to Elaine to mail," his father said, his voice sad.

His father was still trying to absorb everything that had happened, and Bear knew that would take time. A shudder of fear passed over him. They were not safe yet. Down below them, the stained glass mirror glimmered.

Bear realized that the front door was opening and barely had time to push his father down and shield him before the gun went off.

One bullet sank into the wall with a thud and the beams of the house reverberated. The second bullet ricocheted off the marble railing and disappeared into the ceiling. But Bear was unhurt, pressed against the steps, covering his father. He stared down at Elaine, whose jaw was thrust forward, her eyes blue steel as she leveled the semiautomatic at him again.

There was a shout, and Elaine spun around, only to be slammed into by Fish, who flew through the door in a running leap. Both of them fell to the ground, Fish on top, but Elaine's gun arm was pointing out the open door. Through the entranceway, Bear could see Rose standing breathless at the outer door, holding it open. She froze when she saw the gun pointed at her.

"Rose move!" Fish shouted, pinning Elaine's arm to the ground and grabbing at the gun. Elaine shoved her arm free and fired off a shot at Rose. The bullet skittered across the marble tile but Rose had leapt out of the way just in time. Fish, grappling swiftly, tried to force the gun up and away from the doorway, but Elaine changed direction, yanking the gun towards her own head. She broke her arm free of his grip, and viciously cracked him on the side of the face with the gun.

Stunned, Fish fell back and then crawled forwards, disoriented, his face bleeding. But she shoved him aside and got to her feet first, her long black coat whipping around her, two hands on the gun.

"Freeze!" shouted a deep and terrifying voice, and Bear caught a glimpse of Hunter running up the front steps, grabbing Rose and sweeping them both behind the door jamb just as a jumpy Elaine fired another clip at their shadows. Fish tried to grab the gun muzzle, burned his hand on the hot barrel, and released it with a yelp. It was happening too fast. She fumbled with the gun, then leveled it at Fish's head, getting her hand on the trigger...

Bear leapt down the stairs, seizing her from behind and lunging for the gun. He narrowly missed Elaine's wrist as she swung her right hand up over her head to point the gun over her shoulder.

She was trying to shoot him over her back. Quickly he grabbed her waist and the wrist of her gun hand. She fired straight past his face, deafening him. He drove all the force of his arm against her weapon hand, forcing the gun down as she writhed in his grip and shot wildly. Glass shattered and a wild spider web of cracks spread across the mirror's shining surface as a bullet went through.

He was trying to pry her fingers off the handle with one hand. "Elaine, drop the gun!" he grunted in her ear. "Drop it!" But she screamed in answer and suddenly kicked her heel against his left shin, making him stumble. They began to fall, but with vehement tenacity, he didn't let go of her gun hand. She fired again as they fell through the mirror. And again as they hit the floor amidst a shower of broken glass. The last shot sounded strangely muffled.

Silence.

In that catastrophe of shattered glass, he didn't dare to move, more for fear of cutting himself than of gunfire, deafened by the ringing in his ears, completely tense, waiting for Elaine's next move. The smell of blood crept across his nostrils. His left shoulder throbbed and his vision swirled, but he couldn't move. The fall had been hard.

He became aware that Hunter was bending over him warily. He saw the big man step on the gun and slide it away from Elaine's grasp. She did not resist. He realized that her body had become a dead weight.

Tears sprung to his eyes.

Hunter picked up the gun. He was silent for a moment, then his impassive eyes traveled to Bear.

"You okay?" his lips said.

Bear made out what he was saying, and nodded. His ears were still humming loudly. "How's my dad?" he managed to ask, but he couldn't hear his own voice.

Hunter nodded, and spoke again, inaudibly, and, gently pushing the body away, gave Bear a hand up.

Bear staggered to his feet, brushing glass shards away from his clothes and cutting himself in the process. His hands were shaking, and he decided to leave the rest of the glass until he had regained control. Sweeping his eyes around the room, he saw Fish...Rose in the doorway...his father on the steps...all looking at him, and all breathing hard.

His hearing was returning. He saw Hunter punching numbers in his cell phone. Calling the police.

"Are you all right?" his brother asked, and Bear could make out his voice, and nodded.

"When did you get here?" he managed to ask Fish.

"About forty-five minutes ago. But we couldn't get in until Elaine drove up and..." Fish halted as Bear suddenly pivoted and ran out the door and down the steps.

There was a car parked at the curb, a white car. He pulled open the door on the passenger side. A black blanket lay crumpled in the front seat. He yanked it out. The seat was empty.

She could have put Blanche in the front seat, and covered her with the blanket...

Slamming the door, he ran to the front of the car and forced himself to get down on his hands and knees and look at the bumper and front tires. They looked smooth and black. He felt them, trying to see what was on them with only the help of a streetlight. They were dry.

He sensed Fish and Rose coming out. There was a heavy tread beside him, and Hunter stood by him.

"She had taken Blanche with her," Bear made himself say. "She was unconscious. Elaine said she would dump her body on the parkway and run over it..."

Fish and Rose were silent. Hunter squatted down beside him, pulled out a flashlight, and checked the car.

"It doesn't look to me like she ran over anyone with this car tonight," he said.

Bear prayed a silent prayer of thanks and nodded. *But someone else might have run over her by accident*, he told himself.

A patrol car pulled to the curb just as they were standing up, and Hunter took charge of the situation. He talked to the first policeman, who radioed a message immediately for another car to go and look for a body on the parkway. Hunter then led the policeman inside while a second policeman blocked off the area with yellow tape, and an ambulance pulled up behind the police car.

The police took Bear's personal information and a brief statement from him, as well as a gunpowder analysis test to verify who had fired the gun, before sending him off with another policeman to the parkway.

His bleeding hands still shaking, Bear thrust his head out the window as they slowly crept up the ramp, looking for any sign of her, anything—

Up and down the parkway and the surrounding streets, around and around the ramps they went in the night, until Bear was forced to admit the reality.

There was no sign of Blanche. She had vanished again.

Bear was persuaded to go to the hospital to have his cuts treated. While he was waiting for the emergency room doctor, Fish and Rose, who had already been checked over and treated for minor injuries, sat with him. There was still no word about Blanche.

Elaine had been pronounced dead from a self-inflicted wound upon arrival to the hospital. Her husband was in a stable condition, overall, and was being kept overnight for observation.

Breaking a silence of some duration, Bear said, "Fish, thanks again." His brother was still holding an ice pack to his bruised and cut face. "I'm always indebted to you somehow, tonight being no exception."

"Thank Rose," Fish said, unexpectedly.

Rose, surprised, looked up from where she sat on an end table next to Bear. For a moment she looked shocked and disbelieving, not accepting that Fish would be joking about something this significant and recent.

But Fish's face was serious. "I wouldn't have been there, Bear, if Rose hadn't raced up those steps right after Elaine and grabbed the door before it swung shut behind her. We would have been locked out again, and you and Dad probably would have been dead in that hallway."

He stood up, put down the ice pack, and extended a hand to Rose. "I admit it, I was slow to react. You made up for my deficiency. I am sincerely grateful."

She tentatively gave him her hand, and unexpectedly he raised it to his lips and kissed it, then patted it and put it down.

"And thank God for that man, Hunter, getting in when he did. I got his number from the DEA earlier today, and called him as soon as Rose told me where you had gone." Fish replaced his cold pack and turned to Bear again. "He's volunteered to testify on our behalf. Charles told me that he could become the pivotal witness."

"Is that right?" Bear wished for a moment that Fish would see it too, but his brother was facing the other way, seemingly more interested in telling Bear about federal laws concerning agents testifying in court. Rose was transfigured in wonder, holding the hand that Fish had kissed with astonishment. She actually did not speak a single word for several minutes.

*Snow White lay, as still as death, and
nothing could be done for her.*
Grimm

Chapter Twenty-Four

She was floating in the darkness, alternately sinking and rising. Sometimes she drifted to the edges of consciousness and caught snippets of things—a siren, people jabbering, someone sobbing. She thought she recognized a child's voice. Marisol's little girl.

"What happened to you, Princess? What happened to you?"

She fled the child's voice, down the labyrinthine ways back into the suffocating blackness, for fear the child's words would distort into more hallucinations. A scream, a scream that was never going to be heard.

And down, down, into darkness. She hung there for a while, a shy fish terrified of shadows, of the light that gave things form. But she was still breathing, breathing, and her own oxygen drove her back up towards the surface—too fast, too fast.

And then she was halted, gripped by an iron weight freezing her limbs, and something in the darkness laughed maliciously at her. She had not been able to get away.

Why? She asked wearily. *If you knew what was going to happen, God, why didn't you stop this? If he wasn't going to come in time, why did you let me trust him?*

There was nothing but the emptiness of echoes and her own pointless breathing. And the creeping, paralyzing doubt that had been hovering in the corners of her mind came flying out, screaming.

See? There's no one here. This is the darkness. This is the other side, where God is supposed to be. And it's empty.

Empty.

Except for the laughter in the darkness. Elaine's laughter. The delight of destruction.

So there was no point to anything. No platonic ideals, dazzling in the darkness. Just empty shells of people, randomly endowed with strength and weakness. Her sickness had labeled her from birth as one of the weak, which would never be fit to survive anyone's evolutionary scheme.

Only the good die young. Because the good are weak. She huddled in the murky pool and fought desperately against the paralyzing strength of the idea.

Why don't you just give up now? She heard Elaine's voice speaking.

Princes never come. What's the point in being a china doll? Why not be a power goddess, feeding on strength, re-making yourself in the image of every threat to your supremacy that came along? As Elaine had done.

She was being like a silly fainting heroine in some Victorian semi-classic, whimpering and dying of consumption, too fragile to keep herself together for very long, barely suspending disbelief. The weaker vessel.

But she couldn't shed her biology like a cracked eggshell and rise to do battle with nature. She *was* weak. And she was dying. Dying badly, warped by self-pity. As Mr. Fairston had been. Alone.

II

Leon saw the tears creeping from the eyes of the sleeping girl, and gently wiped them away.

Black hair, white skin—still as death, Leon thought. He had sat in the chair by the hospital bed in the ICU through the night, with Brother George. So far, Nora had eluded death, but her future was far from certain. The medications had halted the dangerous arrhythmia, and the cardiograms hadn't shown any major heart damage. But she lay as motionless as if she were indeed dead.

"How is she?" Father Francis asked in a low voice as he joined them on Monday morning. Nora was still attached to an IV and heart monitor. Leon couldn't answer, and the old priest touched his shoulder gently.

"The level of digoxin in her bloodstream is still coming down," Brother George said. "They're pumping it out of her system with dialysis. But they're not sure if she's going to wake up."

"God bless her," Father Francis said quietly. "We've got to find her family."

"Her mom and sister were on vacation. They were coming home tomorrow, I think," Leon said, but added dispiritedly, "But we don't know their names."

George rubbed the cross of his rosary. "The police have put out her information. But I don't know if there's much the doctors can do for her if she doesn't come around."

"Well, we'll just have to be her family until something turns up," Father Francis said briskly. "We'll take turns staying with her. You two go back now and get some sleep. I'll stay here."

Leon slowly got to his feet, grateful for his superior's care. The normally gruff priest surprised him by putting a hand on his shoulder. "There's always hope, Leon. Even in these desperate situations. There's always hope."

III

"Dad is going to be staying with us for a while," Fish informed Bear that afternoon, calling from their apartment. "Is that okay with you?"

"That's fine with me," Bear said, cradling the cell phone as he drove. He was on his way to another hospital, looking for Blanche. "Probably better than him going back to that house."

"No kidding. He was released from Mt. Sinai this afternoon, but he needs a practical nurse right away. Jean and Rose stopped searching to help him get settled in our apartment. Jean said she can stand in as long as she's needed— she still has a few days before she's due back at work—so I suggested she stay here in the apartment, and Rose too. It's pretty tough on both of them right now. I figured you and I could go to a hotel, but Jean wants us to go sleep at her house."

"You can go, but I'm not planning on sleeping tonight," Bear said.

"I understand," Fish said. "Well, I suppose you could call the meeting I had with the Mirror Corporation and Elaine's lawyers 'productive.'"

"Was it?"

Fish blew out his breath. "Well, at least we've found a motive for Elaine's irrational actions. The courts should like this, if we can prove to them that she was the one who framed us. Like Charles told us, if we were convicted for drug possession, we would have been cut out of Dad's will. And everything would have gone to Elaine. It seems he was only going to give her a minimal amount, figuring that she had her investment company to depend on. But now it seems Mirror Corporation is in big, big trouble. There's been some, shall we say, misappropriation of funds going on, and the blame for that seems to be laid at Elaine's office door. I remember that she was a big spender, but this gives a new meaning to the word 'big.' The company would have gone under unless their corporate debts were paid off. All due the first of September."

"She was gambling it would all work out," Bear said. "That Dad would be dead or in a coma by August 15th and that we would be cut out of the will, so she could have all the money to herself."

"That would have balanced the scales, as she would have had power of attorney if he went into a coma. But now, it's a huge mess. Fortunately, Dad isn't liable for most of her losses. He seems to have had the sense to keep his assets away from her control."

"How's he doing?"

"He's handling it okay. Jean and Rose are hanging in there. I have to say that Jean's a great nurse. I have no idea what kind of medical help Elaine hired to take care of him at his home, but they must have been rather lousy. At least he's in good hands now. He's not exactly cheerful, but you can tell the change has been for the better. Mrs. Foster has been reading to him, too, and he seems to appreciate that."

"Good."

"Right now Rose is handling the funeral arrangements for Elaine, and doing quite well."

Bear heard Rose in the background say, "Why thank you, Mr. Fish."

"Good redhead. Helpful redhead," Fish returned. "So any sign of Blanche?"

"No," Bear had expected the question, but wasn't prepared for the sense of failure that overwhelmed him. "She's vanished. I've been checking for a nameless girl with her description, but so far, nothing. I just called the police again to check. No nameless girls at any of the hospitals in Manhattan."

"Did you check under her name? Despite everything, she might have been conscious enough to give a name."

"Yes, but nothing there either."

"Let's hope Elaine didn't dump her in the river," was Fish's grim response. "Rose still thinks Blanche may have come to her senses and been able to escape somehow."

"Rose didn't see her," Bear said in a low voice, and Fish was silent. Bear's heart sickened inside him.

"Well, I'm at the apartment still, and I'll probably be here for a while. The paperwork is pretty hellish. I'm trying to figure it out so I can make sure Dad understands it himself. He was the vice-chairman of Mirror, so they're going to come to him with some of this stuff."

"Do you need me? Should I come back?" Bear asked.

"Are you kidding? No, keep looking. That's the most important thing right now. The money stuff will sort itself out. It always does."

IV

Alone. Cut off from life, but cheated of death. Suspended between two worlds.

She had seen it coming at her for so long, but her foresight had paralyzed her instead of forearming her. And now it had her in its jaws, slowly crushing her.

She was vaguely aware of doctors by her bed, consulting, shaking their heads. And she realized what that meant. A permanent coma. Trapped for life.

No hope.

She spun around in the stillness, trying to find something to hold onto. Was there anything that remained?

...O God, come to my assistance.
O Lord, make haste to help me.
Make haste.

V

By Tuesday morning the digoxin levels were down to normal in Nora's bloodstream, but she remained in a coma. That morning, Father Bernard took over watching Nora so that Father Francis could come back. Matt was to go next. Leon volunteered to pick the priest up after his shift. Father Bernard told him to come early.

"I asked the Catholic chaplain to let us use a small meeting room at the hospital. That way you and I can have our discernment meeting as we planned."

"Sure thing," Leon said, trying to be nonchalant.

But he wasn't prepared for Father Bernard's bombshell, which the older friar quietly dropped in the midst of that meeting.

"What?" Leon stared at his novice master. He was hoping the older friar had been kidding.

But Father Bernard was serious. "I think you should examine your vocation a little more in depth, Leon," he said, his dark eyes looking into the younger friar's. "You have the makings of a good priest in you. I suspect that you haven't thought about it as much as you should."

Leon squirmed. He had always heard Father Bernard had the gift of reading hearts, and suspected that God and his novice master had been talking to each other behind his back. "Father, I just don't think I'm the sort of guy God has in mind when He creates a priest. I'm just—I don't know, too much of a loudmouth."

"Unfortunately, that doesn't seem to be an impediment to ordination," Father Bernard gave a tiny sigh. "But seriously, Leon, after you take your temporary vows, I think you should start taking some introductory courses at the seminary this fall. And while you're doing that, I want you to listen very closely to God. You may find His direction will surprise you."

Leon spread his hands dejectedly. "I promised to be obedient, so I'll obey," he said at last.

"Is there anything that's holding you back?" Father Bernard probed. "Are you afraid of anything?"

"Yes." Leon hung his head, crestfallen.

"Can you tell me what it is?"

"Sure." Leon paused, looked at the ceiling, and then let out his breath. "It's school."

"School," Father Bernard scratched his ear as though he hadn't heard correctly.

"I hate school. I barely survived college. I can't bear the thought of going back, even to become a priest."

"You can't be serious?" Father Bernard asked with a smile.

"You might think it's funny, but it's not," Leon protested. "Four years of seminary—it's like four years of solitary confinement to me. I could put up with the priesthood, but I don't think I could listen to lectures and take notes for one year, let alone four."

Father Bernard crossed his arms and looked at Leon, still chuckling. "It's really not so bad, Leon. But it's not the biggest trial you'll ever face as a priest. I survived it. If God is calling you, you will too." He got to his feet. "Let's go back to see Nora. Then we should leave."

They prayed the rosary beside Nora until Matt arrived. While they were chatting at the doorway of Nora's hospital room, Matt looked over his shoulder. "Oh no." Leon saw Jim Hornberg coming towards them down the hospital hallway.

"There you are!" He came towards them, a solemn expression on his face, but his eyes were a bit more wide-awake. "I heard your distressing news." He looked at Nora's white face, and shook his head, seemingly genuinely sad. "Such a shame," he said. "And so young!"

"How did you find out?" Leon asked.

"Oh, news travels quickly over the grapevine," Jim said. "I was talking to the chaplain here about the diocesan collection, and I thought I would stop by. Is there any chance she's going to come out of it?"

"We don't know," Father Bernard admitted.

"You boys certainly have a way of making waves," Jim shook his head.

Leon cocked his eye suspiciously at Father Bernard.

As Father Bernard and Leon left, Jim followed them out, still asking them questions about Nora's condition. Leon was trying to adjust his attitude towards being friendlier towards Brother Jim, as they walked out into the parking lot.

Brother Jim made as if to take his leave, but then he paused, turned back to Father Bernard, and said, "So, forgive me for saying this at such a hard time, Bernie, but you surely don't expect that the diocese is going to pay for this?"

Brother Leon, who never would have dreamed of calling his novice master "Bernie," stared at the man in stupefaction. Father Bernard also looked a bit disoriented.

"We hadn't exactly considered..." he admitted. "Why are you asking?"

"Well, you should start thinking about that. You know comas can last for years. Does this girl have any family that you know of?"

"I'm sure she does, but..."

"What are you going to do if you can't find her family and she needs hospice care? Who's going to take care of her?"

"We will," Leon said.

Brother Jim looked at him with mixed surprise and amusement. "Oh, really? I hadn't realized this was part of the plan—and neither did the chancery, I'm willing to make a bet. But seriously, Bern, you can't expect to foot someone's medical bills for life, just like that. There's such a thing as Christian charity, but we all know there's harsh reality too. Suppose you find her family, and they turn out to be poor? They're not going to be able to pay for lifelong hospice care, maybe not even her hospital bill."

"So we just starve her to death?" Leon spoke up again fiercely.

"There you go again, Leon, putting things into such judgmental black-and-white terms."

"So what are you suggesting?" Leon repeated, and folded his arms and stared at the man.

"I'm just trying to show you that these situations are far more complex and nuanced than...well, there's the ideal of the sanctity of human life and dignity and then there's the reality: medical bills, quality of life, qualitative care...and you mentioned death. Don't we all believe there's more to life than just this mundane world? Shouldn't we consider whether or not you're keeping someone from fulfilling their appointment with eternal life?"

"If you're talking about your own appointment with eternal life, I agree," growled Leon.

Jim laughed. "Temper, temper, Leon. I always said you weren't cut out for religious life. Just because you managed to get into a renegade order doesn't mean a thing about your psychological fitness, as I'm sure everyone will find out."

Father Bernard said quietly, "I think, Jim, that we're going to use the old-fashioned resource in this case."

"And what's that?" the man smiled at him condescendingly.

"Pray for a miracle," Father Bernard said. "Let's go, Leon."

"A miracle!" Brother Jim hooted. "Holy cards and hand grenades! Storm those heavens!" Chuckling, he turned back to his car, a very nice Cadillac.

Leon called to the older man as he opened the door. "Let me ask you something, Jim."

"What?"

"What exactly do you *do* for a living?"

Brother Leon and Brother Jim, the young friar and the old, exchanged looks for a moment, then Jim's expression soured. He got into the car and turned on the ignition, which answered him smoothly.

"Now Leon," Father Bernard remonstrated with the novice, as he coaxed the engine of their rusty Toyota back to life again. "Patience under trials."

"I suppose I need a penance?" Leon asked, rubbing his forehead.

"Yes. You are to pray for Brother Jim, that he gets to heaven before you do," the older friar directed.

Catching himself, Father Bernard looked quickly back at the novice. "And not because of any direct action on your part!" he added.

"Or yours!" Leon quipped with a smile.

*But she was still black as night and white
as snow, and she lay in her bed, her cheeks
as red as they had been in life,
though she did not move or stir.*
Grimm

Chapter Twenty-Five

Bear stood outside the door of the bedroom that had once been his mother's. He found himself lingering, his hand on the knob, looking up at the ceiling.

Come on, don't wait, he thought to himself. Crashing for a few hours' sleep on the couch had restored some of his physical energy, but he had so little emotional energy left…Still, he had to go in.

"He's not doing so well," Jean had warned him. The digoxin that Elaine had been giving him had weakened his system. And the brain tumor that might take his life any day was still waiting in the wings for its final entrance.

The sick man was lying in the bed that had belonged to his first wife. The silver gray canopy curtains were drawn back to the wall. He was looking out the windows over the cityscape, as though deep in thought, or fighting off pain. But he slowly looked over at Bear when he came in.

"Arthur?"

"Yes," he said. Then he added, "Dad."

"Did you find her?"

"No."

There was a long pause, while the man looked out the window, and Bear wondered for a moment if he had understood. Then he suddenly realized there were tears running down the man's cheeks.

He came closer. "Dad—are you all right?" he asked.

The man spoke without looking at him. "Do you think she's dead?"

Bear shook his head slowly. "No," he said at last. "I don't know if it's because it's still so unreal, but she doesn't feel dead to me."

"I hope you're right," the man said softly. He looked at Bear. "I loved her as though she were my own daughter. I didn't know she was yours. But I loved her."

Bear pulled over a footstool and sat down beside the bed. "Dad, to be honest, I really don't know if she's 'mine.' I don't really know where our relationship is going. I don't know if she—" Bear found he was struggling himself, surprised at how easy and natural it was to converse with his dad. "Let me leave that aside for a minute. Dad, I'm sorry," he said at last. "I've been a real jerk to you."

"Can't say I blame you much," his dad said, after a pause. His breath seemed to have a hard time coming. "I have a lot to ask forgiveness for, don't I?"

"I forgive you, Dad. I've—well, I've been trying to forgive you for a long time." He had to smile, remembering. "Blanche told me I needed to."

"Is that right?"

"Yeah. I didn't see why it would make any difference to us, but now I see it has. She's had a lot to do with this."

"It seems she's been helping both of us." His father looked at him with one eye, but couldn't keep his gaze. *He's still afraid,* Bear thought. "I haven't exactly been much of a role model. More an example of what not to do. I didn't stick to the woman I promised to be faithful to for life, left her to die alone—I would have done more for her, but Elaine made it an issue—said if I went to see Catherine, it was all over between us, and I was too weak to say no. I should have gone anyway—gone back to you and Ben and Catherine. If I had, things might have turned out better for all of us—" his voice died away into despair.

Bear put a hand on his father's shoulder, and the man managed to look him in the eyes once more. "I want you to know that God brought good out of that, Dad, even if you don't see it. I'm just starting to see a lot of it myself. What I'm trying to say is, as big as your shortcomings were, God made up for them. He always will, if we let Him fill in the holes. That's the only way any one of us can say we're men, in the end."

His dad's good eyelid drooped. "I always resented that you boys found more inspiration in a celibate priest than in me. I guess it made me feel inadequate, so I made you suffer for it. I'm sorry."

"I forgive you, Dad."

"Thank you, son," the man whispered. And then put his hand on Bear's arm, "Listen, I know you're worried about me slipping into this coma, but I want you to find Blanche. Just go out and keep looking for her. Don't worry about me. You have to keep after her until you find her." The man pushed Bear's arm away, and then confusingly, grabbed it again, and pulled Bear back towards him.

Bear's father hugged him for a long moment, and Bear felt the strength in his father again, but it was waning. His dad's voice was faint. "Now go."

Bear left.

Despite his words to his father, Bear was afraid that by now, Blanche was dead. At the recommendation of the police department, he forced himself to go to the morgue at the medical examiner's office.

He went alone, not because he wanted to, but because he didn't want to ask Rose or Jean to face the ordeal unnecessarily. If she was dead, he wanted to be the one to find out first, and the one to break the news.

After filling out the paperwork, he waited for a police detective to come and help him go through the files of the recently deceased who might match Blanche's description. He prayed that he would be like steel, and not cave in on himself. Fortunately, the staff member who came to help him was a mild, sensitive man who seemed to understand what he must be going through.

There were only a handful of cases that could have been Blanche, but even going through those four files was numbing. Bear simply prayed the same prayer over and over again: *Lord, have mercy. Christ, have mercy.*

Viewing the photo of the first questionably identified body was the worst, but Bear managed to keep himself steady.

"No," he said. "That's not her."

There was one badly-wounded accident victim who was the same age and hair color as Blanche, so Bear agreed to view the body. He had obtained from Jean a short list of Blanche's identifying marks—a scar on her right wrist from a childhood accident, a small mole on her left leg—that could help him to verify her.

He waited in a small blue and gray room for the body to be brought up on a lift from the morgue in the basement. When the gurney was wheeled up to the viewing window, he knew even before the man removed the sheet from her right arm that it wasn't Blanche. Still, being in the presence of Death was frightening, and silencing.

"No," he said softly, "that's not her."

When he had finished going through the morbid process, Bear realized that there was no real relief. Maybe her body hadn't been found yet, but if and when it was found, he would have to go through the same deadening process again.

"Keep checking the hospitals," the man said to him gently. "You never know. She may turn up alive. Stranger things have happened."

Bear blinked rapidly. He knew the man was trying to show sympathy, but, subdued by the presence of death, he had little hope.

"Thank you," he said.

For hours he drove from hospital to hospital, asking questions and looking at patients that might be Blanche. But the feeling of death was creeping forward in his mind, and he fought against it. Giving up driving, he parked his car and walked around the parkway, searching down alleys and in odd places, any spot where a sick girl might have fainted and lain unnoticed. His search yielded nothing.

He called home to check with Jean, who had been phoning hospitals and drop-in centers. Then he called the police. Still nothing. He was warned that it could take days to find her, even if she were in a hospital.

Heavy with sleep and weak with inner pain, Bear started to drive to the Briers' house. The mental image of death was closing in on him. And weariness lapped dangerously at his limbs.

He couldn't drive any longer. Pulling over to the side of the road, he parked the car, got out, and started walking, forcing his muscles to work and to escape the stalking of death.

By the time he came to a bridge leading to the Bronx, he felt as though he had pulled ahead of his enemy, for a moment. Stumbling off the road down to the bank, he found a dark spot under the bridge pilings uninhabited by muggers. He slept there. He had done it before. There were mosquitoes, and, he was sure, rats, but he was too exhausted to care.

The sun was starting to rise when he woke up with a jerk, aching all over. Blearily he ran his hands through his hair and tried to pat it down. He crawled out from under the bridge, feeling like something that had escaped from a slimy rock, and climbed back up to the road and crossed the bridge. Somehow he formulated a prayer of thanks for at least being alive. And he was hungry. All the same, he ignored his querulous and indignant stomach, and kept walking.

His footsteps took him a long way. Cities are entirely different when you walk through them. Not so long ago, he had walked almost everywhere, because he couldn't afford the subway. Now he started to remember once-familiar things. Memories led to others in an inexorable train.

It seemed like a very short time ago that he and Blanche had driven these streets in a taxi, her in a ripped but lovely green prom dress, him in a ruined tuxedo. That night, which had included a fistfight and an escape from the police, had been their bonding night. He remembered, in the taxi, sensing the closeness between them rising to a crescendo. He could see her fighting it, but didn't want to say anything until she was ready, until she could admit to herself what he had known was going on. On her front steps, she had finally stumbled out some words about loving him, and he had walked on air for days.

He winced now at the recollection and stopped in front of a small diner, open for breakfast. But the memory had stolen his taste for food, and he walked away, his incensed stomach protesting loudly.

If he kept on walking this way, he would come to the Briers' street, the brownstone with the roses in the window boxes. But he wasn't ready to go there yet. At the other end of this path, if he went the right direction, was St. Catherine's, Blanche's old high school, the site of the prom. And St. Lawrence's, the church where Father Raymond had served long ago, in Bear's other life, as he now thought of it. He still had the keys to the church, too—well, at least one key. Blanche had the other one.

No, he couldn't bear any more memories. It was time to retrace his steps, find his car, drive home. He turned around and started wearily back the way he had come.

Rapid steps were padding across the street behind him. He glanced around, and saw a dog. A large, rather ugly Rottweiler.

He halted. The dog, sensing his attention, looked over at him, and barked. Then it leapt back the way it had come.

His memory jarring, Bear ran after the dog. *Blanche, at the airport, grabbing the dog by the collar*—and this dog had the same thick red collar—it might be coincidence, but maybe—

The dog was sprinting towards St. Lawrence's. As Bear closed in on it, the dog sat down on the steps of the church, wagging its tail and looking at Bear expectantly. Apparently this was its home.

Bear didn't know what to do. He patted the dog gingerly on the head, and looked up at his former palace. He remembered being told by the archdiocese that some new order of monks had taken over the church, and had probably changed the locks. But the worn Yale openings looked the same, so out of an abstracted curiosity, he walked up the steps, pulled the key off his neck chain, and tried it in the door. It turned, and the door opened. The dog ran inside and vanished.

He stepped inside the cool darkness, and with a start of indignation, discovered racks of old clothes and piles of garbage bags heaped around the vaults of his old haunt. Someone was making his favorite church into a warehouse.

Feeling bemused by the changes, he let the doors close with a click behind him.

Hesitantly, he opened the door to the sanctuary. The church was vast and empty. But the high altar had been restored to some of its former glory, with gold paint touching up the old worn edges, and a new statue of St. Francis replacing the one of St. Rocco. And the red sanctuary lamp glowed with candlelight again.

Feeling a bit reassured, he crossed himself, genuflected, and slid into a back pew, finally able to rest his aching muscles. Blinking from the relief of sitting still, out of the air, he looked around. There were splattered paint buckets and an orgy of canvas and ladders over part of the sanctuary. But someone was painting an unusually good mural, with lilies, over the Mary altar.

Suddenly reawakening to his cross, he closed his eyes in pain. Everything he was carrying now broke him open, and he slumped his shoulders in defeat. *God, please. Just let me find her. Even if she's dead. Please just let me find her.* There was nothing he could do, except trust.

There were footsteps approaching, and Bear looked up over his hands to see a short young Hispanic man in full Franciscan habit, complete with a rope belt, walking quickly into the church, with an ambling, side-to-side walk that was almost a swagger, pausing only to genuflect before the tabernacle with surprising seriousness. He saw Bear in the corner, nodded, and walked out of the chapel.

Bear took to staring at the dome above the altar, where some ambitious artist had sketched out the outstretched arms and solemn face of a massive Christ in chalk, and wondered what the young monk was saying to the others: *Hey, who's that homeless guy in the chapel?* Bear allowed himself a thin grin, wondering if he should slink away and leave the monks to wonder if he had merely been an apparition of St. Joseph or something.

He tried to guess how high the scaffold would have to be to reach that dome. Or did they use a suspended catwalk of some kind?

Footsteps again. Bear wondered if he should leave, but inertia kept him there. A sigh escaped him. Another eviction was impending. He wondered if he should freak the monk out by telling him that he was the person who had donated thousands of dollars to fix up this church so that it could be used again. It would make a good story. Maybe they would pray extra hard for him.

The young monk returned, casually striding in Bear's direction. *Here comes the interrogation,* Bear thought.

But the monk had some panache, apparently. "How're you doing?" he said familiarly, lounging against the last pew.

I bet he'd say the same thing to an apparition of St. Joseph, Bear guessed. "I've been better," he said, not pretending. The scrub on his cheeks, the worn rumpled clothes, the wild hair and red eyes couldn't have said DISTRESS any more loudly.

"Can I help you with anything?"

"No—" Bear started to get up to go, not anxious to spill his guts. "Sorry. I just thought I'd take a look inside."

"Oh. That's fine. You're not bothering anyone. We sort of encourage people to sit in front of the Eucharist around here." The brother paused, and Bear waited. "So the door was open?" the monk asked.

"I had a key," Bear tried to keep down the sigh unsuccessfully, and handed it to the brother. "There's only one other copy that I know of. Don't worry, they're not selling them on the street these days or anything. I had the key from back when I used to be an altar boy here, and I just figured I'd see if it still worked."

"Oh," the brother said in a strange tone. Bear glanced at him. But the only thing the brother said was, "You were an altar boy and they gave you the keys to the church?" a bit disbelievingly. He was obviously a former altar boy.

"It was a special case. I was really good friends with the priest. I sort of filled in as a sacristan for him a lot of times."

"Boy, you must have been pretty devout."

Bear nodded. "Guess you could say that." He made a half-hearted gesture towards the paintings. "Nice monastery you're putting together here."

"Friary. We're friars, not monks."

"Oh. Sorry."

There was a long pause. The young friar scratched his chin, scratched the back of his head, scratched the back of his neck, and then scratched his chin again. Bear looked at him again oddly, and moved further away.

"You know, this is reeeeally weird," the friar said at last, saying the last two words very slowly. "But you wouldn't happen to know who has the other key?"

Wondering if these brothers were paranoid about burglary, Bear said, reassuringly. "A friend of mine. Don't worry. I doubt she'll ever use it."

"She?" the young brother said in that same strange voice.

"Yes," Bear said. Then, "Why do you ask?"

"Her name wouldn't happen to be Nora?"

Something twinged inside Bear, and he focused in on the situation. "No. It's Blanche. Do you know her? Have you seen her?" He automatically pulled the photograph of Blanche that he had been carrying for verification out of his pocket.

The brother looked at the picture and then back at Bear. "That's her."

"What?" Bear leapt to his feet.

"Except for the hair. It's short. But that's her."

"Do you know where she is?"

"Yes, but hold on—sit back down a moment," the brother said, soberly. "I need to tell you something. You're a friend of hers, right?"

"Yes. My name's Arthur. Arthur Denniston. I know her mom and her sister. Jean and Rose Brier. We've been looking for her for the past week. Is she OK?"

The friar took a deep breath. "She's in a coma."

"I know. But she's alive?"

"You do? Yes. She was attacked—about three days ago. We've been trying to figure out who she is and where she came from." The young monk was animated now, talking at the same time as Bear.

"It was my stepmother who poisoned her—I've been looking for her—So has her family—Where is she?" Bear was saying simultaneously.

"So that's what happened! We've been taking care of her—In Our Lady of Mercy Hospital—Here, I'll take you there."

With one motion, each of them put a hand on the back of the pew and vaulted over, racing through the friary and out the door to the street.

II

In the parking lot, they met Father Francis. Leon yelled an explanation, and the head of the order responded by tossing him the keys. Leon thanked him and raced to join Bear, who was already prowling around, ready to jump into any car Brother Leon indicated. He was sitting in the seat before Leon had opened the door to the driver's side.

Just as Leon started the engine, Bear's cell phone rang. It was Fish. "Where are you?" his brother demanded.

"I found her!" Bear yelled back into the phone.

Fish yelled. "What? Blanche? How? Where? Where are you? How can we get there? Hold on—Rose, yes, yes, yes, he found her, please be quiet for a second—"

Brother Charley, followed by two tail-wagging Rottweilers, had run out to the car and was looking in the window, wanting to know what was going on.

"Our Lady of Mercy Hospital—it's—here—can you explain to him?" Bear shoved the cell phone at a surprised Charley, who took it as Leon threw the car into reverse and screeched back seven feet.

"Uh—hello?" The big friar said into the phone just as Leon shifted again and they pulled away with a roar.

On the way to the hospital, Brother Leon (Bear found out that was his name) talked non-stop about the whole situation. Bear was so absorbed in listening and asking questions of his own that neither of them noticed the traffic accidents they almost caused.

If the friars who followed them in the van hadn't already known the destination, they would have had no trouble figuring out which way Leon and Bear had gone.

After they parked in front of the hospital, Leon leapt out of the car, habit flapping behind him with Bear, his hair flying in all directions, hot on his heels. The odd pair dodged through the halls, Leon waving at the nurses and doctors they passed, not bothering to explain.

But when they reached the door, Leon drew up short and gestured to Bear to go in first.

"After you," Bear said.

"No," said Leon. "She's been waiting for you. You take over from here."

Bear stared at him. "How do you know?"

"Not too hard to put the pieces together. You go."

Looking bewildered, Bear opened the door and went in.

Leon sat down on a nearby chair outside the door, took out his rosary, and in a deep and curious peace, began to pray. He knew his task with Nora, whatever it had been in the Divine Plan, was over.

He crossed himself. *So God, about this priesthood thing...*he began.

III

Bear tentatively stepped inside the room, and looked at her. She lay, deep in stillness, in the hospital bed, her face white as the pillow, but her cheeks were touched with the barest hint of scarlet. Her hair, torn and tattered, lay like a black cloud around her features. She was Blanche, not Nora, and despite her coma, she was still beautiful.

> *Princess, like a rose is her cheek*
> *And her eyes are as blue as the skies...*

He knew then that even if she never woke up from the coma, that he loved her, and that the years would find him sitting by her side, even if she never knew that he was there.

Sitting down beside her bed, he took her hand in his, and closed his fingers over it. His thick bandaged hands around her supple white fingers.

"Blanche," he said to her softly, and he felt a tremor go through her. He had heard that often people in comas could hear, even though their bodies might not be able to respond. *Talk to her as though she can hear you,* he remembered Leon saying in the car. And he sensed that Blanche could hear him, through a cloud of blackness. "Nora," she had called herself, "noir" for "black." Maybe because of the blackness around her. Maybe feeling that she wasn't worthy to be Blanche. But like all humanity, she was both Blanche and Nora, both white and black. And now, wounded by her ordeal, red.

He spoke with her for a long time, as though she could hear him, telling her about how his dad loved her, and how she had saved his dad's life. How he had forgiven his dad. And how his dad wanted Bear to find her.

"Blanche, I'm never going to leave you. I'm sure you'll get better. But even if you never do, I'm staying with you. You know I was thinking God might have had other ideas, but it's clear to me now where He wants me to be. With you."

He leaned close to her and spoke softly, in her ear. "Because...well, you should know this...but in case you don't...I love you."

He paused, his face just an inch above hers. He had never done this before, because he had never been sure it was the right time.

But now it was.

He kissed her.

I give you myself.

Somehow his hand found hers again, and he sat next to her, holding her white fingers. He wiped his eyes, and breathed deeply, feeling the peace. He knew he had done the right thing. What he was supposed to do.

IV

Sometimes it amazes me
How strong the power of love can be
Sometimes it just takes my breath away.

Bear felt her fingers squeeze his faintly, and thought it must have been his imagination. Stirring himself, he looked at her face. Her eyelashes were moving.

Fumbling around with his free hand, he searched for one of those buttons to summon the nurse with, but couldn't find one, and he didn't dare take his eyes off her face. Her fingers were tightening on his other hand, and he knew that she felt him. He had a sense of her rising upward, coming out of deep darkness...

The lashes lifted, and her blue eyes were visible. They found his eyes, and focused. He knew that she saw him at last.

Her lips moved. "Bear," she breathed his name.

Now her grip became stronger and he recognized that it wasn't a dream: she was trying to sit. The next moment she was in his arms as he gathered her up, saying her name over and over.

"It was so dark," she was saying in his ear. "So dark, and I thought I had died, long ago, and far away, but then I heard your voice..." she broke off as he hugged her more tightly.

"Did you hear what I said to you?" he asked, his words muffled by her hair.

"I did."

"I meant it," he said. "I meant every last word. I—"

"I know," she pressed her cheek against his. "Thank you. Thank you so much." Her voice was husky. "I love you."

Now that he knew she was aware, and knew he loved her, and she loved him, he put his hands on her face and kissed her once more. It was only then that they heard and realized that they had an audience.

Bear looked over his shoulders to see the uncommon and extraordinary sight of seven friars minor, young, and old, rejoicing wholeheartedly in a manner that could only be called exuberant in the extreme. He had never seen a bearded friar in full habit dancing, but several of them were, shouting and cavorting and hi-fiving one another. He could have sworn he heard someone doing a rap beat.

He looked back down at Blanche in his arms, and saw her white cheeks blush deep red, but she couldn't keep the smile from her face.

The king's son cried out,
"I love you more than anything in the world.
Come with me to my father's castle
and you shall be my wife."

And she went with him gladly.
Grimm

The End

A Little Bit About This Book:

For some time, I had wanted to do a retelling of the over-familiar tale of Snow White and the Seven Dwarves. This famous Grimm's tale, made more famous by the splendid landmark film by Disney, has all the marks of a folk allegory of the Fall, with the heroine representing the baptized Christian soul, the villainess her demonic counterpart, and the prince as Christ, the savior from the sleep of death. And the seven little men can be thought to represent any number of seven sacred things: the seven virtues, seven gifts of the Holy Spirit, seven sacraments...the number is clearly not accidental.

I was fascinated by the repetition throughout the tale of the colors red, white, and black to represent the heroine. As I worked and reworked the story, which underwent a full fourteen major plot changes, I tried to use images of many things that are black, white, and red, like playing cards, chess games, and tapestries. In the end I assigned each of the three temptations of Snow White (variously interpreted as temptations of the flesh, mind, and soul) one of the three colors, and matched them with three (twisted) versions of womanhood that the mortal woman must reject.

The book turned out to have a great deal to say about vocations and life paths, which I hadn't expected. Making the "seven little men" into seven "friars minor" was one character choice that paid off quite well. And I enjoyed the chance to get inside Bear's head, and flesh out the characters of Mrs. Foster, Jean, Rose, and especially Fish a little further.

On a lighter note, I tried to pay homage to the Disney Snow White film in various subtle (and not so subtle) ways. The rambunctious and physical slapstick of the friars owes a lot to the famous Disney dwarves, and although there is no one-to-one correspondence, readers will doubtless see some similarities between the eventually heroic Grumpy and the surly Brother George, as well as between lovable Dopey and the short, (relatively) beardless, outrageous (but hardly mute) Brother Leon. To answer queries some have made, many of the friars are based on composites of actual friars I knew while living in New York City, where I was a lay volunteer with the Community of the Friars of the Renewal. Of course, I took liberal poetic license with their original characters when writing the book. I've written two reflections about the writing of this book, both of which can be found on the book's website, www.blackasnight.com.

Many people helped make this book into what it is through contributing their information and expertise on certain topics. I want to particularly thank:

Ed Childress from the Washington branch of the Drug Enforcement Agency, and Liz Jordan from the New York Branch for information on agency procedure.

Captain Schiro, Captain Stephen Marchi, Sergeant Mark Werner, and Chief Dispatcher Jamie of the Front Royal, Virginia police department for their help with police procedure questions and fact checks.

For location details, Sharon Perry, Airport Airspace Analysis Specialist, of the Federal Aviation Administration and Marie Riseman of the Public Relations Department at John F. Kennedy International Airport.

Ted Bowen from the Metro North Customer Service, for his helpful descriptions of New York trains and train tunnels and his enthusiasm.

Ellen Borakove, director of Public Affairs for the New York City Medical Examiner's Office for explaining their procedures to me.

For information about medical matters, I am indebted to my friend Ceril Khoury, pharmacist, for her advice on drugs and comas; also to Sharon Jones, ER nurse at Warren Memorial Hospital for information on medical procedures. Also to Dr. Frank, for his extremely useful information on almost all of the above.

Numerous thanks goes to my "violence experts"–Andrew O'Neill and Benjamin Hatke, for their equally numerous fact checks. Also I am in debt to my friend Jason Manak, judo practitioner and computer animator, who was invaluable in helping me "choreograph" the fight scenes, since I still would have not the least idea of what to do if confronted with a villain in a dark tunnel, or a villainess with a semi-automatic.

For language help, I want to thank Maria Hambric, Joseph Meaney, and Mariangelis Burger for translations into Spanish, my aunts Charlotte Corrigan and Pamela Spinelli for phrases in Italian, and Geoffrey Douglas and Nicole Hamilton for Jamaican translations (And my brother David, who put me in contact with the last two).

I wish to thank Fr. Glenn Sudano, Community of the Franciscans of the Renewal, Fr. Peter Giroux of the Franciscans of the Primitive Observance, Fr. Bernard Murphy, CFR, and Brother Shawn O'Connor, CFR, for their insights into religious life.

And thanks to attorney Stephen Jerome and his lovely wife Kristin for help with final legal details.

Special thanks to:

Marie Meaney for proofreading and critique, poetic advice, and refreshing my information on Santa Cecilia with postcards from Rome.

Ben and Anna Hatke for babysitting help, Italian phrases, discussions, and proofreading.

Stratford Caldecott for some poetic advice and encouragement.

Barbara Nicholosi for mentioning Emily Dickinson at precisely the right moment.

Alan Gordon, New York lawyer and mystery novelist, for his important legal advice on several questions.

Sonia Tate Cousins, Esq., for referring me to Alan Gordon.

My wonderful aunt and attorney Pamela Spinelli, who not only gave me advice on Italian and legal help, but also searched out lawyers in the precise area of law that I needed to consult. Thanks so much Aunt Pam!

Having acknowledged the contributions of all of the above, I want to claim any factual or informational errors in the book as my own, as many times I extrapolated from data that was provided to me for the purpose of the plot.

For babysitting and tutoring my children on various occasions during the long process of this book, I want to thank Mary Accetullo, Erica Zepeda, Jaimie Berger, Anna Hatke, Christin McCaffrey and Jamie Dresch.

My friends Ben and Anna Hatke, Andy and Heather O'Neill, Nick Marmalejo, and my brothers and sisters all helped me work through various snarls and problems in the plot.

A most particular thanks to my "emergency Jamies," Jaime Berger and Jamie Dresch, for the late-night phone calls and endless debates over tea at times when I had written myself into a corner and had no idea what to do next. And also Mandy Hains and Katie von Shaijik.

Albert Zuckerman, for his very useful book *Writing the Blockbuster Novel.* Not that this will be one, necessarily, but his book was able to explain to me when others couldn't, just what was wrong with my manuscript.

I also want to thank those who willingly read the manuscript in its various incarnations, including my mother Michele Doman, Mary and Karim Accetullo, Joe Sharpe, Alicia Van Hecke, Eileen Cummings, Elizabeth McShurley, Christine Dalessio, and my family members Jennifer Doman, Mike Schmiedicke, Gretchen Nelson, Matthew Schmiedicke, and John Doman.

And last but not least, for all those who attended my reading of the final draft over the course of two weeks, including Anna Hatke, Joseph and Marie Meaney, Kathleen Blum, Sophia Cuddeback, Jamie Dresch, Linda Antunes, Lewis Kappell, Dr. Patrick Keats of Christendom College, students Julia Peterson, Amy Raab, Elizabeth Stephens, Rita Traugott, Elizabeth Black, Emma Fritcher, and Emily Griswold, Ben Bielinski, Adrienne Smith, and Mary Akers. Also Sharon Higby for announcing it to her classes, even though she couldn't attend.

Great thanks must go to my editors and dare I say, friends and kindred spirits: Jean Ann Sharpe, Peter Sharpe, Lydia Reynolds, and the others in the Bethlehem Community who gave me the primary support I needed to finish this book and who published the original edition. Not to mention Francis Philips, who helped me along the home stretch.

As always, a deep debt of gratitude goes to my husband Andrew, who worked with me on this project 24/7 on several occasions to see it done. And my children, Caleb, Rose, Marygrace, Joshua, and baby Thomas, who were very understanding with a constantly-occupied mommy.

And for all the fans who wrote to me to ask about the progress of the book, and who promised their prayers to see it through–thank you. This is the result of your prayers. I hope you enjoy it thoroughly.

For this second edition of the book, I want to additionally thank my daughter Joan for her patience with Mommy, and for my son Joshua, who now, I know, prays for me from heaven. I want to thank my friend Joan Coppa Drennen, who created the lovely chapter headings. And I must especially thank my husband Andrew, my "secret weapon," who spent much time trimming fat from the book, which had swelled disproportionately in the final days of writing the first edition. I hope this makes for a slimmer, trimmer story that moves more quickly and is more satisfying in the end.

For the 2009 cover makeover, I am indebted to my friends Veronica Randolph, who posed for the cover, to Craig Spiering, who took the new photo, and Theodore Schleunderfritz, who made the whole thing look beautiful. Also grateful thanks to Patrick Rose who stepped in at the last minute as the model for Bear on the back cover, and to Katherine and Elizabeth Sartor who helped me find him.

Regina Doman
Shirefeld, Strasburg, Virginia
2009

About the Author

Regina Doman lives near Front Royal, Virginia with her husband
and their five children.

More information about her Fairy Tale Novel series can be found at
www.fairytalenovels.com. Regina always welcomes email, feedback, and
questions from readers.

www.fairytalenovels.com

CPSIA information can be obtained
at www.ICGtesting.com
Printed in the USA
FFOW01n1406240414
5005FF